THE
GUN
CONTROL
DEBATE

Contemporary Issues

Series Editors: Robert M. Baird
                 Stuart E. Rosenbaum

Other titles in this series:

Animal Experimentation: The Moral Issues
edited by Robert M. Baird and Stuart E. Rosenbaum

Are You Politically Correct: Debating America's Cultural Standards
edited by Michael Bauman and Francis J. Beckwith

Bigotry, Prejudice, and Hatred: Definitions, Causes, and Solutions
edited by Robert M. Baird and Stuart E. Rosenbaum

The Ethics of Abortion: Pro-Life vs. Pro-Choice
edited by Robert M. Baird and Stuart E. Rosenbaum

Euthanasia: The Moral Issues
edited by Robert M. Baird and Stuart E. Rosenbaum

Morality and the Law
edited by Robert M. Baird and Stuart E. Rosenbaum

Philosophy of Punishment
edited by Robert M. Baird and Stuart E. Rosenbaum

Pornography: Private Right or Public Menace?
edited by Robert M. Baird and Stuart E. Rosenbaum

Sexual Harassment: Confrontations and Decisions
edited by Edmund Wall

Suicide: Right or Wrong?
edited by John Donnelly

THE GUN CONTROL DEBATE

YOU DECIDE

EDITED BY
LEE NISBET

CONTEMPORARY ISSUES

PROMETHEUS BOOKS
BUFFALO, NEW YORK

Dedication

To my best friend, my lover,
and strongest supporter—my wife, Lynette.

Thanks for everything, Baby!

Published 1990 by Prometheus Books

With editorial offices located at 700 East Amherst Street, Buffalo, New York 14215, and distribution facilities at 59 John Glenn Drive, Amherst, New York 14228.

Copyright © 1990 by Lee Nisbet

Library of Congress Cataloging-in-Publication Data

The gun control debate : you decide / edited by Lee Nisbet.
    p.   cm.—(Contemporary issues in philosophy)
Includes bibliographical references.
ISBN 0-87975-618-7 (pbk.)
1. Gun control—United States. I. Nisbet, Lee. II. Series.
HV7436.G866   1990
363.3′3′0973—dc20   90-9138
                                                                      CIP

Printed on acid-free paper in the United States of America

Acknowledgments

This book could not have been completed without the valuable advice and assistance of a number of people who made my work so much easier.

I am grateful to Ms. Gwen Fitzgerald, Assistant Director of Communications for Handgun Control Inc., and Paul H. Blackman, Ph.D., Research Coordinator for the Institute for Legislative Action, National Rifle Association, for providing me with vital materials and valuable references to important research.

Mr. Joseph Tartaro, President of the Second Amendment Foundation and Executive Editor of *Gun Week,* as well as Ms. S. Bird and Mr. C. Spector, gave of their valuable time to help identify issues, research, scholars, and scholarship that added immeasurably to the quality of the volume.

My secretary, Ms. Lynette Herron, deciphered my miserable handwriting to produce a beautiful manuscript.

Thanks goes to my editor, Steven L. Mitchell of Prometheus Books, for proposing this project in the first place, in addition to making insightful editorial improvements in the manuscript as well as in the construction and arrangement of this anthology.

Without the encouragement and enthusiasm of my parents, Dr. Dorothea E. and Arthur M. Nisbet, my project would have been all the more difficult to complete.

And to Master Jeffrey Lee Nisbet, age 7, who not only exhibited extreme patience concerning missed fishing time with his dad but still managed to catch the biggest bass in Willow Island Lake.

Contents

PART TWO: CONTROLLING CRIME AND VIOLENCE

PART THREE: GUNS FOR SELF-DEFENSE: PROTECTION OR MENACE?

PART FOUR: INTERPRETING THE SECOND AMENDMENT: CULTURE CONFLICT REVEALED

Introduction

(September 1989) *Worker Kills 5, Self in Kentucky* (A.P.)

Louisville, Ky. "A printing company employee with an assault rifle and a handgun opened fire in the plant today, killing at least five and wounding 14 before taking his own life, police said.

" 'It looks like a battle zone . . . with the blood and people involved here,' Mayor Jerry Abramson said. . . ."

(April 1990) *Freed Mental Patient Kills 1, Wounds 4* (A.P.)

Atlanta, Ga. "A smiling gunman recently released from a mental hospital opened fire (with a handgun) in the food court of a suburban shopping mall Tuesday, killing one man and wounding four people before calmly walking outside to surrender.

"He held up his hands and said, 'I'm the one you're looking for,' said Police Chief M. F. Feugerson. . . ."

(April 1990) *Case Called Replay of the Goetz Drama—Woman Faces Weapons Counts* (Karen Tumulty, *Los Angeles Times*)

"In a case that is being billed as a replay of the Bernhard Goetz drama that gripped this city five years ago, a three-time mugging victim is fighting to escape prosecution after shooting (with a handgun) an armed man who attempted to rob her and a friend.

"Ms. Bureau, 20, has even retained Goetz's lawyer to defend her. 'It's our intention not to lie down, but to fight,' attorney Barry Slotnik said Monday, 'Yvonne fought back. She's alive today because she did.' "

What do these headlines and news clips mean? Should we ban certain kinds of firearms? Should more citizens, male and female, be armed to better fend off or deter muggers, murderers, burglars, and rapists? Let's look at the following statistics compiled by the federal government and leading criminologists: Each year, approximately 30,000 Americans are killed with firearms. Suicides claim 15,000 to 16,000 lives, homicides account for 12,000 more, and gun accidents add another 2,000. Gun-related injuries, whether intentional or accidental, are inflicted upon 40,000 Americans every year. Meanwhile, in any given year, there are up to one million crimes committed involving guns. A 1990 Justice Department study covering the years 1979 to 1987 estimates that 44 percent of all homicides during this period were committed with handguns. Furthermore, in 27 percent of *all* crimes involving weapons of *any* sort, the "weapon of choice" was the handgun. Yet, as criminologist Gary Kleck argues in chapter 9 of this volume (using data drawn from surveys), although handguns are involved in approximately 580,000 instances of criminal misuse each year, they are also used approximately 645,000 times in the same period to defend against criminal incursion. Kleck goes on to point out that 99 percent of those who legally own firearms never commit any crime with these weapons.

What do these statistics mean? Do they "speak for themselves" as many believe? Do the figures on deaths and injuries involving guns tell us what the problems are or how to solve them? Should we have more gun control or less? What does "gun control" mean anyway, and how does the Second Amendment to the Constitution bear upon gun control issues? These are difficult questions because they deal with very complex issues.

The goal of this volume is to introduce readers to the fundamental questions at the core of one of America's most emotionally divisive social and political battles. The often conflicting points of view of historians, criminologists, sociologists, legal experts, and medical researchers will help us reach the central issues of the gun control debate. These experts stand outside of the well-known advocacy organizations that lobby federal and state legislatures and finance expensive public awareness campaigns. Some of these reseachers have actually changed their minds on various gun control issues as a result of their investigations. The selections offered here provide access to material not available to those who, for the most part, follow the debate in popular magazines, newspapers, or on the nightly news. The materials in this volume are not only crucial to understanding what the gun control debate is about but vital for evaluating the relative merits of the opposing points of view.

Understanding what America's gun control debate is about requires that we first come to know what it is *not* about. The gun control debate is *not* about whether government, at any level, has the legal authority and ethical obligation to *regulate* the sale, possession, and use of firearms. All contending parties in the debate recognize the government's legitimate power to so do. The fact that there are presently over 20,000 federal, state, and local laws to accomplish such regulation would make a debate on this score irrelevant in any case. The debate is also *not* about whether government has the legal power to prohibit certain categories of people, such as felons and mental incompetents, from owning firearms or to legislate additional penalties for criminal activities involving firearms. Even the National Rifle Association (NRA), for example, supports government efforts in this direction; in fact, it promotes mandatory licensing* for the carrying of concealed weapons as well as mandatory sentencing and additional penalties for criminal misuse of firearms. In short, everyone involved in the gun control debate agrees that since firearms can be used wittingly or witlessly as lethal weapons, it is both legally and ethically essential to regulate and hence restrict firearm possession and use.

If there is so much agreement about regulating guns, what *is* the debate about? It's about *how much* regulation and *what kinds* of regulations there ought to be. Specifically, the gun control controversy concerns proposals and arguments whose assumptions and evidence would seriously restrict or prohibit mentally competent adult noncriminals from owning firearms that are presently legally obtainable. The controversy focuses on proposals that would markedly restrict access to, or legally ban and confiscate, whole classes of firearms such as handguns, "assault"-style semi-automatic rifles, and "Saturday Night Specials." In short, the controversy centers on proposals that would require many Americans to give up freedoms—believed by many to be constitutionally guaranteed—that they now enjoy. Criminologists, using the results of surveys, estimate that upwards of 70 million Americans own about 150 to 200 million firearms—that is, up to 50 percent of American households contain guns, and half of these homes contain the estimated 70 million handguns currently in private hands. The political, legal, ethical, and economic implications and consequences of such restrictive gun control proposals are therefore enormous. The burden of demonstrating that further restrictions (or complete prohibition) are both necessary and feasible relative to public safety and order lies squarely on gun control advocates; it's a challenge that the proponents of gun control readily acknowledge.

Now, as the reader may suspect, it is not merely the number of people affected by these proposals that explains the virulence of the gun control debate or the importance attached to its outcome. Like many volatile social controversies, whole systems of values—political, social, personal, and aesthetic—are in conflict. Firearms *mean* different things to different groups of Americans, hence they are valued in radically different ways by these groups. Therefore, proposals that appear to have as their aim severely restricting or prohibiting access to firearms that are at present legally obtainable will be perceived by many to strike at the very heart of a constitutionally guaran-

---

*Mandatory licensing systems provide specific criteria for screening applicants which, if met, *legally require* the issuing of a permit to carry a concealed weapon.

teed freedom, one that is personally cherished and revered. On the other hand, such proposals are perceived by equally caring and dedicated people as necessary and eminently sensible approaches to eliminating a dire threat to public and personal safety. Succinctly put, millions of Americans are fearful and contemptuous of exactly what millions of other Americans love and cherish. The fierceness of the debate over every gun control proposal, however innocuous it may appear, is explained by these deeply conflicting meanings and valuations of "the gun."

Millions of Americans not only own firearms, they *love* them. "The gun" is a treasured source of recreation, a cherished instrument of sport, and a valued source of security in a crime-ridden world. Furthermore, for many of these enthusiasts "the gun" is a venerated aesthetic object to be collected and traded as well as written and read about for its impact on history, politics, and warfare. Books devoted to the development and historical impact of a specific firearm become collector's items in their own right. Beyond their utility and history, a great many Americans own and collect firearms for purely aesthetic reasons: the beautiful integration of form, substance, and function. Others are attracted to the power of firearms—the sounds and results of shooting. Millions of Americans consume the many monthly publications devoted to every conceivable aspect of firearm use and lore. Many experienced hunters and target shooters "hand load"—that is, assemble—their own ammunition as a special hobby. They learn the theory and mathematics of ballistics and purchase expensive electronic equipment to monitor and improve the results of the ammunition they fabricate. These devotees maintain memberships in shooting clubs, write and exchange newsletters, "talk guns" at gun shops, and attend local and national gun shows. They are the people who have made big-game hunting with handguns one of the fastest growing types of hunting activity. Handguns chambered for such powerful cartridges as the .44 Magnum and the .454 Casull and equipped with scopes put even more challenge into hunting deer and grizzly.

These are the enthusiasts: guns are an integral part of their lives; in fact, firearms here constitute a way of life. They are gas station attendants and corporate executives, presidents of sportsmen's clubs, and leaders of some of the most important conservation organizations in the country. They constitute what some have referred to as the "gun culture."

It was the nineteenth-century members of this "gun culture" who, in 1871, formed the National Rifle Association to promote shooting proficiency and safety. It is the contemporary members of this culture who, while retaining the NRA's traditional functions, transformed it during the 1960s and 1970s into a vehicle for political action in response to prohibitionist gun control proposals that followed in the wake of political assassinations and highly publicized gun violence. Such proposals were perceived by many firearm enthusiasts as nothing more than attempts to eliminate their constitutionally guaranteed freedom to own firearms on grounds that were both factually unsubstantiated and politically suspect. In short, as long as gun control remains cast in restrictivist or prohibitionist terms, gun enthusiasts will continue to respond by forming an ever-expanding and unyielding political counterforce to protect their collective interests. At the forefront of this political struggle is the NRA, the "gun lobby." Today, 2.8 million strong, with a membership that leans toward political and social conservatism, the NRA is arguably the most potent single-issue lobbying organization in the history of American democracy. It is no coincidence, therefore, that in the age of radical gun control, not only are Presidents Reagan and Bush members of the NRA, but so were Nixon, Eisenhower, and Kennedy.

On the other side of the gun control debate stands a large group of politically active and socially concerned Americans who perceive criminal and negligent use of firearms in this country to be a problem of major dimensions. They believe large-scale public ownership and access to firearms, especially handguns and "assault"-style semi-automatic long guns, to be both a social anachronism and a major public safety menace. All available evidence suggests that this sector of the population is well educated and politically and socially liberal. They are supported in their views by the giants of the American media: national magazines, nearly all metropolitan newspapers, and the major television networks promote additional and sometimes far-reaching restrictions on ownership of these classes of firearms. Such restrictions are advocated as the only effective means of keeping lethal weapons out of the hands of criminals, lunatics, political assassins, and especially gun owners who, in times of emotional distress, kill spouses, relatives, acquaintances, and/or themselves and whose negligence often allows guns to kill their children. Supporters of restrictive gun control emphasize the claim that firearm ownership, especially of handguns, constitutes a much greater menace to family safety and home security than do intruders and burglars.

Responding to the public safety issue and the success of the "gun lobby" (most notably the NRA), the proponents of gun control have formed their own political action organizations. These groups advocate a prohibitionist or restrictivist approach to gun control and emphasize the view that there is no constitutional guarantee for individual citizens to own firearms, especially handguns. The most effective of these organizations, Handgun Control Inc., has a membership of one million. It was founded in the 1970s by Pete Shields after his son was killed by a pistol-wielding black terrorist. The present leader of the organization is Sarah Brady, whose husband, James, was permanently disabled in the attempted handgun assassination of Ronald Reagan.

It is in this emotionally charged, politically and culturally polarized atmosphere that gun control proposals and the evidence in their behalf are debated in the popular media and fought over on the political battlefields of federal, state, and local government. The polarized nature of the gun control

debate has important consequences. Highly organized and financially powerful advocacy groups are able to gain media attention and, in so doing,
define the debate in terms of contrary propositions: far-reaching restrictions
on firearms are both constitutional and necessary versus the view that such
restrictions are unconstitutional and unworkable. Each side marshals arguments
and makes selective use of studies that support its position, while large segments
of the public support the view most in agreement with their attitudes, values,
and interests. Further, the organized advocacy groups, assisted by the popular media, have successfully made each other the issue. For many, the gun
control debate reduces to a hostile attitude toward either the "gun lobby"
or the "anti-gunners."

By presenting some of the most important contemporary studies and the
most persuasive arguments developed by experts on both sides of the issue,
this volume avoids as much as possible the selectivity that polarization
engenders. It is noteworthy that none of the authors represented are connected with the major organized advocacy groups. The sources and impact
of political and cultural polarization cannot be ignored, however, for they
rule the gun control debate as it is popularly engaged in and significantly
influence the form it assumes in academic circles. Selections are provided that
explain not only *why* the debate has taken its present course but also the
consequences of this course for identifying and resolving actual problems. At
the same time, the selections included here identify key questions as well as
the controversies they generate; both are empirically independent of social
and political agendas and must be resolved before any "solution" to firearm-
related problems can be entertained.

Specifically, what problems do gun control proposals seek to remedy?
What is the magnitude and significance of these problems and to what extent
can gun control resolve them? In sum, after reading this volume, you, the
reader, will have the opportunity to form your own judgments on the relative merits of the gun control proposals, based upon your assessment of the
often conflicting answers given by experts to the following key questions:

Does the present freedom to own firearms constitute a threat to political and social stability?

Is the debate over gun control influenced by political, cultural, and
sociological factors?

Are the gun control policies and experiences of other countries relevant to the problems we face in the United States?

Is contemporary research at odds with the findings and conclusions
of earlier scholarship on the necessity for and workability of gun
control?

Would further restrictions on public access to handguns, or the banning of them altogether, prevent more criminals and mentally unstable people from obtaining these weapons?

Would banning handguns lead criminals to use more or less lethal weapons?

Is the availability of guns causally related to levels of violence?

Does gun ownership deter such crimes as mugging, burglary, and rape?

Are firearms in the hands of ordinary citizens effective or ineffective as a means of self- and home defense?

Does possession of firearms by ordinary law-abiding citizens place them and/or their relatives, acquaintances, and children at significant risk?

Should "Saturday Night Specials" be banned?

Would mandating additional jail terms for crimes involving firearms deter their use in crime, and is this approach politically and economically feasible?

What gun control measures are likely to be effective and why?

What are the prospects for significantly more restrictive gun control in the United States?

Do individual Americans have a constitutional right to own firearms?

Has scholarship on the Second Amendment been influenced by political and social concerns?

Readers will not find here a discussion of the "assault" rifle controversy that has drawn so much recent media attention and sparked heated debate among advocacy organizations and legislators. At present there exist no reliable data on the degree of criminal misuse of these semi-automatic replicas of true assault rifles (a rifle having the capacity to be fired fully automatically and hence presently illegal, except to holders of a federal machine gun permit). That the fate of these weapons can be discussed with such fervor in the popular media and on the floor of the Congress in the absence of data is a phenomenon that will be fully understood by those who complete this volume. The opinion of experts in any case is that handguns, because they can be so readily concealed, will remain the "weapon of choice" for criminal abuse and will continue to be the object of the most intense and sustained gun control efforts.

One final note to the reader. The selections and studies contained in this volume represent but a fraction of the writing and research done on the subject of gun control. How then was the material for this volume selected?

First, representatives of the two major organized advocacy groups were asked to identify the best writing and research that supported their position but which was conducted by experts not connected with their organization. Both Handgun Control Inc. and the National Rifle Association responded with great enthusiasm to this request.

Second, my conversations with experts in the field, together with my own reading and research in the area, formed the second criterion. Outside the obvious limitations of space, which eliminated significant amounts of excellent material, I am solely responsible for any bias or omissions.

Part One

A Culture in Conflict

Introduction

The gun control movement in America has been a twentieth-century response to the problems of urban crime and domestic violence. The movement's traditional target was, and continues to be, the readily concealed weapon—the handgun. The fact that it can be easily carried and concealed has made the handgun the "weapon of choice" for those who use firearms for illicit purposes. In urban areas these same qualities have also made the handgun the preferred weapon for those who desire a means to defend themselves against criminals. In such settings the effective distances at which deadly encounters take place are short. The long barrels of shotguns (unless shortened or "sawed off") and rifles are a disadvantage in these encounters, and the fact that they cannot be easily concealed eliminates the advantage of surprise.

Technical factors alone, however, do not explain why the handgun has become so controversial in contemporary American urban areas, unlike their European counterparts. One difference is the availability of such weapons. There are roughly 70 million handguns in the United States at the present time: the ratio of existing handguns to the total population has remained relatively constant over the last century. Availability, of course, is in part a function of demand. But why do large numbers of Americans—honest citizens comprising 99 percent of handgun owners—feel the need to own these weapons?

One reason is heritage: as noted historian Richard Hofstadter documents, the early frontier experience, the role (actual and idealized) of the citizen-soldier in the Revolutionary War, the continued wars against Indian tribes and bandits while settling the nation's frontier, together with America's hunting tradition, gave the gun an honored place in our culture. Hofstadter and other historians who analyze the role of firearms in American life agree, however, that this heritage alone does not explain why Americans remained heavily armed after the frontier was closed and especially after millions of people settled in large eastern cities. One hypothesis of particularly contemporary relevance centers on nineteenth-century urban crime, social unrest, and the public's perception that the police could not effectively protect citizens from criminals. Historians Lee Kennett and James Anderson, in their classic volume *The Gun in America: The Origins of a National Dilemma,* point out that the gun habits of nineteenth-century *urban* Americans (like their twentieth-century counterparts) had more to do with crime than frontier nostalgia:

> The general tendency to keep arms or carry them on the person may well be linked to the "urban explosion" that transformed American cities in the period 1820–1860. Its mechanism of everyday law enforcement did not keep pace with its growth so that the inhabitant felt an increased need to fend for himself. . . . This sense of personal insecurity in the face of crime probably did more to hasten the trend toward personal armament than anything else. . . .[1]

It should be noted that most police forces in eastern and midwestern urban areas were not permitted to carry weapons until the latter part of the nineteenth century. Throughout the 1800s, Americans distrusted a standing armed police force as much as eighteenth-century Americans distrusted a standing or professional army. This mistrust, when combined with America's individualistic "self-help" ethic, the availability of weapons, and most of all the existence of chronic, violent urban criminal activity, contributed both to the ideal and the fact of an armed citizenry. In sum, the tradition of citizens being armed, which permeated nineteenth-century America, together with the continued explosive growth of cities, violent gun-related urban crime, and social unrest, set the stage for both the contemporary gun control movement and the debate it has fostered.

The debate began, not surprisingly, in New York City during the turn of the century. At this time in our nation's history, the fact that citizens carried handguns was both commonplace and noncontroversial in urban areas throughout the country. In 1911, however, the Sullivan Law—the most significant gun control legislation of the next half-century—was passed in New York State.* How did this extraordinary legislation come to pass?

Prominent political, civic, religious, and financial leaders in New York City mobilized newspaper support for a campaign that portrayed handgun control as vital in fighting the city's growing criminal and domestic violence. Newspapers inundated the public with feature stories on gun accidents and incidents

---

*The Gun Control Act of 1968, a *federal* act, is the most important legislation regulating firearms passed to date. The act prohibited the importation of surplus military weapons and small, short-barrelled, cheap foreign handguns popularly referred to as "Saturday Night Specials." Most importantly, however, it outlawed the interstate retailing of all firearms. This last provision aimed at preventing criminals and assassins like Lee Harvey Oswald from ordering firearms through the mails under assumed names. Earlier federal acts in 1934 and 1938 effectively prohibited the possession of machine guns, assault rifles, sawed-off shotguns, and silencers. This legislation also required the licensing of firearms manufacturers and dealers.

of gun violence. In addition, as Kennett and Anderson note, gun control was promoted by the press, prominent citizens, and civic groups as a statement affirming America's resolve to become a sane, civilized, cosmopolitan nation, no longer to be embarrassed by its crude and violent frontier past.

The ideal of the citizen armed for self-defense in an age of a modern police force was ridiculed as a dangerous anachronism, a throwback to those bygone days of the old frontier. Gun control was also advocated as a way to disarm what was regarded as a suspect new wave of immigrants. Taking a stand against gun control was condemned as advocating crime, barbarism, and ethnic violence. Through the efforts of New York City's major newspapers, the Sullivan Law passed the state legislature with little opposition. The law was significant for the future of gun control debate for several reasons:

(1) For the first time a state had made a serious legislative commitment to regulate the handgun. A permit was now required to purchase, own, and possess such a weapon. Carrying an unlicensed handgun became a felony. The permit was issued at a local authority's discretion and could be denied or revoked for criminal behavior or suspect character.*

(2) The rationale for such regulation firmly linked handgun control to crime control and the civilizing process. The handgun lost its traditional place of honor and was now officially regarded as a potential menace, with citizens being required to prove their fitness and need for ownership.

(3) Despite the law, the handgun violence in New York City continued to rise, which encouraged both critics and advocates of the statute. Critics argued that the law served only to disarm the law-abiding public while doing nothing to keep handguns out of criminal hands. Criminals, it was observed, were not likely to apply for handgun permits. Supporters countered that the Sullivan Law's failure to stem gun violence only proved the need for stricter controls in neighboring states or, better yet, federal controls.

(4) All of the arguments for and against the Sullivan Law would be echoed from the 1960s on into the 1990s as the movement grew for stricter regulation, if not the outright banning of handguns.

---

*Discretionary licensing, as opposed to mandatory licensing (supported by the NRA), does not presume that an applicant has a right to a license unless there is a specified cause for denial. The applicant must prove that he/she has a "reasonable need" to own and carry a concealed handgun. The issuing authority alone decides if the applicant has made his/her case. In New York City, for example, the discretionary permit system is used effectively to preclude the average citizen from owning and carrying a handgun.

Most importantly, the Sullivan Law, along with its advocates and critics, marked the emergence of the firearm as a symbol of a much larger ongoing political, social, and cultural struggle—*kulturkampf*—to define the kind of nation America should be. Specifically, the gun control debate can be viewed as part of a larger social struggle between an urban, well-educated, politically liberal class and one with more traditional political and social views. The conflict of values will provide important insights into the nature, course, and meaning of "gun control." Knowledge of the political and social agendas involved in this controversy will help us to understand why the "facts of the case" mean different things to different people depending upon the specific issue: gun-crime control, self-defense, or the meaning of the Second Amendment (Parts Two, Three, and Four). The readings in Part One, therefore, have been selected not only to acquaint readers with the classic positions for and against strict gun control, but also to demonstrate how political and social agendas sometimes influence the debate.

Historian Richard Hofstadter (selection 1) and Congressman Robert F. Drinan (selection 3) present the classic liberal position, mustering historical, political, and social evidence to make their case for strict gun control, especially as that view was advanced in the 1970s in response to political assassinations, social unrest, and increasing rates of criminal and domestic violence involving handguns.

B. Bruce-Briggs's work (selection 4) is another classic from the 1970s. Here, however, for the first time, a social scientist takes a skeptical look at the various arguments advanced to support restrictive gun control policies. He wonders how such definitive policy recommendations can be made when, in his view, no credible social science research had ever been done on the subject. Bruce-Briggs's challenge touched off the movement in the decade of the 1980s to do the needed research. His work reinforces the hypothesis that the gun control debate is symptomatic of a much wider cultural skirmish.

The selection by social scientist William R. Tonso (number 2) takes aim at Hofstadter's historically based recommendations for gun control. More importantly, Tonso broadens the context of the gun control debate by focusing on the impact of political and social agendas influencing both research and policy recommendations on gun control issues.

NOTE

1. Lee Kennett and James Anderson. *The Gun in America: The Origins of a National Dilemma* (Westport, Conn.: Greenwood Press, 1975), p. 148.

1

America as a Gun Culture

Richard Hofstadter

Senator Joseph Tydings of Maryland, appealing in the summer of 1968 for an effective gun-control law, lamented: "It is just tragic that in all of Western civilization the United States is the one country with an insane gun policy." In one respect this was an understatement: Western or otherwise, the United States is the only modern industrial urban nation that persists in maintaining a gun culture. It is the only industrial nation in which the possession of rifles, shotguns, and handguns is lawfully prevalent among large numbers of its population. It is the only such nation that has been impelled in recent years to agonize at length about its own disposition toward violence and to set up a commission to examine it, the only nation so attached to the supposed "right" to bear arms that its laws abet assassins, professional criminals, berserk murderers, and political terrorists at the expense of the orderly population—and yet it remains, and is apparently determined to remain, the most passive of all major countries in the matter of gun control. Many otherwise intelligent Americans cling with pathetic stubbornness to the notion that the people's right to bear arms is the greatest protection of their individual rights

From *American Violence: A Documentary History,* edited by Richard Hofstadter and Michael Wallace. Copyright © 1970 by Richard Hofstadter. Reprinted by permission of Alfred A. Knopf, Inc.

and a firm safeguard of democracy—without being in the slightest perturbed by the fact that no other democracy in the world observes any such "right" and that in some democracies in which citizens' rights are rather better protected than in ours, such as England and the Scandinavian countries, our arms control policies would be considered laughable.

Laughable, however, they are not, when one begins to contemplate the costs. Since strict gun controls clearly could not entirely prevent homicides, suicides, armed robberies, or gun accidents, there is no simple way of estimating the direct human cost, much less the important indirect political costs, of having lax gun laws. But a somewhat incomplete total of firearms fatalities in the United States as of 1964 shows that in the twentieth century alone we have suffered more than 740,000 deaths from firearms, embracing over 265,000 homicides, over 330,000 suicides, and over 139,000 gun accidents. This figure is considerably higher than all the battle deaths (that is, deaths sustained under arms but excluding those from disease) suffered by American forces in all the wars in our history. It can, of course, be argued that such fatalities have been brought about less by the prevalence of guns than by some intangible factor, such as the wildness and carelessness of the American national temperament, or by particular social problems, such as the intensity of our ethnic and racial mixture. But such arguments cut both ways, since it can be held that a nation with such a temperament or such social problems needs stricter, not looser, gun controls.

One can only make a rough guess at the price Americans pay for their inability to arrive at satisfactory controls for guns. But it can be suggested in this way: there are several American cities that annually have more gun murders than all of England and Wales. In Britain, where no one may carry a firearm at night, where anyone who wants a long gun for hunting must get a certificate from the local police chief before he can buy it, and where gun dealers must verify a buyer's certificate, register all transactions in guns and ammunition, and take the serial number of each weapon and report it to the police, there are annually about .05 gun homicides per 100,000 population. In the United States there are 2.7. What this means in actual casualties may be suggested by the figures for 1963, when there were 5,126 gun murders in the United States, twenty-four in England and Wales, and three in Scotland. This country shows up about as badly in comparative gun accidents and, to a lesser degree, in suicides. There is not a single major country in the world that approaches our record in this respect.

Americans nowadays complain bitterly about the rising rate of violent crime. The gun is, of course, a major accessory of serious premeditated crime. Appealing for stronger gun controls in 1968, President Johnson pointed out that in the previous year there had been committed, with the use of guns, 7,700 murders, 55,000 aggravated assaults, and more than 71,000 robberies. Plainly, stronger gun controls could not end crime, but they would greatly enhance enforcement of the law (as New York's Sullivan Law does) and would reduce fatalities. Out of every one hundred assaults with guns, twenty-one led to death, as compared with only three out of every one hundred assaults committed by other means. In five states with relatively strong gun laws the total homicide rate per 100,000 population—that is, homicides from all causes —runs between 2.4 and 4.8. In the five states with the weakest gun laws this rate varies from 6.1 to 10.6.

In 1968, after the assassinations of Robert F. Kennedy and Martin Luther King, Jr., there was an almost touching national revulsion against our own gun culture, and for once the protesting correspondence on the subject reaching senators and representatives outweighed letters stirred up by the extraordinarily efficient lobby of the National Rifle Association. And yet all that came out of this moment of acute concern was a feeble measure, immensely disappointing to advocates of serious gun control, restricting the mail-order sales of guns. It seems clear now that the strategic moment for gun controls has passed and that the United States will continue to endure an armed populace, at least until there is a major political disaster involving the use of guns.

Today the *urban* population of the nation is probably more heavily armed than at any time in history, largely because the close of World War II left the participating countries with a huge surplus of militarily obsolescent but still quite usable guns. These could be sold nowhere in the world but in the United States, since no other country large enough and wealthy enough to provide a good market would have them. More weapons became available again in the 1950s, when NATO forces switched to a uniform cartridge and abandoned a stock of outmoded rifles. These again flooded the United States, including about 100,000 Italian Carcanos of the type with which John F. Kennedy was killed. Imported very cheaply, sometimes at less than a dollar apiece, these weapons could be sold at enormous profit but still inexpensively—the one that killed Kennedy cost $12.78.

It has been estimated that between five and seven million foreign weapons were imported into the United States between 1959 and 1963. Between 1965 and 1968 handgun imports rose from 346,000 to 1,155,000. Domestic industries that make cheap handguns are approaching an annual production of 500,000 pistols a year. Thus a nation in the midst of a serious political crisis, which has frequently provoked violence, is afloat with weapons—perhaps as many as fifty million of them—in civilian hands. An Opinion Research poll of September, 1968, showed that 34 percent of a national sample of white families and 24 percent of blacks admitted to having guns. With groups like the Black Panthers and right-wing cranks like the Minute Men, not to speak of numerous white vigilante groups, well armed for trouble, the United States finds itself in a situation faced by no other nation. One must ask: What are the historical forces that have led a supposedly well-governed nation into such a dangerous position?

It is very easy, in interpreting American history, to give the credit and the blame for almost everything to the frontier, and certainly this temptation is particularly strong where guns are concerned. After all, for the first 250 years of their history Americans were an agricultural people with a continuing history of frontier expansion. At the very beginning the wild continent abounded with edible game, and a colonizing people still struggling to control the wilderness and still living very close to the subsistence level found wild game an important supplement to their diet. Moreover, there were no enforceable feudal inhibitions against poaching by the common man, who was free to roam where he could and shoot what he could and who ate better when he shot better. Furthermore, all farmers, but especially farmers in a lightly settled agricultural country, need guns for the control of wild vermin and predators. The wolf, as we still say, has to be kept from the door.

Finally, and no less imperatively, there were the Indians, who were all too often regarded by American frontiersmen as another breed of wild animal. The situation of the Indians, constantly under new pressures from white encroachments, naturally commands modern sympathy. But they were in fact, partly from the very desperation of their case, often formidable, especially in the early days when they were an important force in the international rivalries of England, France, and Spain in North America. Like the white man they had guns, and like him they committed massacres. Modern critics of our culture who, like Susan Sontag, seem to know nothing of American history, who regard the white race as a "cancer" and assert that the United States was "founded on a genocide," may fantasize that the Indians fought according to the rules of the Geneva Convention. But in the tragic conflict of which they were to be the chief victims, they were capable of striking terrible blows. In King Philip's War (1675–76) they damaged half the towns of New England, destroyed a dozen, and killed an estimated one out of every sixteen males of military age among the settlers. Later the Deerfield and other frontier massacres left powerful scars on the frontier memory, and in the formative days of the colonial period wariness of sudden Indian raids and semimilitary preparations to combat them were common on the western borders of settlements. Men and women, young and old, were all safer if they could command a rifle. "A well grown boy," remembered the Reverend Joseph Doddridge of his years on the Virginia frontier, "at the age of twelve or thirteen years, was furnished with a small rifle and shot-pouch. He then became a fort soldier, and had his port-hole assigned him. Hunting squirrels, turkeys, and raccoons, soon made him expert in the use of his gun."

That familiarity with the rifle, which was so generally inculcated on the frontier, had a good deal to do with such successes as Americans had in the battles of the Revolution. The Pennsylvania rifle, developed by German immigrants, was far superior to Brown Bess, the regulation military musket used by British troops. This blunt musket, an inaccurate weapon at any considerable distance, was used chiefly to gain the effect of mass firepower in open field maneuvers at relatively close range. The long, slender Pennsylvania rifle, which had a bored barrel that gave the bullet a spin, had a flatter and more direct trajectory, and in skilled hands it became a precision instrument. More quickly loaded and effective at a considerable distance, it was singularly well adapted not only to the shooting of squirrels but to the woodsman's shoot-and-hide warfare. It struck such terror into the hearts of British regulars as to cause George Washington to ask that as many of his troops as possible be dressed in the frontiersman's hunting shirt, since the British thought "every such person a complete Marksman." The rifle went a long way to make up for the military inconsistencies and indifferent discipline of American militiamen, and its successes helped to instill in the American mind a conviction of the complete superiority of the armed yeoman to the military professionals of Europe.

What began as a necessity of agriculture and the frontier took hold as a sport and as an ingredient in the American imagination. Before the days of spectator sports, when competitive athletics became a basic part of popular culture, hunting and fishing probably were the chief American sports, sometimes wantonly pursued, as in the decimation of the bison. But for millions of American boys, learning to shoot and above all graduating from toy guns and receiving the first real rifle of their own were milestones of life, veritable rites of passage that certified their arrival at manhood. (It is still argued by some defenders of our gun culture, and indeed conceded by some of its critics, that the gun cannot and will not be given up because it is a basic symbol of masculinity. But the trouble with all such glib Freudian generalities is that they do not explain cultural variations: they do not tell us why men elsewhere have *not* found the gun essential to their masculinity.)

What was so decisive in the winning of the West and the conquest of the Indian became a standard ingredient in popular entertainment. In the penny-dreadful Western and then in films and on television, the western man, quick on the draw, was soon an acceptable hero of violence. He found his successors in the private eye, the FBI agent, and in the gangster himself, who so often provides a semilegitimate object of hero worship, a man with loyalties, courage, and a code of his own—even in films purporting to show that crime does not pay. All mass cultures have their stereotyped heroes, and none are quite free of violence; but the United States has shown an unusual penchant for the isolated, wholly individualistic detective, sheriff, or villain, and its entertainment portrays the solution of melodramatic conflicts much more commonly than, say, the English, as arising not out of ratiocination or some scheme of moral order but out of ready and ingenious violence. Every Walter Mitty has had his moment when he is Gary Cooper, stalking the streets in *High Noon* with his gun at the ready. D. H. Lawrence may have had something, after all, when he made his characteristically bold, impressionistic, and unflattering judgment that "the essential American soul is hard, isolate, stoic, and a killer." It was the notion cherished also by Hemingway in his long romance with war and hunting and with the other sports that end in death.

However, when the frontier and its ramifications are given their due, they fall far short of explaining the persistence of the American gun culture. Why is the gun still so prevalent in a culture in which only about 4 percent of the country's workers now make their living from farming, a culture that for the last century and a half has had only a tiny fragment of its population actually in contact with a frontier, that, in fact, has not known a true frontier for three generations? Why did the United States alone among industrial societies cling to the idea that a substantially unregulated supply of guns among its city populations is a safe and acceptable thing? This is, after all, not the only nation with a frontier history. Canada and Australia have had theirs, and yet their gun control measures are far more satisfactory than ours. Their own gun homicide rates, as compared with our 2.7, range around .56, and their gun suicide and accident rates are also much lower. Again, Japan, with no frontier but with an ancient tradition of feudal and military violence, has adopted, along with its modernization, such rigorous gun laws that its gun homicide rate at .04 is one of the world's lowest. (The land of hara-kiri also has one of the lowest gun suicide rates—about one-fiftieth of ours.) In sum, other societies, in the course of industrial and urban development, have succeeded in modifying their old gun habits, and we have not.

One factor that could not be left out of any adequate explanation of the tenacity of our gun culture is the existence of an early American political creed that has had a surprisingly long life, albeit much of it now is in an underground popular form. It has to do with the anti-militaristic traditions of radical English Whiggery, which were taken over and intensified in colonial America, especially during the generation preceding the American Revolution, and which became an integral part of the American political tradition. The popular possession of the gun was a central point in a political doctrine that became all but sacrosanct in the Revolution: a doctrine that rested upon faith in the civic virtue and military prowess of the yeoman; belief in the degeneration of England and in the sharp decline of "the liberties of Englishmen" on their original home soil; and a great fear of a standing army as one of the key dangers to this body of ancient liberties. The American answer to civic and military decadence, real or imagined, was the armed yeoman.

By the same reasoning the answer to militarism and standing armies was the militia system. It had long been the contention of those radical Whig writers whose works did so much to set the background of American thought, that liberty and standing armies were incompatible. Caesar and Cromwell were commonly cited as the prime historical examples of the destructive effects of political generals on the liberties of the people. The Americans became confident that their alternative device, an armed people, was the only possible solution to the perennial conflict between militarism and freedom. Their concern over the evils of repeated wars and institutionalized armies was heightened by the eighteenth-century European wars in which they were inevitably involved. Blaming the decay that they imagined to be sweeping over England in good part on the increasing role of the military in the mother country, they found their worst fears confirmed by the quartering of troops before the Revolution. John Adams saw in the Boston Massacre "the strongest proof of the danger of standing armies." The Virginian George Mason, surveying the history of the nations of the world, remarked: "What havoc, desolation and destruction, have been perpetrated by standing armies!" The only remedy, he thought, reverting to one of the genial fictions of this school of thought, was the ancient Saxon militia, "the natural strength and only stable security of a free government." Jefferson reverted to the idea of a popular Saxon militia by providing in his first draft of the Virginia Constitution of 1776 that "no freeman shall ever be debarred the use of arms."

Washington, who had to command militiamen, had no illusions about them. He had seen not a single instance, he once wrote, that would justify "an opinion of Militia or raw Troops being fit for the real business of fighting. I have found them useful as light Parties to skirmish in the woods, but incapable of making or sustaining a serious attack." Despite the poor record of militia troops in the Revolution, as compared with the courage and persistence of Washington's small and fluctuating Continental Army, the myth persisted that the freedom of America had been won by the armed yeoman and the militia system, and the old fear of a standing army was in no way diminished now that it was not to be under the command of an English aristocracy but of native American generals. In the mid-1780s, when the Americans had won their independence and were living under the Articles of Confederation, Secretary of War Henry Knox found himself the administrator of an army of about seven hundred men. In the 1790s, when it was proposed under the Constitution to add only about five hundred more, Pennsylvania Democrat Senator William Maclay anxiously observed that the government seemed to be "laying the foundation of a standing army"! Only the disastrous performance of militiamen in the War of 1812 persuaded many American leaders that the militia was a slender reed upon which to rest the security of the nation.

In the meantime the passion for a popular militia as against a professional army had found its permanent embodiment in the Second Amendment to the Constitution: "A well regulated Militia, being necessary to the security of a free State, the right of the people to keep and bear Arms, shall not be infringed." By its inclusion in the Bill of Rights, the right to bear arms thus gained permanent sanction in the nation, but it came to be regarded as an item on the basic list of guarantees of *individual* liberties. Plainly it was not meant as such. The right to bear arms was a *collective*, not an individual right, closely linked to the civic need (especially keen in the absence of a sufficient national army) for "a well regulated Militia." It was, in effect, a promise that Congress would not be able to bar the states from doing whatever was necessary to maintain well-regulated militias.*

The Supreme Court has more than once decided that the Second Amendment does not bar certain state or federal gun controls. In 1886 it upheld an Illinois statute forbidding bodies of men to associate in military organizations or to drill or parade with arms in cities or towns. When Congress passed the National Firearms Act of 1934 forbidding the transportation in interstate commerce of unregistered shotguns, an attempt to invoke the Second Amendment against the law was rejected by the Court in what is now the leading case on the subject, United States v. Miller (1939). In this case the Court, ruling on the prosecution of two men who had been convicted of violating the National Firearms Act by taking an unregistered sawed-off shotgun across state lines, concluded that the sawed-off shotgun had no "reasonable relationship to the prevention, preservation, or efficiency of a well-regulated militia." The Court ruled that since the gun in question was not part of ordinary military equipment, its use was unrelated to the common defense. The Court further found that the clear purpose of the Second Amendment was to implement the constitutional provision for "calling forth the Militia to execute the Laws of the Union, suppress insurrections and repel invasions" and declared that the Second Amendment "must be interpreted and applied with that end in view."

While the notion that "the right to bear arms" is inconsistent with state or federal gun regulation is largely confined to the obstinate lobbyists of the National Rifle Association, another belief of American gun enthusiasts enjoys a very wide currency in the United States, extending to a good many liberals, civil libertarians, and even radicals. It is the idea that popular access to arms is an important counterpoise to tyranny. A historian, recently remonstrating against our gun policies, was asked by a sympathetic liberal listener whether it was not true, for example, that one of the first acts of the Nazis had been to make it impossible for the nonparty, nonmilitary citizen to have a gun—the assumption being that the German people had thus lost their last barrier to tyranny. In fact Nazi gun policies were of no basic consequence: the democratic game had been lost long before, when legitimate authorities under the Weimar Republic would not or could not stop uniformed groups of Nazi terrorists from intimidating other citizens on the streets and in their meetings and when the courts and the Reich Ministry of Justice did not act firmly and consistently to punish the makers of any Nazi Putsch according to law. It is not strong and firm governments but weak ones, in-

---

*For a more detailed discussion of issues related to the Second Amendment, see Part Four of this volume.—Ed.

capable of exerting their regulatory and punitive powers, that are overthrown by tyrannies. Nonetheless, the American historical mythology about the protective value of guns has survived the modern technological era in all the glory of its naïveté, and it has been taken over from the whites by some young blacks, notably the Panthers, whose accumulations of arms have thus far proved more lethal to themselves than to anyone else. In all societies the presence of small groups of uncontrolled and unauthorized men in unregulated possession of arms is recognized to be dangerous. A query therefore must ring in our heads: Why is it that in all other modern democratic societies those endangered ask to have such men disarmed, while in the United States alone they insist on arming themselves?

A further point is of more than symptomatic interest: the most gun-addicted sections of the United States are the South and the Southwest. In 1968, when the House voted for a mild bill to restrict the mail-order sale of rifles, shotguns, and ammunition, all but a few of the 118 votes against it came from these regions. This no doubt had something to do with the rural character of these regions, but it also stems from another consideration: in the historic system of the South, having a gun was a white prerogative. From the days of colonial slavery, when white indentured servants were permitted, and under some circumstances encouraged, to have guns, blacks, whether slave or free, were denied the right. The gun, though it had a natural place in the South's outdoor culture, as well as a necessary place in the work of slave patrols, was also an important symbol of white male status. Students in the Old South took guns to college as a matter of course. In 1840 an undergraduate at the University of Virginia killed a professor during a night of revelry that was frequently punctuated by gunfire. Thomas Hart Benton, later to be a distinguished Missouri senator, became involved, during his freshman year at the University of North Carolina, in a brawl in which he drew a pistol on another student, and was spared serious trouble only when a professor disarmed him. He was sixteen years old at the time. In the light of the long white effort to maintain a gun monopoly, it is hardly surprising, though it may be discouraging, to see militant young blacks borrowing the white man's mystique and accepting the gun as their instrument. "A gun is status—that's why they call it an equalizer," said a young Chicago black a few years ago. "What's happening today is that everybody's getting more and more equal because everybody's got one."

But perhaps more than anything else the state of American gun controls is evidence of one of the failures of federalism: the purchase and possession of guns in the United States is controlled by a chaotic jumble of twenty thousand state and local laws that collectively are wholly inadequate to the protection of the people and that operate in such a way that areas with poor controls undermine those with better ones. No such chaos would be tolerated, say, in the field of automobile registration. The automobile, like the gun, is a lethal instrument, and the states have recognized it as such by requiring that each driver as well as each car must be registered and that each driver must meet certain specified qualifications. It is mildly inconvenient to conform, but no one seriously objects to the general principle, as gun lobbyists do to gun registration. However, as the United States became industrial and urban, the personnel of its national and state legislatures remained to a very considerable degree small town and rural, and under the seniority system that prevails in Congress, key posts on committees have long been staffed by aging members from small-town districts—worse still, from small-town districts in regions where there is little or no party competition and hence little turnover in personnel. Many social reforms have been held back long after their time was ripe by this rural-seniority political culture. Gun control is another such reform: American legislators have been inordinately responsive to the tremendous lobby maintained by the National Rifle Association, in tandem with gunmakers and importers, military sympathizers, and far-right organizations. A nation that could not devise a system of gun control after its experiences of the 1960s, and at a moment of profound popular revulsion against guns, is not likely to get such a system in the calculable future. One must wonder how grave a domestic gun catastrophe would have to be in order to persuade us. How far must things go?

2

Social Problems and Sagecraft: Gun Control as a Case in Point

William R. Tonso

This essay is not about the gun control issue per se. It is about the way the issue has typically been dealt with by those social scientists who, in one social scientific capacity or another, have had occasion to be concerned with it. Or, more accurately, this essay focuses on the more publicized social scientific treatments of the gun control issue—those passed on to college students through social problems texts, anthologies, and monographs, and to the general public through magazine articles and the published findings of various social science assisted federal commissions on crime, violence, and civil disturbances. The objective is to point out some of the shortcomings of what will be referred to as the conventional social scientific approach to controversial social issues and social problems.

While the controversial issue examined here is gun control, other examples could conceivably have been used to make the same points: issues such as school busing, pornography, or the legalization of marijuana, or social problems

From *Firearms and Violence: Issues of Public Policy,* edited by Don B. Kates, Jr. (San Francisco, Calif.: Pacific Research Institute for Public Policy). Copyright © 1984 by the Pacific Research Institute for Public Policy. Reprinted by permission of the publisher.

such as discrimination, pollution, poverty, unemployment, or crime. There is a missionary aspect to the conventional approach to such issues and problems in that it often goes beyond analysis to lend, subtly or otherwise, supposedly scientifically based support to one means or other of coping with these phenomena. This support is disseminated through textbooks, commission findings, and so forth, and being "scientifically" based can be ignored only at the risk of one's being considered unenlightened. It will be argued, therefore, that the conventional social scientific treatments of controversial social phenomena often have much more in common with the work of those to whom Florian Znaniecki referred as "sages" than they have with social science, and consequently that such treatments obscure more than they reveal about the issues or problems with which they are dealing. The first part of the essay describes the conventional social scientific treatment of the gun issue, places this treatment into social-cultural context, and finally links it to Znaniecki's comments on the social role of the sage. The second part points out, through a critique of the conventional treatment of the gun issue, how the concerns of the sage affect the social scientific enterprise, here defined broadly enough to include social history.[1]

SOCIAL SCIENCE OR SAGECRAFT?

It seems to be generally accepted that the civilian possession of firearms in the United States is widespread, but whether or not this state of affairs is desirable has been the subject of much controversy since the early part of the twentieth century.[2] The side of this controversy that has received the most publicity through the media, however, maintains that this widespread possession constitutes, if not a social problem unto itself, a major contributing factor to other social problems such as crime, violence, and civil disorder. It is hardly surprising, then, that efforts to bring the civilian possession of firearms under strict control and to reduce the number of firearms in civilian hands have also received a great deal of publicity through the media.

A perusal of the *Reader's Guide to Periodical Literature's* "Firearms—Laws and Regulations" section can give one some indication of the magnitude of this media support for gun controls. Since the latest major push for controls began in the early 1960s, articles on the subject in such news and general interest magazines as *Life, Time, Newsweek, The Saturday Evening Post, Reader's Digest, Harper's, Saturday Review, The Nation,* and *The New Republic* have been almost unanimous in their strong support of gun controls, with only the outdoor, gun, and libertarian magazines consistently taking an anti-control stand. The national television networks have also been almost unanimous in their support of controls through various documentaries on the subject as well as through [popular] television [dramas and sitcoms]. The leading urban newspapers have all editorialized in favor of controls, the *Washington Post* once doing so for seventy-seven straight days,[3] as have many medium- and small-town newspapers and the syndicated columnists and political cartoonists appearing in them—Ann Landers, Art Buchwald, Jack Anderson, and Herblock, among others. Newspapers and magazines have also helped publicize the works of such procontrol authors as Carl Bakal and Robert Sherrill.[4] And even comic strips, such as "Goosemyer," "Tank McNamara," and "Doonesbury," have supported gun controls by ridiculing the anticontrol position.

While those responsible for the various newspaper editorials, columns, magazine articles, and TV documentaries that have over the years argued for controls have often looked to the "experts" on man and society—psychiatrists, psychologists, and sociologists—for assistance, by the middle 1960s the social sciences were starting to get more directly involved in the controversy. In response to the political assassinations and civil disturbances of the period, a number of federal commissions aimed at discovering and eradicating the causes of crime, violence, and civil disturbances were established, and these commissions were invariably assisted by social scientists. The commissions also invariably ended up recommending that strict gun controls be enacted as one means of reducing the amount of crime, violence, and civil disorder.[5]

Beginning with the federal commissions, the social scientific involvement with the gun control issue has extended increasingly to monographs, textbooks, and anthologies which deal with various social problems and are aimed at the college market. Based on commission reports and the treatment that the gun issue has received in the various texts, and so forth, that have dealt with it, the sentiments concerning civilian firearms possession and gun control that have been transmitted through these various social science sources can be summarized as follows:

1. When the United States was being transformed from a raw wilderness to a modern, urban, industrial nation, passing through a rural, agricultural stage along the way, private citizens often had use for firearms if they were to provide themselves with food and/or protection.[6]

2. The United States no longer has a frontier, and in fact, it is now primarily urban and industrial rather than rural and agricultural. Consequently, the large number of firearms that have gotten and continue to get into civilian hands no longer serve any useful purpose and are more trouble than what they are worth. They no longer contribute to the establishment of law and order but actually undermine efforts to establish order, as the high rate of firearms-related crime shows.[7]

3. The United States is the only modern, urban, industrial nation that does not strictly regulate the civilian possession of firearms. The effectiveness

of such controls is demonstrated by the fact that other modern, urban, industrial nations, all of which have them, have violent crime rates far lower than those of the United States.[8]

4. It is obvious, therefore, that the United States is badly in need of strict gun controls that at a minimum would require the registration of all privately owned firearms, and licenses and identification cards for all firearms owners, plus a drastic reduction of the number of privately owned handguns.[9]

5. The pollsters have shown that considerably more than half of the populace supports all of these measures and that as many as three fourths support some of them.[10]

6. The only reason that such regulations have not been enacted into law is that the domestic firearms industry and the National Rifle Association have, through well-organized lobbying efforts, been able to take advantage of the weaknesses of the federal system of government to block such legislation.[11]

7. This opposition to obviously needed firearms regulations, though thus far effective, is self-serving, irresponsible, irrational, unenlightened, reactionary, uninformed, etc.[12]

The impression given by the foregoing is that through historical research, cross-cultural comparisons of crime rates, and the scientific analysis of public opinion, social scientists have been able to establish definitely that the United States would benefit significantly from gun controls, that the majority of Americans want such controls, and consequently, that opposition to such controls is self-serving or unreasonable. But there are things about the conventional social scientific analysis of the gun control issue that make one wonder about the impartiality of those engaged in it. First, it should be noted that the conventional social science position on gun control summarized earlier is identical to the position that procontrollers have taken for years without social scientific assistance. In fact, it is not uncommon for nonsocial scientific, non-scholarly, procontrol, antigun polemics such as *The Right to Bear Arms,* by irate citizen Carl Bakal, and *Saturday Night Special,* by "investigative reporter" Robert Sherrill, to be cited in social science textbook analyses of the gun issue.[13] And when such sources are cited, no mention is made of the acknowledged procontrol, antigun sentiments of their authors.

A second interesting aspect of the conventional social scientific treatment of the gun issue is that qualification of the material presented on the subject is rare to nonexistent. Poll findings are accepted at face value, although there is good social scientific cause to do otherwise.[14] Similarly, cross-cultural comparisons of firearms-related crime rates are made with no consideration given to factors having little or nothing to do with gun controls that might help account for cross-cultural differences between such rates.[15]

Finally, it is worthy of consideration that the conventional social scientific treatment of the gun issue makes no attempt to put the control controversy into social, cultural, and historical perspective in order to foster nonjudgmental understanding of the sentiments and vested interests of both those who support controls and those who oppose them. Occasional attempts are made to present the anticontrol position along with the procontrol position,[16] but no effort is made to uncover the vested interests of the people who subscribe to these conflicting views of control, and one is seldom left in doubt concerning which position is the most sophisticated, informed, and logical. Similarly, the gun's place in American history is sometimes examined by conventional social scientists,[17] but its survival is obviously viewed as unfortunate and is explained in terms of cultural lag.

In other words, the conventional social scientific treatment of gun control leaves much to be desired if its goal is the scientific illumination of this controversial issue. Why? To answer this question it is helpful to put both the issue and those studying it into social, cultural, and historical context, as the conventional have been so reluctant to do; a very unconventional work by social historians Lee Kennett and James LaVerne Anderson provides a starting point for such an effort. In *The Gun in America: The Origins of a National Dilemma,* Kennett and Anderson make no policy recommendations or insinuations. They simply fit the gun into American history, demonstrating along the way how the pro- and anticontrol factions evolved and came into conflict with each other as the United States became ever more urban and industrial, and less rural and agricultural. They conclude that the trends are against the gun, but they do not hint that American society will be either better or worse off if this is the case.

While Kennett and Anderson make no attempt to delineate the role that the social sciences have played in the gun control controversy, their treatment of the phenomenon in terms of culture conflict is quite suggestive along these lines. Taking their lead from a *Wall Street Journal* article dealing with gun control, they argue that the controversy is best seen "as a skirmish in the larger battle over the nation's cultural values, a battle in which 'cosmopolitan America' is pitted against 'bedrock America.' "[18] Expanding on the differences between the worldviews of these two Americas and commenting on the appropriateness of the labels applied to them, Kennett and Anderson continue:

The terms are apt; they could be used to describe the protagonists when the Sullivan Law was debated fifty years ago. Pro-gun spokesmen have long been addicted to those assaults on the liberal establishment in which Spiro Agnew excelled, and those in the other camp have not always concealed their contempt for the "shirtsleeve crowd." Cosmopolitan America foresees a new age when guns and the need for them will disappear; bedrock America conceives of it as 1984. Cosmopolitan America has always been concerned about its international image;

bedrock America has always been nativist. Shortly after Robert Kennedy's assassination, Gunnar Myrdal reportedly said that if the Constitution allowed such indiscriminate ownership of guns, "then to hell with the Constitution." Cosmopolitan America would have found this food for sober reflection; bedrock America, without reflection, would have said: "To hell with Gunnar Myrdal."[19]

If, as Kennett and Anderson argue, the gun controversy is "a skirmish in the larger battle over the nation's cultural values," a battle pitting cosmopolitan America's lifestyles, worldviews, and ways of interpreting reality against those of bedrock America, it is hardly surprising that the conventional social scientific treatment of the control issue amounts to an unquestioning scientific stamp of approval of the media-supported procontrol stand. Kennett and Anderson make no claim that the "cultural battle lines" between the two Americas are rigidly fixed. In fact, they claim that "sophisticated America and shirtsleeve America war in all of us."[20]

While the two Americas may war in many of us—all is surely an exaggeration—one gets the impression that the purest cosmopolitanism is likely to be found in the urban, highly educated (degreed might be more appropriate), philosophically and politically liberal, upper-middle class; the purest bedrockism is likely to be found in the rural and small-town, less degreed, philosophically and politically conservative, lower-middle and working classes.[21] If this is the case, at the very cosmopolitan-sophisticated core of cosmopolitan-sophisticated America, along with those who control the nation's media—or at least the national television networks, large circulation metropolitan newspapers, general interest periodicals, and major publishing houses—are the American intellectual elite. And of course, the American intellectual elite includes not only the nation's "top" writers, journalists, and other such literary folk, but its "top" educators, scholars, and scientists, social and otherwise, as well. Cosmopolitan America, therefore, is not only generally more adept at articulating its views than is bedrock America; it also possesses the means to place its views before bedrock as well as cosmopolitan America; *Reader's Digest* and TV for the former; *New Republic* and college social science courses for the latter. Through its scholarly and scientific connections, cosmopolitan America can also coat these views with a thick veneer of what passes for impartial scientific authority: consider the gun control issue and the conventional social scientific treatment of it as a case in point.

That the media, the scholarly-intellectual community, and even the social scientific subcommunity of the latter are, for the most part, part of what the *Wall Street Journal* and Kennett and Anderson have referred to as cosmopolitan America, rather than impartial observers and interpreters of and reporters on the passing scene, has been noted by a number of maverick social scientists. Sociologist, Roman Catholic priest, and columnist Andrew Greeley, himself a strong supporter of strict gun controls, has claimed that the intellectual community—social scientists not excluded—has all the characteristics of an ethnic group, including divisive factions and an ethnocentrism that encourages it to look down upon rather than attempt to understand the nonintellectual "masses."[22] Michael Lerner, while a graduate student in political science and psychology at Yale, claimed in an even more scathing polemic that the "upper classes" are extremely prejudiced against the lower-middle class and that "one of the strongest supports for this upper-class, 'respectable' bigotry lies in the academic field of psychology."[23] Clearly including social scientists, sociologist Stanislav Andrzejewski has noted that liberal intellectuals are not as tolerant as they think they are when it comes to dealing with those who do not subscribe to their Liberal-Humanitarian religion or participate in their "supranational culture."[24] And sociologist Peter Berger has written about the rising "New Class" of knowledge producers, symbol- rather than thing-manipulators, who have class vested interests of their own. According to Berger, "institutionally, prestige universities and other centers of knowledge production (such as think tanks) are centers of New Class power, while publishing houses, periodicals, and foundations serve as distributing agencies."[25] He goes on to point out that the New Class has a vested interest in government intervention because the greater part of its livelihood is derived "from public-sector employment. . . . Because government interventions have to be legitimated in terms of social ills, the New Class has a vested interest in portraying American society as a whole, and specific aspects of that society, in negative terms."[26]

In other words, to these critics and analysts of the knowledge-producing and disseminating class to which they themselves belong, knowledge producers and disseminators in general tend to be so bound up with the worldviews, lifestyles, values, and vested interests of their own urban, upper-middle class, degreed, liberal, sophisticated, cosmopolitan lives that their analyses of various controversial social issues and problems might be expected to be somewhat one-sided and aimed at promoting their own cosmopolitan interests. If this is the case, such knowledge producers and disseminators are involved in what might be called "sagecraft" in behalf of the cosmopolitan America of which they are not only an integral but a central part. "The original status of the sage lies within his party," according to Florian Znaniecki, "and his original function consists in rationalizing and justifying intellectually the collective tendencies of his party. It is his duty to 'prove' by 'scientific' arguments that his party is right and its opponents are wrong."[27]

In order to perform his duty, the sage must demonstrate that his party's position is right because it is based on truth, and that the opposition's stand is wrong because it is based on error. "There is no doubt but that he can perform this task to the satisfaction of himself and his adherents," says Znaniecki, "for in the vast multiplicity of diverse cultural data it is always possible to find facts which, 'properly' interpreted, prove that the generalizations he accepts as true are true and that those he rejects as false are false."[28] Of course, the sage is likely to be opposed by the sages of the other side. Unless opposition sages can be silenced, the sage must call their reasoning and/or facts into question.

If the knowledge producers and disseminators form the core of cosmopolitan America, as suggested in the aforementioned, it is hardly surprising that the social scientific treatment of the gun issue that has been publicized through federal commissions and college social problems books is identical to the procontrol stand almost unanimously supported by the media. Neither is it surprising that such treatments do not critically examine poll findings, cross-cultural comparisons of crime rates, and so forth, that can be used to support controls; nor that they invariably fail to put the control controversy into social, cultural, and historical context examining the vested interests of the pro- as well as the anticontrol factions. That sagecraft, purposeful or the inadvertent product of cosmopolitan ethnocentrism, helps account for such oversights is suggested by statements made by two prominent sociologists associated with a federal commission headed by Milton Eisenhower. In spite of the fact that his own research ten years earlier had found no correlation between the availability of guns and the incidence of gun crime, one of these, Marvin E. Wolfgang, stated in a letter to the editor of *Time* magazine: "My personal choice for legislation is to remove all guns from private possession. I would favor statutory provisions that require all guns to be turned in to public authorities."[29] The other, Morris Janowitz, is in complete agreement: "I see no reason . . . why anyone in a democracy should own a weapon."[30]

Inadvertent or otherwise, a sage orientation results in social scientific analysis that is social scientific in name only. The social scientist who is primarily concerned with "rationalizing and justifying intellectually the collective tendencies of his party," rather than with shedding as much light as possible on a complex social phenomenon is quite limited. He or she is not likely to consider personal position as part of the phenomenon being studied, or to recognize how one's ideological position restricts one's vision.

SAGECRAFT AND THE SOCIAL SCIENTIFIC ENTERPRISE

While it is being suggested that those social scientists responsible for the conventional social scientific treatment of the gun control issue are acting as sages in behalf of a cosmopolitan America that is generally anti-gun, no claim is made that they are, in most cases at least, consciously doing so. It would not be surprising to find that most of those social scientists assisting federal commissions or passing information concerning the phenomenon to students through textbooks actually feel that they are letting the facts—crime rates, poll results, and so forth—speak for themselves. The point being made is that such social scientists have been inclined to take too much for granted about the gun issue, possibly due to their own cosmopolitan worldviews, life-styles, values, and vested interests, and in doing so they have provided "scientific" support—sage fashion—for the cosmopolitan tendencies that they not only share but help to create. A few examples should suffice to demonstrate how such cosmopolitan ethnocentrism and the sage orientation it encourages can affect the social scientific enterprise.

Consider the late Richard Hofstadter's attempt to explain the widespread civilian possession of firearms in the United States. Along the way, as he attempted to discredit the "frontier past" explanation for a state of affairs that he clearly considered to be deplorable, Hofstadter noted that the American frontier experience could not account for the persistence of what he referred to as the American gun culture, since the frontier faded away several genera-tions ago. "Why," Hofstadter asked, "did the United States alone among indus-trial societies cling to the idea that a substantially unregulated supply of guns among its city populations is a safe and acceptable thing."[31] Canada and Austra-lia have had frontiers, and Japan has had a violent past, he reminds us, yet the gun homicide, suicide, and accident rates for these nations are far lower than those for the United States. Hofstadter credits the "rigorous gun laws" that Japan (the land of hara-kiri) has adopted as it has modernized with produc-ing that country's extremely low gun homicide and suicide rates. "In sum," he states, "other societies, in the course of industrial and urban development, have succeeded in modifying their old gun habits, and we have not."[32]

The preceding is typical of the conventional social scientific use of cross-cultural comparisons to support gun controls. The facts have apparently been allowed to speak for themselves. But interestingly enough, the conventional never tell us anything about the "old gun habits" of other nations that gun controls have supposedly modified. In fact, the conventional not only do not tell us anything about these "old gun habits," but they show no sign that they are familiar with them or that they have made any attempt to become so. Hofstadter, for example, simply assumed that Japan's "old gun habits" were similar to ours because of that nation's tradition of feudal and military violence, and that Australia's and Canada's were similar to ours because both nations have had frontiers. Such assumptions certainly amount to convenient lapses of scholarly curiosity, since the works of various scholars who have not involved themselves with the gun control controversy—firearms historians, students of Japanese history, and those who have compared frontiers—give us no reason to believe that the "old gun habits" of these nations were anything like ours.

With respect to Japan, if we are to accept what other scholars have written on the subject, firearms were used extensively in the feudal wars after having been brought to Japan by the Portuguese toward the middle of the sixteenth century, but the populace as a whole never seemed to have become familiar with them.[33] The sword remained the most respected weapon through the

250 years of relatively peaceful Tokugawa rule down to rather recent times. During this period, partly due to traditional concerns and partly due to official policy, little or no effort was made to improve firearms, and when Perry "reopened" Japan to the rest of the world in the middle of the nineteenth century, the Japanese were still using matchlock guns of the same basic variety as those to which they had been introduced by the Portuguese 300 years earlier. What "old gun habits" did the Japanese have to modify as they became urban and industrial? Why should "rigorous gun laws" that came with "modernization" be credited with producing a low gun-related homicide rate when, prior to "modernization," Japan had relegated the gun to the status of plaything of the wealthy and had shown little or no concern for developing it as a weapon? Similarly, how can such laws be credited with producing a low gun-related suicide rate in a traditionbound land where the honored way to commit hara-kiri was with a knife?

With regard to Canada and Australia, scholars who have compared them have found many differences between the Canadian and Australian frontiers and our own—differences that may account for dissimilar patterns of firearms usage between those of our frontiers and the others. Except for the trouble that the French experienced with the Iroquois Confederacy in eastern Canada during the eighteenth century, for instance, neither Canadian nor Australian frontiersmen encountered the formidable aboriginal opposition that Americans encountered on the fringes of settlement for some 250 years of "recurring pioneering experience."[34] In fact, neither the Canadian nor the Australian frontier experience could even be described as recurring. Part of the Canadian east was simply transported west after the railroads penetrated the Laurentian Shield in the late nineteenth century; in Australia, pioneer expansion was stopped short in the mid-nineteenth century by the uninhabitable interior deserts.[35] Centralized police forces, for another example, were reasonably effective in Canada[36] and Australia, though hardly popular in the latter,[37] while "law and order" was often brought to American frontier communities through vigilante action,[38] a phenomenon hardly known on the other two frontiers. In short, it would seem that American frontiersmen over a period of 250 or so years were required to rely more heavily on their firearms for their own protection than were their Canadian and Australian counterparts.

But Hofstadter not only was not aware of, or conveniently overlooked, differences between frontiers that might have produced dissimilar "old gun habits" in these various ex-frontier nations; he also overlooked differences that developed behind the frontiers in these nations—differences that also might have had some bearing on the forms these "habits" took and on their preservation. To compare modern firearms-related crime rates of formerly frontier nations without considering the differences in the magnitude of the transformations that these nations have experienced is to "stack the deck" sage-fashion in favor of one's own cause rather than to attempt to foster understanding. When one considers that the United States, 3,615,122 square miles in area to Canada's 3,851,809 and Australia's 2,967,909, has almost five times the population and over eight times the Gross National Product of Canada and Australia combined, it is obvious that much more has occurred behind the frontier here than in either of the other nations. And it seems generally agreed that this American transformation generated much more social disruption and civil strife than has resulted from the lesser transformations in Canada and Australia. What were the Canadian or Australian equivalents of our Revolutionary and Civil Wars, for example—conflicts that set neighbor against neighbor and lasted at that level long after the battlefields had grown silent? When did either Canada or Australia have racial, ethnic, or labor wars to approach those that Americans have waged against each other behind the frontier?

In other words, the passing of the frontier in the United States did not appreciably reduce the risk to life and limb that Americans have created for each other, so, given the political nature of law enforcement that conflict theorists take such delight in exploring, why is it surprising that many Americans continue to look to the gun for protection as well as for recreation? How can Canadian and Australian gun laws be credited with producing lower gun-related crime rates than ours by modifying "old gun habits" assumed to have been similar to ours, when there seems to be good reason to believe that neither their frontiers nor what came afterward actually produced "old gun habits" like ours?

Hofstadter's comments on the modified "old gun habits" of other nations appeared in an *American Heritage* article entitled "America as a Gun Culture." This article developed a theme first mentioned in Hofstadter's introduction to an anthology he and Michael Wallace edited, entitled *American Violence: A Documentary History.*[39] If his assumptions concerning the "old gun habits" of other nations have been challenged in the scholarly literature on the gun issue published to date, such challenges have received little publicity.

Another example of the selective perception that scholarly supporters of gun controls carry into their cross-cultural comparisons of crime rates is provided by a social science assisted staff report submitted to the National Commission on the Causes and Prevention of Violence, headed by Milton Eisenhower. This report, directed by George D. Newton and Franklin E. Zimring, pointed out that of the four homicides per 100,000 persons recorded in England and Wales in 1967, only one out of each four involved the use of a firearm.[40] In the United States during the same period, sixty-one crimes of this sort were recorded per 100,000 persons, with thirty-eight of each sixty-one involving the use of firearms. Similarly, in England and Wales, ninety-seven robberies per 100,000 persons were recorded, with only six of each ninety-seven involving firearms, while in the United States 1020 robberies per 100,000 persons were recorded, with 372 out of each 1020 involving the use of firearms.

To the extent that one is inclined to take statistics at face value, these figures are interesting. Suppose that no American citizen had possessed a firearm in 1967, and let us assume that none of the crimes in which firearms were used that year would have been committed if a firearm had not been available—a questionable assumption, to say the least. Subtracting the firearms-related crimes from the others, we find that the United States still would have led England and Wales in homicides twenty-three to four per 100,000 (5.8 to 1) and in robberies 648 to ninety-seven per 100,000 (6.7 to 1). A scholar interested in shedding light on a complex issue might wonder, then, if it is English gun laws or the differences between English and American societies that are responsible for the lower rate of firearms-related crime in England and Wales. Newton and Zimring acknowledge this possibility but do not dwell on it, since they are building the case for controls. A scholar might also point out that the passing of the frontier has not, according to these figures, removed the sorts of threats that humans create for one another from the United States (and these threatening conditions have continued not simply because of the absence of strong firearms regulations). A procontrol sage, of course, would hardly be expected to consider seriously either of these issues, but Newton and Zimring and the social scientists who assisted them were supposedly searching for "truths" upon which to base policy recommendations.[41] It should be mentioned that Marvin Wolfgang, whose strong procontrol sentiments have been mentioned, was one of the social scientists associated with the report.

As the conventional have been inclined to take too much for granted about firearms use, past and present, in other parts of the world, they have also been inclined to accept uncritically and pass on Gallup and Harris poll results that invariably show that there is a great deal of public support for various gun control measures. Sociologist Rodney Stark, for example, wrote the following in his college-level social problems text: "The failure of national, state, and local governments to enact strict gun-control legislation offers considerable insight into the American political process. For decades a dedicated minority has had its will over an apathetic majority. What does the majority believe?"[42] Looking to the public opinion polls for the answer to his question, Stark noted that 84 percent of those polled on gun control by Gallup in 1938 believed that " 'all owners of pistols and revolvers should be required to register with the Government' "; that 75 percent of those polled in 1959 "(and 65 percent of gun owners) believed no one should be permitted to buy a gun without a police permit"; and that "no poll conducted in the United States has ever found that more than a third of those polled opposed tough gun controls."[43] This same message, as has been noted, can be found in other social problems texts and anthology readings, always presented in a matter-of-fact manner as if the poll findings are indisputable. But poll findings are not indisputable, as anyone familiar with the measurement and interpretation problems encountered by survey researchers is likely to be aware.

To claim that the "apathetic majority" believes that we should have "tough gun controls" of some type or other implies that we know that the people concerned have seriously considered the issue, taken a stand in favor of controls, but been unwilling to put forth the effort required to get them enacted. But might we not just as easily conclude that the majority is inactive because most of those who are a part of it have seldom given any consideration at all to the issue and are really not particularly committed to controls? The apparent overwhelming procontrol support reported by the polls does not preclude this interpretation. The appearance of support might be the product of one or both of the following:

1. Even if an individual has given little or no consideration to the gun control issue, and consequently is not committed to either a pro- or anticontrol stand, once he has decided to cooperate with the pollsters, he or she must make some effort to answer their questions. And, given the situation, it would hardly be surprising for the responses to support tough gun laws. Though not committed, the individual may quite understandably feel that this is the response expected. Survey researchers are familiar with the measurement problems posed by "social desirability" responses,[44] and with the overwhelming media support for controls, the possibility that such responses may have inflated the procontrol column of the polls can scarcely be dismissed. The way the questions are posed, the demeanor of the interviewer, and recent news events may also tend to make the procontrol response seem to be the expected response. Who but the most dedicated opponent of controls could tell an urbane interviewer that he or she was against tough gun controls after a presidential assassination involving the use of a firearm?

2. Apart from the social desirability response issue, the way that single questions or a series of questions are posed can, inadvertently or otherwise, elicit the responses desired by those commissioning the polls. Thus the Harris and Gallup polls, commissioned by the procontrol media, ask whether the respondent is for tough gun controls and invariably find that most Americans want the controls that the media support. On the other hand, the less-publicized survey conducted for the anticontrol National Rifle Association by Decision/Making/Information (DMI), a California-based opinion measuring firm, asking simply "What should be done to reduce crime?" When only 11 percent suggested that gun laws were needed, DMI reported that "the lack of gun control laws is not spontaneously mentioned as either a national problem or a local problem by a significant number of citizens. Their attention had to be called to the issue before they expressed an opinion."[45] Once their attention was called to the issue, 73 percent answered that they did not believe that even firearms confiscation would reduce crime, and 68 percent answered that they felt that most gun owners would not turn in their guns if the federal government demanded that they do so. Not surprisingly, the bias built into the DMI poll

satisfied the NRA. When NBC made the mistake of asking similar questions, they found that 59 percent of those polled answered that a handgun ban would not reduce crime and 11 percent answered that it would increase crime.[46] Certainly this was a tactical error in the war between the sages.

Even if we assume that the interviewer's questions have tapped the "true feelings" of the American public on a given issue, however, we are still faced with the problem of interpretation. It may be that the majority of Americans, after carefully thinking over the issue, support tougher gun controls. It may also be, given what appears to be an American, or at least a bedrock, tendency to view crime in terms of "us good guys" against "those bad guys,"[47] that many such supporters, particularly those who are firearms owners, do not consider the possibility that they themselves may be adversely affected by such laws. After all, the police would never deny them permission to acquire or possess the firearm of their choice—only the "bad guys" would be affected. This assumption may shed light on the apparent paradox noted by Kennett and Anderson: according to the polls, most Americans support gun controls at the same time that most would use their guns against urban rioters.[48] What response would Gallup and Harris receive if they asked those being interviewed if they would support firearms regulations even though there was a good chance that those regulations would restrict their own possession and usage of firearms?

Many social scientists are aware of the problems associated with polls and survey research in general, and in fact, the preceding commentary is largely based on Armand L. Mauss and Milton Rokeach's critique of a 1976 Gallup poll. The purpose these two sociologists give for their critique is as follows: "We would like to suggest a number of considerations that should be kept in mind by the intelligent and sophisticated reader in assessing the significance of survey results like these, and then offer a few opinions of our own about their meanings."[49] This objective could certainly be considered praiseworthy, an example of the scientific, inquiring mind at its best, taking for granted no more than necessary, and helping others to examine that which they might have overlooked. The poll findings being critiqued, however, had nothing to do with gun control. Significantly, the poll chosen for critical examination dealt with religious beliefs and had found, among other things, "that 94 percent of Americans still believe in God," and that "69 percent believe in immortality." Bedrock America, of course, might be expected to revel in these findings, but ultra-cosmopolitan America would probably find them disconcerting. And also significantly, the critique appeared in *The Humanist,* the journal of the ultra-cosmopolitan secular humanists. When poll findings indicating that the majority of Americans favor strong gun controls are cited in texts and commission reports, they are not accompanied by "considerations that should be kept in mind by the intelligent and sophisticated reader in assessing the significance of survey results."

As the conventional have been inclined to take too much for granted about the use of firearms past and present in other parts of the world, and to accept uncritically and pass on Gallup and Harris poll findings, so have they been reluctant to treat the gun issue as some of their number have treated other controversial social issues. Edwin M. Schur, for example, has claimed that categories of victimless crimes have been created through the outlawing of abortion, homosexuality, and the use of certain drugs. He has argued that such laws are unenforceable, and that they may have unwelcome side effects —the establishment of "the economic basis for black-market operations," or the production of "situations in which police efficiency is impaired and police corruption encouraged."[50] While bedrock America might find such an argument hard to accept, cosmopolitan America would probably tend to agree with it.

If the argument holds for laws against the use of certain drugs, and so forth, does it not also hold for attempts to regulate firearms possession? Those who do not register their guns when registration is required, or who do not turn in their handguns when handgun possession is banned become classifiable as criminal even though they have not misused firearms or committed other acts classifiable as serious crimes. How would gun control affect police efficiency? The more difficult it becomes to acquire firearms legally, the more valuable supposedly confidential firearms registration and owner registration lists become to professional burglars who wish to locate firearms for illegal sale; hence, more temptation is placed in the way of those officials charged with guarding such records. If an attempt is made to disarm the populace, the guns that the police are able to confiscate become valuable items. How many will be filtered back into private hands via the black market? How could gun controls not foster official and police corruption? When laws are difficult to enforce, as attorney Don B. Kates, Jr., has noted, "enforcement becomes progressively more haphazard until at last the laws are used only against those who are unpopular with the police."[51] How could gun control not lead to selective enforcement and discrimination against minorities and the poor? It would seem that Schur, of all people, would be in a position to recognize that if this argument concerning the creation of victimless crime categories and their side effects holds for any attempts to regulate behavior, it holds as well for gun control. But not surprisingly, the recognition seems to have escaped him, as it has other social scientists, and he has even indicated that he believes gun controls could play a significant part in reducing violence and civil disorder.[52] Need more be said concerning the restricted vision that cosmopolitan ethnocentrism and sagecraft can impose on the social scientific enterprise?

SUMMARY

Using the gun control issue as a case in point, this essay has argued that the conventional social scientific treatment of controversial social phenomena often has much more in common with sagecraft than it does with social science. The social scientific treatment of the gun issue passed on to the general public through magazine articles, textbooks, and the published findings of various social science assisted federal commissions is identical to the pro-gun control argument generally accepted by that segment of American society with which the more prominent social scientists are more likely to identify—urban, degreed, philosophically and politically liberal, upper-middle class, or cosmopolitan America. While the cosmopolitan ethnocentrism of the social scientists involved may help to account for their treatment of the control issue, in lending "scientific" support to the pro-gun control position of cosmopolitan America, these social scientists are still serving the vested interests of their party.

Firearms historians, students of frontiers, and other scholars not dealing directly with the gun control issue have shown in various ways that patterns of firearms use and the social factors accounting for them have differed significantly from one part of the world to another. Textbook and federal commission treatments of the gun issue, apparently completely oblivious to such considerations, continue to credit gun controls with "modifying the old gun habits" of other modern nations and thereby reducing their gun crime rates. Many social scientists are aware of the problems associated with public opinion polls and survey research in general, but textbook and commission citations of poll results supportive of gun controls are never accompanied by hints to the "intelligent and sophisticated reader" interested "in assessing the significance of survey results." Some social scientists have concerned themselves with making students and the public aware of the social repercussions arising from the creation of victimless crime categories, but these same individuals do not seem to believe that attempts to regulate firearms possession would create such a category. It would certainly appear that cosmopolitan ethnocentrism and the sage orientation that it fosters do little to encourage the intellectual curiosity and skepticism so vital to ᴛe social scientific enterprise.

NOTES

1. While the tone of this essay might seem polemical in places, its aim is not to argue against gun control. Though the author does personally oppose such controls, whether or not they are necessary or desirable is a political issue to him, rather than a social scientific issue. The essay's polemics are not aimed at gun control, therefore, but at one-sided social science, which in this case is pro-gun control.

2. Lee Kennett and James LaVerne Anderson, *The Gun in America: The Origins of a National Dilemma* (Westport, Conn.: Greenwood Press, 1975), ch. 7.

3. Ibid., pp. 239, 312.

4. Carl Bakal, *The Right to Bear Arms* (New York: McGraw-Hill, 1966); Robert Sherrill, *The Saturday Night Special* (New York: Charter House, 1973).

5. See George D. Newton and Franklin E. Zimring, *Firearms and Violence in American Life,* a staff report to the National Commission on the Causes and Prevention of Violence (Washington, D.C.: GPO, 1969). This work is a prime example of such commission reports, and it includes a summary of several others. pp. 151–62.

6. See Richard Hofstadter, "America as a Gun Culture," *American Heritage* (October 1970): 7, 10; Richard Hofstadter and Michael Wallace, eds., *American Violence: A Documentary History* (New York: Vintage Books, 1970), p. 24; Eugene W. Hollon, *Frontier Violence: Another Look* (New York: Oxford University Press, 1974), pp. 121–22; Charles H. McCaghy, *Deviant Behavior: Crime, Conflict, and Interest Groups* (New York: Macmillan, 1976), p. 125; Joseph Boskin, "The Essential American Soul: Violent," in Joseph Boskin, ed., *Issues in American Society* (Encino, Calif.: Glencoe, 1978), p. 43; Daniel Glazer, *Crime in Our Changing Society* (New York: Holt, Rinehart and Winston, 1978), p. 201; Charles E. Silberman, *Criminal Violence, Criminal Justice* (New York: Vintage Books, 1978), pp. 48–49; and Newton and Zimring, *Firearms and Violence in American Life.*

7. See Kenneth Westhues, *First Sociology* (New York: McGraw-Hill, 1982), pp. 457, 460–62; Newton and Zimring, *Firearms and Violence in American Life;* Hofstadter, "America as a Gun Culture"; Hofstadter and Wallace, *American Violence,* pp. 25–26; Hollon, *Frontier Violence,* pp. 121–22; McCaghy, *Deviant Behavior,* p. 125; Boskin, "The Essential American Soul," p. 48; Glazer, *Crime in Our Changing Society,* p. 260; and Silberman, *Criminal Violence,* pp. 80–81.

8. See Amitai Etzioni, "Violence," in Robert K. Merton and Robert Nisbet, eds., *Contemporary Social Problems* (New York: Harcourt Brace Jovanovich, 1971), p. 740; Lamar Empey, "American Society and Criminal Justice Reform," in Abraham S. Blumberg, ed., *Current Perspectives on Criminal Behavior: Original Essays in Criminology* (New York: Oxford University Press, 1974), pp. 295–96; Arthur S. Shostak, ed., *Modern Social Reforms: Solving Today's Social Problems* (New York: Macmillan, 1974), p. 291; Rodney Stark, *Social Problems* (New York: Random House, 1975), p. 226; Martin R. Haskell and Lewis Yablonsky, *Crime and Delinquency* (Chicago: Rand McNally, 1978), pp. 340–41; Michael S. Bassis, Richard J. Gelles, and Ann Levine, *Social Problems* (New York: Harcourt Brace Jovanovich, 1982), p. 477; Donald Light, Jr., and Suzanne Keller, *Sociology,* 3rd ed. (New York: Alfred A. Knopf, 1982), p. 254; Newton and Zimring, *Firearms and Violence in American Life,* pp. 119–28; Hofstadter, "America as a Gun Culture," p. 82; Hofstadter and Wallace, *American Violence,* p. 26; and Hollon, *Frontier Violence,* p. 122.

9. See Joseph Julian, *Social Problems* (New York: Appleton-Century-Croft, 1973), pp. 481–82; Marvin E. Wolfgang, "Violent Behavior," in Abraham S. Blumberg, ed., *Current Perspectives on Criminal Behavior: Original Essays on Criminology* (New York: Oxford University Press, 1974), p. 246; Frank Scarpitti, *Social Problems* (New York: Holt, Rinehart and Winston, 1974), p. 431; President's Commission on Law Enforcement and the Administration of Justice, "Control of Firearms," in Rose Giallombardo, ed., *Contemporary Social Issues: A Reader* (Santa Barbara, Calif.: Hamilton, 1975), pp. 176–77; Hugh Barlow, *Introduction to Criminology* (Boston: Little, Brown and Company, 1978), p. 116; Jeffrey H. Reiman, *The Rich Get Richer and the Poor Get Prison: Ideology, Class, and Criminal Justice* (New York: John Wiley and Sons, 1979), pp. 192–93; Newton and Zimring, *Firearms and Violence in American Life,* pp. 139–48; Hofstadter, "America as a Gun Culture"; Hofstadter and Wallace, *American Violence,* pp. 25–26; Etzioni, "Violence," p. 740; Empey, "Criminal Justice Reform," p. 296; Stark, *Social Problems,* pp. 226–27; McCaghy, *Deviant Behavior,* p. 126; Boskin, "The Essential American Sour," p. 48; Glazer, *Crime in Our Changing Society,* pp. 260–64; Haskell and Yablonsky, *Crime and Delinquency,* p. 752; and Bassis, Gelles, and Levine, *Social Problems,* p. 477.

10. See Michael J. Harrington, "The Politics of Gun Control," in Phillip Whitten, ed., *Readings in Sociology: Contemporary Perspectives* (New York: Harper and Row, 1979), p. 257; Newton and Zimring, *Firearms and Violence in American Society,* p. 152; Shostak, *Modern Social Reforms,* p. 292; President's Commission, "Control of Firearms," p. 174; Stark, *Social Problems,* p. 227; McCaghy, *Deviant Behavior,* p. 126; and Glazer, *Crime in Our Changing Society,* p. 262.

11. See Hofstadter, "America as a Gun Culture," p. 85; Etzioni, "Violence," pp. 739–40; Julian, *Social Problems,* p. 481; Scarpitti, *Social Problems,* p. 431; President's Commission, "Control of Firearms," pp. 174–75; Stark, *Social Problems,* p. 227; McCaghy, *Deviant Behavior,* pp. 127–29; Barlow, *Introduction to Criminology,* p. 115; Glazer, *Crime in Our Changing Society,* p. 262; Haskell and Yablonsky, *Crime and Delinquency,* p. 341; and Harrington, "The Politics of Gun Control."

12. See Newton and Zimring, *Firearms and Violence in American Life,* pp. 195–99; Hofstadter, "America as a Gun Culture"; Hofstadter and Wallace, *American Violence,* p. 25; Etzioni, "Violence," pp. 739–40; Julian, *Social Problems,* p. 481; Shostak, *Modern Social Reforms,* pp. 278–92; President's Commission. "Control of Firearms," pp. 174–75; Stark, *Social Problems,* p. 227; McCaghy, *Deviant Behavior,* pp. 127–29; Barlow, *Introduction to Criminology,* p. 115; Haskell and Yablonsky, *Crime and Delinquency,* p. 341; and Harrington, "The Politics of Gun Control."

13. See Hofstadter and Wallace, *American Violence*, p. 26; Barlow, *Introduction to Criminology*, p. 143; Glazer, *Crime in our Changing Society*, pp. 213, 261, 262, 263; Haskell and Yablonsky, *Crime and Delinquency*, p. 340; and Joseph F. Sheley, *Understanding Crime: Concepts, Issues, Decisions* (Belmont, Calif.: Wadsworth, 1979), p. 229.

14. See President's Commission, "Control of Firearms," p. 174; Glazer, *Crime in Our Changing Society*, pp. 261–62; Shostak, *Modern Social Reforms*, p. 292; McCaghy, *Deviant Behavior*, p. 126; and Harrington, "The Politics of Gun Control," p. 257.

15. See Newton and Zimring, *Firearms and Violence in American Life*, pp. 119–28; Hofstadter, "America as a Gun Culture," p. 82; Hofstadter and Wallace, *American Violence*, p. 26; Etzioni, "Violence," p. 740; Empey, "American Society," pp. 95–96; Hollon, *Frontier Violence*, p. 122; Stark, *Social Problems*, p. 226; Haskell and Yablonsky, *Crime and Delinquency*, pp. 340–41.

16. See Shostak, *Modern Social Reforms*, pp. 287–92; and McCaghy, *Deviant Behavior*, pp. 124–29. McCaghy handles the gun control issue in a more evenhanded manner in a recent textbook, *Crime in American Society* (New York: Macmillan, 1980), pp. 112–15. Though he still accepts much that is questionable about public opinion polls, handgun usage, and so forth, in this book McCaghy does question the practicality and effectiveness of gun controls.

17. See Hofstadter, "America as a Gun Culture"; and Hollon, *Frontier Violence*, pp. 106–23.

18. Kennett and Anderson, *The Gun in America*, p. 254.

19. Ibid., pp. 254–55.

20. Ibid., p. 255.

21. Ibid., p. 254; and *American Rifleman* Staff, "Pro-gun Poll Comes as Revelation," *The American Rifleman* (February 1976): 16–17.

22. Andrew M. Greeley, *Why Can't They Be Like Us?* (New York: Dutton, 1970), ch. 10.

23. Michael Lerner, "Respectable Bigotry," *The American Scholar* (Autumn 1969): 608.

24. Stanislav Andrzejewski, *Military Organizations and Society* (London: Routledge and Kegan Paul, 1954), pp. 13–14.

25. Peter L. Berger, "Ethnics and the Present Class Struggle," *World View* (April 1978): 7.

26. Ibid., p. 10.

27. Florian Znaniecki, *The Social Role of the Man of Knowledge* (New York: Harper & Row, 1968), pp. 72–73.

28. Ibid., p. 74.

29. Marvin E. Wolfgang, "Letters to the Editor," *Time* (July 5, 1968): 6.

30. See "The Gun Under Fire," *Time* (June 21, 1968): 17.

31. Hofstadter, "America as a Gun Culture," p. 82 [see p. 30 in this volume].

32. Ibid.

33. See Noel Perrin, *Giving Up the Gun: Japan's Reversion to the Sword, 1543–1879* (Boston: Godine, 1979). See also Georges Sansom, *Japan: A Short Cultural History* (New York: D. Appleton-Century, 1936), pp. 412–13; and *A History of Japan 1334–1615*, vol. 2 (Stanford, Calif.: Stanford University Press, 1961), pp. 263–64.

34. Ray Allen Billington, "Frontiers," in C. Vann Woodward, ed., *The Comparative Approach to American History* (New York: Basic Books, 1968), p. 79. See also Richard A. Preston and Sydney F. Wise, *Men in Arms: A History of Warfare and Its Interrelationships with Western Society* (New York: Praeger Publishers, 1970), pp. 165–66.

35. Billington, "Frontiers," p. 79.

36. See Seymour Martin Lipset, "The 'Newness' of the New Nations," in C. Vann Woodward, ed., *The Comparative Approach to American History* (New York: Basic Books, 1968), p. 70; and Paul F. Sharp, *Whoop-Up Country: The Canadian American West, 1865–1885* (Minneapolis: University of Minnesota Press, 1955), p. 110.

37. See H. C. Allen, *Bush and Backwoods: A Comparison of the Frontier in Australia and the United States* (Sydney: Angus and Robertson, 1959), p. 103; and Russel Ward, *The Australian Legend* (New York: Oxford University Press. 1958), p. 144.

38. See Richard Maxwell Brown, *Strains of violence: Historical Studies of American Violence and Vigilantism* (New York: Oxford University Press, 1975).

39. Hofstadter and Wallace, *American Violence*, pp. 5, 25–27.

40. Newton and Zimring, *Firearms and Violence in American Life*, p. 124.

41. Ibid., p. iii.

42. Stark, *Social Problems*, p. 227.

43. Ibid.

44. See Derek L. Phillips, *Abandoning Method: Sociological Studies in Methodology* (San Francisco: Jossey-Bass, 1973). pp. 38–59.

45. *American Rifleman* Staff, "Pro-gun Poll," p. 16.

46. NBC Special, "Violence in America," 1977.

47. Kennett and Anderson, *The Gun in America,* p. 252.

48. Ibid., p. 255.

49. Armand Mauss and Milton Rokeach, "Pollsters as Prophets," *The Humanist* (May-June 1977): 48-51.

50. Edwin M. Schur, *Crimes Without Victims: Deviant Behavior and Public Policy—Abortion, Homosexuality, Drug Addiction* (Englewood Cliffs, N.J.: Prentice-Hall, 1965), p. 6.

51. Don B. Kates, Jr., "Handgun Control: Prohibition Revisited," *Inquiry* (December 5, 1977): 21.

52. Edwin M. Schur, *Our Criminal Society: The Sociological and Legal Sources of Crime in America* (Englewood Cliffs, N.J.: Prentice-Hall, 1969), pp. 143, 237.

3

The Good Outweighs the Evil*

Robert F. Drinan

One central question dominates any discussion of civil liberties and legislation to prohibit the private possession of handguns: do the benefits of such a law outweigh the potential costs in terms of the threats to civil liberties? In his negative response to this question, Don B. Kates, Jr., has ignored the obvious benefits of such a law and has grossly exaggerated its costs. In fact, the benefits of a ban on handguns are enormous, while the civil libertarian costs are virtually nonexistent. It is astonishing that objections should be raised against such urgent legislation on such ephemeral and illogical grounds.

Prof. Kates states at the outset that he responds to questions from liberals concerning his opposition to gun control by asking them the following question: "How can a civil libertarian trust the military and the police with a monoply on arms and with the power to determine which civilians may have them?"

This response contains the same unwarranted suppositions and flawed reasoning that characterize the arguments which follow. Prof. Kates's rhetor-

From "Gun Control: The Good Outweighs the Evil," *The Civil Liberties Review* (August/September 1976): 44–59.

*This essay is a response to an article titled "Why A Civil Libertarian Opposes Gun Control" by Don B. Kates, Jr.

ical question—and his entire essay—assumes the following: that handgun prohibition and long-gun licensing and registration would give the police and the military a monopoly of arms, which is not true; that possible "selective non-enforcement" of gun control laws poses a serious threat to the rights of dissenters, which it would not; and that handguns are valuable tools of self-defense, which they are not.

An analysis of these three basic assumptions, and of several related issues, constitutes an answer to Prof. Kates's initial rhetorical question and a thorough refutation of his argument that gun control legislation is objectionable on civil libertarian grounds.

While the title of Prof. Kates's essay refers only to handgun prohibition, he proceeds to rest much of his argument on the assumption that gun control would completely "disarm" the public. Even the most dedicated advocates of gun control legislation, however, do not call for a ban on the sale or possession of all firearms.

If the most far-reaching gun control legislation introduced in this Congress were enacted, all so-called long guns (that is, all firearms except handguns) would remain lawful. The only encumbrances upon their possession would be a system of licensing and registration to aid in the tracing of firearms used in the commission of crimes. Such a system would also prevent the purchase of such weapons by convicted felons, mental incompetents, or other individuals who are, by objective standards, not qualified to own a firearm. Presumably, those people prevented from purchasing guns by a registration and licensing system would include many of the violence-prone individuals who, as Prof. Kates points out, threaten the rights of dissenters.

Only handguns, which are concealable and hence perfect for criminal assaults, would be subject to an outright ban. Those individuals who, like Prof. Kates, persist in the belief that firearms are desirable for self-defense purposes would remain perfectly free to purchase a rifle or shotgun for the protection of their homes, offices, or meeting places. Prof. Kates's specter of a totally disarmed citizenry at the mercy of a police force which enjoys a monopoly on all firearms is highly misleading.

The most serious libertarian issue raised by Prof. Kates, and in many ways the most important point in his entire essay, is the relationship between what he calls the right to self-defense and the right to dissent. "The right to self-defense" is, given the facts about gun control, a somewhat misleading phrase. First, since only handguns would be prohibited, dissenters would still be able to avail themselves of rifles and shotguns if they choose to do so. Thus, we are not dealing with any absolute "right to self-defense" in the context of firearms. Second, as I will demonstrate shortly, the defensive value of owning a gun is far outweighed by the frequency with which the weapon is, accidentally or otherwise, turned against its owner, his family, or his friends.

Prof. Kates's central point is the fear that gun control laws would be selectively enforced. This would supposedly enable individuals or groups not objectionable to law enforcement organizations to purchase and use firearms against dissenters, while the dissenters would be unable to obtain weapons for their own defense.

There are several major flaws in this line of reasoning. The most obvious is that if stringent gun control laws were enforced, there would be a general decline in the availability of firearms to violence-prone individuals and groups. While one might concede that isolated instances of selective nonenforcement are possible, there would certainly be far more instances in which violence-prone people would be denied access to firearms. To the extent that this would occur, dissenters and other unpopular targets of such individuals would enjoy greater protection from harassment through the operation of stringent gun control laws. In the absence of any firearms controls (a situation apparently considered desirable by Prof. Kates), the Ku Klux Klan and other such groups would obtain and, of greater importance, actually would use guns to a far greater extent than the normally nonviolent dissenters whom Prof. Kates would protect.

Another fundamental problem with Prof. Kates's argument is his conclusion that selective nonenforcement is inevitable. Several states have had experience with gun control laws which are considerably tougher than existing federal standards. To date it appears that selective nonenforcement in order to benefit or punish particular groups has not been a serious problem. Indeed, the broad nationwide support for handgun prohibition among law enforcement officials suggests that enforcement would be both tough and fair.

Even if one admits that occasional instances of unfair enforcement of the law are possible, one can hardly conclude, as Prof. Kates does, that the proper remedy is the removal of the law. We are all familiar with the carnage caused by the virtually unlimited availability of firearms, particularly handguns, in our country. Atlanta Public Safety Commissioner A. Reginald Eaves recently told a congressional committee that "three out of four deaths could have been prevented, were a handgun not available." Boston Police Commissioner Robert diGrazia added that "the unavailability of handguns would lead to the noncommission of many crimes."

The rising rate of crimes involving handguns has spurred continually rising levels of public support for tough gun control legislation. A Gallup poll released in June 1975 indicates that two-thirds of all Americans favor the licensing and registration of all firearms, and 41 percent favor a ban on the private possession of handguns. A poll conducted by the National Opinion Research Center for CBS News, released in June 1975, indicates that 51 percent of the American public favors such a ban—the first time a survey has revealed that a majority of all Americans favors such action. Where such legitimate public interest exists, possible unfair enforcement of laws designed to achieve that interest does not lead us to abrogate the laws.

The proper response is to endeavor to eliminate the isolated instances of unfair enforcement.

Prof. Kates's admirable efforts to aid in the fight for civil rights in the South in the early 1960s have apparently exerted a great influence on his views regarding gun control, dissent, and self-defense. The experience of confronting an armed mob acting with the tacit approval of the local police is certainly a powerful and searing memory, and one which can be expected to instill strong feelings in support of the right to purchase arms for self-defense. It must be conceded, however, that such abdications of responsibility by the police are highly unusual, particularly in the light of civil rights progress in the South.

For each example of attacks on unarmed minorities by armed people against whom the police did not enforce anti-gun laws (and most of these instances cited by Prof. Kates occurred in foreign countries), one could list hundreds of deaths caused by the unlimited availability of handguns. The solution to the problem of occasional, isolated nonenforcement of the law is not to advocate, as Prof. Kates apparently does, a society in which everyone gets armed in the interest of self-defense, but rather to embark on the far less dangerous and far more sensible course of drafting an impartial and fair law and then seeing to it that the law is enforced with strict objectivity.

Prof. Kates raises the related point of impossibility of enforcement. He claims that the police would be no more successful in enforcing a prohibition against handguns than they were in enforcing the prohibition against the manufacture, sale, or importation of alcoholic beverages.

While one can argue that an analogy does exist between the Volstead Act and a ban against handguns, prohibition was absolute in the case of alcoholic beverages, while in the case of firearms, such a ban would be partial; individuals who have legitimate sporting or self-defense interests will be able to purchase long guns. Moreover, the human proclivity to consume alcoholic beverages is surely more powerful than the desire to own handguns (particularly when long guns are available). It seems highly unrealistic to expect the same sort of difficulty in enforcing a law which, unlike prohibition in the 1920s, does not outlaw absolutely a very powerful human desire. That enforcement would not be completely effective is irrefutable; this cannot, however, serve as the rationale for abandoning the law. Many existing laws, such as those outlawing larceny or the possession of heroin, are difficult to enforce, but no one suggests that for this reason they be rescinded.

Prof. Kates suggests that the ban on handguns would be particularly difficult to enforce because a gun can be bought in a single transaction and may last for a generation or more. A machine gun, however, shares these same characteristics and we have declared it illegal because its destructive power, particularly suited for criminal assaults, is not matched by any countervailing legitimate use. The same is true of the handgun.

A related argument offered by Prof. Kates is that the enforcement of a prohibition on the possession of handguns would produce major additional strains on the Fourth Amendment privilege against unreasonable searches and seizures. Given the enormous number of items currently prohibited by law, it seems highly unlikely that the addition to the list of one more illegal commodity would lead to a significant increase in the incidence of police searches. Gun control advocates do not envision or support massive police intrusions into private homes in search of handguns; the constitutional requirement of a specific warrant obtained as a result of corroborating evidence and signed by an impartial magistrate would remain in force to preclude unreasonable searches.

The alleged value of handguns as tools for self-defense is a major underpinning of Prof. Kates's argument. In support of this position he cites a number of isolated examples in which handguns were effective in defense against attacks. These graphic examples of individual instances of self-defense are hardly persuasive. For each such example, there are literally thousands of accidental and deliberate homicides and assaults in which a handgun was used against the owner of the firearm, his family, or his friends.

No real point is proved by compiling long lists of examples on either side of the self-defense question. Only overall statistics can provide an accurate estimate of the real value of handguns as weapons of self-defense—and these statistics clearly demonstrate the bankruptcy of the self-defense argument. An FBI report, *Crime in the United States, 1973*, reveals that a firearm kept in the home for self-defense is six times more likely to be used in a deliberate or accidental homicide involving a relative or a friend than against a burglar or unlawful intruder.

A National Crime Panel Survey in 1973 entitled "An Analysis of Victimization Survey Results from the Eight Impact Cities" indicates that only 3.5 percent of those owning guns even had the *opportunity* to use their firearms when they were assaulted or robbed either at home or on the street. This study was based on data in Atlanta, Baltimore, Cleveland, Dallas, Denver, Newark, Portland, and St. Louis.

All of this is hardly surprising in light of the FBI estimate in 1973 that 99 percent of all burglaries occur when no one is at home. Contrary to Prof. Kates's assertion, it would seem that the presence of a gun in the home, if this is known to a prospective burglar, would probably constitute an inducement, rather than a deterrent, to the commission of a crime. A gun in an empty house is a lure. A 1973 study by the Criminal Justice Coordinating Council of New York City estimates that half-a-million handguns were stolen during burglaries in the previous year.

Shopowners, too, are safer if they do not court armed attacks by keeping guns in their stores. Patrick B. Murphy, president of the Police Foundation and former police commissioner of New York City, stated: "I've always recommended to shopkeepers that they not have guns because, in my experience, what happens more often than not, is that violence begets violence. When we look at the total picture, I think that shopkeepers are killed more often or injured more often when they draw a gun. . . . I think you're safer as a small store owner not to have a gun."

These and other recent studies confirm the conclusion of the Eisenhower Commission that "the gun is rarely an effective means of protecting the home." Prof. Kates's dismissal of the commission's report for "lack of evidence" is unwarranted. The evidence is now in, and it is convincing: the frequent absence of any opportunity to utilize firearms in such situations, the danger involved in doing so, and the staggering number of accidental and passion-inspired injuries to relatives and friends directly attributable to the easy availability of handguns destroy the myth of self-defense. The conclusion is inescapable: those who own handguns for self-defense are engaging in dangerous self-deception.

In order to buttress his self-defense argument, Prof. Kates suggests that those most likely to be victimized by criminal assaults, the poor people living in the central cities, are opposed to gun control legislation, particularly those proposals which would deprive them of their right to purchase handguns for self-defense. The rich, who have escaped the crime-infested central cities and have less need for handguns, Prof. Kates asserts, are the prime advocates of gun control.

This position is directly contradicted by several public opinion polls which demonstrate that support for stringent gun control laws is highest in the high-crime areas of the central cities. For example, a Gallup poll survey released in June 1975 indicates that 66 percent of the American people living in cities with populations over one million favor banning handguns. Clearly, those most familiar with the problem of our nation's soaring crime rate, its most frequent victims, are the strongest advocates of gun control. Those who might be expected to adopt Prof. Kates's self-defense argument most fervently in fact reject it most overwhelmingly.

One of Prof. Kates's most outrageous suggestions is the notion that women are particularly in need of handguns for self-defense. In making this assertion, he ignores the central fact that a principal reason for the extraordinary level of violence in our society is the virtually unparalleled availability of firearms, particularly handguns, which are the weapons most commonly used in street assaults.

It is noteworthy that women are consistently more supportive of tough gun control legislation than men; indeed, in the most recent Gallup poll survey on this subject, women advocated tough gun control legislation in greater numbers than any other group. A survey of metropolitan Chicago residents (conducted by Marke-Trends, Inc., assisted by the National Opinion Research Center and Prof. James Wright of the University of Chicago, released in

November, 1975) demonstrates that women are consistently among the most enthusiastic supporters of gun control. On the subject of an outright ban on the possession of handguns, 52 percent of the women polled were in favor of such a law, while only 37 percent of the men favored it. Among the women 86 percent, as against 72 percent of the men, agreed with the observation that control of guns would reduce street crime.

Many women's groups have taken positive action to speed the enactment of a ban on the sale or possession of handguns. They include the American Association of University Women; B'nai B'rith Women; the International Ladies' Garment Workers Union; the Massachusetts League of Women Voters; the National Council of Jewish Women; the National Council of Negro Women; the Women's Division, Board of Global Ministries, United Methodist Church; and the Young Women's Christian Association of the U.S., National Board. The Massachusetts League of Women Voters has led an apparently successful petition drive to place the issue of a handgun ban on the ballot in that state.

It is clear that the women of this country are more sensitive than Prof. Kates is to the dangers of unrestricted access to handguns. Existing statistics and common sense indicate that for each instance of successful self-defense, there would be many unsuccessful attempts leading to serious injuries and deaths, accidental and passion-inspired shootings, and thefts of guns by violence-oriented individuals. Former Police Commissioner Murphy summed up the situation well: "Anyone who goes out on the street armed with a handgun for self-defense is courting disaster."

Prof. Kates's arm-the-women campaign is simply a part of his overall arm-the-citizenry syndrome, and it has no more merit than does his general theory.

Prof. Kates asserts that there is no demonstrable need for a prohibition of handguns, that existing firearms control efforts suggest that such legislation is not effective, and that civil liberties would be jeopardized by a handgun prohibition. I have already dealt extensively with the civil liberties argument. Before proceeding to a brief analysis of the overwhelming need for firearms control, I would like to make one final point with regard to the civil liberties issue.

The availability of cheap, easily concealable handguns is, I believe, one of the principal reasons for the intolerable crime rate in this country. This rising crime rate not only deprives many of our citizens of the right to walk the streets without fear; it also helps to foster the political climate in which "law and order" is elevated above the protection of certain civil liberties. Thus, a prohibition on the possession of handguns would reduce the fear which prevents many people from exercising their most basic rights, and would help to reverse the "law and order" trend which dominates domestic politics and threatens civil liberties. These positive effects of gun control legislation depend upon the belief that such laws would, in fact, reduce the rate of violent crime. This belief, as I shall attempt to explain, is an eminently well-founded one.

Prof. Kates seriously distorts the views of gun control advocates, asserting that they believe ". . . crime will cease when its victims are deprived of the means of self-defense." No one believes that crimes will cease upon the enactment of gun control legislation. It is clear, however, that firearms play a grossly disproportionate role in crimes of violence. The statistics are familiar, and the facts which they reveal have led a growing number of Americans to favor stringent gun control measures.

● According to FBI crime statistics (*Crime in the U.S., 1973*), the handgun, with little legitimate sporting capability and representing only 20 percent of all firearms, accounts for 53 percent of all murders and 95 percent of all armed robberies in the United States.

● According to the same FBI study, over 65 percent of all murders involve family members or friends and are not the result of criminal design, but rather are crimes of passion in which the ready availability of the handgun is surely a major factor. As Judge George Edwards of the Sixth Circuit Court of Appeals put it: "Most murder in real life comes from a compounding of anger, passion, intoxication and accidents—with the victims being wives, husbands, girl friends, boy friends, prior friends, or close acquaintances. . . . A loaded handgun, alcohol, and passion in the same home are a time bomb."

● The 1973 FBI study documents 30,000 firearm deaths, 160,000 armed robberies, and 100,000 armed assaults, mostly involving handguns. Addressing the enormity of the firearms crisis in the United States, former Washington, D.C., Chief of Police Jerry V. Wilson stated: "Nothing less than a drastic reduction of the handgun presence will take and keep pistols out of the hands of criminals who use them to rob and terrorize our communities, and of honest citizens who use them to kill their families and friends and themselves."

These shocking (and still rising) figures are many times greater than corresponding totals in other Western countries which, uniformly, have enacted stringent gun control laws. The positive experience of these nations is also an indication of the effectiveness of tough firearms control legislation.

Prof. Kates's criticism of the results of existing state gun control programs is not persuasive. "Project Identification," a nationwide survey conducted by the Bureau of Alcohol, Tobacco, and Firearms of the U.S. Department of the Treasury (ABT), released in February 1976, reveals that the ease with which guns are transported from one jurisdiction to another frustrates the existing laws. Prof. Kates cited the relative ineffectiveness of New York's tough state law, but the ABT study shows that over 90 percent of the handguns used in crimes in New York were purchased in other states. Studies of state firearms control laws actually demonstrate only one thing: the need for national legislation.

The data contained in the Bureau of Alcohol, Tobacco, and Firearms study render worthless the conclusions of the University of Wisconsin study so heavily relied on by Prof. Kates. The Wisconsin analysis was based upon comparisons between each state's gun control law and its crime rate. The ABT report, however, demonstrates that the case of interstate purchase and transport of firearms dramatically reduces the effectiveness of tough local gun control legislation. Indeed, the report concludes: "The percentage of crime handguns purchased interstate was directly proportionate to the degree of local control." As long as there is no national gun control law and there are states in which the purchase of firearms is virtually unencumbered, state-by-state comparisons such as that employed by the Wisconsin study are of little value.

It is common knowledge that a large percentage of handguns used in crimes are stolen. Prof. Kates's apparent advocacy of an armed citizenry would only increase the number of weapons subject to theft, accidents, and crimes of passion. The massive evidence linking handguns with crimes of violence cannot be dismissed as "mere hopeful speculation." Alone among the Western nations, the United States permits the unrestricted availability of handguns, and alone it suffers an astronomical crime rate. The only sensible solution, in the interest of civil liberties as well as public safety, is to reject the notion that we can fight violence with more violence (a notion whose results we have seen), and choose instead to attack violence at its source by banning the private possession of handguns.

4

The Great American Gun War

B. Bruce-Briggs

For over a decade there has been a powerful and vocal push for stricter government regulation of the private possession and use of firearms in the United States—for "gun control." The reader cannot help being aware of the vigorous, often vociferous debate on this issue. Indeed, judging from the amount of energy devoted to the gun issue—Congress has spent more time on the subject than on all other crime-related measures combined—one might conclude that gun control is the key to the crime problem. Yet it is startling to note that no policy research worthy of the name has been done on the issue of gun control. The few attempts at serious work are of marginal competence at best, and tainted by obvious bias. Indeed, the gun control debate has been conducted at a level of propaganda more appropriate to social warfare than to democratic discourse.

No one disagrees that there is a real problem: Firearms are too often used for nefarious purposes in America. In 1974, according to the FBI's Uniform Crime Reports, 10,000 people were illegally put to death with guns, firearms were reportedly used in 200,000 robberies and 120,000 assaults, as

Reprinted with permission of the author from *The Public Interest,* No. 45 (Fall 1976): 37–62. Copyright © 1976 by National Affairs, Inc.

well as in a small number of rapes, prison escapes, and other crimes. There is universal agreement that it would be desirable, to say the least, that these numbers be substantially reduced. So everybody favors gun control. But there is widespread disagreement about how it can be achieved. Two principal strategies are promoted. To use the military terminology now creeping into criminology, they can be called "interdiction" and "deterrence."

Advocates of deterrence recommend the establishment of stricter penalties to discourage individuals from using firearms in crimes. But "gun control" is usually identified with interdiction—that is, the reduction of the criminal use of firearms by controlling the access of all citizens to firearms. The interdictionist position is promoted by a growing lobby, supported by an impressive alliance of reputable organizations, and sympathetically publicized by most of the national media. Every commission or major study of crime and violence has advocated much stricter gun control laws. The only reason that this pressure has failed to produce much tighter controls of firearms is a powerful and well-organized lobby of gun owners, most notably the National Rifle Association (NRA), which has maintained that improved interdiction will have no effect on crime, but will merely strip away the rights and privileges of Americans—and perhaps even irreparably damage the Republic. The organized gun owners advocate reliance on deterrence.

The debate between the "gun controllers" (as the interdictionists are generally identified) and the "gun lobby" (as the organized gun owners have been labeled by a hostile media) has been incredibly virulent. In addition to the usual political charges of self-interest and stupidity, participants in the gun control struggle have resorted to implications or downright accusations of mental illness, moral turpitude, and sedition. The level of the debate has been so debased that even the most elementary methods of cost-benefit analysis have not been employed. One expects advocates to disregard the costs of their programs, but in this case they have even failed to calculate the benefits.

THE PREVALENCE OF FIREARMS

While estimates vary widely, it can be credibly argued that there are at least 140 million firearms in private hands in the United States today. This number has been expanding rapidly in recent years.[1] Since 1968, 40 million firearms have been produced and sold. And these counts do not include the millions of guns brought back from the wars and/or stolen from military stocks. These figures are usually cited by advocates of interdiction as demonstrative of the enormity of the problem and as implying the dire necessity for swift and positive action. But they also demonstrate the incredible difficulty of dealing with the problem.

In the gun control debate, the most outlandishly paranoid theories of gun ownership have appeared. Some people seem to believe that private arsenals exist primarily for political purposes—to kill blacks, whites, or liberals. But of course, the majority of firearms in this country are rifles and shotguns used primarily for hunting. A secondary purpose of these "long guns" is target and skeet shooting. Millions of gun owners are also collectors, in the broad sense of gaining satisfaction from the mere possession of firearms, but even the serious collectors who hold them as historical or aesthetic artifacts number in the hundreds of thousands.

The above uses account for the majority of firearms owned by Americans. Weapons for those purposes are not intended for use against people. But there is another major purpose of firearms—self-defense. In poll data, some 35 percent of gun owners, especially handgun owners, indicated that at least one reason they had for possessing their weapons was self-defense. A Harris poll found two-thirds of these people willing to grant that they would, under certain circumstances, kill someone with their weapon. This sounds very ominous, but it is such a widespread phenomenon that interdictionists have felt obliged to conduct studies demonstrating that the chance of being hurt with one's own weapon is greater than the chance of inflicting harm upon an assailant. The studies making this point are so ingeniously specious that they are worth expanding upon.

For example, the calculation is made that within a given jurisdiction more people are killed by family and friends, accidents, and sometimes suicide, than burglars are killed by homeowners. In a Midwestern county it was found that dead gun owners outnumbered dead burglars by six to one. Both sides of that ratio are fallacious. People do not have "house guns" to kill burglars but to prevent burglaries. The measure of the effectiveness of self-defense is not in the number of bodies piled up on doorsteps, but in the property that is protected. We have no idea how many burglars are challenged and frightened off by armed householders. And, of course, there is no way to measure the deterrent effect on burglars who know that homeowners may be armed. Though the statistics by themselves are not particularly meaningful, it is true that the burglary rate is very low in Southern and Southwestern cities with high rates of gun ownership. Burglary in Texas would seem a risky business.

The calculation of family homicides and accidents as costs of gun ownership is equally false. The great majority of these killings are among poor, restless, alcoholic, troubled people, usually with long criminal records. Applying the domestic homicide rate of these people to the presumably upstanding citizens whom they prey upon is seriously misleading.

Other studies claim to indicate that there is little chance of defending oneself with a weapon against street crime or other assaults. But almost without exception, such studies have been held in cities with strict gun control laws. My favorite study was the one purporting to show that it was very dangerous to attempt to defend yourself with a gun because the likelihood of suffering harm in a mugging was considerably higher if you resisted. But the data indicated only that you got hurt if you yelled, kicked, or screamed —but not if you used a gun.

GUN OWNERS VERSUS INTERDICTION

All this, of course, is begging the question. Why do people feel it necessary to obtain firearms to defend themselves? The rising crime rates would suggest it is not lunacy. But the data are improperly understood. Despite the high crime rates, there is a very small chance of being attacked or robbed in one's home, or even during any given excursion into the highest crime area. But the average citizen does not make such calculations and certainly would not have much faith in them if he did. He is scared. The gun, if it does nothing else, gives the citizen reassurance.

This last is a reason for large numbers of guns being owned—not quite defense, but insurance. Many people have weapons tucked away with no explicit idea of how they might be used except "you never know when you might need one." No violent intent is implied, any more than a purchaser of life insurance intends to die that year. It is pure contingency.

Apparently most owners care little about their firearms *per se*, considering them as mere tools, to be properly cared for—and, because they are potentially deadly, to be handled with caution. Yet within the ranks of the gun owners is a hard core of "gun nuts" (they sometimes call themselves "gunnies") for whom firearms are a fanatic hobby. To them, the possession, handling, and use of guns are a central part of life. They not only accumulate guns, but also read books and magazines about firearms and socialize with kindred spirits in gun clubs and gun stores. Many such people combine business with pleasure as gun dealers, gunsmiths, soldiers, policemen, and officials of gun owners' organizations. All this is symptomatic of the earnest devotees of any hobby—there are similar ski nuts, car nuts, boat nuts, radio nuts, dog nuts, even book nuts. In this case, however, the "nuts" have political importance because they are the core of the organized gun owners, easily aroused and mobilized to thwart the enemies of their passion.

Polls are unreliable on this point, because internal inconsistencies in the data and common sense suggest that many respondents won't admit to gun ownership, but it appears that at least one half of all American households are armed. They own guns for recreation or self-protection. The principal form of recreation, hunting, has deep cultural roots. In rural areas and small towns, a boy's introduction to guns and hunting is an important rite of passage. The first gun at puberty is the *bar mitzvah* of the rural WASP. Possession of a gun for self-protection is based upon a perception of a real or potential threat to personal, family, or home security that is beyond the control of the police. Very rarely is there criminal or seditious intent. Yet these people are told by the interdictionists that their possession of weapons is a threat to public safety and order, that they must obtain permits, fill out forms, pay taxes and fees, and keep and bear arms only by leave of the state. Inevitably, some of them have organized themselves against such interdiction. With a million members [in 1976], the NRA is the largest and most effective consumer lobby in America. It maintains its morale and membership by broadcasting the statements in favor of "domestic disarmament" by extreme and loose-mouthed interdictionists and by publicizing the legislative attempts to restrict gun ownership as merely part of a fabian strategy—to use the interdictionists' code words, a "step in the right direction"—toward liquidating the private ownership and use of firearms in America.

The interdictionist position rests on the self-evident proposition that if there were no guns, there would be no crimes committed with guns. But few are sanguine about achieving that situation. Instead, their argument is that if there were fewer guns and/or if gun ownership were better controlled by the government, there would be fewer crimes with guns.

Can interdiction work? Let us examine what is proposed. Guns and control are subdivided in several ways. Usually there is an attempt to distinguish between mere possession and use. Furthermore, different controls are suggested for different types of weapons—"heavy stuff" (machine guns and cannon); long guns (rifles and shotguns); handguns (revolvers and pistols); and "Saturday Night Specials" (cheap handguns). The levels of possible control can be roughly ranked by degree of severity: market restrictions, registration, permissive licensing, restrictive licensing, prohibition.

Market restrictions seek to limit the number of manufacturers, importers, or retailers of firearms, in order to keep better track of them. As in all areas of economic regulation, a principal effect is to promote the interests of the favored outlets, at the cost of the consumer. They do not deny anyone access to guns, but push up the cost—both the money cost and the personal inconvenience—thereby presumably discouraging some marginal purchasers, but surely few criminals, lunatics, and terrorists.

"Registration" is widely discussed, but no one is really advocating it. To register is merely to enroll, as a birth is registered. Merely to enroll weapons would be costly, to little or no purpose. What goes by the label of registration is actually "permissive licensing" whereby anyone may obtain a firearm except certain designated classes—minors, convicted criminals, certified lunatics.

"Restrictive licensing," such as New York's Sullivan Law, permits only people with a legitimate purpose to own a firearm. Police, security guards, hunters, target shooters, and collectors are obliged to demonstrate their bona fides to the licensing authorities. Typically, personal or home defense is not ordinarily considered a legitimate purpose for gaining a license.

Prohibition is self-defined. If there were no or few firearms already in circulation, a simple ban would be sufficient. But with tens of millions out there, prohibition would require buying or collecting existing weapons or some more complicated policy intended to make them useless.

The preferred program of most interdictionists today contains four elements, most of which have been attempted one way or another in one jurisdiction or another: (1) continuing and tightening all existing laws, (2) permissive licensing for long guns, (3) restrictive licensing for all handguns, and (4) prohibition of cheap handguns, the so-called "Saturday Night Specials."

The third element is currently considered most important. Because the great majority of gun crimes are committed with handguns, control of them would presumably promote domestic tranquility. Concentration on handguns is also politically useful. Relatively few of them are used for recreation, so this would seem to outflank the objection of sportsmen to restrictions.*

EXISTING GUN CONTROL

There are reportedly some 20,000 gun control ordinances in the various jurisdictions of the United States. Most are prohibitions against discharging a weapon in urban areas or against children carrying weapons, and are trivial, reasonable, and uncontroversial. Most states and large cities have laws against carrying concealed weapons, the rationale being that no person has a legitimate reason to do so. In a few large cities and states, particularly in the Northeast, a license is required to buy or possess a handgun, and in a very few but growing number of Northeastern cities and states a permit or license is required to possess any sort of firearm.

At first sight, licensing seems eminently reasonable. Dangerous criminals should not have weapons, nor should the mentally disturbed. But the administrative "details" of licensing become incredibly difficult. It is fairly easy to check out an applicant for a criminal record, which can be a legitimate reason for denying a license. But many criminals, judging from the comparison between reported crime and conviction rates, are not convicted of crimes, especially violent crimes, so the difficulty exists of whether to deny people the privilege of purchasing weapons if they have merely been arrested, but then set free or acquitted. Civil libertarians should be taken aback by this prospect. The question of mental competence is even nastier to handle. Is someone to be denied a firearm because he sought psychiatric help when his wife died?

From the point of view of the organized gun owners, licensing is intolerable because of the way that it has been enforced in the past. One of the peculiarities of most local licensing is the lack of reciprocity; unlike marriage

---

*In the 1980s handguns, due to improved cartridge technologies, became extremely popular as long-range target and hunting arms. Their popularity for such purposes continues in the 1990s.—Ed.

licensing, what is recogized in one jurisdiction is not in another. In the Eastern states it is nearly impossible to travel with a firearm without committing a felony (not, of course, that this troubles many people). Also many police agencies, particularly in the Northeastern states with restrictive licensing, have engaged in some extremely annoying practices. Not only do they load up questionnaires with many superfluous personal questions, but they also require character witnesses to provide intimate information. When the police wish to restrict privately owned firearms, they resort to all manner of subterfuge. In a test of the local licensing procedure some years ago, the Hudson Institute sent several female staff members to try to make the necessary application. The forms were not available and the people responsible for the forms were absent.

Even when the applications are submitted, the waiting period is often deliberately and inordinately long. I have a friend on Long Island who spent three years getting a pistol permit for target shooting. Influence is useful, but even it is not necessarily sufficient. A staff aide to a leading New York politician who has frequently been threatened applied for a permit to carry a handgun as his boss's bodyguard. Even a letter to the Police Commissioner of New York City on the gentleman's stationery was inadequate; a personal phone call had to be made—and that has not speeded up the process very much. The system is not much better with long guns and sympathetic police. Immediately after New Jersey required the licensing of rifles, I happened to be in a police station in a suburb of Philadelphia when a young man came in to get his license. The process had taken six weeks. He commented bitterly, "It's a good thing that I planned well in advance for my Maine hunting trip." (By the way, if he had lost or damaged his weapon during a hunting trip, the Federal Gun Control Act of 1968 would have made it extremely difficult for him to get a replacement out of state.)

This sort of anecdotal evidence can be continued almost indefinitely. It suggests to the organized gun owners that licensing systems are a screen not against criminals but against honest citizens, and that licensing authorities are not to be trusted with any sort of discretionary power. It is certainly an inefficient system that dribbles out gun permits and refuses to recognize self-defense as a legitimate reason for owning a gun, while muggers operate with impunity, illicit pistols are exchanged openly on the streets, and penalties for gun-law violations—even by people with criminal records—are very rarely imposed.[2]

Among the most unproductive local gun control measures are the moratoria permitting individuals to surrender their firearms without fear of prosecution. The police will then investigate such people to make sure they are not wanted by some other agency, and they are then entered in police files. (Obviously, if you really wish to dispose of an illegal weapon, you merely disassemble it and throw the parts from a bridge.) The number of weapons delivered under such programs is infinitesimal. An extension of such programs is the buying of weapons by police departments. This was attempted in Baltimore and obtained a substantial number of guns. But the total collected is a matter of simple economics: Large numbers of guns worth much less than the price offered will be obtained. Few valuable weapons will be turned in—and it is perhaps needless to note that there has been no perceptible effect on the crime rate.

The latest innovation in local gun control is a sort of interdiction through deterrence. Massachusetts recently passed a law mandating a minimum jail term of one year for possession of an unlicensed weapon. This reflects an interesting set of social values, because there are no such mandated sentences for burglary, armed robbery, rape, or even murder in Massachusetts. Every hunter who passes through the state on the way to Maine is risking a year in prison. What is happening is predictable: The law is not enforced.

The Massachusetts experience is both a caution to the interdictionists and a reassurance to the organized gun owners. If restrictive gun legislation is passed, the police will be hesitant to arrest ordinary citizens, prosecutors will be loathe to prosecute, juries will be unwilling to convict, and judges will devise ingenious loopholes.

Most of the existing interdiction laws have been in effect for many years, yet it is not possible to make any sort of estimate as to whether they do any good in reducing crime. Attempts have been made to correlate gun ownership and/or gun control laws with gun-related crimes, but they are singularly unconvincing for the very simple reason that the data are so miserable —we have no firm estimate even of the number of guns available nationwide, much less in any given community, and it seems that the gun laws now on the books are rarely enforced. Some ingenious attempts to use regression analyses are easy to demolish.

In any event, no serious student of the subject would disagree that regional, racial, and cultural factors completely swamp the effects of gun control laws. It is true that places with gun control laws tend to have lower violent crime rates, but it happens that these are Northern communities with a long tradition of relative nonviolence, and the existence of gun control laws on the statute books is merely evidence of the same relative peaceableness that is also reflected in the low rates of violent crime. The gun-toting states are also the gun-using states and the violent states, mostly in the South. And where Southerners or ex-Southerners are in the North, there are high violence rates regardless of laws. In recent years a few Northern states have imposed stricter licensing and use laws, with no perceptible effect on the crime rate. As with so many things, the laws on the books don't matter as much as their application. People in these states claim that any effects of their laws are spoiled by the spillover of easily available weapons from outside the state, which certainly sounds eminently reasonable. But if the economists are right, the gun control laws should at least increase the cost or the inconvenience of getting guns, and therefore discourage their use. Retail handgun price differentials between open sources in the South and the black market in New York prove that the Sullivan Law does pass the cost of a less efficient transportation system onto the consumer. But we have no idea of the effect of these increased costs upon the demand for guns. Presumably, those who want to buy guns for illicit purposes are not likely to be much affected by an extra $25 or $100 on the price tag.

The spillover effect has led many public officials in the gun controlling states to advocate essentially the extension of their systems of licensing to the entire nation. It is easy to sneer at this approach as the characteristic reflex of failed government programs—X didn't work, so let's try 10X. But the thesis seems plausible. If one could cut off the supply of guns from, say, South Carolina, they would be more difficult to obtain in, say, New York; that is, they would be more difficult to obtain *casually*. So the principal interest of gun controllers is in national legislation.

FEDERAL FIREARMS CONTROL

National firearms control legislation is a relative innovation. The first important law passed was the Federal Firearms Act of 1934, which was allegedly a response to the wave of gangsterism that swept the country in the depths of the Depression. Originally the Roosevelt administration attempted to require national licensing of all weapons, but it was thwarted by a previously quiescent organization, the NRA. The watered-down version that passed Congress effectively prohibited (through punitive taxes) the private possession of submachine guns, silencers, sawed-off rifles and shotguns, and other weapons presumably of use only to gangsters. While there appears to be no information whatever on the effectiveness of this law, it seems to have been reasonably successful. Submachine guns are rarely used in crimes. That success, however, may simply reflect the fact that very few such weapons were in circulation, and their rarity gives them too much value to be risked in crime. (We know, of course, that there certainly are tens of thousands of unregistered automatic weapons in the United States, largely war souvenirs. Vietnam veterans brought back thousands of M-16s and Kalchnikov assault rifles in their duffel bags. But most of these gun owners have no criminal intent or any intention of selling such weapons to criminals.) Sawed-off shotguns and rifles may be made illegal, but they are impossible to prohibit; all that is needed is a hacksaw and a few minutes' time.

The second federal effort was the National Firearms Act of 1938. Again, this took the form of a revenue measure, requiring the licensing of firearms manufacturers and dealers. The law requires the firearms trade to keep records of the purchasers of weapons, and prohibits sales to known criminals. But only a simple declaration on the part of the buyer is required. These records are useful for tracing firearms. If a weapon needs checking, it is merely necessary to go back to the original manufacturer or importer and trace it through the serial number to the dealer. Although these records are not yet centralized, *in effect there has been registration of every new weapon sold in the United States since 1938.* How many crimes have been solved through this means, or how it has otherwise been effective to law enforcment, is by no means clear. It would not be difficult to find out, but no one has really tried to. Presumably, such registration is of some help to the police—though it seems to have had no effect on the crime rate or the conviction rates.

The most important national measure is the Gun Control Act of 1968, the immediate result of the disturbances in the 1960s and the assassinations of Robert Kennedy and Martin Luther King, Jr. The Act raised taxes on firearms dealers, added cannon to the list of weapons subject to punitive taxes, prohibited the importation of surplus military firearms and "Saturday Night Specials," and prohibited the interstate retailing of all firearms. The last provision is the most important. The purpose was to prevent individuals like Lee Harvey Oswald from ordering weapons by mail under phony names. But it also has more annoying side effects. For example, if you live in Kansas City, Kansas, and wish to give your brother, who lives in Kansas City, Missouri, a .22 caliber rifle for his birthday, it is illegal for you to do so. If you are traveling in another state and see a weapon you wish to buy, you must go through the rigamarole of having it sent to a dealer in your own state. So far as one can determine, the law has had no perceptible effect in slowing down the interstate sale of arms.

Enforcement of federal firearms laws was given to what is now the Bureau of Alcohol, Tobacco, and Firearms (BATF) of the Department of the Treasury. These are the famous "revenuers" whose most important function was stamping out moonshining. But for economic and social reasons, the illicit liquor trade is fading and the BATF needs other things to do than break up stills. Since 1968 they have rapidly expanded their funding and activity in firearms control and now devote about half their personnel and budget to that function. BATF seems to be a crude and unsophisticated police agency, more like the Bureau of Narcotics and Dangerous Drugs or the Border Patrol than the FBI or the Secret Service. For example, it says it has no idea how many of the 250,000 licensed Title II firearms (i.e., machine guns, cannon, etc.) are held by police or other public agencies and how many by private citizens; nor has it any information on how many unlicensed Title II firearms were used for criminal purposes. Some of its methods of operating have been irritating to legitimate gun owners.[3] The Gun Control Act of 1968 says that BATF shall have access to the premises of a gun dealer during normal business hours, which BATV interprets to mean that there must be a business premises separate from, for example, a private residence, and that there shall be ordinary posted business hours. BATF also took upon itself the enforcement of local zoning laws. This problem arises because many gun owners have taken advantage of simple and cheap licensing procedures to obtain dealer licenses so they can buy firearms wholesale. The majority of the nearly 150,000 dealers operate from their homes.

The organized gun owners see the activities of the BATF as a plot against them, not realizing that its habits and state of mind are not much different from other regulatory agencies. Once an activity has been licensed, it becomes a privilege; a citizen is obliged meekly to petition the regulator for the boon and to modify his behavior to suit the needs of the bureaucracy. At the present time, the Department of the Treasury is asking for a large increase in the licensing fee of gun dealers in order to reduce the number of license holders—not for any public benefit but because it will make the job of regulation easier for BATF.*

"SATURDAY NIGHT SPECIALS"

The "Saturday Night Special" is the latest target of the interdictionist. It is identified as a cheap, unreliable, inaccurate, and easily concealed handgun, allegedly employed for large numbers of "street crimes." Because it is impossible to define a "Saturday Night Special" precisely, the NRA claims that the concept is fraudulent—but any definition in practice or law is necessarily arbitrary. Concentration on the "Saturday Night Special" has definite political advantages. Firearms enthusiasts scorn it as sleazy junk quite unsuited for serious work. Nevertheless, the organized gun owners are making an effective fight against banning the "Saturday Night Special." They were unable to block prohibition of its importation in 1968, but have resisted attempts to ban domestic manufacture and the assembly of imported parts.

It has been said against the "Saturday Night Special" that it is employed to commit a disproportionately large number of street crimes, and that getting rid of it would cut substantially into those crimes. A BATF study claimed that 65 percent of "crime guns" used for street crime in sixteen major cities were cheap "Saturday Night Specials." Unfortunately, the text of the report reveals that these weapons were *not* those used in crimes but all those handguns collected by police, and anyone who knows anything about how reliable the police are in handling contraband knows that the chances of a quality firearm like a good Smith and Wesson finding its way into the reporting system are infinitesimal. Because the principal sanction against the illegal carrying of guns is on-the-spot seizure by the police, it stands to reason that individuals would pack the cheapest effective gun.

---

*The Department of Treasury is still seeking such licensing increases.—Ed.

But even if "Saturday Night Specials" are used for some half of crimes with handguns, their elimination is hardly likely to reduce handgun crime by that much. People buy them because they are cheap. If people want a weapon, and if their demand for handguns is highly inelastic, this only means that whatever guns fell outside of whatever arbitrary definition of a "Saturday Night Special" that was adopted would sell more. Perhaps this is recognized by the proponents of banning the "Saturday Night Special," because they have written bills to give the Secretary of the Treasury sufficient discretion to ban all handguns.

Actually, neither side cares much about the "Saturday Night Special" one way or another. The interdictionists advocate its regulation as a stepping stone toward tight licensing of handguns or the licensing of all guns, while the organized gun owners fear it as a camel's nose in the tent. It is difficult to escape the conclusion that the "Saturday Night Special" is emphasized because it is cheap and is being sold to a particular class of people. The name is sufficient evidence—the reference is to "nigger-town Saturday night."

CRACKPOT SCHEMES

Some other suggestions for gun control are simply silly. One idea is to have all weapons locked up in armories of various sorts, to be drawn by hunters or target shooters when they are needed. But most hunters and gun owners perform ordinary maintenance on their own weapons, so that a storage facility would have to provide room for that. The most overwhelming drawback against the idea is the enormous cost of providing such facilities—no one has calculated how much, and they would, of course, be targets for anyone who wished to obtain illicit firearms.

Another crackpot scheme is to record the ballistics of all weapons, rather like fingerprints. This would not be enormously expensive, costing only a few million a year for new weapons only. But it is physically impossible. The pattern that the rifling of a barrel imprints on a bullet is not consistent and can be simply modified by changing the barrel. Ballistics is excellent at a one-to-one comparison between bullets, but cannot be employed for a general identification search.

Perhaps the most peculiar gun control proposal to date was made by the Department of Justice in 1975. It recommended that, when the "violent crime rate has reached the critical level," possession of handguns outside the home or place of business be banned altogether. This assumes that those areas where law enforcement is least efficient could enforce a handgun ban, and that where the forces of public order are weakest citizens should be denied the means to defend themselves. In almost all high-crime areas the carrying—or at least the concealed carrying—of handguns is already illegal. (Hard data are necessarily spotty, but it now appears likely that the widespread private ownership of handguns for self-protection among crime-liable populations leads to some transfer to criminals, principally by theft. If this is true, it would not seem unreasonable to dry up the demand for guns by providing security to these people.)

THE LIMITS TO INTERDICTION

So the utility of interdiction has not and perhaps cannot be demonstrated. While the lack of evidence that a policy can be effective should make prudent men wary of promoting it, that does not mean the policy is necessarily without merit. Nevertheless, in the case of gun control it is possible to identify some weaknesses in the principles behind the policy.

To begin with, gun control as a general anticrime strategy is flawed because most crimes, including many of the crimes most feared, are not committed with guns. Firearms are rarely employed for rape, home burglary, or street muggings. On the other hand, a good portion of the most heinous crime, murder, is not a serious source of social fear. The majority of murders are the result of passionate argument, and although personal tragedies, are not a social concern—ditto for crimes committed by criminals against one another. Furthermore, the worst crimes, involving the most dangerous and vicious criminals, will not be affected by gun control. No serious person believes that an interdiction program will be effective enough to keep guns out of the hands of organized crime, professional criminals, or well-connected terrorists and assassins. And almost all the widely publicized mass murderers were eligible for licensed guns.

Gun control advocates grant this, and emphasize the need to limit spontaneous murders among "family and friends" that are made possible by the availability of firearms. But the commonly used phrase "family and friends" is misleading. The FBI's Uniform Crime Reports classify relationships between murderers and victims as "relative killings," "lovers' quarrels," and "other arguments." The last can be among criminal associates, as can the others. Nor can we necessarily conclude that such murders are spontaneous. The legal distinction between premeditated and nonpremeditated murder prompts killers (and their lawyers) to present murders as unplanned.

The very nature of interdiction suggests other weaknesses. It is a military term used to describe attempts, usually by aerial bombing, to impede, not halt, the flow of enemy supplies to the battlefield. Interdiction has been the principal strategy used in drug control; it works only when pressure is being applied at the street level at the same time that imports and production are being squeezed. If there are 140 million privately owned firearms in the United States and guns can last centuries with minimum maintenance, merely cutting off the supply will have little or no effect for generations, and if the supply is not cut off entirely (which no serious person believes it can be), an interdiction policy is hardly likely to have a major effect even over the very long run. To my knowledge, no interdiction advocate has given a plausible answer to the very simple question of how to get 140 million firearms out of the hands of the American people.

Even more to the point, is it cost-effective to try to deal with 140 million weapons when you are presumably concerned with a maximum at the outside of 350,000 weapons used in violent crimes? The odds of any gun being criminally used are roughly on the order of one in 400. For handguns the rate is considerably higher; for rifles and shotguns considerably lower. I estimate that in 1974, roughly one of every 4,000 handguns was employed in a homicide, compared with one in 30,000 shotguns and one in 40,000 rifles. There are probably more privately owned guns in America than there are privately owned cars, and with the obvious exception of murder, the rate of criminal use of firearms is almost certainly less than the rate of criminal use of automobiles. How are we to control the 400 guns to prevent the one being used for crime? And if we decide the only way is to reduce the 400, to what must we reduce it? It must be assumed that the one gun used for crime will be the 400th.

Moreover, interdiction is a countermeasure against crime. Countermeasures provoke counter-countermeasures: Substitution is the most obvious strategy. If guns cannot be bought legally, they can be obtained illegally—organized crime is ready to cater to any illicit demand. If cheap handguns are unobtainable, expensive handguns will be used. If snub-nosed pistols and revolvers are banned, long-barreled weapons will be cut down. If the 40-million-odd handguns disappear, sawed-off rifles and shotguns are excellent substitutes. If all domestic production is halted, we will fall back on our tradition of smuggling. If all manufactured weapons vanish, anyone with a lathe and a hacksaw can make a serviceable firearm. In the 1950s, city punks produced zip guns from automobile aerials. A shotgun is easily made from a piece of pipe, a block of wood, several rubber bands, and a nail.

A more promising variation is to go after the ammunition rather than the gun. Whereas firearms are easily manufactured and last indefinitely, modern ammunition requires sophisticated manfuacturing facilities and has a shorter shelf life. Recently the interdictionists attempted to get the Consumer Product Safety Commission (CPSC) to prohibit the sale of handguns on the basis of their being inherently unsafe. This was certainly the most intelligent gun control tactic attempted so far; yet it failed because Congress explicitly prohibited CPSC from meddling in firearm matters. But a strategy directed against ammunition is also flawed. Hundreds of thousands of Americans "hand load" ammunition at home from commercially purchased shells, powder, and bullets in order to obtain substantial cost savings and to get precisely the sort of load they desire. Shell cartridges last forever and there are untold billions in circulation. Lead and steel bullets can be made by anyone with a stove or a file. So it would be necessary to close off powder sales as well. Smokeless powder would be extremely difficult to make at home, but the old-style black powder that fired weapons for 500 years can be manufactured by any kid with a chemistry set. Besides, any ammunition cutoff would be preceded by a long debate and bitter fight—during which time everyone would stock up. Also, thefts from the military, National Guard, and police would continue to be a major source of ammunition.

THE COSTS OF INTERDICTION

Against the unconvincing or unsupported benefits of any interdiction law, one must count the costs; practically no attention has been paid to them. BATF is now [1976] expending $50 million per annum on enforcement of federal laws. Local police, court, and corrections expenditures are buried in budgets. The only serious accounting of costs was prepared for the Violence Commission of 1968 and was downplayed in the final report. New York's Sullivan Law licensing cost about $75 per permit in 1968; double that for current levels of expenditure; assume that a maximum of half the households in the country will register their weapons; the cost is therefore in excess of $5 billion—or more than one-third of the present cost of the entire criminal justice system, from police to prisons. Simple "registration" on the model of auto registration would cost proportionately less, but the numbers are always in the hundreds of millions of dollars.

The financial costs do not exhaust the potential expense of gun control laws. It is too much to expect government to count as a cost the time and trouble to a citizen of registering a gun, but we might look at the price of diverting police and other law enforcement officials from potentially more rewarding activities.

But the worst cost is that of widespread flouting of the law. Existing gun controls are now being disobeyed by millions. More severe restrictions will be widely disregarded by tens of millions, including a huge group of stalwart citizens whose loyalty and lawfulness we now take for granted. Needless to say, the organized gun owners cite the Prohibition experience.

THE LIMITS TO DETERRENCE

Organized gun owners, on the other side of the issue, advocate enforcing the existing gun control laws. I suggest that they do not take this recommendation seriously; the existing laws are not enforceable. Another suggestion would appear to be more credible at first glance—to employ deterrence by having add-on sentences for the use of guns in crime. But such laws are on the books in several states and are not enforced, for a fairly obvious reason: Americans are not concerned with the use of a gun in a crime, but with the crime itself. The murder or armed robbery is objectionable, not the gun. *Illegal gun ownership is a victimless crime.*

Several practical problems make a deterrence strategy extremely difficult. There is trouble putting anyone away these days, and enforcement of existing gun laws or of new laws would add to the overload of an already jammed criminal justice system. Perhaps most important of all, when the effective sentence for premeditated murder is seven or eight years in a penitentiary,[4] how much leeway is there to add to sentences for lesser crimes? Given the advantages of a firearm to a robber, a few more weeks or months of jail is hardly likely to deter him from using it.

The organized gun owners also claim that the widespread possession of firearms in itself deters crime; criminals are likely to be restrained by an armed citizenry. Perhaps—but consideration of criminal tactics suggests the idea is limited in application. Take burglars—by definition they prefer stealth, choosing unoccupied houses. If the owner is at home it is unlikely that he will awaken. A noise that arouses him will also alert the burglar. Should the householder awake, the burglar will probably hear him—especially if he is fumbling for a gun that is, as it should be, secured. In a confrontation, the burglar is alert, while the householder is sleepy-eyed. It is far more likely that a gun will be stolen than that it could be used against a burglar.

In store robberies, the robber also has the advantage. Guns are clearly not a deterrent, since the armed stores are those most often hit—because to use Willie Sutton's phrase, "that's where the money is." Arming stores will certainly dissuade nongun robberies, obliging robbers to escalate to firearms. Street robberies offer a similar tactical imbalance: the mugger has the initiative. It is not unknown for even police to be disarmed by criminals.* It is true that areas with high gun ownership tend to have less crime against property, but this is probably largely the result of cultural factors. In any event the low quality of data on crime rates and gun ownership makes rigorous examination impossible.

INTERNATIONAL EXPERIENCE

Many peripheral arguments used in the gun control debate have little relevance to the issue, but must be addressed. Both sides will deploy the testimony of police chiefs on the desirability or futility of gun control laws. Liberal

---

*See Parts Two and Three for the latest research findings on these issues.—Ed.

interdictionists often cite the testimony of those gentlemen who have most illiberal views on most other law enforcement matters. Most, but not all, big-city chiefs favor interdiction, while small-town chiefs generally oppose it, both nicely reflecting the views of their political superiors. But, for what it is worth, one can cite the Sheriff of Los Angeles County staunchly demanding stricter gun control laws and the Chief of Police of Los Angeles City saying that public order has broken down so far that only a fool would not arm himself. The gun owners gained strong reinforcement when the Superintendent of Scotland Yard recently pointed out that the number of guns available in America makes an interdiction strategy impossible.

A surprising amount of attention has been paid in the gun control debate to international experience. In the world of gun control there seem to be only three foreign countries: Great Britain, Japan, and Switzerland. British gun control is taken by the interdictionists as the model of a desirable system. Guns are tightly regulated in the United Kingdom, violent crime is trivial by United States standards, and even the police are unarmed. But, as James Q. Wilson recently pointed out in this journal, the English situation is slowly eroding. The key to the low rates of personal violence in England is not in rigorous gun control laws (which only date from 1920), but in the generally deferential and docile character of the populace. Perhaps it is significant that interdictionists point to "Great Britain" as their model; gun control laws are even stricter in the other part of the United Kingdom, Northern Ireland.

Japan is an even more gun-free country. Not only does it restrict the ownership of weapons, but it has prohibited the ownership of handguns altogether, and the rates of violent crime are so low as to be hardly credible to Americans. To which the organized gun owners reply that Japanese-Americans have even lower rates of violence than Japanese in Japan.

The third international comparison is used by the organized gun owners. Switzerland has a militia system: 600,000 assault rifles with two magazines of ammo each are sitting at this moment in Swiss homes. Yet Switzerland's murder rate is 15 percent of ours. To which the interdictionists respond that the Swiss have strict licensing of weapons, though this would seem to have very little to do with the thesis that the mere availability of weapons provokes murder and other crimes with guns.

It is not entirely clear what these very different countries—with very different histories, political systems, and national character—have to do with the United States. Those interdictionists who defend civil liberties would be appalled at the suggestion that even the English system of justice be applied to the United States, much less the Swiss civil law or the authoritarian Japanese judicial system—none of which provides the criminal with the rights and privileges he has in the United States.

But let me muddy these waters by introducing two other countries of great interest. Israel is mostly inhabited by a people who have no tradition whatever of using firearms in self-defense and whose compatriots in America are for the most part unarmed and have little taste for hunting. But the objective political conditions of Israel have required them to arm in self-defense and the country bristles with public and private weapons. In addition to the armed forces, soldiers on pass or in casual transit in border areas carry their small arms with them. There is a civil guard in the tens of thousands. Every settlement has an arsenal, and individual Israelis are armed. The government requires registration of all weapons, but the system is very lenient on handguns (for Jews, of course; considerably tighter for Arabs) and very tough on rifles and shotguns, which might be used for military purposes. Israeli gun control policy is directed toward internal security, not against crime. But despite these restrictions, the Israelis have accumulated huge numbers of privately owned military weapons, including automatics, in various wars and raids. These are held "just in case" they may be needed. But strangely, hunting is on the increase in Israel, as are target shooting and gun collecting, and there is talk of forming an Israeli national rifle association. Needless to say, the crime rate in Israel is much lower than in the United States.

The special conditions of Israel are too obvious to note, but Canada is closer to home, and it is odd that so little attention has been paid it. Since the early 1920s, Canada has registered all pistols on what is essentially the same basis as New York's Sullivan Law. Rifles and shotguns are sold freely, even through mail order. Canada's crime rate is much lower than the United States'. Here, too, cultural factors seem to predominate. It is not usually observed that without the South and Southerners (black and white) transplanted to the North, the United States would have crime rates comparable to other industrial nations. In fact, there is no appreciable difference in murder rates for "Yankee" whites in states and provinces on either side of the 49th parallel.

The best point of the interdictionists is that America is an exception to the international system of strict restrictive licensing. To which the "gunnies" reply that our ancestors came here to free themselves and us from the tyrannies of the Old World.*

THE SECOND AMENDMENT

One reason the organized gun owners have had bad public relations is that they take an absolutist position regarding the Constitution, relying on the Second Amendment of the Bill of Rights: "A well regulated Militia, being

---

*See Part Two for further discussion of international comparisons. See also Tonso, "Social Problems and Sagecraft."—Ed.

necessary to the security of a free State, the right of the people to keep and bear Arms, shall not be infringed."

To the NRA and other organizations this is an unqualified right, like the freedom of the press, not to be compromised on any grounds. To the interdictionists, the amendment merely guarantees the right of the states to maintain what is now called the National Guard. Actually, the status and meaning of the Second Amendment can be the subject of debate among reasonable men. It is certainly true that the original intention of the Second Amendment was that there be an armed citizenry. A "militia" as understood in the eighteenth century was indeed the people armed with their own weapons, and the inclusion of the Second Amendment in the Bill of Rights was meant to protect the independence of the states and the people against the threat of the central government's employing the standard instrument of baroque tyranny, the standing army. However, there was no intention of the Founding Fathers to guarantee the use of firearms for recreation, nor for self-defense against criminals (although of the thirty-eight states that have similar "right to bear arms" provisions in their constitutions, eighteen specifically provide for personal defense, and one, New Mexico, for recreation).

The supreme arbiter of the Constitution has never ruled directly on the matter. The four cases that have come before the Supreme Court have been decided on narrow technical issues. Three nineteenth-century cases seem to support the view that states have the right to regulate firearms, and the one twentieth-century case, which rose out of the Federal Firearms Act of 1934, was decided on the very narrow ground of whether a sawed-off shotgun was a weapon suitable for a well-regulated militia.*

Gun-owning lawyers claim that the doctrine of "incorporation" to the states of Bill-of-Rights restraints protect gun owners from state controls. This is reasonable on the face of it. However, the Supreme Court, as it was intended to do, applies the standards of an enlightened public opinion to the law. If the dominant elements in the country favor gun control, it is to be expected that the courts will rule accordingly.

The organized gun owners also see the armed citizenry as a last line of defense against insurrection. This idea has roots in the disturbances of the 1960s. While many Americans viewed the urban riots as the inevitable outcome of centuries of repression, many more merely saw police standing aside while looters cleaned out stores and homes, then envisioned the same happening to *their* stores and homes, and armed themselves. They did not understand that the looting was permitted only so long as it was contained to black neighborhoods; any attempted "breakout" would have roused the forces of public order from their lethargy. Indeed, the contingency plans have been prepared.

---

*See Part Four for an extended discussion of Second Amendment issues.—Ed.

The gun owners claim that any registration lists would be used by a conqueror or tyrant to disarm the potential resistance. A minor debate has grown up over what the Nazis did in occupied Europe, especially in Norway. A source in the Norwegian Defense Ministry says the Nazis did not make use of registration lists but rather offered to shoot anyone who failed to turn in his weapons.

But there are examples of the use of registration lists to disarm the public. All handguns were called in following the assassination of the governor of Bermuda a few years ago. And the late, unlamented regime of the Greek colonels ordered the registration of all hunting weapons, followed by their confiscation, in order to disarm the royalists. Although the guns were later returned by the colonels, the present republican regime is continuing the control apparatus, presumably "just in case." When the IRA* began its offensive in Ulster earlier in the decade, the Irish Republic used registration lists to confiscate all privately owned firearms in the South.

PHALLIC NARCISSISM

A common assertion in the dispute is that gun owners are somehow mentally disturbed. The weapon is said to be a phallic symbol substituting for real masculinity, for "machismo." The historian Arthur Schlesinger, Jr., has written of "the psychotic suspicion that men doubtful of their own virility cling to the gun as a symbolic phallus and unconsciously fear gun control as the equivalent of castration." When queried about the source of this suspicion, he responded that he thought it was a "cliché." Such statements never cite sources because there are no sources. Every mention of the phallic-narcissist theory assumes it is well known, but there is no study or even credible psychoanalytical theory making the point. The germ of the idea derives from the 10th lecture in Sigmund Freud's *General Introduction to Psychoanalysis*, where he maintains that guns can symbolize the penis in dreams—as can sticks, umbrellas, trees, knives, sabers, water faucets, pencils, nail files, hammers, snakes, reptiles, fishes, hats and cloaks, hands, feet, balloons, aeroplanes, and Zeppelins. In other words, any long object can represent a phallus in a dream. Gun owners laugh at the thesis, or are infuriated. One said to me, "Anybody who associates the discharge of a deadly weapon with ejaculation has a *real* sexual problem."

Studies of hunters reveal that they are not much interested in guns or in killing but in the package of skills and camaraderie involved in the hunt. No one has studied the psychology of gun owners or even hard-core gun nuts, nor are there studies of gun phobia. Fortunately, there is a reason-

---

*The Irish Republican Army—Ed.

able amount of sociological data available, in the form of public opinion polls, which are believable because they give support to ordinary observation. Gun ownership is more prevalent among men, rural and small-town residents, Southerners, veterans, and whites. Except for the lowest income groups (who may not be willing to admit ownership), guns are fairly evenly distributed by income. Education, occupation, and politics make little difference. Protestants are more likely to be armed than other religious groups. When asked why they own guns, most people respond that they hunt or target shoot. But most handgun owners have them for self-defense, and long-gun owners admit to defense as a secondary purpose of their firearms.

Two generations of good data show that substantial majorities of the populace support gun registration, and this is cited fervently by individuals who prefer not to cite similar data favoring, e.g., maintaining prohibitions on marijuana, having courts get tougher with criminals, and restoring capital punishment. Of course, questions on "registration" are considerably misleading, because no one is advocating the mere registration of weapons, but rather licensing. Most people live in places where there is no licensing and have no idea of the difficulty and expense this would impose upon public authorities and gun owners if the standards of New York or Connecticut were aplied nationwide. Gun owners and people with knowledge of existing gun control laws are considerably less enthusiastic for registration. Supporters of interdiction are more likely to be young, single, prosperous, well-educated, liberal, New England nongun owners with little knowledge of existing gun control laws.

THE REAL ISSUES

The main point that emerges from any serious analysis is that the gun control issue, under conditions that exist in the United States today, has practically nothing to do with crime control. I think that there are other issues at stake.

In 1967, armed robbers with pistols killed two policemen in London. There was a wide outcry to "bring back the noose." The Labour government, opposed to capital punishment, responded by extending strict licensing requirements to small-bore shotguns used in rural areas for shooting birds and rodents. In Canada in 1974, there were two incidents of boys running amok with rifles in schools. There was wide agitation to restore capital punishment. The Liberal government, opposed to capital punishment, proposed a far-reaching program to eliminate registered pistols in private ownership and to register all rifles and shotguns. It is possible that gun control is, at least in part, a strategy to divert the mob away from the issue of capital punishment.

Political factors are clearly important. The assassinations of the 1960s and 1970s rather unnerved the politicians. But the wide social unrest of the

1960s probably had more impact. In 1939, George Orwell noted, "When I was a kid you could walk into a bicycle shop or ironmonger's [hardware store] and buy any firearm you pleased, short of a field gun, and it did not occur to most people that the Russian revolution and the Irish civil war would bring this state of affairs to an end." There is a remarkable coincidence between gun control agitation and periods of social upheaval. English and Canadian gun laws date from the "red scare" following the First World War, and the original United States national controls are the product of the violent days of the New Deal.

But underlying the gun control struggle is a fundamental division in our nation. The intensity of passion on this issue suggests to me that we are experiencing a sort of low-grade war going on between two alternative views of what America is and ought to be. On the one side are those who take bourgeois Europe as a model of a civilized society: a society just, equitable, and democratic; but well ordered, with the lines of responsibility and authority clearly drawn, and with decisions made rationally and correctly by intelligent men for the entire nation. To such people, hunting is atavistic, personal violence is shameful, and uncontrolled gun ownership is a blot upon civilization.

On the other side is a group of people who do not tend to be especially articulate or literate, and whose worldview is rarely expressed in print. Their model is that of the independent frontiersman who takes care of himself and his family with no interference from the state. They are "conservative" in the sense that they cling to America's unique pre-modern tradition—a nonfeudal society with a sort of medieval liberty writ large for every man. To these people, "sociological" is an epithet. Life is tough and competitive. Manhood means responsibility and caring for your own.

This hard-core group is probably very small, not more than a few million people, but it is a dangerous group to cross. From the point of view of a right-wing threat to internal security, these are perhaps the people who should be disarmed first, but in practice they will be the last. As they say, to a man, "I'll bury my guns in the wall first." They ask, because they do not understand the other side, "Why do these people want to disarm us?" They consider themselves no threat to anyone; they are not criminals, not revolutionaries. But, slowly, as they become politicized, they find an analysis that fits the phenomenon they experience: Someone fears their having guns, someone is afraid of their defending their families, property, and liberty. Nasty things may happen if these people begin to feel that they are cornered.

It would be useful, therefore, if some of the mindless passion, on both sides, could be drained out of the gun control issue. Gun control is no solution to the crime problem, to the assassination problem, to the terrorist problem. Reasonable licensing laws, reasonably applied, might be marginally useful in preventing some individuals, on some occasions, from doing violent harm to others and to themselves. But so long as the issue is kept at white heat, with everyone having some ground to suspect everyone else's ultimate intentions, the rule of reasonableness has little chance to assert itself.

NOTES

1. One obvious reason for the growing gun sales is that the prices of firearms, like most mass-produced goods, have not risen as fast as incomes. The classic deer rifle, the Winchester 94, in production since 1894, cost 250 percent of an average worker's weekly take-home salary in 1900, 91 percent in 1960, and 75 percent in 1970. The relationship to annual median family income has been even more favorable —from 2.8 percent in 1900 to 1.4 percent in 1960 and 1.0 percent in 1970. More important, increased competition during the past decade has lowered the absolute price of handguns.

2. The Police Foundation is currently engaged in a study of the details of local handgun-law enforcement. Unfortunately, because its head is known as a vocal interdictionist, the credibility of its results will necessarily be somewhat compromised.

3. The BATF also made the grave error of providing the organized gun owners with their first martyr. In Maryland, in 1971, a local pillar of the community—a Boy Scout leader, volunteer fireman, and gun collector—was in his bathtub when a group of armed men in beards and rough clothes—BATF agents— broke through the door. Understandably, he reached for a handy antique cap-and-ball pistol and was shot four times and left on the floor while his wife, still in her underwear, was dragged screaming from the apartment. What had happened was that a local boy reported a hand grenade in the apartment. There was, but it was only the shell of a hand grenade. A simple records check would have been adequate to establish the resident's bona fides, and if there was an interest in following up the matter, someone might have come and knocked on his door. He is now crippled for life.

4. The assassin of George Lincoln Rockwell was released from prison last year.

Selected Bibliography

Allen, H. C. *Bush and Backwards: A Comparison of the Frontiers in Australia and the United States.* Sydney, Australia: Angus and Robertson, 1959.

Billington, Ray Allen. "Frontiers," in C. Vann Woodard, ed., *The Comparative Approach to American History.* New York: Basic Books, 1975, pp. 75–90.

Kennett, Lee, and James Anderson. *The Gun in America: The Origins of an American Dilemma.* Westport, Conn.: Greenwood Press, 1975.

Newton, George D., and Franklin Zimring. *Firearms and Violence in American Life.* A staff report of the Task Force on Firearms, National Commission on the Causes and Prevention of Violence. Washington, D.C.: Government Printing Office, 1969.

Tonso, William R. *The Gun Culture and Its Enemies.* The Second Amendment Foundation. Bellevue, Wash.: Merril Press, 1990.

United States Congress, Committee on the Judiciary, Subcommittee on Juvenile Delinquency. *Handgun Crime Control: 1975–1976,* hearings to examine the adequacy of federal firearms controls in restricting the availability of handguns for criminal use. Washington, D.C.: 94th Congress, First Session, 1975.

Part Two

Controlling Crime and Violence

Introduction

In 1978, the National Institute of Justice funded a study that critically evaluated all the existing research done on guns and their relation to crime and violence in America. The final report was authored by two prominent sociologists, James D. Wright and Peter Rossi. Wright, a contributor to Part Two, acknowledges that, before this survey, he though it self-evident that if fewer guns were available, there would be less crime and violence. During the course of his research, however, he changed his mind. Wright and Rossi's findings were first published as a three-volume report in 1981 and subsequently as a book in 1983 titled *Under the Gun.* They challenged every major empirical assumption justifying strict gun control as a method for reducing criminal and domestic violence. Their work stimulated further critical inquiry and additional studies by other criminologists, who also reached skeptical conclusions as to the feasibility and even the desirability of restricting public access to firearms, especially handguns, as an effective response to the 1 to 2 percent of the population who criminally misuse firearms. In 1986, Wright and Rossi dropped another bombshell: they investigated *how* and *why* criminals obtain guns, surveying two thousand felons serving sentences in ten state prisons in the United States. The results, published in *Armed and Considered Dangerous,* created even more skepticism concerning attempts to deny criminals access to handguns by restricting public access to these weapons. The work of Wright and Rossi, along with other criminologists such as Gary Kleck and Don B. Kates, Jr.—selections from their work are included in this Part—raise further disturbing questions. Would a successful handgun ban lead criminals to use even more lethal weapons such as "sawed-off" shotguns and, therefore, increase the number of gun-related fatalities (Wright and Rossi, selection 6; and Kleck, selection 9)? Did earlier studies showing correlations between high levels of gun ownership and high rates of gun violence demonstrate only that as the rate of violent crime rises, more honest citizens buy guns to defend themselves (Kleck, selection 7)? Beyond such questions, these criminologists advance the hypothesis that the causes of violent crime are social, political, economic, and cultural in nature. They view firearm violence therefore as a *consequence* of these factors rather than firearms being a *cause* of violence (Wright, selection 5; Wright and Rossi, selection 6; Kleck, selection 9; and Kates, selection 13).

Specifically, these criminologists dispute the claim that the more handguns are possessed by the *general public,* the more these weapons will be involved in crime and violence. The objections to this linkage center on the differences between criminals and noncriminals, relative to how these groups obtain weapons (Wright and Rossi, selection 6), the different ways these groups use weapons (Wright and Rossi, selction 6; Cook, selection 8), and Kleck's research (selection 7), which makes the case that rising rates of gun ownership on the part of the noncriminal is a *response* to, not a cause of, rising violent crime rates.

These criminologists further argue that the marked differences in the gun habits of noncriminal and criminal populations have important implications for gun control measures. They favor "moderate" or selective measures, which target only identifiable "high risk" groups—e.g., young, urban people with criminal records—for exclusion from firearms ownership through a permit system. The noncriminal adult population would have free access to both long guns and handguns through such a system (Wright and Rossi, selection 6; Cook, selection 8; and Kleck, selections 7 and 9).

In sum, the work of these and other noted researchers reversed a trend that developed in the 1960s and 1970s. For nearly twenty years scholarly research had overwhelmingly supported strict gun control. The findings from these studies were eagerly used by gun control advocates and completely ignored by the "gun lobby." Now the advocates of gun ownership enthusiastically embrace the new research that bolsters their position, namely, that restrictive or prohibitionist gun control would be ineffective and even counterproductive in the battle against crime and the criminal misuse of firearms. The reader, however, will note that some of the gun control measures recommended by this recent research go beyond what is presently acceptable to the gun lobby (e.g., the licensing of long guns).

The new research has created serious problems for strict gun control advocates, who base their case on the idea that reducing public access to firearms, especially handguns, will reduce violent crime. The burden of proof is obviously on those who would ask others to give up legally obtainable firearms in the name of public safety. If the recent work of criminologists is sustained, skepticism over whether that proof is convincing is certainly warranted.

Also included in Part Two are selections that challenge the new research. Professor Franklin Zimring, who, along with George Newton, authored *Fire-*

arms and Violence in American Life: A Staff Report Submitted to the National Commission on Causes and Prevention of Violence in 1969 and subsequent research making the case for strict handgun control, challenges the skeptics' research assumptions, methodologies, and conclusions.

Professor Zimring's reply to his critics in Part Two is especially important to the gun control debate. His 1969 research and subsequent work in the 1970s continues to be cited as primary evidence in both popular and scholarly movements to ban or restrict public access to handguns. A successful defense of his investigations and conclusions therefore is vital to the credibility of stricter gun control approaches.

In Zimring and Hawkin's work titled *The Citizen's Guide to Gun Control* (1987), he stands by his earlier research (1969) and continues to maintain that there are "significant links between general handgun availability and the use of handguns in violent crimes," and "that periods of increased handgun acquisition appear to be associated with increases in firearm violence."[1] Specifically, he claims that the more handguns are available to and purchased by the *public,* the higher the rates of gun violence.

Zimring disputes the claim of Wright and Rossi, Kleck, and Kates that, since the causes of America's crime and violence are social and cultural in nature, a reduction of firearm availability would not *appreciably* lessen levels of violence (selection 11). He maintains that his earlier research, which found that handguns were five times more dangerous than knives when used in crimes, is correct. He had concluded that, because of firearms' increased degree of lethalness—their "instrumentality effect"—mortality would decline if their numbers were reduced (selection 11). Zimring disputes Wright's and Kleck's arguments against his calculation of the relative lethality of handguns, arguing that critics like Kates and Wright and Rossi are mistaken in their conclusions that restricting public access to firearms would do little to reduce the availability of guns to criminals (selection 10). He also contests investigations by Wright and Rossi (selection 6) and Kleck (selection 9), which suggest that criminals would use more lethal weapons, such as sawed-off shotguns, if handguns were banned (selection 11).

Zimring favors a federal gun control approach that would emulate on the national level the restrictive or prohibitionist policies currently in place in New York City and in Washington, D.C. (selection 12).

Further perspectives on these issues will be gained through Philip Cook's essay (selection 8), in which he discusses how availability of firearms to criminals affects not only homicide rates but also the kinds of victims selected for attack, the kind of assaults engaged in, and the rates of criminal success. Cook agrees with Zimring that the handgun's greater lethal power (its "instrumentality effect") has a substantial impact on mortality when firearms are used criminally. However, Cook sides with those of Zimring's critics who contend that restricting the public's access to firearms would have little effect in reducing violent crime. He therefore is a supporter of selective or "moderate" gun control measures.

The last issue addressed in Part Two involves comparing the higher levels of gun availability and associated violence in the United States, which lacks restrictive federal controls, to the lower levels of gun availability and gun violence in selected foreign countries, which feature restrictive national firearms controls. The conclusion that many gun control advocates draw from these studies is just this: restrictive federal gun controls would reduce gun violence.

These comparisons were mainstays in the academic and popular arguments advanced in the 1960s and 1970s for strict federal gun regulations. However, criticisms of methodological difficulties in these studies (see selections by Bruce-Briggs and Tonso in Part One; Wright, selection 5) cost them considerable credibility. Simply put, nations differ in so many respects, including history, culture, racial problems, ethnicity, crime rate, and the like, that it is impossible to draw valid conclusions linking gun availability and gun laws to levels of gun violence. Such criticisms extend even to comparing different regions of the *same* country. These criticisms, however, have not deterred their continued use in the gun control debate. They figure prominently in the contemporary popular campaign for strict gun control.

Included here in the work of John Henry Sloan and his associates (selection 14) is a contemporary attempt to overcome the pitfalls of making international comparisons. The preceding selection by Kates (13) details the historical and methodological problems of such attempts. The reader must judge whether Sloan and his coauthors have succeeded in demonstrating that stricter gun control reduces criminal violence involving guns.

NOTE

1. Franklin E. Zimring and Gordon Hawkins. *The Citizen's Guide to Gun Control* (New York: Macmillan, 1987), p. 53.

5

Second Thoughts about Gun Control

James D. Wright

Gun control, it has been said, is the acid test of liberalism. All good liberals favor stricter gun controls. After all, doesn't the United States have the most heavily armed population on earth? Are we not the world's most violent people? Surely these facts must be causally connected. The apparently desperate need to "do something" about the vast quantity of firearms and firearms abuse is, to the good liberal, obvious.

At one time, it seemed evident to me, we needed to mount a campaign to resolve the crisis of handgun proliferation. Guns are employed in an enormous number of crimes in this country. In other countries with stricter gun laws, gun crime is rare. Many of the firearms involved in crime are cheap handguns, so-called Saturday Night Specials, for which no legitimate use or need exists. Many families buy these guns because they feel the need to protect themselves; eventually, they end up shooting one another. If there were fewer guns around, there would also be less crime and less violence. Most of the public also believes this, and has supported stricter gun control for as long as pollsters have been asking the question. Yet Congress has refused to act

Reprinted with permission of the author from *The Public Interest,* No. 91 (Spring 1988): 23–39.
Copyright © by National Affairs, Inc.

in a meaningful way, owing mainly to the all-powerful "gun lobby" headed by the National Rifle Association. Were the power of this lobby somehow effectively countered by the power of public opinion, stricter gun laws would follow quickly, and we would begin to achieve a safer and more civilized society.

When I first began research on the topic of private firearms, in the mid-1970s, I shared this conventional and widely held view of the issue. Indeed, much of it struck me as self-evidently true. My initial interest in the topic resulted from a life-long fascination with the bizarre: I certainly did not own a gun (I still don't), and neither, as far as I knew, did many of my friends. Still, readily available survey evidence showed that half the families in the United States did own one, and I wondered what unspeakable oddities or even pathologies an analysis of this half of the American population would reveal.

My first scholarly paper on the topic, "The Ownership of the Means of Destruction," appeared in 1975. This demographic comparison between gun-owning and non-gun-owning households revealed shocking information. Gun owners, it turned out, were largely small-town and rural Protestants of higher-than-average income. Fear of crime, interestingly enough, did not seem to be related to gun ownership. The general tone of my piece remained unmistakably "anti-gun," but the findings did not provide much new information to strengthen the "anti-gun" lobby's arguments. At about the same time, I prepared a more polemical version of the paper, which was eventually published in the *Nation*. The General Counsel of the National Rifle Association described the piece as "emotionally supercharged drum-beating masquerading as scholarly analysis." Clearly, I was on the right track; I had managed to offend the right people.

The *Nation* article was abridged and reprinted in the Sunday Chicago *Tribune*, a newspaper read by about two million people, many of whom saw fit to write me after the piece appeared. Almost all the letters I received were provocative; some were very favorable, but most were vitriolic attacks from gun nuts. The first wave of correspondence over the *Tribune* piece affirmed my assumption that many gun owners were crazy. Subsequent waves, however, convinced me that many were indeed thoughtful, intelligent, often remarkably well-read people who were passionately concerned about their "right to keep and bear arms," but were willing, nonetheless, to listen to reason.

Two years later, in 1977, my colleague Peter Rossi and I received a grant from the National Institute of Justice to undertake a comprehensive, critical overview of the research literature on guns, crime, and violence in America. The results of this overview were published in 1981 in a three-volume government report and in 1983 as a commercial monograph, entitled *Under the Gun*. Subsequent to this work, we received another grant to gather original data on gun acquisition, ownership, and use from about 2,000 men doing felony time in ten state prisons all over the United States. We assembled this information in a government report and later in a monograph, *Armed and Considered Dangerous*. The felon survey marked the temporary end of my firearms research program, one that ran roughly from 1974 through 1986, when *Armed and Considered Dangerous* was finally published.

As I have already suggested, at the outset of the research program I had a strong feeling that the pro-gun control forces had never marshalled their evidence in the most compelling way, that they were being seriously undercut by the more artful polemics of the National Rifle Association and related pro-gun groups. That the best available evidence, critically considered, would eventually prove favorable to the procontrol viewpoint was not in serious doubt—at least not to me, not in the beginning.

In the course of my research, however, I have come to question nearly every element of the conventional wisdom about guns, crime, and violence. Indeed, I am now of the opinion that a compelling case for "stricter gun control" *cannot be made*, at least not on empirical grounds. I have nothing but respect for the various pro-gun control advocates with whom I have come into contact over the past years. They are, for the most part, sensitive, humane, and intelligent people, and their ultimate aim, to reduce death and violence in our society, is one that every civilized person must share. I have, however, come to be convinced that they are barking up the wrong tree.

WHAT IS "GUN CONTROL"?

Before I describe the intellectual odyssey that led to my change in thinking, it is critical to stress that "gun control" is an exceedingly nebulous concept. To say that one favors gun control, or opposes it, is to speak in ambiguities. In the present-day American political context, "stricter gun control" can mean anything from federal registration of firearms, to mandatory sentences for gun use in crime, to outright bans on the manufacture, sale, or possession of certain types of firearms. One can control the manufacturers of firearms, the wholesalers, the retailers, or the purchasers; one can control the firearms themselves, the ammunition they require, or the uses to which they are put. And one can likewise control their purchase, their carrying, or their mere possession. "Gun control" thus covers a wide range of specific interventions, and it would be useful indeed if the people who say they favor or oppose gun control were explicit about what, exactly, they are for and against.

In doing the research for *Under the Gun*, I learned that there are approximately 20,000 gun laws of various sorts already on the books in the United States. A few of these are federal laws (such as the Gun Control Act of 1968), but most are state and local regulations. It is a misstatement to say, as pro-gun control advocates sometimes do, that the United States has "no meaningful gun control legislation." The problem is not that laws do not exist but that the regulations in force vary enormously from one place to the next, or, in some cases, that the regulations carried on the books are not or cannot be enforced.

Much of the gun legislation now in force, whether enacted by federal, state, or local statutes, falls into the category of reasonable social precaution, being neither more nor less stringent than measures taken to safeguard against abuses of other potentially life-threatening objects, such as automobiles. It seems reasonable, for example, that people should be required to obtain a permit to carry a concealed weapon, as they are virtually everywhere in the United States. It is likewise reasonable that people not be allowed to own automatic weapons without special permission, and that felons, drug addicts, and other sociopaths be prevented from legally acquiring guns. Both these restrictions are in force everywhere in the United States, because they are elements of federal law. About three-fourths of the American population lives in jurisdictions where the registration of firearms purchases is required. It is thus apparent that many states and localities also find this to be a useful precaution against something. And many jurisdictions also require "waiting periods" or "cooling off" periods between application and actual possession of a new firearms purchase. These, too, seem reasonable, since there are very few legitimate purposes to which a firearm might be put that would be thwarted if the user had to wait a few days, or even a few weeks, to get the gun.

Thus, when I state that "a compelling case for 'stricter gun control' cannot be made," I do not refer to the sorts of obvious and reasonable precautions discussed above, or to related precautionary measures. I refer, rather, to measures substantially more strict than "reasonable precaution," and more specifically, to measures that would deny or seriously restrict the right of the general population to own a firearm, or that would ban the sale or possession of certain kinds of firearms, such as handguns or even the small, cheap handguns known colloquially as "Saturday Night Specials."

EFFECTS OF GUN LAWS

One wonders, with some 20,000 firearms regulations now on the books, why the clamor continues for even more laws. The answer is obvious: none of the laws so far enacted has significantly reduced the rate of criminal violence. *Under the Gun* reviewed several dozen research studies that had attempted to measure the effects of gun laws in reducing crime; none of them showed any conclusive long-term benefits.

As it happens, both sides of the gun control debate grant this point: they disagree, though, as to why there is no apparent connection between gun control laws and crime rates. The NRA maintains that gun laws don't work because they can't work. Widely ignored (especially by criminals) and unenforceable, gun control laws go about the problem in the wrong way. For this reason, the NRA has long supported mandatory and severe sentences for use of firearms in felonies, contending that we should punish firearms abusers once it is proven that an abuse has occurred, and leave legitimate users alone until they have actually done something illegal with their weapon.

The procontrol forces argue that gun laws don't work because there are too many of them, because they are indifferently enforced, and because the laws vary widely from one jurisdiction to the next. What we need, they would argue, are federal firearms regulations that are strictly enforced all across the nation. They would say that we have never given gun control a fair test, because we lack an aggressive *national* firearms policy.

This example illustrates an important point that I have learned and relearned throughout my career in applied social research: the policy consequences of a scientific finding are seldom obvious. On this particular point, the science is reasonably clear-cut: gun control laws do not reduce crime. But what is the implication? One possible implication is that we should stop trying to control crime by controlling guns. The other possible implication is that we need to get much more serious than we have been thus far about controlling guns, with much stricter, nationally standardized gun control policies. There is little or nothing in the scientific literature that would allow one to choose between these possibilities; either could well be correct.

GUNS, CRIMES, AND NUMBERS

What is the annual firearms toll in this country? Our review of the data sources revealed that some components of the toll, especially the annual fatality count, are well known, whereas other components are not. In recent years, the total number of homicides occurring in the United States has been right around 20,000. Of these, approximately 60 percent are committed with firearms. There are somewhat fewer than 30,000 suicides committed in an average recent year, of which about half involve a firearm. Deaths from firearms accidents have represented about 2 percent of the total accidental deaths in the nation for as long as data have been collected, and add about 2,000 deaths per year to the toll. Taken together, then, there are about 30,000 deaths from firearms in an average year; this amounts to some 1-2 percent of all deaths from any cause.

Both camps in the gun control war like to spew out exaggerated rhetoric. In the case of gun deaths, the anticontrol forces shout that the total deaths due to firearms in a year are less than the deaths due to automobile accidents (about 50,000)—"but nobody wants to ban cars!" To counter, the procontrol people express the gun toll as a number of deaths per unit of time. The resulting figure is dramatic: on average, someone in the United States dies from a firearm every seventeen or eighteen minutes.

Death is not the whole story, of course. One must also include nonfatal but injurious firearms accidents, crimes other than homicide or suicide committed with guns, unsuccessful suicide attempts involving firearms, and so on. None of these things is known with much precision, and the lack of firm data is an invitation to exuberant formulations on both sides. Still, reasonable compromise values for the various components suggest a total incident count of fewer than a million per year—that is, incidents in which a firearm of some sort was involved in some way in some kind of violent or criminal incident (intentional or accidental, fatal or not). Pro-gun people have dismissed this estimate as much too high, and anti-gun people have dismissed it as much too low, so I figure it can't be too far off.

When we shift to the guns side of the "guns and crime" equation, the numbers jump by a few orders of magnitude, although here, too, some caution is needed. In the course of the twentieth century, so far as can be told, some 250 million total firearms (excluding military weapons) have been manufactured in or imported into the United States. Published guesses about the number of guns in private hands in this country ran upwards to a billion—an absurd and inconceivably large estimate. Most of the published estimates are produced by advocates and thus are not to be trusted, most of all since both sides have vested interests in publishing the largest possible numbers: the pro-gun people, to show the vast number of people whose rights would be infringed by stricter gun controls; the anti-gun people, to show the obvious urgency of the situation.

It is not known for certain how many of the 250 million guns of the twentieth century remain in private hands; 150 million is a sensible guess. Survey evidence dating from at least 1959 routinely shows that about 50 percent of all American households possess at least one firearm, with the average number owned (among those owning at least one) being just over three. Whatever the exact number, it is obvious that there are lots and lots of guns out there—many tens of millions at the very least.

Both sides trumpet these large numbers with relish. To the NRA, these big numbers show clearly that "nothing can be done." The vast size of the private U.S. arsenal renders any effort to control it utterly futile. To the procontrol forces, these same numbers demonstrate, with equal clarity, that "something must be done." The vast size of the private U.S. arsenal makes the effort to control it essential.

The numbers do speak clearly to at least one point: if we are going to try to "control" guns as a means of controlling crime, then we are going to have to deal with the guns already in private hands; controls over new purchases alone will not suffice. Taking the highest plausible value for the number of gun incidents—1 million per year—and the lowest plausible value for the number of guns presently owned—say, 100 million—we see rather quickly that the guns now owned exceed the annual incident count by a factor of at least a hundred; in other words, the existing stock is adequate to supply all conceivable nefarious purposes for at least the next century.

These figures can be considered in another way. Suppose we did embark on a program of firearms confiscation, with the ultimate aim of achieving a "no guns" condition. We would have to confiscate at least a hundred guns to get just one gun that, in any typical year, would be involved in any kind of gun incident; several hundred to get just one that would otherwise be involved in a chargeable gun crime; and several thousand to get just one that would otherwise be used to bring about someone's death. Whatever else one might want to say about such a policy, it is not very efficient.

DEMAND CREATES ITS OWN SUPPLY

One of the favorite aphorisms of the pro-gun forces is that "if guns are outlawed, only outlaws will have guns." Sophisticated liberals laugh at this point, but they shouldn't. No matter what laws we enact, they will be obeyed only by the law-abiding—this follows by definition. If we were to outlaw, say, the ownership of handguns, millions of law-abiding handgun owners would no doubt turn theirs in. But why should we expect the average armed robber or street thug to do likewise? Why should we expect felons to comply with a gun law when they readily violate laws against robbery, assault, and murder?

For the average criminal, a firearm is an income-producing tool with a consequent value that is several times its initial cost. According to data published by Phillip Cook of Duke University, the average "take" in a robbery committed with a firearm is more than $150 (in 1976 dollars) and is three times the take for a robbery committed with any other weapon; the major reason for the difference is that criminals with guns rob more lucrative targets. Right now, one can acquire a handgun in any major American city in a matter of a few hours for roughly $100. Even if the street price of handguns tripled, a robber armed with a handgun could (on the average) recoup his entire capital outlay in the first two or three transactions.

As long as there are *any* handguns around (and even "ban handgun" advocates make an exception for police or military handguns), they will obviously be available to anyone *at some price.* Given Cook's data, the average street thug would come out well ahead even if he spent several hundred—perhaps even a few thousand—on a suitable weapon. At those prices, demand will always create its own supply: just as there will always be cocaine available to anyone willing to pay $200 a gram for it, so, too, will handguns always be available to anyone willing to pay a thousand dollars to obtain one.

The more militant "ban handgun" advocates urge what is easily recognized as the handgun equivalent of Prohibition. Why would we expect the outcome of "handgun prohibition" to differ from its 1920s predecessor? A black market in guns, run by organized crime, would almost certainly spring up to service the demand. It is, after all, no more difficult to manufacture a serviceable firearm in one's basement than to brew up a batch of home-made gin. Afghani tribesmen, using wood fires and metal-working equipment much inferior to what can be ordered from a Sears catalogue, hand-manufacture rifles that fire the Russian AK-47 cartridge. Do we ascribe less ability to the Mafia or the average do-it-yourselfer?

A recent poll of the U.S. adult population asked people to agree or disagree with this proposition: "Gun control laws affect only law-abiding citizens; criminals will always be able to find guns." Seventy-eight percent agreed. There is no reasonable doubt that the majority, in this case, is right.

CRIMES OF PASSION

Sophisticated advocates on both sides by now grant most of the preceding points. No one still expects "stricter gun control" to solve the problem of hard-core criminal violence, or even make a dent in it. Much of the argument has thus shifted toward violence perpetrated not for economic gain, or for any other good reason, but rather in the "heat of the moment"—the so-called "crimes of passion" that turn injurious or lethal not so much because anyone intended them to, but because, in a moment of rage, a firearm was at hand. Certainly, we could expect incidents of this sort to decline if we could some-how reduce the availability of firearms for the purpose. Or could we?

Crimes of passion certainly occur, but how often? Are "heat of the moment" homicides common or rare? The fact is, nobody knows. The assumption that they are very common, characteristic of the procontrol worldview, is derived from the well-known fact that most homicides involve persons known to one another before the event—typically family members, friends, or other acquaintances. But ordinarily, the only people one would ever have any good reason to kill would be people known intimately to oneself. Contrary to the common assumption, prior acquaintance definitely does *not* rule out willful, murderous intent.

The "crime of passion" most often discussed is that of family members killing one another. One pertinent study, conducted in Kansas City, looked into every family homicide that occurred in a single year. In 85 percent of the cases examined, the police had previously (within the prior five years) been called to the family residence to break up a domestic quarrel; in half the cases, the police had been there five or more times. It would therefore be misleading to see these homicides as isolated and unfortunate outbursts occurring among normally placid and loving individuals. They are, rather, the culminating episodes of an extended history of violence and abuse among the parties.

Analysis of the family homicide data reveals an interesting pattern. When women kill men, they often use a gun. When men kill women, they usually do it in some more degrading or brutalizing way—such as strangulation or knifing. The reason for the difference seems obvious: although the world is full of potentially lethal objects, almost all of them are better suited to male than to female use. The gun is the single exception: all else held constant, it is equally deadly in anyone's hands. Firearms equalize the means of physical terror between men and women. In denying the wife of an abusive man the right to have a firearm, we may only be guaranteeing her husband the right to beat her at his pleasure. One argument against "stricter gun control" is thus that a woman should have as much right to kill her husband as a man has to kill his wife.

Some will gasp at this statement; no one, after all, has a "right" to kill anyone. But this, of course, is false: every jurisdiction in the United States recognizes justifiable homicides in at least some extenuating circumstances, and increasingly a persistent and long-standing pattern of physical abuse is acknowledged to be one of them. True, in the best of all possible worlds, we would simply do away with whatever gives rise to murderous rage. This is not, regrettably, the world in which we live.

INTERNATIONAL COMPARISONS

Comparing the United States with other civilized nations in terms of guns, crime, and violence is the "service revolver" in the procontrol armament, the first line of defense against all disputation. The essentials are well-known: there are, in the United States, no strict federal controls over civilian arms, vast numbers of firearms in private hands, and an enormous amount of gun crime and violence. In other nations (England and Japan, for example), there are strict national controls, few guns, and little or no gun crime. Is this not conclusive evidence that strong gun laws reduce gun violence? One would be hard-pressed to find a single example of procontrol writing in which these points are not featured prominently.

It does not take advanced training in research methods to see that in the absence of more detailed analyses, such comparisons are vacuous. Any two nations will differ along many dimensions—history, culture, social structure, and legal precedent, to name a few—and any of these differences (no less than the difference in gun laws or in the number of guns available) might well account for the difference in violent crime rates. Without some examination of these other potentially relevant factors, attributing the crime difference to the gun-law or gun-availability difference begs the question.

The English case is commonly cited. It is quite clear, however, that the rates of firearm ownership and violent crime were both extremely low in England for decades *before* that nation's strict gun law was passed, and also that the gun laws have not prevented a very sharp increase in gun crime in England in the past decade. Japan is also commonly cited. In fact, the rate of *non-gun* homicide in the United States is many times higher than the total homicide rate of Japan, so there is also much more to the U.S.-Japan difference than meets the eye.

What is true of comparisons among nations is equally true of other geographic aggregates—for example, regions, states, or counties. Any two aggregates, like any two countries, will have any number of differences—differences that must somehow be held constant in order to make any sense of the differences in crime rates. The methodological point is easy to demonstrate with a single example: it is well known that gun ownership is much more widespread in small towns and rural areas than in big cities. Violent crime, in contrast, is disproportionately a big-city problem. Should we therefore conclude from this evidence alone that guns are not the cause of crime, or that high rates of gun ownership actually reduce crime? Probably not: rather, we should demand something more from the analysis. Without that "something more," nothing of value can be inferred; this is also the case with crude comparisons between the United States and other countries.

PUBLIC OPINION

Public opinion has always played a key role in the case for stricter gun control. If the effectiveness of "gun control" in reducing crime is in some doubt, as it obviously is, at least little apparent harm would be done by such controls, and the public clearly favors them. If the majority sentiment has counted for little or nothing, it is only because of the Machiavellian workings of the gun lobby.

The first "gun control" question in a national poll was apparently asked in the 1930s. Even at that early date, large majorities responded favorably. In 1959, Gallup instituted what is now the standard "gun control" question, asking whether one would favor or oppose a law that required a person to acquire a police permit before purchasing a gun. In the original study, and in many subsequent studies, the proportions favoring such a law have seldom dropped below 70 percent.

These large majorities are interpreted by gun control advocates as evidence of wide popular demand for stricter gun controls, but the fact is that two-thirds to three-quarters of the American population resides in political jurisdictions in which something similar to the Gallup "police permit" mechanism is *already* in force. The majority sentiment may only represent an endorsement of the status quo, not a demand for bold new gun control initiatives.

Other gun control measures that are sometimes asked about—those substantially more stringent than registration or permit requirements—are not, in general, received with much popular enthusiasm. Bans on the manufacture, sale, or ownership of handguns, for example, are rejected by good-sized majorities; government use of public funds to buy back guns and destroy them is rejected by an even larger majority. Mandatory sentencing for the criminal use of a firearm is enormously popular; mandatory sentencing for the illegal carrying or possession of a firearm is less so. In general, the poll evidence suggests that most people support most of the "reasonable social precautions" I discussed earlier, but do not wish to see government go much further. Not incidentally, immense majorities of the population, approaching 90 percent, believe that the Constitution guarantees them the right to own a gun. Procontrol advocates who effusively cite "public opinion" as a principal rationale for stricter gun control rarely comment on this finding.

THE SATURDAY NIGHT SPECIAL

The notorious Saturday Night Special has received a great deal of attention. The term is used loosely: it can refer to a gun of low price, inferior quality, small caliber, short barrel length, or some combination of these. The attention is typically justified on two grounds: first, these guns have no legitimate sport or recreational use, and second, they are the firearms preferred by criminals. Thus, the argument goes, we could just ban them altogether; in doing so, we would directly reduce the number of guns available to criminals without restricting anyone's legitimate ownership rights.

The idea that the Saturday Night Special is the criminal's gun of choice turns out to be wrong. Our felon survey showed, overwhelmingly, that serious criminals both prefer to carry and actually do carry relatively large, big-bore, well-made handguns. Indeed, not more than about one in seven of these criminals' handguns would qualify as small and cheap. Most of the felons wanted to be and actually were at least as well armed as their most likely adversaries, the police. There may well be good reason to ban Saturday Night Specials, but the criminal interest in such weapons is not one of them. Most serious felons look on the Saturday Night Special with considerable contempt.

It is too early to tell how these data will be interpreted among "Ban Saturday Night Special" advocates. The most recent wrinkle I have encountered is that they should be banned not because they are preferred or used by criminals, but because, being cheap, they tend to be owned by unknowledgeable, inexperienced, or irresponsible people. One may assume that cheap handguns, like cheap commodities of all sorts, tend to be owned by poor people. The further implication—that poor gun owners are less knowledge-able, experienced, or responsible than more affluent owners—has, however, never been researched; it is also the sort of "elitist" argument that ordinarily arouses liberal indignation.

What about the other side of the argument—that these guns have no legitimate use? It is amazing how easily people who know little about guns render such judgments. When I commenced my own research, it occurred to me that I ought to find out what gun owners themselves had to say on some of these matters. So I picked up the latest issues of about a half-dozen gun magazines. It is remarkable how informative this simple exercise turned out to be.

One magazine that surfaced is called *Handgunning*, which is specifically for devotees of handgun sports. Every issue of the magazine is full of articles on the sporting and recreational uses of handguns of all kinds. I learned, for example, that people actually hunt game with handguns, which never would have occurred to me. In reading a few articles, the reason quickly became obvious: it is more sporting than hunting with shoulder weapons, and it requires much more skill, which makes a successful handgun hunt a much more satisfying accomplishment.

In my journey through this alien turf, I came upon what are called "trail guns" or "pack guns." These are handguns carried outdoors, in the woods or the wilds, for no particular reason except to have a gun available "just in case" one encounters unfriendly fauna, or gets lost and needs small game for food, or is injured and needs to signal for help. The more I read about trail guns, the more it seemed that people who spend a lot of time alone in the wilds, in isolated and out-of-the-way places, are probably being pretty sensible in carrying these weapons.

One discussion went on in some detail about the characteristics to look for in a trail gun. It ought to be small and light, of course, for the same reason that serious backpackers carry nylon rather than canvas tents. "Small and light" implies caliber (a .22 or .25), a short barrel, and a stainless-steel frame (to afford greater protection from the elements). The article mentioned that some of the finest weapons of this sort were being manufactured in Europe, and at very reasonable prices. And suddenly it dawned on me: the small, low-caliber, short-barreled, imported, not-too-expensive guns the article was describing were what are otherwise known as Saturday Night Specials. And thus I came to learn that we cannot say that Saturday Night Specials have "no legitimate sport or recreational use."

It would be sophistic to claim that most Saturday Night Specials are purchased for use as trail guns; my point is only that some are. Most small, cheap handguns are probably purchased by persons of modest means to protect themselves against crime. It is arguable whether protection against crime is a "legitimate" or "illegitimate" use; the issues involved are too complex to treat fairly in this article. It is worth stressing, however, that poor, black, central city residents are by far the most likely potential victims of crime; if self-protection justifies owning a gun, then a ban on small, cheap handguns would effectively deny the means of self-protection to those most evidently in need of it.

There is another argument against banning small, cheap handguns: a ban on Saturday Night Specials would leave heavy-duty handguns available as substitute weapons. It is convenient to suppose that in the absence of small, cheap handguns, most people would just give up and not use guns for whatever they had in mind. But certainly some of them, and perhaps many of them, would move up to bigger and better handguns instead. We would do well to remember that the most commonly owned handgun in America today is a .38 caliber double-action revolver, the so-called Police Special that functions as the service revolver for about 90 percent of American police. If we somehow got rid of all the junk handguns, how many thugs, assailants, and assassins would choose to use this gun, or other guns like it, instead? And what consequences might we then anticipate?

The handgun used by John Hinckley in his attack on President Reagan was a .22 caliber revolver, a Saturday Night Special. Some have supported banning the Saturday Night Special so as to thwart psychopaths in search of weapons. But would a psychopath intent on assassinating a President simply give up in the absence of a cheap handgun? Or would he, in that event, naturally pick up some other gun instead? Suppose he did pick up the most commonly owned handgun available in the United States, the .38 Special. Suppose further that he got off the same six rounds and inflicted the same wounds that he inflicted with the .22. A .38 slug entering Jim Brady's head where the .22 entered would, at the range in question, probably have killed him instantly. The Washington policeman would not have had a severed artery, but would have been missing the larger part of his neck. The round deflected from its path to President Reagan's heart might have reached its target. One can readily imagine at least three deaths, including the President's, had Hinckley fired a more powerful weapon.

REACTIONS

The preceding does not exhaust my skepticism about gun control doxology; it merely illustrates some of the doubts I have come to entertain. As far as I can tell, the arguments in favor of "stricter gun control" fail nearly every empirical test, although in many cases, I hasten to add, the "failure" is simply that the appropriate research is not available.

There is an interesting asymmetry in the gun control debate. For rather obvious reasons, the procontrol people want to change things, and the anticontrol people are happy enough with the status quo. This implies that the burden of proof typically rests on the procontrol side; they have to show that the suggested changes, whatever they are, would improve conditions. Thus, the procontrol argument is far more commonly advanced via recitation of research findings, statistics, and the like; in many cases, the anticontrol argument involves nothing more complicated than a reference to the Second Amendment.

My gun research has been more enthusiastically received in anticontrol circles than among procontrol advocates. One prominent procontrol luminary described some of the research in *Under the Gun* as "constructed on an incomplete and misconceived reading of the relevant research, an unwillingness to cumulate circumstantial evidence, and standards of proof that inherently rule out nonexperimental conclusions." The NRA reaction was more positive although not uncritical; the entry on *Under the Gun* in the *American Rifleman* read: "Although the authors' anti-gun bias leads them to exaggerate the amount of gun abuse and to praise too readily some poor research, this book is fairly objective and probably the best summary of scholarly research on the issue." Much to my relief, however, the reactions of putatively neutral outsiders were neither harsh nor guarded. Thus the review in *Contemporary Sociology* described it as "the most comprehensive review of gun control research yet published," and noted later that "it is the highest compliment to say that this book should have something to offend, or at least annoy, everyone. Both 'gun nuts' and 'gun control nuts' will be discomfited."

Armed and Considered Dangerous came out several years later, in 1986, so all the returns are not yet in. I have taken some fairly hard knocks from procontrol people for believing too literally what the felons in the survey told me—a criticism I accept. And in general, the reaction in pro-gun circles was along the lines of "we told you so," with a subtext that, once again, the sociologists had spent hundreds of thousands of dollars belaboring some very obvious points. But here, too, the reaction in the professional social science community was largely favorable. The review in *Contemporary Sociology* called it "a must for those interested in firearms, crime, or policy research" and concluded that "the gun control debate will never be the same again."

Grateful though I am for this last comment, it is assuredly wrong. In the "Great American Gun War," as B. Bruce-Briggs has described it in *The Public Interest* (Fall 1976),* as in most other areas of public policy, relatively little turns on factual matters that could be resolved through more and better research; most of what is at issue turns on values, ideologies, and world views that are remarkably impervious to refutation by social science research. No one who believes deeply that gun control would make this a better world —or that it wouldn't—will be persuaded otherwise by any of the research I or anyone else has done.

---

*See selection 4 in Part One of this volume.—Ed.

Applied social research can often describe a problem well, but it can seldom suggest a viable solution. Most of the implications I have seen fit to draw from my gun research are negative in character: this won't work for this reason, that won't work for that reason, and so on. What to do about guns, crime, and violence in America is a question that has occupied many intelligent and capable people for decades, and no one has yet come up with a compelling, workable, legal answer. It is unlikely that "research" will provide that answer. As for social scientists with an interest in the topic, I think we ought simply to resign ourselves to doing what we do best—capable, informative research—and leave the search for "solutions" to the political process itself. Few of us will be entirely satisfied with the outcome; but a political process that proceeds in ignorance of or contempt for the best information we can provide is undesirable. On the other hand, to make too much of the "policy implications" of our research is to suggest that we command an expertise that is not usually at our disposal.

6

The Great American Gun War: Some Policy Implications of the Felon Study

James D. Wright and Peter H. Rossi

INTRODUCTION

In an oft-quoted article published in 1976, Bruce-Biggs (1976) characterized the perennial debate in American political life over what to do about firearms as "The Great American Gun War," suggesting, correctly in this case, a rather more rancorous and hotly contested arena of public policy than one normally might expect to encounter. There may be some issues in American politics where feelings run more strongly (abortion being one, nuclear power perhaps another), but not many; few issues evoke such passion or have had a longer run on the political playbill than what to do about crime and the guns with which crimes are committed.

A session of the Congress seldom passes without at least a few new "gun control" measures being introduced, be they amendments to existing regulations

Reprinted with permission from James D. Wright and Peter H. Rossi, *Armed and Considered Dangerous: A Survey of Felons and Their Firearms* (New York: Aldine de Gruyter). Copyright © 1986 by James D. Wright and Peter H. Rossi.

or proposals for entirely new policies. Almost invariably, these initiatives are warmly received in some quarters and bitterly denounced in others. What seems to one group a reasonable method of reducing criminals' access to guns seems to another an unconscionable infringement upon the legitimate rights of the American gun-owning public.

It is worth stressing at the outset of a discussion of the policy implications of our results that the key issues in "The Great American Gun War" rarely turn on matters of empirical fact. As Bruce-Biggs correctly observed, the policy debate concerns styles of life and corresponding value systems as much as it concerns the equipment of crime and how to control it. In some segments of American society, guns of all sorts are loathsome objects utterly devoid of redeeming social value; in other segments, guns and the activities that guns make possible are an integral and highly valued aspect of day-to-day existence. Neither segment will be dissuaded from its views by the results of empirical research, no matter how sound or well-conducted.

Although there is no love lost among the contestants in this particular public policy arena, there is at least some agreement among all contending groups that one policy goal should be to reduce significantly the use of firearms in crimes of all sorts. No one denies that the American crime rate is unacceptably high or that the use of firearms to commit crimes is a pressing national problem. The issues at the heart of contention are whether and how this goal can best be reached.

Broadly speaking, the methods available to achieve the agreed-upon goal fall into two categories: (1) reducing the ability of criminals to obtain firearms in the first place; and/or (2) reducing the criminals' use of guns in committing crime once guns have been obtained. Clearly, the issues are closely related: if we could accomplish (1), (2) would then be moot. Hence, the second issue is only an issue because of the presumption that complete success at preventing criminals from obtaining firearms will probably not be possible.

Both available methods are rife with considerable complexity, even ambiguity. It is easy to agree, for example, that one goal of policy should be to "keep guns out of the hands of criminals." Indeed, other than the criminals themselves, it is hard to imagine anyone who would not agree. But this presumes that criminals can somehow be easily identified before the fact, a task that has occupied criminologists for a century with little notable success. It is, of course, very easy to identify criminals after they have committed crimes and have been convicted and sentenced for them; thus, after the fact, it is always easy to say that "that man should not have been allowed to own a gun." Identifying the people who "should not be allowed to own a gun" before they have acquired one and inflicted harm on others is an immeasurably more difficult and perhaps intractable problem.

It is of some interest that partisans on both sides of the gun debate, or some of them at least, both recognize and accept the fact just noted (namely, that criminals are hard to identify in advance of their actually committing crimes). One side infers from this that the appropriate strategy, therefore, is to keep guns (or at least handguns or certain kinds of handguns) out of everybody's hands, which would assure (assuming a 100 percent success rate) that they were being kept from criminal hands in the process. The other side infers that the appropriate strategy, therefore, is to forego any effort to interdict before the fact and simply punish abuses as they occur. In the interpretation, in other words, the same fact subtends two entirely different implications. It should be noted that this area of social policy is no different in this respect from others: The same empirical facts can be accommodated within a variety of widely differing policies.

Other complications are introduced by the unintended side consequences of policies that are or may be enacted. The best of all imaginable firearms policies enacted to reduce gun crime would clearly be ones that somehow impacted only on criminals and on no others. Furthermore, such policies would be ones that had only the intended effect on the target population and no other effects. The ideal policy, in short, complicates the life of the gun-wielding felon but not the lives of legitimate firearms users, at least not unduly.

Unfortunately, it is hard to target any social policy with a high degree of accuracy; serious definitional questions arise, particularly at the margins. To illustrate, the United States Olympic pistol shooting team represents an obviously legitimate body of handgun owners whose right to own and use handguns can be taken as given; likewise, an urban street thug with a lengthy criminal record and overt sociopathic tendencies is obviously a person who has long since foregone any claim to legitimate handgun ownership. At the extremes, the categories of legitimate and illegitimate are easy to recognize. But what of the adolescents who may someday grow up to become either Olympic shooters if all goes well or street thugs if all does not? Or of young men in urban slums who today may feel they need a gun to defend against the thugs but who tomorrow might be thugs themselves? What, for that matter, of the outwardly placid and upstanding citizen who buys a shotgun to hunt quail but who, in an alcohol-induced fit of psychotic anger, barricades himself in his house and kills everything in sight?

Unacceptably adverse consequences to noncriminal gun owners represent the single greatest barrier to the design of effective policy in the "gun crime" area. A stiff tax on handguns imposed at the point of production would no doubt raise the price of handguns enough to drive some criminals out of the handgun market, but it would also drive millions of noncriminals out of the market as well. The cheap, low-quality handgun that is not available for use in crime is also not available to impoverished families in high-crime neighborhoods who feel (correctly or otherwise) that they need a gun to defend against the predation rampant on their streets. A jurisdiction that requires a week-long waiting period to obtain a handgun while the police run the appropriate criminal records check will come across an occasional criminal attempting to obtain a handgun through customary channels and enormous numbers of other people for whom both the waiting period and the records check were altogether immaterial.

Aside from the spill-over of effects onto the noncriminal population, there is also the problem of unintended effects on the target (criminal) population. A policy designed to prevent the transfer of firearms to felons through customary retail channels (such as the Gun Control Act of 1968) might only result in an increase in the rate of gun thefts by felons from nonfelon owners or an increased level of activity in the informal nonretail market. A policy intended to prevent criminals from carrying small, cheap handguns might cause them to carry big, expensive, and more lethal handguns instead.

The intended effect of virtually every piece of "gun-crime" legislation enacted in the twentieth century has been along one or the other of the lines suggested earlier: to prevent criminals from obtaining guns or to prevent them from using guns once obtained. And yet, the number of armed criminals and the amount of armed crime has tended to increase, not abate. What has happened is not what was intended. We do not mean to suggest that gun control legislation has caused crime, in some way, to increase, only that the hoped-for reduction in armed crime has not occurred.

One final and long-standing complication, of course, has been the well-known Second Amendment to the Constitution of the United States and the apparent ambiguity about what rights it grants to whom. In the current epoch of nuclear weaponry, for example, what meaning should be construed for the phrase, "an armed militia"? Does the "right to keep and bear arms" include the right to target practice? To own a gun for self-defense? To keep loaded firearms in the home with children present? Surely, in a democratic society, every right comes with certain corollary obligations. But what, then, are the obligations that come with the right "to keep and bear arms"?*

The last few pages are not intended to create despair, and much less to enumerate exhaustively all of the complications that are inherent in this particular public-policy area. Our point, rather, is to illustrate that the issues involved go well beyond anything that can be learned from data supplied by a sample of state prisoners. Much, in fact, goes well beyond what could be learned from any study; and many relevant empirical questions cannot be answered with data on prisoners alone.

This study, of course, was not designed to answer all the relevant empirical questions, only to provide baseline information about the acquisition, ownership, and use of guns among a criminal population, information that could be useful in discussing the appropriate policy issues. Although seldom in an

---

*For a more detailed discussion of issues related to the Second Amendment, see Part Four of this volume.—Ed.

explicit fashion, all policies and policy recommendations make assumptions about the "facts" concerning the area of human behavior in question. Clearly, the chances of successful policy are higher the more accurate these assumptions turn out to be. A policy based on the assumption that criminals prefer small, cheap handguns can hardly be successful if in fact they do not. Our point in undertaking this study, in short, was to test some common assumptions and provide useful descriptive data, assuredly not to evaluate the wisdom of one or another "gun control" measure.

Research is often very good in describing the nature of a problem and rather poor in suggesting adequate solutions. This study is no exception: We have tried to obtain reasonably accurate readings on certain facets of the criminal acquisition and use of guns, but by themselves, the findings of the research do not immediately suggest any effective solutions. "Policy implications" are just that: implications that derive from one particular interpretation of a set of research findings, certainly not policy conclusions or recommendations whose wisdom is self-evident now that the findings are in hand. Policymaking is the rightful domain of policymakers: Our intention is that policymaking be informed, but not overly constrained, by the results and interpretations we have reported.

In order to prevent criminals from obtaining guns, we need to know where and how their guns are obtained; to prevent them from carrying guns and using them in crime, we need to know why they carry and how they use them, or in short, the roles that firearms play in the lifestyles of the felon population. Most of the policy implications of this study derive from the information we have assembled on these topics.

THE NATURE OF THE ILLICIT FIREARMS MARKET

Firearms manufacturers are, of course, the ultimate source of virtually all the guns that are ever used for any purpose, since the home maufacture of firearms is apparently rare. This obvious fact means that guns come into the hands of criminals by means of a system of distribution that connects manufacturers and criminals through a chain of transfers. The early links in this chain ordinarily involve firearms wholesalers and retailers, a fact that tempts policymakers to consider using these intermediaries as points to detect potential firearms abusers and thereby to prevent firearms from falling into improper hands. The ultimate efficacy of such an approach depends to a considerable extent on the length of the chain of transfers and the location of retail outlets within the chain.

The findings from our study cast some light on the nature of the transfer chain: We cannot reconstruct the complete chain from manufacturer to criminal consumer, but we have considerable detail on the last link in the chain, the transfer of a firearm into criminal hands. From the viewpoint of policy, two features of these data stand out, and these are discussed in the next sections.

Deterring the Acquisition of Firearms

Legitimate firearms retailers play a minor and unimportant role as direct sources of the criminal handgun supply. Not more than about one in six of the most recent handguns acquired by our sample was obtained through a customary retail transaction involving a licensed firearms dealer; the market into which criminals are tied, rather, is dominated by informal, off the record, transactions, mostly involving friends and associates, family members, and various black-market sources. The means of acquisition from these informal sources include cash purchase, swaps and trades, borrowing and renting, and often theft. (Indeed, our impression is that the verbs, "borrow," "take," "steal," and "rent" were blurred and indistinct in the vocabularies of our respondents.) Whatever the verbal ambiguities, however, it is clear that our sample was enmeshed in a largely informal market in firearms that served as the immediate source of their supply.

The implication of this result is probably not that we should simply give up on our efforts to interdict criminal acquisition of handguns at the point of retail sale. To so argue would be equivalent to arguing that we should stop the airport metal searches because they only rarely detect a weapons-carrying passenger. Restrictions at the point of retail sale, that is, may serve a useful preventive function; at minimum, the acquisition of a firearm by a felon should be somewhat more complicated than just walking into a gun shop and buying one. The implication, rather, concerns the ultimate effect of such efforts, which is not to prevent the acquisition of guns by criminals but rather to force them out of the retail market and into other, less formal channels of distribution.

One tempting way to intervene between the manufacturer and the criminal end-user is to raise the price of weapons entering the market, perhaps by taxing handguns heavily. Eventually, a sharp rise in handgun prices would be reflected on the gray and black markets as well as in the retail stores. Our data do not allow any calculations of how high prices on the legitimate market would have to go to affect those on the gray and black markets, but we suspect that a dollar increase on the former most likely means considerably less on the latter. Furthermore, it is not at all clear how price-elastic the criminal demand for handguns is; price increases may affect criminal gun acquisition only once they reach very high levels.

Moreover, although exceptionally high prices might drive some criminals out of the handgun market altogether, it would also increase the attractiveness of gun theft and, therefore, might draw some criminals *into* the market, as procurers of stolen handguns. Furthermore, there would also be a large price burden placed on literally millions of legitimate handgun users, some of whom might then be tempted to become buyers on the gray and black markets.

The further implication of our results, of course, is that if we do intend seriously to complicate the acquisition of guns by felons, then methods must be found for intervening in the informal firearms market. As we have already noted, the transfer of a firearm to a felon, whether formal or informal, is already illegal, so legislation to make it illegal is clearly not the answer. By their very nature, such transactions are difficult or impossible to detect, so "stricter enforcement" of existing laws is also probably chimerical. One might require, as a matter of federal policy, that every firearms transaction be reported to the cognizant authorities and the appropriate criminal records check undertaken; but one quickly senses that this measure would have virtually no effect on the criminal users we are trying to interdict and a considerable effect on legitimate users among whom a large informal market also exists.

There is, in short, some reason to doubt whether any politically acceptable, implementable, effective, and constitutional method of intervening in the informal market can be found; the implication of our results is not a method by which this could be done but rather the information that it must be done if we are to prevent or even seriously hamper the acquisition of firearms by criminals.

The Role of Gun Theft

Our study also confirms beyond serious doubt the important role that gun theft plays in connecting the criminal market to its firearms supply. One-half the men in this sample had stolen at least one gun at some time in their lives; many had stolen more than one; a few had stolen guns in extremely large numbers. At least 40 percent, and perhaps as much as 70 percent, of the most recent handguns owned by this sample were stolen weapons.

We indicated earlier that the ideal "gun-crime" policy is one that impacts directly on the illicit user but leaves the legitimate user pretty much alone. This presupposes a sharp distinction between the licit and illicit markets, a distinction that is made tenuous by the apparently heavy volume of gun theft. To leave the legitimate user "pretty much alone" at least implies a guarantee of the right to acquire firearms under some set of prescribed conditions; and yet, all else equal, any gun that can be legitimately possessed by a legal and law-abiding owner can be stolen from its owner and subsequently fall into criminal hands.

Again, our data suggest little by way of a method through which the gun theft problem could be attacked. In terms of the total number of thefts, thefts from homes and apartments are clearly the most numerous, which suggests, as one approach, that legitimate gun owners be made more aware of the problem and the strategies available to them to prevent theft of their weapons. Police chiefs who are empowered to issue permits to own or purchase firearms might be one point at which this information could be imparted; information booklets produced by the manufacturers for inclusion with shipped weapons would be another.

Legitimate gun owners might also be induced to exercise greater caution in storing their weapons in relatively theft-resistant ways—for example, by tax credits or insurance discounts similar to those given for energy conservation measures or the installation of home fire detectors.

Finally, some jurisdictions have begun to consider the liability of a legitimate owner whose gun is stolen and subsequently used to commit a crime. Our data do not speak to the advisability or likely consequences of such measures, but certainly, as we have already said, the right to own guns must be accompanied by certain corollary responsibilities, and perhaps these responsibilities include all *reasonable* precaution in storing one's weapons in relatively theft-proof ways. (To be sure, one would still want to insist that the liability of the thief greatly exceeded the liability of his victim.)

Although house and apartment break-ins appear to account for the largest number of thefts, they may not account for the largest number of stolen weapons that enter the illicit market. A distressingly large number of our respondents also reported having stolen guns from potential high-volume sources: manufacturers, shippers, wholesalers, retailers, and even military establishments. Our impression is that security measures in these quarters are already pretty tight, but perhaps they could be increased even further.

The "scale" problem is pertinent in this case: One successful hijacking of a truck during shipment could well net as many total firearms as would be netted in a few thousand household thefts; consequently, the prevention of one hijacking is as useful to society as a whole as the prevention of a few thousand household thefts. All else equal, then, resources might be directed disproportionately to preventing thefts from high-volume sources. Unfortunately, our data do not show that high-volume sources account for more of the total volume than housebreaks, only that they may; this, therefore, is an area that requires further research before the policy implication is obvious.

At minimum, of course, society as a whole could increase the penalty for the crime of gun theft, perhaps by making gun theft a felony whatever the other circumstances of the crime. In most jurisdictions at present, the theft of a gun from a household or store is considered to be a no more serious crime than the theft of any other object of equivalent value.

Whatever the methods one might imagine, however, the nature of the task that society confronts is made reasonably clear by our results: If we are to make headway in preventing the acquisition of guns by criminals, we must find some way to intervene in the informal gun market, a market that, under present conditions, is supplied in substantial part by firearms obtained through theft.

CRIME GUNS: QUALITY AND PRICE

Many "gun-crime" proposals that have surfaced in recent years have been targeted to particular classes of firearms: to handguns in general or, somewhat more commonly, to certain restricted classes of handguns, particularly those of the small, cheap, low-quality variety: the "snubbies" or the so-called Saturday Night Specials (SNS). The rationale for such proposals is twofold: (1) legitimate owners have little or no need for such firearms, and (2) illegitimate owners do.

To assess the nature of the criminal demand for these kinds of handguns, we asked for considerable information both on the characteristics our sample preferred in a handgun and on the characteristics of the most recent handgun they had actually possessed. Neither of these sources of information represents perfect data on the nature of the criminal handgun demand: The "preferred-characteristics" questions may tell us more about our sample's fantasies concerning the "perfect" handgun than about the true nature of their demand; the characteristics of the most recent handgun may or may not generalize to the typical handgun that felons own, carry, and use to commit crimes. Still, neither source of data suggests much interest among felons in small, cheap handguns; such interest as we observed was concentrated primarily among felons who had never used firearms to commit crimes. The criminals in our sample both preferred to own, and actually owned, relatively large, well-made weapons.

The average price paid by our felons for their most recent handguns was not especially high, falling in the $100-$150 range; still, the average quality was well beyond the level of the "cheapies." The most common among the recent handguns was a Smith and Wesson .38 equipped with a 4-inch barrel; no more than about 15 percent of the most recent handguns would qualify as SNSs. A comparison between the average dollar cost and the average apparent quality suggests that prices in the informal, gray, and black markets are heavily discounted, in all likelihood because of the predominance of stolen weapons in these markets.

Whatever the price paid or the mode of acquisition, however, one result is clear: The more a felon used his guns in crime, the higher the quality of th equipment he possessed. Among the truly predatory criminals in the sample, the small, cheap handgun was not the weapon of choice.

Given the rate of gun theft reported by the sample, it is also of no surprise that the price was not a very important consideration. Our interpretation of a question on how much they would be willing to pay for a suitable handgun is that felons are willing to pay the going rate. For what it is worth, far more interest was shown in matters such as accuracy, firepower, untraceability, and quality of construction than in price.

The implication of these findings is that the strategy of purging the market of small, cheap weapons may simply be irrelevant, most of all to predatory felons who are more likely to use their guns to commit crimes. In addition, the apparent price insensitivity argues against a policy that stresses raising the price of guns to keep them from criminal hands. Either or both of these strategies may well prove advisable for other reasons; it is possible, for example, that small, cheap handguns are much more important to first offenders, juveniles, or other classes of criminals who are on average younger, less hardened, and less violent than the men in our sample. So far as the sorts of men who end up doing time in state prisons are concerned, however, it is fairly clear that they do not have much interest in small, cheap firearms in the first place.

WHY CRIMINALS CARRY AND USE GUNS

> As long as you got a lot of fire power, you're all right. There was a rule with me that I always have a gun at all times, 'cause sometimes you'd be out in the street and the opportunity just presents itself where you see a lot of money. Then you want to be armed. (. . .) So I had the gun always on me to take advantage of opportunities—and to protect myself. A gun is like a part of me. I could wake up in the morning, and before I get out of the bed to go into the bathroom, I strap my shoulder holster over my shoulder. I never would go out of the house without it.

The preceding is not a quotation from one of our respondents, although it certainly might have been. It is, rather, a passage from John Allen's *Assault with a Deadly Weapon: The Autobiography of a Street Criminal* (Allen, 1977, pp. 179–80). John Allen is typical of the predatory felons in our sample in many ways: He is urban, black, and uneducated, commenced his life of crime in his early teens, acquired his first firearm at age thirteen by stealing it from his grandfather, was a heroin addict on several occasions and a heavy abuser of drugs, had a lengthy criminal record as both a juvenile and an adult, spent much of his life in prison, was prone to fits of violent rage, and seldom passed by an opportunity to commit a crime, be it armed robbery, car theft, drug dealing, pimping, housebreaking, or whatever. His motives for owning and carrying guns, as expressed in the above passage, are also typical of the motives expressed by our sample: When armed, one is prepared "for anything that might happen"—an opportunity to commit a crime or a need to defend oneself against the assaults or predations of others. His behavior in regard to the weapon is also perhaps typical: As his comment concerning the morning regimen indicates, carrying a gun was an habitual part of his daily routine.

The possession and carrying of handguns (and other weapons: John Allen also kept a sawed-off shotgun at hand for truly serious work) by felons is part and parcel of their day-to-day existence, no more unusual in their circles than the carrying of wallets or purses would be in others. The motivation to do so goes well beyond the instrumental use of guns in committing crimes, although as Allen's testimony and our data make clear, this is assuredly one important motive. Survival in an uncertain but hostile and violent world is, with equal assurance, another.

Most of the gun-owning felons in our sample grew up around guns, were introduced to guns at an early age, and had owned and used guns ever since. Most also hung around with other men who owned and carried guns. In such circles, a handgun is at least an acceptable article of attire, if not a *de rigeur* requirement. Not to suggest that these handguns are strictly ornamental: Our felons tended in the majority to keep their guns loaded at all times and to fire them at a fairly regular rate, often enough at other people: One-half the men claimed to have fired a gun at someone at some time; one-half also claimed to have been fired upon.

It is, therefore, no surprise that one of their major acknowledged motives for acquiring and carrying guns was for the purpose of self-protection. In an environment where crime and violence are pervasive, and where many of one's friends and associates routinely carry guns, there is plenty to "protect" oneself against. "Self-protection," in this context at least, must be interpreted with some caution, of course. Part of it no doubt implies protection against being preyed upon or continually hassled by others who are better armed; another part, perhaps the larger part, means protection against armed innocents, against the police, against the prospects of apprehension during a crime, etc. The "insurance" that many of these men seek in carrying a gun is only the insurance that they will always be the perpetrator and not the victim of the sorts of crimes they so regularly commit.

A third of our sample (of gun criminals), like John Allen, made it a practice to carry a gun more or less all the time; one-half carried whenever the circumstances seemed to suggest it: when doing a drug deal, when going out at night, when they were with other men who were carrying guns, or more generally, whenever their ability to defend themselves might be at issue. Only one in five of the gun criminals in our sample carried just when they intended to commit a crime.

Since it follows directly from this finding that most of the guns used to commit crime are not carried *specifically* for the purpose, the implication is that the decision to carry is the critical decision point, not the decision to use the gun in a crime. This is to suggest only that the decision to carry guns regularly by men prone to criminal acts is causally prior to the actual uses of these weapons on victims and, therefore, may represent the theoretically most effective point of intervention.

How one might intervene in the decision to carry, however, is a rather depressing question to contemplate. Unlicensed carrying of concealed weapons is already illegal everywhere. Stricter enforcement of the relevant laws prohibiting concealed carrying of weapons—for example, by periodic shakedowns of people on the streets or in the bars—is a theoretical possibility but raises obvious constitutional issues; such dragnets would also net large numbers of otherwise legitimate people who are carrying a weapon out of fear. The largest handguns, and even some sawed-off shoulder weapons, can be carried more or less unobtrusively; the smaller the weapon, the more true this becomes. A patrol officer might have some suspicions about a particular person, but anything short of open display might fail the criterion of probable cause.

If one accepts the idea that self-protection in a hostile and dangerous world is a principal motive for the ownership and carrying of guns among felons, then it follows that relevant policies to discourage the practice are those that would reduce the hostility and danger endemic to the social worlds inhabited by these men, that is, poor, urban neighborhoods in the main. As is well known, these neighborhoods produce not only most of the perpetrators but also most of the victims of crime; crime, violence, and routine handgun carrying are distinguishing features of urban slum existence. Unfortunately, there are few issues in law enforcement that seem more intractable than that of substantially reducing violent crime in high crime areas: it is not at all clear just how such a goal might be attained, nor is it clear that communities would support the effort by paying the added taxes that would be required.

Outright neglect is, of course, one possibility, one that, in fact, has been followed in at least some of our major cities from time to time. Here, the strategy is for the police to withdraw in force, hoping to contain the crime problem within certain boundaries. (Some have also charged, perhaps with reason, that a second hope is that the criminals within the boundaries will kill or maim each other in sufficient numbers that the rest of us could walk our own streets in peace.) "Containment" has not proven to be a very effective strategy, however; crime has a habit of spilling over into the more affluent (and politically powerful) communities. A humane society should also not be indifferent to the victimization by crime of those who can least afford it and who are also victimized by many of society's other institutions and practices as well.

We conclude that a viable policy designed to reduce the criminal use of guns will have to find means of reducing the violence that is characteristic of many urban neighborhoods. We recognize the circularity of this reasoning: What we are suggesting is that the way to get criminals to stop carrying guns is to get criminals to stop carrying guns! Our point, however, is not entirely tautological: What we are suggesting is that the reduction of crime in high-crime neighborhoods has to be as much in the center of law enforcement concern as protecting middle-class citizens from the incursions of predatory criminals.

One might also simply give up dealing with the causes of gun carrying among felons and deal directly with the behavior itself, for example, through policies designed to encourage criminals to leave their weapons at home when they "go to work." Here, the effort would be concentrated on making the carrying and use of guns as difficult and as costly to the felon as possible.

One strategy presently in use in many jurisdictions, one that also enjoys overwhelming popular support (Wright, Rossi, and Daly, 1983: ch. 12) is to provide enhanced (mandatory "add-on") penalties for the use of a gun (or other weapon) in committing crime (or, as in the Massachusetts case, a mandatory penalty for unlicensed carrying, whatever the actual usage or intent).

How successful this tactic has been in reducing the use of guns in crime has yet to be assessed definitively. Often, or so it appears, judges working with mandatory add-ons reduce the sentence for the main charge by an equivalent number of years, so that the total penalty remains much the same. Moreover, the add-on is often a small fraction of the main charge: A typical sentence for an armed robbery (assuming a lengthy prior record) might be 10–30 years; a 1- or 2-year mandatory sentence enhancement might not alter the sentence enough to make any difference in the subjective calculations of the criminal. Ultimately, increased sentencing runs up against prison overcrowding as the limiting condition: It does no good to add additional years to a felon's sentence when the state corrections system has no prison space for him in any case. The overcrowding situation is such that many prisons now find every reason for early release (e.g., time off for good behavior, lenient parole) simply to make sufficient room for the "new arrivals" from the courts.

Another problem in using mandatory add-ons for felonious gun use as a deterrent to the practice of carrying weapons is that most criminals do not expect to be caught in any case; what might happen to them once they are caught, therefore, cannot be much of a concern. (It should be added, nonetheless, that many of the non-gun criminals in our sample mentioned the prospect of a stiffer sentence when caught with a weapon as a very important reason not to carry one.)

A final problem in deterring the routine carrying of guns (whether through sentencing or through other measures), at least among the more predatory men in our sample, is that many of the crimes these men commit are directed toward victims who may be armed themselves. John Allen notes: "During the times when I was down, though, I would mainly rob the other dealers to get the drugs or the scratch I needed to buy my drugs" (1977, p. 176). Why an addict would rob his own dealer (or fellow dealers) is not hard to fathom: They have the drugs, and they carry a lot of money. But to do so unarmed would be the height of folly, since the dealer being robbed doubtlessly will be armed himself. [In discussing one robbery of a fellow dealer, Allen notes, "This was a way we often got weapons—we'd take people's guns when we robbed them" (p. 177).]

More generally, the presence of firearms among a felon's associates and potential victims is probably a much greater threat to his well-being than the prospect of an extra one or two years in prison. It would be sensible, therefore, to run the risk of an enhanced prison term by carrying a firearm oneself. In this sense, the predatory gun-wielding felon must be considered to be largely indifferent to deterrence through after-the-fact punishments; relative to what might happen if he needed a gun but did not have one, most after-the-fact punishments would pale to relative insignificance.

SUBSTITUTION AND OTHER NEUTRALIZING SIDE EFFECTS

. . . Some of the more commonly advocated "gun-crime" policies could well prove to have negative and unwantd side consequences. Bans on certain kinds of weapons, assuming a reasonable success rate, will cause some criminals not to commit the crimes they would have committed otherwise and will cause other criminals to commit the same crimes but armed with different weapons. The relative sizes of these two groups is a pertinent issue; so, too, is the question of what these "different weapons" would be.

All the data we have presented on this issue are conjectural, and so their implications are even "iffier" than usual. Still, the large majority of the more predatory felons in our sample told us they would respond to various partial or total handgun bans with either lateral or upward substitution—the weapons they said they would carry under these hypothetical conditions were either just as lethal as, or more lethal than, the weapons they would have otherwise carried in any case. One may properly quarrel with some of the details, doubt the practicalities, or debate the probity and realism of these responses, but the major message comes through clearly: The felonious activities of these men will not suffer for lack of the appropriate armament; their intent, so far as we can tell, would be to find substitutes that may be somewhat inconvenient but nevertheless highly effective.

Given our results, we think it likely that the major effects of partial or total handgun bans would fall more on the shoulders of the ordinary gun-owning public than on the felonious gun abuser of the sort studied here. The people most likely to be deterred from acquiring a handgun by exceptionally high prices or by the nonavailability of certain kinds of handguns are not felons intent on arming themselves for criminal purposes (who can, if all else fails, steal the handgun they want), but rather poor people who have decided they need a gun to protect themselves against the felons but who find that the cheapest gun in the market costs more than they can afford to pay. . . . It is therefore also possible that one side consequence of such measures would be some loss in the crime-thwarting effects of civilian firearms ownership.

Perhaps the most telling implication of our data on weapons substitution is not in the substance of the results but in the more general lesson that any social policy can have consequences that no one foresaw, intended, or wanted—consequences that, under the right conditions, worsen rather than improve the problem being addressed. Anticipating these untoward side consequences, and avoiding them, requires above all else a detailed empirical understanding of the nature of the problem; "solutions" that are implemented before the problem is reasonably well understood rarely solve anything.

Clearly, this study has not "solved" the problem of gun crime in American society; indeed, it has not even exemplified what the solution would look like. But it has provided some information about the nature of the problem itself, information that we hope others will use to formulate workable solutions to the problem of gun crime, thereby improving the collective existence of us all.

7

The Relationship Between Gun Ownership Levels and Rates of Violence in the United States

Gary Kleck

How are levels of gun ownership and rates of violence related? If we are to believe the conclusions of the Task Force on Firearms of the 1968 Eisenhower Commission, the answer is a simple one: "More Firearms—More Firearms Violence."[1] However, it is worth noting that even in their enthusiastically pro-gun control report nowhere is it explicitly stated that increases in gun ownership *caused*, even partially, the increases of violent crime of the 1960s, although it is certainly implied throughout. The slogan just quoted is carefully phrased in such a way as to clearly suggest such an interpretation to the casual reader, without actually committing its authors to a claim they could not (or at least did not) support. Virtually all of the evidence marshalled to establish the association between gun ownership and violence could just as easily be interpreted as showing that more gun violence leads to more

From *Firearms and Violence: Issues of Public Policy*, edited by Don B. Kates, Jr. (San Francisco, Calif.: Pacific Research Institute for Public Policy). Copyright © 1989 by the Pacific Research Institute for Public Policy. Reprinted by permission of the publisher.

people acquiring guns for defensive purposes rather than the reverse (see especially their chapter 7). Yet the authors never acknowledged this alternative interpretation, despite devoting an entire chapter to the subject of firearms and self-defense, where they noted that home defense is a major reason why many people acquire and own guns!

There is no logically necessary relationship between levels of gun ownership and interpersonal violence, or even between levels of gun ownership and gun violence. Clearly, most people who own guns do not use them for inflicting harm on others, and many people commit acts of violence without using guns. It is possible for gun violence to decrease while at the same time gun ownership is increasing, as indeed happened in the United States during the 1950s.[2] Gun ownership can increase among people who are very unlikely to be violent, with or without weapons, while remaining constant among those social groups where interpersonal violence is relatively common, producing no change in the homicide rate. Guns, like other objects, do not have any meaning in themselves but only the meaning that is attached to them by people, a meaning that varies between social groups and between social situations. Some people, in some situations, may identify a gun as an instrument of interpersonal violence, a way of establishing dominance, or a method of settling a dispute; other people, in other situations, may not attach any such meaning. The mere possession of a gun alone does not necessarily make deadly violence more likely, and thus the connection between levels of gun ownership and violence is one that must be evaluated empirically.

This discussion is in part an update and elaboration of an earlier investigation of the relationship between trends in gun ownership and homicide rates in the United States.[3] Two questions are addressed:

1. To what extent, if any, do levels of gun ownership in the general population affect U.S. homicide rates?

2. To what extent, if any, do crime rates affect levels of gun ownership?

The earlier paper covered the 1947–1973 period, while this discussion covers five additional years, spanning the period from 1947 to 1978. This change has not been a trivial one, as it has resulted in the need to modify some of the earlier paper's findings regarding the effect of gun ownership on homicide rates. . . .

THE CHANGING CHARACTER OF U.S. GUN OWNERSHIP

Why is it that in a data set dominated by years prior to 1964, gun ownership in the general population appeared to have a significant positive effect on the homicide rate, while in the 1947–1978 set, dominated by cases from the 1960s and 1970s, there was no such effect apparent? I propose that the apparent discrepancy is due to a change in the pattern of ownership of firearms that occurred in the 1960s.

The vast majority of gun owners never commit a serious crime of violence with their guns. Although at least half of America's 80 million households own a gun, and there may be more than 160 million guns in circulation by now, it is doubtful if even 200,000 different guns or gun owners are involved in serious violent gun crimes in any given year.[4] Since our measure of gun ownership describes the general population rather than any crime-prone segment of it, it is largely a measure of gun ownership among the law-abiding and nonviolent. Levels of *legal* gun ownership have been found to be unrelated to rates of violent crime in a cross-sectional analysis.[5] Therefore the only reason why such a measure would show an effect of gun ownership on homicide would be if it served as an indicator of ownership within the violence-prone segment of the population. The difference in results found between data sets could be due to the possibility that trends in general gun ownership and ownership among the violence prone roughly paralleled each other up until the 1960s, but that they no longer did so in more recent years. In particular, it seems likely that ownership among low income and nonwhite people began to increase even faster than in the rest of the population around the mid-1960s. Thus, as time went on, the general level of gun ownership became an increasingly poor indicator of gun ownership among the violence prone and consequently showed less of a relationship with the homicide rate for time periods dominated by later years.

The best evidence of changing firearms ownership patterns would be national survey evidence which compared reported gun ownership among persons with arrest or conviction records for crimes of violence with ownership among those without such records. Unfortunately, I know of no published national survey that has made such a comparison, and there certainly are not enough of such surveys to show whether trends among the two groups differ. A second-best strategy would involve examination of reported gun ownership among the poor and among blacks. Between 1952 and 1978, from 49 to 66 percent of homicide arrestees were black, although blacks constituted only 11 to 12 percent of the U.S. population.[6] For seventeen cities studied in 1967, 87 percent of homicide arrestees were blue-collar workers, service, farm or domestic workers, housewives (presumably most of these were wives of men with occupations similar to the male arrestees), or were unemployed.[7] Serious violence, including gun violence, is heavily concentrated among low-income and nonwhite people, and thus gun ownership trends among these groups are especially crucial.

Before 1966 there were almost no national surveys that included a gun ownership question which would allow us to establish some benchmark levels of ownership, and after 1966, although I know of at least twenty such surveys, there have been almost no analyses that published breakdowns by income groups.[8] A few breakdowns by race have been published, but these show extremely erratic trends; this is not surprising, since typical national surveys, with a total sample size of 1,200, often contain only about 30 to 70 gun-owning black households. Reported handgun ownership in U.S. white households increased from 16 percent in 1972 to 25 percent in 1978, while it increased even more sharply in black households over the same period, from 11 percent in 1972 to 23 percent in 1978, supporting the hypothesis that gun ownership trends in groups with high rates of violence were diverging from those for the rest of the population.[9]

A more indirect, but perhaps more reliable kind of evidence of changing ownership patterns is found in data on the criminal use of firearms. Trends in the relative frequency with which homicides are committed with a fire-arm can serve as a rough indicator of trends in the relative availability of firearms among the violence prone, although it is also a product of weapon preference. The relative frequency of gun use in homicide remained almost constant until 1964, then increased sharply, from 57.5 percent in 1964 to a peak of 68.7 percent in 1974. Further, the percentage of gun use increased far more among blacks than among whites. Because over 90 percent of homicides are intraracial, the victim's race can be used to indicate the offender's race with little error.[10] Therefore vital statistics data on weapon use in homicide deaths can accurately indicate trends in the relative use of guns in homicides among whites and blacks. The percent of homicides committed with guns among blacks increased by 17 percentage points, from 56.8 to 73.8 percent between 1964 and 1972, while the increase was only 5.5 percentage points among whites over the same period.

Criminals' proportional use of guns increased in connection with aggravated assaults as well during this period, according to FBI data. While only 15 percent of aggravated assaults reported to the police in 1964 were committed with a gun, this figure reached a peak of 25.7 percent in 1973.[11] Parallel figures on the percentages of robberies that were armed robberies indicate an increase after 1967, peaking in 1972. Thus the use of guns by criminals in general was increasing from 1964 to the early and mid-1970s.

There is also some indirect evidence that the frequency of the carrying of firearms and other weapons increased in a manner that almost exactly paralleled the trends in relative gun use in crimes. Arrests on illegal weapons charges rarely occur other than as a result of an arrest or search regarding some other crime, that is, "incident" to some other matter.[12] Therefore, weapons arrests as a percentage of total arrests can serve as a rough indicator of the relative frequency with which police found persons searched to be illegally carrying weapons. Data for this indicator show a sharp increase beginning in 1964 and a peak in 1974. If these trends regarding weapons in general apply to guns as well, it suggests that illegal carrying of firearms, as well as ownership of guns, increased during this period among those people most inclined to commit acts of violence. Thus the hypothesis that gun ownership was increasing faster among the violence prone during the 1960s and 1970s than within the general population is consistently, albeit indirectly, supported.

CONCLUSIONS

The general level of gun ownership in our society has no direct effect on the homicide rate (although it has an indirect effect on homicide through its significant positive effect on robbery rates, which in turn positively affect homicide rates). How can such a statement be true when over 60 percent of the homicides committed in the United States in the last thirty years were committed with firearms? These seem to be mutually incompatible observations, especially to people who believe the latter fact to be prima facie evidence of the need for highly restrictive versions of gun control. A few simple statements can summarize and tie together the available evidence in a way which makes it clear that there are no contradictions between these observations.

The following statements seem to be supported by, or at least consistent with, the best available evidence regarding the effects of gun ownership on homicide rates:

1. Most gun ownership is for legal purposes. Most of the guns owned are long guns, which are primarily owned for recreational reasons unrelated to crime. Only a small percentage of guns or gun owners are involved in crimes; this is true even for handguns.

2. Gun ownership among the law-abiding has no effect on the homicide rate. Killers almost invariably have records of prior violence, and it is a myth that guns are commonly used in family arguments and assaults between previously law-abiding people.

3. From (1) and (2) we should expect that *general* levels of gun ownership should show no effect on the homicide rate, and this is indeed what our analysis has found.

4. Ownership of guns among the violence prone *is* related to homicide rates, because when an assault occurs (for reasons largely unrelated to gun ownership) it is somewhat more likely to produce a fatality if it involves a gun. However, we have no direct measure of such ownership levels; the only measure we *do* have is of general, largely noncriminal ownership.

These conclusions imply that gun ownership among the law-abiding poses no direct risk of crime or violence in the community. Thus the only justification for disarming the majority of the population is for the sake of denying violence prone persons easy access (presumably mostly through theft) to firearms owned by the law-abiding. In effect, the justification runs this way: we must deny guns to the 99 percent of the population who will never commit a serious act of violence in their lives in order to produce some marginal reduction in the ease of access to guns among the 1 percent who will commit such an act. Understandably, the argument is rarely phrased quite so baldly by advocates of gun or handgun prohibition, or of near approximations such as restrictive licensing.

On the other hand, these conclusions are perfectly compatible with more moderate gun control strategies, such as permissive licensing or laws restricting the open or concealed carrying of firearms. Such laws have the potential of being both just and at least modestly effective precisely because they are focused and concentrated in their intended impact in a way that corresponds with the way in which the problem of violence, both gun and nongun, is focused and concentrated. Violence is not uniformly or randomly distributed through the population, nor should its remedies be so distributed.

Regarding the effect of homicide and other crimes on levels of gun ownership, our conclusions are straightforward. General levels of ownership either of all gun types, handguns only, or long guns only are all positively affected by crime rates. Either the homicide rate or the robbery rate shows a significant positive effect on gun ownership levels (although both cannot be included in the same equation and still show positive effects, due to the problem of multicollinearity). These aggregate-level findings accord well with the best of the individual-level studies, in particular that of Lizotte and Bordua.[13]

It seems clear that, although most gun ownership is motivated by recreational and sport concerns, a significant part of it is oriented toward protection of the self, family, and home, and is a response to reported rates of crime, sometimes to prior victimization, and to the fear of victimization that these engender. The conclusions probably apply to both the law-abiding and the non-law-abiding, although no study of this subject has distinguished between the two groups. However, logically we would expect that if there is any difference between the two groups, it is the non-law-abiding whose gun ownership is most strongly motivated by victimization and fear of future victimization, simply because they are the most likely to live in dangerous neighborhoods, among other people as dangerous as themselves.

NOTES

1. George D. Newton and Franklin Zimring, *Firearms and Violence in American Life*. A Staff Report of the Task Force on Firearms, National Commission on the causes and Prevention of Violence (Washington, D.C.: GPO, 1969), p. xiii.

2. Gun ownership increased from an estimated 38,127 guns per 100,000 resident population in 1950 to an estimated 43,061 in 1960, while homicide deaths from firearms declined from 2.75 per 100,000 resident population in 1950 to 2.57 in 1960, and total homicides per 100,000 resident population declined from 5.23 to 4.09 during the same period.

3. Gary Kleck, "Capital Punishment, Gun Ownership, and Homicide," *American Journal of Sociology* 84 (January 1979): 882–910.

4. Hazel Erskine, "The Polls: Gun Control," *Public Opinion Quarterly* 36 (Summer 1972): 455–69.

5. David J. Bordua and Alan J. Lizotte, "A Subcultural Model of Legal Firearms Ownership in Illinois," *Law and Policy Quarterly* 2 (April 1979): 147–75.

6. U.S. FBI, *Uniform Crime Reports, 1953–1979*.

7. D. J. Mulvihill and M. M. Tumin, with L. A. Curtis, *Crimes of Violence*. Task Force on Individual Acts of Violence, National Commission on the Causes and Prevention of Violence (Washington, D.C.: GPO, 1969), p. 27.

8. The study by Wright and Marston, "The Ownership of the Means of Destruction," is a prominent exception.

9. Gallup poll no. 852 in George H. Gallup, *The Gallup Poll: Public Opinion, 1972–1977* (Wilmington, Del.: Scholarly Resources, 1978): Cambridge Reports, Inc., *An Analysis of Public Attitudes Toward Handgun Control* (Philadelphia, Pa.: Center for the Study and Prevention of Handgun Violence, 1978).

10. U.S. FBI, *Uniform Crime Reports, 1979*, p. 10.

11. U.S. FBI, *Uniform Crime Reports, 1965; 1974*.

12. David J. Bordua et al., *Patterns of Firearms Ownership, Use, and Regulation in Illinois* (Springfield, Ill.: Illinois Law Enforcement Commission, 1979), Sec. 3.

13. Alan J. Lizotte and David J. Bordua, "Firearms Ownership for Sport and Protection: Two Divergent Models," *American Sociological Review* 45 (April 1980): 229–43; Alan J. Lizotte et al., "Firearms Ownership for Sport and Protection: Two Not So Divergent Models," *American Sociological Review* 46 (August 1981): 499–503.

8

The Effect of Gun Availability on Violent Crime Patterns

Philip J. Cook

The debate over the appropriate degree of governmental regulation of firearms has been a prominent feature of the political landscape for the last two decades. The claims and counterclaims for various gun control strategies have been bruited in congressional and state legislative hearings, political campaigns, editorials, and bumper strips. The issues are by this time familiar to even disinterested bystanders: the proper interpretation of the Second Amendment; the value of guns as a means of defense against burglars, or foreign invaders, or local tyrants; the difficulty of depriving criminals of guns without depriving the rest of us of basic rights; and so forth. This "great American gun war"[1] clearly involves both value questions and questions of fact, and the latter have been the subject of numerous statistical skirmishes. Strangely, however, the relevant factual questions have not attracted much attention from scholars until very recently. The role of guns—and other types of weapons—in violent crime is a fit and important subject for scientific inquiry. No etiological theory of violent crime is complete without due consideration of the technology of

Reprinted from *The Annals* of the American Academy of Political and Social Science, No. 455 (May 1981): 63-79. Copyright © 1981. Reprinted by permission of the author and publisher.

violent crime. This would be true even in the absence of political interest in gun control.

Each of the major categories of violent crime—criminal homicide, aggravated assault, robbery, and rape—is committed with a variety of weapons. Guns are used in a minority of violent crimes, but are of special concern because they are used in almost two thirds of the most serious events, criminal homicides, and because, unlike most other commonly used weapons (hands, kitchen knives, and baseball bats), it is conceivable that we might reduce the availability of guns without imposing unacceptable costs on the public. The principal factual question in the gun control debate is whether reducing gun availability would reduce the amount and seriousness of violent crime. Can potential violent criminals be deterred from obtaining guns, carrying guns, and using guns in crime? If so, will this reduction in gun use make any difference, or will criminals simply substitute other weapons to equal effect? The answers to these questions are crucial to policy evaluation. Our ability to answer these questions—to make accurate predictions about the effects of legal interventions in this area—is one measure of our scientific understanding of the role of weapons in violent crime.

At the sacrifice of some dramatic tension, I provide a preview of my results here. The type of weapon used in a violent crime is in part determined by the nature of the victim; guns are most likely to be used against the least vulnerable victims in robbery and homicide. The type of weapon used in a violent crime influences the outcome of the crime: gun robberies, when compared with other types of robbery, are more likely to be successful, less likely to result in injury to the victim, and more likely to result in the victim's death; gun assaults are more likely to result in the victim's death than knife assaults, *ceteris paribus*. A general increase in gun availability would probably have little effect on the overall robbery rate, but would increase the homicide rate, including the rate of robbery murder, and possibly reduce the number of aggravated assaults. These and other predictions emerge from the empirical results presented here. My overall conclusion is that the technology of violent crime matters a great deal in a number of dimensions, with important implications for the gun control debate.

THE BASIC ISSUES

Gun control measures come in a variety of forms, but most share the objective of reducing the availability of guns for the use in violent crime. Most federal and state gun regulations in the United States are moderate interventions intended to reduce criminal use while preserving the majority's access to guns for legitimate uses. Washington, D.C., and New York City have adopted a much broader attack on the handgun problem, with a ban on sales to all but a few people. Whether the regulations are moderate or extreme, some opponents of gun control insist that a regulatory approach will be ineffective in reducing criminal violence. Their position is summarized in two bumper strips: "When guns are outlawed, only outlaws will have guns," and "Guns don't kill people—people kill people." The formers suggests that "outlaws" will acquire guns, despite whatever steps are taken to stop them, that is, that criminals will continue to do what is necessary to obtain guns, even if the price, hassle, and legal threats associated with obtaining a gun are increased substantially. The latter bumper strip apparently is meant to suggest that people who decide to kill will find a way even if they do not have access to guns. This is one aspect of a more general issue, the degree of "substitutibility" between guns and other weapons in homicide and other violent crimes. In short, does the type of weapon matter?

Supposing that we were somehow successful in discouraging some violent people from obtaining guns and using them in crime, how might violent crime patterns change? Three dimensions of the violent crime problem are important: (1) the *distribution* of robberies, aggravated assaults, rapes, and homicides across different types of victims, for example, commercial versus noncommercial robbery; (2) the *seriousness* of robberies, rapes, and aggravated assaults; and (3) the overall *rates* of each of these crimes. These three dimensions are considered in turn in the next three sections.[2]

DISTRIBUTION: THE VULNERABILITY PATTERN

People who attempt robbery or homicide are more likely to succeed with a gun than with other commonly used weapons. A gun is particularly valuable against victims who are physically strong, armed, or otherwise relatively invulnerable—the gun is "the great equalizer." The patterns of weapon use in criminal homicide and robbery demonstrate that perpetrators are most likely to use guns against victims who would have the best chance of defending themselves against other weapons; that is, the likelihood of a gun being chosen by a robber or killer increases with the value of a gun in effecting a successful completion of the crime. These observations suggest that a program that is successful in reducing the rate of gun ownership by potential robbers or killers will change the relative distribution of these crimes among different types of victims. The evidence and implications of the vulnerability pattern are presented in the following sections, beginning with criminal homicide.

Criminal Homicide

A decision to kill is easier and safer to implement with a gun than with other commonly available weapons—there is less danger of effective victim resistance during the attack, and the killing can be accomplished more quickly and impersonally, with less sustained effort than is usually required with a knife or blunt object. A gun has greatest value against relatively invulnerable victims, and the vulnerability of the victim appears to be an important factor in determining the probability that a gun will be used as the murder weapon.

The least vulnerabile victims are those who are guarded or armed. All presidential assassinations in U.S. history were committed with a handgun or rifle. Almost all law enforcemnt officers who have been murdered in recent years were shot: in 1978, 91 of 93 murdered officers were killed by guns.[3]

Physical size and strength ar also components of vulnerability. In 1977, 68.5 percent of male homicide victims were shot, compared with only 51.0 percent of female homicide victims.[4] The victims' age pattern of gun use also reflects the vulnerability pattern: about 70 percent of victims aged 20-44 are shot, but this fraction drops off rapidly for younger and older—that is, more vulnerable—victims.[5]

Vulnerability is of course a relative matter. We would expect that the lethality of the murder weapons would be directly related to the difference in physical strength between the victim and killer, other things being equal. To investigate this hypothesis, I used FBI data coded from the supplemental homicide reports submitted for 1976 and 1977 by police departments in 50 large cities. These data include the demographic characteristics of the victim and, where known, the offender, as well as the murder weapon, immediate circumstances, and apparent motive of the crime. The results calculated from these data tend to confirm the relative vulnerability hypothesis. First, women tend to use more lethal weapons to kill their spouses than do men: 97 percent of the women, but only 78 percent of the men, used a gun or knife. The gun fractions in spouse killings are 67 percent and 62 percent, respectively— not a large difference, but one that is notable, since women typically have less experience than men in handling guns and are less likely to think of any guns kept in the home as their personal property. It is also true that women who kill their "boyfriends" are more likely to use a gun than men who kill their "girlfriends."

Table 1 focuses on killings resulting from arguments and brawls in which both the killer and the victim were males. The gun fraction increases with the age of the killer and is inversely related to the age of the victim: the highest gun fraction—87 percent—involves elderly killers and youthful victims; the lowest gun fraction—48 percent—involves youthful killers and elderly victims. Since age is highly correlated with strength and robustness, these results offer strong support for the relative vulnerability hypothesis.

Why are less vulnerable murder victims more likely to be shot than relatively vulnerable victims? A natural interpretation of this result is that intended victims who are physically strong or armed in some fashion are better able to defend themselves against homicidal assault than more vulnerable victims—unless the assailant uses a gun, the "great equalizer." The "vulnerability pattern" can

TABLE 1

GUN USE IN MURDERS AND NONNEGLIGENT HOMICIDES RESULTING FROM
ARGUMENTS OR BRAWLS, MALE VICTIM AND MALE OFFENDER

	OFFENDER'S AGE		
VICTIM'S AGE	18–39	40–59	60+
18–39 (in percentage)	68.0	79.6	87.2
N*	1906	368	47
40–59 (in percentage)	54.5	64.1	66.7
N	398	245	57
60+ (in percentage)	48.3	49.2	63.3
N	58	61	30

SOURCE: FBI Supplemental Homicide Reports, 50 large cities, 1976 and 1977 combined (unpublished). *N = the sample size, that is, the denominator of the fraction. Cases in which the age of the killer is not known are excluded.

then be explained as resulting from some combination of three mechanisms. (1) Homicidal attacks are more likely to fail against strong victims than weak ones, and the difference in the likelihood of failure is greater for non-gun attacks than attacks with a gun. (2) The likelihood that an individual will act on a homicidal impulse depends in part on the perceived probability of success. The intended victim's ability to defend himself acts as a deterrent to would-be killers—but this deterrent is much weaker if the killer has a gun than otherwise. (3) In the case of a planned murder, the killer will have the opportunity to equip himself with a tool that is adequate for the task. Against well-defended victims, the tool chosen will almost certainly be a gun, if one can be obtained without too much difficulty.

Each of these mechanisms is compatible with the prediction that a reduction in gun availability will cause a reduction in homicide, a reduction that will be concentrated on killings that involve a victim who is physically stronger than the killer. A number of specific hypotheses are suggested by this observation, including the following: a reduction in gun availability will reduce the male:female victimization ratio in killings of spouses and other intimates, reduce the fraction of homicide victims who are youthful males, and reduce the fraction of killers who are elderly.

Robbery

Robbery is defined as theft or attempted theft by means of force or the threat of violence.[6] The robber's essential task is to overcome through intimidation or force the victim's natural tendency to resist parting with his valuables. A variety of techniques for accomplishing this task are used in robbery, including actual attack—as in "muggings" and "yokings"—and the threatening display of a weapon such as a gun, knife, or club. Whatever the means employed, the objective is to quickly gain the victim's compliance or to render him helpless, thereby preventing the victim from escaping, summoning help, or struggling. The amount of what could be called "power"—capability of generating lethal force—the robber needs to achieve these objectives with high probability depends on the characteristics of the robbery target—victim—and in particular on the vulnerability of the target. The most vulnerable targets are people who are young, elderly, or otherwise physically weak or disabled—for example, by alcohol—who are alone and without ready means of escape. The least vulnerable targets are commercial place, especially where there are several customers and clerks and possibly even armed guards—a bank being one extreme example.

A gun is the most effective tool for enhancing the robber's power. Unlike other common weapons, a gun gives a robber the capacity to threaten deadly harm from a distance, thus allowing him to maintain a buffer zone between himself and the victim and to control several victims simultaneously. A gun serves to preempt any rational victim's inclination to flee or resist.[7] Wesley Skogan documented the effectiveness of a gun in forestalling victim resistance in his analysis of a national sample of victim-reported robberies:[8] only 8 percent of gun robbery victims resisted physically in noncommercial robberies, compared with about 15 percent of victims in noncommercial robberies involving other weapons.[9] Other types of resistance—arguing, screaming, and fleeing—were also less common in gun robbery than in robbery involving other weapons.

It seems reasonable to assume that, from the robber's viewpoint, the value of employing a gun tends to be inversely related to the vulnerability of the target. A gun will cause a greater increase in the likelihood of success against well-defended targets than against more vulnerable targets. A strong-arm technique will be adequate against an elderly woman walking alone on the street—a gun would be redundant with such a victim—but a gun is virtually a requirement of successful bank robbery. Skogan provides evidence supporting this claim: he finds little relationship between robbery success rates and weapon type for personal robbery, but a very strong relationship for commercial robbery. He reports that success rates in commercial robbery were 94 percent with a gun, 65 percent with a knife, and 48 percent with other weapons.[10]

In economic terms, we can characterize robbery as a production process with weapons, robbers, and a target as "inputs."[11] The "output" of the production process can be defined as the probability of success. This probability increases with the number and skill of the robbers, the vulnerability of the target, and the lethal effect of the weapons. For given robber and target characteristics, the "marginal product" of a gun can be defined as the increase in probability of success if the robber(s) substitute a gun for, say, a knife. The evidence presented in the preceding paragraphs suggests that the marginal product of a gun is small against vulnerable targets and is relatively large against well-defended targets. We can go one step further and define the "value of a gun's marginal product" as its marginal product (increase in success probability) multiplied by the amount of loot if the robbery is successful. Since for obvious reasons, targets with greater potential loot tend to be better defended against robbery,[12] the *value* of the gun's marginal product is even more strongly related to target vulnerability than is the marginal product of the gun. The conclusion can be put in the form of a proposition:

> The economic value of a gun in robbery tends to be greatest against commercial targets and other well-defended targets, and least against highly vulnerable targets.

It makes good economic sense, then, for gun use in robbery to be closely related to target vulnerability. This is indeed the case, as demonstrated in Table 2, which is based on tabulating results of more than 12,000 robbery reports taken from victim survey data gathered in 26 large cities.

From Table 2, we see that 55 percent of gun robberies committed by adults, but only 13 percent of other adult armed robberies, involve commercial targets. Those relatively few gun robberies that were committed against people on the street are concentrated on relatively invulnerable targets—groups of two or more victims or prime-age males—while street robbery with other weapons was more likely to involve women, children, and elderly victims. Skogan provides further detail for commercial robberies, reporting that the likelihood that a gun is present in such robberies is only 44 percent for commercial places that have only one employee, but 68 percent for commercial places with two or more employees.[13]

What is the causal process that produces these patterns in gun robbery? There are two plausible explanations, both compatible with the evidence presented in the preceding paragraphs: (1) robbers who aspire to well-defended, lucrative targets equip themselves with a gun in order to increase their chance of success or (2) robbers who happen have a gun are more tempted to rob lucrative, well-defended targets than robbers who lack this tool. In short, the question is whether the weapon is chosen to suit the task or, rather, the available weapon helps define the task. There is doubtless some truth in both explanations.

The first explanation suggests that the observed relationship between gun use and target choice is the result of differences between the kinds of people that rob lucrative targets and those who commit relatively petty street robberies—a difference reminiscent of John Conklin's distinction between "professionals" and "opportunists."[14] Victim survey evidence does suggest that gun robbers as a group have more of the earmarks of professionalism than other

TABLE 2

DISTRIBUTION OF ROBBERIES (IN PERCENTAGE)

ALL ROBBERIES ACROSS LOCATIONS

	GUN	KNIFE OR OTHER WEAPON	UARMED
Commercial	55.1	13.3	19.3
Residence	6.4	10.4	8.3
Street, vehicle, and so forth	38.5	76.3	72.4
Total	100.0	100.0	100.0

STREET ROBBERIES BY VICTIM CHARACTERISTICS

	GUN	KNIFE OR OTHER WEAPON	UNARMED
Male victim age 16–54	59.8	53.8	41.1
Two or more victims	10.5	5.8	3.7
All others (young, elderly, and/or female victim)	29.7	40.4	55.2
Total	100.0	100.0	100.0

SOURCE: Adapted from Philip J. Cook, "Reducing Injury and Death Rates in Robbery," p. 43. © 1980 by the Regents of the University of California. Reprinted from *Policy Analysis,* volume 6, no. 1 (Winter 1980), by permission of the Regents. The distributions are calculated from National Crime Panel victimization survey data of 26 cities.

NOTE: All incidents involved at least one male robber age 18 or over. Entries in the table reflect survey sampling weights.

armed robbers: besides the fact that they make bigger "scores," gun robbers are older, less likely to rob acquaintances, and less likely to work in large groups of three or more. The factors that determine a robber's choice of weapon have some tendency to persist: a cohort of adult men arrested for gun robbery in the District of Columbia showed a greater propensity to use guns in subsequent robberies than the corresponding cohort of non-gun robbery arrestees.[15]

It seems reasonable to hypothesize, then, that robbers who engage in planning and who seek out big scores will take pains to equip themselves with the appropriate weapon—usually some type of firearm. The frequency with which other less professional robbers use guns, and hence the kinds of targets they choose, may be more sensitive to the extent to which such people have access to guns and are in the habit of carrying them, for whatever reason. Increased availability of guns may then result in some target switching by this group—substitution of more lucrative, better-defended targets for more vulnerable targets. Increased gun availability may also result in weapon substitution for a given type of target, implying an increase in the fraction of street robberies committed with a gun; that is, guns will be put to less valuable uses, as guns become "cheaper." These hypotheses can be stated more precisely as follows:

> An increase in gun availability in a city will (1) increase the fraction of non-commercial robberies committed with a gun and (2) increase the fraction of robberies committed against commercial and other well-defended targets.

In an earlier study of robbery patterns across 50 cities,[16] I found some confirmation for the first of these two predictions; controlling for other robbery-related variables, the fraction of robberies committed with a gun increases with the density of gun ownership in a city. A 10 percent increase in the fraction of households that owns guns is associated with approximately a 5 percent increase in the rate of gun robbery.

Conclusions

The preceding evidence demonstrates the existence of an important vulnerability pattern in weapon choice in homicide and robbery. Guns give assailants the power to succeed in killing or robbing relatively invulnerable victims who would have a good chance of fending off attack with a less lethal weapon. If some potential killers were deprived of guns, the criminal homicide rate would be reduced. The reduction would be concentrated among the least vulnerable types of potential victims—law enforcement officers, people with bodyguards, husbands of homicidal women, youthful men, and so forth. If robbers were deprived of guns, there would be a reduction in robberies against commercial places and other well-defended victims. In general, a reduction in gun availability would change the distribution of violent crimes, with greater concentration on vulnerable victims.

SERIOUSNESS: THE OBJECTIVE DANGEROUSNESS PATTERN

Recall that I am concerned with three dimensions of violent crime: the distribution, the seriousness, and the number of incidents. The vulnerability pattern suggests that gun availability will in certain respects influence the distribution of robberies and homicides across different categories of victims. I now turn to the seriousness dimension of violent crime. "Seriousness" in this discussion will be defined as the degree of injury to the victim. A violent or potentially violent confrontation, as in robbery, rape, or assault, can result in a range of possible outcomes, from no physical harm up to serious injury or death of the victim. The likelihood that the victim will be killed is influenced by the lethal effects of the weapon used by the perpetrator. The evidence on this "objective dangerousness" pattern is presented first for serious assaults, and subsequently for robbery.

Serious Assaults

The fraction of serious gun assaults that result in the victim's death is much higher than for assaults with other weapons. Richard Block, for example, found that of all aggravated assaults resulting in injury to the victim—and reported to the Chicago Police—14 percent of the gun cases, but only 4 percent of the knife cases, resulted in the victim's death.[17] In part, this difference is the result of differences between gun and knife attacks in intent and capability. An assailant who intends to kill his victim, and who has some chance to prepare, is more likely to equip himself with a gun than an assailant who merely intends to hurt his victim. Furthermore, an attack that is intended to kill is more likely to be successful if perpetrated with a gun than with a knife or other weapons—especially against victims who are capable of defending themselves. But differences in intent and capability are not the whole story.

Franklin Zimring has demonstrated that a large proportion of murders are similar to serious assaults in that the attacks are unsustained[18]—the assailant does not administer the *coup de grâce,* the blow that would ensure the death of his victim. Indeed, the victim was shot only once in about two thirds of the gun homicides in Zimring's Chicago samples. These cases differ very little from serious assaults: for every death resulting from a single wound in the head or chest, Zimring found 1.8 victims with the same type of wound who did not die[19]—victims who were clearly not saved by any differences in the gunman's intent or capability, but rather just by good luck with respect to the precise location of the wound.

Evidently, some proportion of gun murders are not the result of a clear intent to kill; given that the majority of murders are the immediate result of altercations, often involving alcohol and rarely much thought, it seems unlikely that many killers have any clearly formulated "intent" at the time of their attack. The assailant's mental state is characterized by an impulse—to punish, avenge an insult, or stop a verbal or physical attack—backed by more or less cathexis. The immediate availability of a gun makes these circumstances more dangerous than would a less lethal weapon because an unsustained attack with a gun—a single shot—is more likely to kill than an unsustained attack with another weapon.

Zimring buttressed the conclusions from his first study, which compared knife and gun attacks, with a later study comparing large and small caliber gun attacks. Even after controlling for the number and location of wounds, he found that .38 caliber attacks were more than twice as likely to kill as .22 caliber attacks.[20] It appears, then, that weapon dangerousness has a substantial independent impact on the death rate from serious assaults.

Zimring's seminal work in this area supports several important propositions, including:

1. A restrictive gun control policy that causes knives and clubs to be substituted for guns will reduce the death rate in serious assault.

2. A gun control policy that focuses on handguns may increase the death rate from gun assault if shotguns and rifles are substituted for handguns as a result.[21]

3. In setting prosecution and sentencing priorities for aggravated assault cases, gun assaults should be viewed as more serious than assaults with other weapons, *ceteris paribus,* since there is a higher probability of the victim's dying in the gun assaults. This is Zimring's "objective dangerousness" doctrine.[22]

Richard Block extended Zimring's work on instrumentality by comparing death rates in aggravated assault and robbery cases. He concludes that "the relative fatality of different weapons in violent crime may be a technological invariant— . . . the probability of death given injury and a particular weapon remains relatively constant and unrelated to the type of crime committed."[23]

The notion that the number of deaths per 100 injuries is a "technical" constant, largely determined by the lethality of the weapon, is not supportable, however. Zimring demonstrated that the type of weapon was one important determinant of the outcome of serious attacks, but did not claim it was the only determinant. Presumably the weapon-specific death rates in such attacks will differ across jurisdictions and vary over time depending on the mix of circumstances, the quality of medical care, and so forth. Arthur Swersey presents an interesting case in point.[24]

Swersey reports that the number of assaultive—as opposed to felony— gun homicides in Harlem increased from 19 in 1968 to 70 in 1973, and then fell back to 46 in 1974. Much of the change between 1968 and 1973 was from an increase in intentional killings resulting from disputes involving narcotics activities. The importance of changes in the intent of violent perpetrators during this period is indicated by the fact that the death rate in gun attacks doubled between 1968 and 1973, and then fell back in 1974. Swersey concludes that more than 80 percent of the rise and fall in Harlem homicides was due to changes in the number of deliberate murders. He finds a similar pattern for the rest of New York City.[25]

Swersey's findings do not undermine Zimring's position. Zimring did not deny that some killings were unambiguously motivated, or that the importance of intent in murder was subject to change over time, or that it might be more important in Harlem than in Chicago. In any event, Swersey's results are useful in documenting these possibilities.

My conclusions can be briefly stated. The likelihood of death from a serious assault is determined, *inter alia,* by the assailant's intent and the lethal nature of the weapon he uses. The type of weapon is especially important when the intent is ambiguous. The fraction of homicides that can be viewed as deliberate—unambiguously intended—varies over time and space, but is probably fairly small as a rule. The fraction of gun assaults that results in the death of the victim is one indication of the relative prevalence of deliberate gun murders.

Robbery

The principal role of a weapon in robbery is to aid the robber in coercing the victim—either by force or threat—to part with his valuables. If the threat is sufficiently convincing, physical force is not necessary. For this reason, it is hardly surprising that the use of force is closely related to the weapon type in robbery, being very common in unarmed robbery and rare in gun robbery. Table 3 documents this pattern for both commercial and noncommercial robberies committed by adult males. As shown in this table, gun robberies are less likely than other armed robberies to involve physical violence and, furthermore, are less likely to injure the victim.[26] These patterns are compatible with the notion that violence plays an instrumental role in robbery—that it is employed when the robber believes it is needed to overcome or forestall victim resistance and that this need is less likely to arise when the robber uses a gun than otherwise.

There is evidence, however, that this "instrumental violence" pattern can account for only a fraction of the injuries and deaths that result from robbery. Three observations are relevant in this respect. First, over two thirds of victims injured in noncommercial gun robberies do not resist in any way—even after the attack;[27] similarly, 20 out of 30 victims killed in gun robberies in Dade Country between 1974 and 1976 did not resist the robber. Second, the likelihood that the victim will be injured in an armed robbery is much higher if the robbery is committed by a gang of three or more than otherwise; since victims are less likely to offer resistance to a group of three or four robbers than to a lone robber, this result is clearly incompatible with the "instrumental violence" hypothesis. Third, judging from re-arrest statistics for a large cohort of adult robbery arrestees in Washington, D.C., it appears that robbers who injure their victims tend to be more violence prone than other robbers.[28]

These findings are different aspects of an "excess violence" pattern: much of the violence in robbery is not "necessary," in the sense of being an instrumental response to anticipated or actual resistance by the victim. Rather, it is motivated by objectives or impulses that have little to do with ensuring successful completion of the theft. In particular, the high incidence of violence in street robberies committed by larger groups—which typically have a low "take"—is best viewed as a form of recreation, and the gratuitous violence against the victim may be just part of the fun.

TABLE 3

LIKELIHOOD OF PHYSICAL ATTACK AND INJURY IN ROBBERY (IN PERCENTAGE)

	GUN*	KNIFE†	OTHER WEAPON	UNARMED
Noncommercial robbery**				
Victim attacked	22.1	39.4	60.4	73.5
Victim required medical treatment†	7.2	10.9	15.5	11.1
Victim hospitalized overnight	2.0	2.6	2.7	1.6
Number of cases (not in percentage)	892	841	1060	1259
Commercial robbery				
Victim required medical treatment	4.8	10.8	17.9	5.1
Victim hospitalized overnight	1.5	3.5	6.0	0.4
Number of cases (not in percentage)	2307	288	117	570

*Many robberies involve more than one type of weapon. Incidents of that sort were classified according to the most lethal weapon used.

†Only about one third of the injured gun robbery victims were actually shot. Two thirds of the injured knife robbery victims were stabbed.

**Robberies occurring on the street, in a vehicle, or near the victim's home.

SOURCE: National Crime Panel victimization surveys of 26 cities. This table is excerpted from Philip J. Cook, "Reducing Injury and Death Rates in Robbery," Table 2. © 1980 by The Regents of the University of California. Reprinted from *Policy Analysis*, volume 6, no. 1 (Winter 1980), by permission of The Regents.

NOTE: All incidents included in this table involved at least one male robber age 18 or over. Entries in the table do not reflect the survey sampling weights, which differed widely among the 26 cities.

Given these findings, it is useful to attempt a distinction between "robbery with intent to injure" or kill and robbery without such intent—in which violence would only be used to overcome victim resistance. The latter form of robbery dominates the statistics—most victims are not in fact injured, and the likelihood of injury is less with guns than with other weapons. However, the more violent strain of robbery, involving an intent to injure, apparently accounts for a high percentage of the serious injuries and deaths that do occur in the robbery context. Furthermore, the incidence of excess violence in robbery is subject to change over time, as Zimring demonstrated in his study of robbery murder in Detroit.[29] He found a sharp discontinuity in 1972 in the fraction of victims killed in armed robbery: after 10 years of stable weapon-specific death rates, this fraction doubled between 1971 and 1973 for gun robberies and increased even more during this period for other armed robberies.

Are gun robberies more dangerous than other armed robberies, in the sense of being more likely to result in the victim's death? Victims are killed in a higher fraction of gun robberies than others: based on victim surveys and homicide data in eight cities, I calculated that there are 9.0 victim fatalities for every 1000 gun robberies, compared with 1.7 victim fatalities per 1000 non-gun armed robberies.[30] Furthermore, it appears that the type of weapon plays an independent role in determining the likelihood of robbery murder; in a cross-sectional analysis of 50 cities, I found that the fraction of robberies resulting in the victim's death is closely related to the fraction of robberies that involve firearms.[31] Thus the objective dangerousness pattern applies to robbery as well as assault, for reasons that remain a bit obscure.

Why does the presence of a loaded authentic gun in robbery increase the probability of the victim's death? My studies of robbery murder in Atlanta and Dade County[32] indicated that in at least half of the cases the killing was deliberate: for example the victim was tied and then executed, or shot several times from close range. But insofar as intent could be ascertained from police reports, it appears that these intentional killings were not pre-meditated, but rather decided on during the course of the robbery. Perhaps the explanation for why these spontaneous decisions are more likely to occur when the robber is holding a gun is related to Marvin Wolfgang's suggestion: "The offender's physical repugnance to engaging in direct physical assault by cutting or stabbing his adversary, may mean that in the absence of a firearm no homicide occurs."[33]

Two conclusions can be inferred from the preceding discussion:

1. A reduction in gun availability will increase the robbery injury rate,[34] but reduce the robbery murder rate.

2. Given the excess violence pattern in robbery, the robbery cases in which the victim is injured should be allocated special emphasis in establishing criminal prosecutions and sentencing priorities.[35] In a high proportion of these crimes, the attack that caused the injury was not instrumental to the robbery, but rather was a distinct act. A relatively severe judicial response to such cases might act as a deterrent to excess violence in robbery.

Coercion and Assault

Does the instrumental violence pattern in robbery have any parallel in assault? I suspect the answer is yes, but I know of no empirical evidence.

Some unknown fraction of assault cases are similar to robbery in that the assailant's objective is to coerce the victim's compliance—the assailant wants the victim to stop attacking him, physically or verbally, or stop dancing with his girlfriend, or get off his favorite barstool, or turn down the stereo. And, as in the case of robbery, the probability of a physical attack in such cases may be less if the assailant has a gun than otherwise because the victim will be less inclined to ignore or resist a threat enforced by the display of a gun.

It may also be true that the assailant would be more hesitant to use a gun than another weapon to make good his threat. If this reasoning is correct, then a general increase in gun availability may reduce the number of assault-related injuries.

INCIDENCE: THE SUBSTITUTION PATTERN

The preceding evidence suggests that gun availability has a substantial effect on the distribution and seriousness of violent crime. The third dimension of the violent crime problem is incidence—the number of violent confrontations and attacks. For each of the crimes under consideration—assault, robbery, and homicide—a reduction in gun availability to criminals would presumably cause a reduction in the number of incidents involving guns. But for each crime there is a real possibility that the number of incidents involving weapons other than guns would increase as a result of the reduction in gun availability. If this weapon substitution does occur, the net effect of reduced gun availability on crime rates could be either positive or negative.

First, consider the crime of assault. In an environment in which a high percentage of the violence prone people carry guns, it is possible that a sort of mutual deterrent is created, whereby a rational person would think twice before picking a fight. A protagonist that is foolish enough to start a fight in such an environment may be persuaded to back off if his intended victim pulls a gun. When physical attacks do occur, they are likely to be perpetrated with a gun and to be serious. This line of argument may explain why the Bartley-Fox Amendment in Massachusetts—an anticarrying law that was apparently quite effective—may have resulted in an increase in the rate of aggravated assaults—the gun assault rate went down substantially following implementation, but the non-gun assault rate increased even more.[36] A legal intervention that is successful in getting guns off the streets may encourage relatively harmless fights with fists and broken bottles. Definitive results in this area are hard to come by, in part due to the difficulty in measuring the assault rate in a consistent manner over time or across jurisdictions.

My cross-sectional analysis of robbery in 50 cities found that one measure of gun availability—the density of gun ownership—was statistically unrelated to the overall robbery rate when other causal factors were taken into account.[37] By way of illustration, the two cities with the highest robbery rates—Detroit and Boston—differed markedly in gun ownership. Boston was one of the lowest, and Detroit was above average. The same study demonstrated that the fraction of robberies committed with a gun was closely related to the density of gun ownership in the city. Apparently robbers tend to substitute guns for other weapons as guns become readily available, but with little or no change in their rate of commission.

If guns were less widely available, the criminal homicide rate would fall. This prediction is justified by three distinct arguments developed in this essay: (1) knives and clubs are not close substitutes for guns for implementing a decision to kill, especially when the intended victim is relatively invulnerable; (2) Zimring's "objective dangerousness" results demonstrate that a reduction in gun use is serious—but ambiguously motivated—assaults will reduce the homicide rate, and (3) my results on robbery murder in the 50-cities study indicate that the fraction of robberies that result in the victim's death is closely related to the fraction of robberies involving guns. A final bit of evidence comes from evaluations of the Bartley-Fox Amendment, which suggest that it reduced the criminal homicide rate in Massachusetts. The tough new handgun law in the District of Columbia has also apparently been effective in this regard. It should be noted that a crackdown focused on the least lethal type of gun—small caliber handguns—might not have the desired effect on criminal homicide if perpetrators substituted large caliber handguns or long guns.

My conclusion is that effective gun control measures are unlikely to reduce the total number of violent confrontations and attacks, but may well reduce the criminal homicide rate.

CONCLUSIONS

The type of weapon matters in violent crime, both in terms of its seriousness and its distribution. If robbers could be deprived of guns, the robbery murder rate would fall, the robbery injury rate would rise, and robberies would be redistributed to some extent from less to more vulnerable targets. The assaultive murder rate would decline, with the greatest reductions involving the least vulnerable victims. The overall assault rate might well increase. These predictions are based on common sense and a variety of empirical observations. None of this evidence is conclusive, but it is the best that is currently available.

Is it reasonable to suppose that moderate gun control measures have the potential to discourage some violent criminals—potential or active—from obtaining guns? No doubt there are some active criminals and other violence prone people who have the incentive and resources required to acquire a gun even in the face of substantial legal barriers. But such determined people do not figure importantly in the violent crime statistics—indeed, most assaults and robberies do not even involve guns now, despite the fact that guns are readily available in most jurisdictions. A gun control measure that increases the average cost and hassle of a youthful urban male acquiring his first handgun may at least delay acquisition for a year or two—with noticeable effect on the gun crime rate. A vigorous crackdown on carrying concealed weapons may have a similar beneficial effect.

Not all of the predicted effects on violent crime of a reduction in gun availability are attractive. None of these predictions can be made with a high degree of certainty. But it is not unreasonable to suggest that a moderate, vigorously enforced program for regulating the sale and use of guns would save a substantial number of lives. Gun control is not "the solution" to America's violent crime problem, but perhaps it should be one aspect of the effort to find a solution.

NOTES

1. A phrase coined by B. Bruce-Briggs, "The Great American Gun War," *The Public Interest*, 45:1–26 (fall 1976).
2. I am indebted to Mark Moore for this approach to carving up the violent crime problem. In the review that follows I omit any discussion of rape, since relevant empirical studies are lacking for this crime.
3. FBI, *Crime in the United States, 1978* (Washington, D.C.: U.S. Government Printing Office).
4. U.S. Department of Commerce, Bureau of the Census, *Statistical Abstract of the U.S., 1978* (Washington, D.C.: U.S. Government Printing Office).
5. FBI.
6. The perspective of this section was first developed in John Conklin's seminal work on robbery in Boston: *Robbery and the Criminal Justice System* (Philadelphia, Pa.: J. B. Lippincott, 1972).
7. Ibid., pp. 110–11; Conklin analyzes a gun's usefulness in terms of the ability it provides the robber to (1) maintain a buffer zone; (2) intimidate the victim; (3) make good the threat, if necessary; and (4) ensure escape.
8. Wesley Skogan, "Weapon Use in Robbery: Patterns and Policy Implications," unpublished manuscript (Northwestern University: Center for Urban Affairs, 1978). He used the robbery incident reports collected from the National Crime Panel, which occurred during calendar year 1973. It should be noted that any analysis of victim survey data relies on the victim's impression of the nature of the weapon that was employed in the robbery. In some cases the "gun" may be a toy, or simulated; Floyd Feeney and Adrianne Weir, "The Prevention and Control of Robbery: A Summary," unpublished manuscript (University of California, Davis: Center on Admin. of Criminal Justice, 1974) report that of 58 "gun" robbers interviewed in Oakland, 3 claimed to have used toys and 4 to have simulated the possession of a gun.
9. Richard Block (*Violent Crime* [Lexington, Mass.: Lexington Books, 1977]) found from studying robbery police reports in Chicago that victims who resisted with physical force typically (68 percent) did so in response to the robber's use of force. Other types of resistance typically (70 percent) preceded the robber's use of force.
10. Skogan, "Weapon Use in Robbery."
11. This perspective is further developed in Philip J. Cook, "The Effect of Gun Availability on Robbery and Robbery Murder: A Cross Section Study of Fifty Cities," in *Policy Studies Review Annual*, eds. Robert H. Haveman and B. Bruce Zellner, vol. 3 (Beverly Hills, Calif.: Sage, 1979), pp. 752–53 (hereafter cited as "The Effect of Gun Availability").
12. It is obvious that commercial targets tend to be more lucrative than noncommercial and that a group of two or more victims will be more lucrative on the average than a single victim. Feeney and Weir (p. 24) report the not-so-obvious result that robberies of male victims resulted in a much higher median take ($50) than robberies of female victims (less than $20).
13. Ibid., calculated from figures in his Table 3.
14. Ibid.
15. Philip J. Cook and Daniel Nagin, *Does the Weapon Matter?* (Washington, D.C.: Institute for Law and Social Research, 1979). The results cited here are based on 541 adult male gun robbery arrestees and 761 nongun robbery arrestees. This cohort, which was arrested in 1973, was tracked through 1976 through Prosecutor's Management Information System (PROMIS). The robbery re-arrest rate for the gun cohort was 43 percent, of which 58 percent were gun robberies. The robbery re-arrest rate for the non-gun cohort was 45 percent, of which 40 percent were gun robberies. The two cohorts had the same re-arrest rate for burglary (13 percent), but the non-gun cohort was much more likely to be re-arrested for assaultive crimes (22 percent, as opposed to 13 percent for the gun cohort); see Table 9 of Cook and Nagin.
16. Cook "The Effect of Gun Availability."
17. Ibid., p. 33.

18. Franklin Zimring, "The Medium is the Message: Firearm Calibre as a Determinant of Death from Assault," *Journal of Legal Studies* 1, no. 1 (January 1972): 97–124; and idem, "Is Gun Control Likely to Reduce Violent Killings?" *University of Chicago Law Review* 35 (1967) :721-37.

19. Ibid. computed from Table 7, p. 104.

20. Ibid., 1972.

21. This implication has been pointed out by Gary Kleck, "The Assumptions of Gun Control" (Tallahassee, Fla.: Florida State University, 1980) (unpublished).

22. "In the generality of cases, how likely is it that conduct such as that engaged in by the offender will lead to death?" Zimring, "The Medium Is the Message," p. 114.

23. Block, *Violent Crime,* p. 32.

24. "A Greater Intent to Kill: The Changing Pattern of Homicide in Harlem and New York City" (New Haven, Conn.: Yale School of Organization and Management, 1980) (unpublished).

25. Swersey also notes several other indications of an increasing fraction of deliberate murders in the homicide statistics for New York City as a whole. During the 1970s, the clearance rate declined for homicide, as did the fraction of homicides occurring on the weekend and the fraction involving family members.

26. Other sources on this pattern include Conklin; Skogan; and Philip J. Cook, "A Strategic Choice Analysis of Robbery," in *Sample Surveys of the Victims of Crimes,* ed. Wesley Skogan (Cambridge, Mass.: Ballinger, 1976).

27. Philip J. Cook, "Policies to Reduce Injury and Death Rates in Robbery," *Policy Analysis* 6, no. 1 (Winter 1980): 36 (hereafter cited as "Policies to Reduce Injury and Death Rates").

28. Cook and Nagin, p. 39.

29. Franklin Zimring, "Determinants of the Death Rate from Robbery: A Detroit Time Study," *Journal of Legal Studies* 6, no. 2 (June 1977): 317-32.

30. Cook, "Policies to Reduce Injury and Death Rates," p. 39.

31. Cook, "The Effect of Gun Availability," p. 775. The regression equation is as follows:

$$\frac{\text{Robbery murders}}{\text{1000 robberies}} = \underset{(1.16)}{1.52} + \underset{(2.38)}{5.68} \frac{\text{Gun robberies}}{\text{Robberies}}$$

A closely related result uses the per capita, rather than "per robbery," murder rate:

$$\frac{\text{Robbery murders}}{100,000} = \underset{(.232)}{-.284} + \underset{(.089)}{.907} \frac{\text{Gun robberies}}{1000} + \underset{(.072)}{.136} \frac{\text{Nongun robs.}}{1000}$$

(Numbers in parentheses are the standard errors of the ordinary least squares regression coefficients.) The data for 50 cities are 1975-76 averages. The second equation has an $R^2 = .82$, suggesting that robbery murder is very closely linked to robbery. Inclusion of the assaultive murder rate in this equation as an independent variable does not affect the other coefficients much—and the coefficient on the murder variable is not statistically significant. I conclude that robbery murder is more robbery than murder.

32. Cook, "Policies to Reduce Injury and Death Rates."

33. Marvin Wolfgang, *Patterns in Criminal Homicide* (Philadelphia, Pa.: University of Pennsylvania, 1958), p. 79.

34. See Skogan.

35. Cook, "Policies to Reduce Injury and Death Rates."

36. Glenn L. Pierce and William J. Bowers, "The Impact of the Bartley-Fox Gun Law on Crime in Massachusetts," unpublished manuscript (Northeastern University: Center for Applied Social Research, 1979).

37. Cook, "The Effect of Gun Availability."

9

Policy Lessons from
Recent Gun Control Research

Gary Kleck

INTRODUCTION

In 1976, a review of policy research on gun control concluded that "the few attempts at serious work are of marginal competence at best and tainted by obvious bias."[1] It is hard to quarrel with this assessment, especially as it is applied to the most important and widely cited of the pre-1976 studies, the procontrol report to the Eisenhower Commission written by George Newton and Franklin Zimring.[2] Since that time, however, considerable scholarly work has been completed, much of it of high quality and relevant to policy-related questions surrounding the legal regulation of firearms.

Some researchers make the policy implications of their work explicit, while others modestly choose to "let the facts speak for themselves." All too often, policy-relevant gun control research has been characterized by perfectly respectable data and research methods, but also by interpretations of the find-

From *Law and Contemporary Problems* 49, no. 1 (Winter 1986): 35–43, 48–52, 59–62. Copyright © 1986, Duke University School of Law. Reprinted by permission of the author and the publisher.

ings which either do not follow from the evidence or which are too vaguely and generally phrased to be useful in making policy. This discussion reviews the body of recent gun control research and points out some of the more important, albeit tentative, implications for public policy.

Although a broader definition could be employed, the term "gun control" is used here to refer to laws aimed at limiting possession of firearms, either among the general public or among specific segments of the population. This definition includes laws requiring a license or permit to purchase, own, or possess guns and laws totally prohibiting civilian ownership of all guns or of specific types of guns such as handguns in general or "Saturday Night Specials" in particular. The term as used here does not cover laws regulating the *use* of guns, such as prohibitions against carrying them, firing them within city limits, or using them to further a crime (for example, laws mandating additional or enhanced penalties for use of a gun in the commission of a felony). Most such measures are not a significant part of the gun control debate. Indeed, the generally anti-gun control National Rifle Association strongly supports additional penalties for the use of guns in crimes.

THE RELATIONSHIP BETWEEN VIOLENCE AND THE AVAILABILITY OF GUNS

The first issue which must be addressed is why society should want to regulate firearms. This question is not as foolish as it may seem, since it is by no means obvious how, or even whether, the availability of firearms affects levels of violence. There are three ways in which the availability of guns might increase crime and violence: assault-instigating effects, crime-facilitating effects, and assault-intensifying effects. The term "assault-instigating effects" refers to the possibility that the sight of a gun, or possession of a gun, could stimulate or trigger assaults which otherwise would not have occurred. It has been asserted that stimuli commonly associated with aggression, such as guns, can elicit aggression from people ready to act aggressively, especially angry people. The literature on this subject has been reviewed elsewhere,[3] so only brief remarks are necessary here. The studies are almost equally divided between those concluding that there *is* a "weapons effect" and those indicating that there is not. In any case, the bulk of this literature is irrelevant to concerns about the effect of guns in actual assaults because of the artificiality of the circumstances in which the weapons effect experiments were conducted. Most of the studies involved laboratory experiments in which confederates of the experimenters angered subjects, who were then given an opportunity to act aggressively toward the confederates, for instance, by giving them electrical shocks during a "learning experiment." A gun would be present for some subjects and was either left unexplained (not associated with anyone in the experiment) or was associated with the confederate, the "victim" of the subjects' aggression. Even when experiments were done in naturalistic field conditions, the gun was never in the possession of, or otherwise associated with, the subjects whose aggression was being measured. Consequently, these studies at best simulate aggression *against* persons with guns. Even for this limited use, however, it is highly doubtful that many people will accept the conclusion that angry people will be *more* likely to attack another person if the potential victim is armed. This conclusion contradicts too much real-life experience of police officers, soldiers, criminals, and ordinary civilians, who have successfully inhibited the aggression of others by the display of a firearm.

The weapons-effect literature sheds little light on whether a person's possession of a gun or other weapon can trigger his or her *own* aggression. Currently, the available evidence is compatible with the assertion that guns are as likely to inhibit aggression as to stimulate it.[4] Although his finding may have other explanations, Philip J. Cook observed that robbers armed with guns are far less likely to assault their victims than either robbers armed with other weapons or unarmed robbers. Twenty-two percent of robbers with guns, 39 percent of those with knives, 60 percent of those with other weapons, and 74 percent of unarmed robbers attacked their victims.[5] This is a commonplace finding, which agrees with earlier studies.[6] If guns trigger assaults among people ready to act aggresively in real life, this tendency certainly is not in evidence among robbers.

The term "crime-facilitating effects" refers to the possibilty that the possession of a gun may make possible or make easier a crime that a criminal already wanted to commit but might not have committed without the gun. For example, a gun can make it possible for a small man to attack a bigger man: "Colonel Colt made every man six feet tall." Similarly, a gun could facilitate an attack by a woman against a man. A gun may also make it possible for a man to commit a specific robbery even though he might not have thought that he would have had a reasonable chance of pulling it off without a gun. In these situations, the gun does not affect motivation or drive to commit the crime, but rather provides a tool that reduces risk to the criminal and improves chances for successfully manipulating the victim.

Cook has shown that guns are most likely to be used in assaults involving "weak" attackers and "strong" victims—attacks by females against males are more likely to involve guns than attacks with other gender combinations, and attacks by elderly persons against victims in their "prime" are more likely to involve guns than attacks with other age combinations.[7] While it is impossible to know from these facts whether some weak attacker-strong victim assaults would not have occurred in the absence of guns, the findings are compatible with the facilitation hypothesis. Gun availability could increase the overall frequency of attacks by enabling weaker people to attack stronger ones.

Cook has also provided some indirectly relevant evidence about robberies. A series of studies found that availability of guns has no effect on the robbery rates in large cities[8] but that it does appear to affect the *kinds* of targets robbed.[9] Gun possession seems to provide the tactical edge that allows robbers to attack more lucrative, but less vulnerable targets—such as commercial targets rather than individuals on the street, males rather than females, groups of victims rather than single victims, and victims in their middle years rather than the very young or the very old.[10] These findings strongly suggest that reducing gun ownership among the crime prone, even if it could be achieved, would result in no change in the frequency or number of robberies but would shift the burden of robbery from those best able to bear it to those least able to do so—a policy outcome of dubious value.

The term "assault-intensifying effects" refers to the assertion that when assaults occur, for whatever reason and in whatever circumstances, the use of a gun increases the severity of any resulting injuries and the probability of the victim's death, compared to what would have occurred had a likely substitute weapon, such as a kinfe or fists, been used. This is the least controversial of the possible effects of guns on crime, yet it too is subject to dispute concerning its magnitude.

How much deadlier are guns compared to probable substitute weapons such as knives? The most widely cited estimate is *implied* in the conclusions of George Newton and Franklin Zimring regarding assaults: "When a gun is used, the chances of a death are about five times as great as when a knife is used."[11] Perhaps what is most noteworthy about this statement is its misleading phrasing. While leading many readers to believe that guns are five times as deadly as knives, the authors avoid saying so in any explicit way. Critics have pointed out that much of the difference in fatality rates between gun assaults and knife assaults could be due to the greater seriousness of intent to injure or kill among users of guns.[12] People choose more serious methods of assault when they are more serious about hurting their victims, even when there is little premeditation or conscious weighing or self-examination of motives by assaulters.[13] Since more seriously inclined attackers can be expected to injure more seriously, regardless of weapon choice, the fact that fatality rates in gun assaults are higher than in knife assaults does not necessarily indicate that guns themselves are even slightly more deadly than knives, regardless of how self-evident the greater deadliness of guns may seem.

A meaningful comparison of weapon deadliness requires some comparability of intent and motive between users of different weapons. There is no reason to believe that such comparability prevailed in the heterogenous samples of assaults examined in the Newton and Zimring discussion and in the study by Zimring[14] on which it was based. For example, in one of Zimring's own tables, a simple recomputation of his percentages shows that gun assaulters are substantially more likely to be male than knife assaulters (eighty-seven percent and sixty-five percent, respectively),[15] a difference of obvious significance given the enormous difference in homicidal behavior between men and women.[16]

Another way of validating the assault-intensifying hypothesis would be to demonstrate a positive correlation between aggregate levels of gun ownership and homicide rates. Studies of this issue have produced mixed results.[17] In this author's studies,[18] the pattern of findings suggested that gun ownership in the general public has no effect on homicide rates, although ownership within violence prone groups may well affect homicide rates.[19] It was not possible to determine if the result was due to an assault-intensifying effect, although this explanation seems plausible.

This discussion focuses exclusively on assaultive crimes and robbery for the simple reason that gun use in other crimes is slight. For example, in 1979 only about 9 percent of rape offenders were armed with a gun.[20] The presence of a gun in even these few rapes was often incidental and not necessary in the commission of the crime when rapists could rely on their superior size and strength to overpower their victims. Guns are also unnecessary in the commission of burglary because it is a crime of stealth. Although there is little solid information on the subject, it seems that few burglars carry firearms, based on the extremely small number of victims who are shot when a confrontation with the burglar occurs. In New York City, for example, only twenty burglary victims were killed (and not necessarily with guns) between 1958 and 1967, even though there were 150,000 burglaries reported in 1967 alone.[21] It has been estimated that by 1973 a million New York City residents owned guns.[22] Consequently, gun availability likely has only a negligible effect on increasing rape or burglary.

The relationship between gun availability and crime and violence is still very much in doubt, but can be summarized as follows. No reliable evidence indicates that guns have any net assault-instigating effects, or that aggression-eliciting effects are any more common than inhibiting effects. Guns probably have a crime-facilitating effect on robberies against less vulnerable targets, but no effect on the overall robbery rates. In other words, guns cause some robbers to shift from one target type to another, without, however, increasing the frequency with which they rob. Evidence is consistent with the idea that guns facilitate some assaults and thus gun availability could conceivably increase assault frequency. Finally, although an assault-intensifying effect of gun availability is plausible, there is no compelling evidence demonstrating its existence or magnitude.

WHOSE GUN OWNERSHIP SHOULD BE CONTROLLED?

Gun control measures can be aimed at preventing gun possession either among the general public or by individuals in some more restricted, presumably high-risk, subset of the population. A prohibition on private ownership of hand-guns or a restrictive licensing or permit system administered to reduce drastically possession by ordinary citizens would be examples of the former, while a permissive licensing or permit-to-purchase system from which only high-risk groups are excluded would exemplify the latter. The first alternative, the "blunderbuss" approach, makes more sense to people who believe that it is impossible to distinguish between low-risk and high-risk candidates for gun ownership, that everyone is a potential killer, and that serious acts of violence and other criminal acts committed with guns are common among people with no previous record of violence. Gun control advocates like to proclaim that domestic homicides and other killings involving persons who know each other are common. The implication is that such killings involve people who could not have been identified in advance as anything other than ordinary citizens, who one day got angry and went over the edge. The policy implications of such a picture are twofold: that all citizens must be excluded from gun ownership to prevent such tragedies, and that gun control laws can be effective even if hardcore criminals ignore them, since compliance among "ordinary people" will produce significant reductions in numbers of homicides.

In fact, very few homicides are committed by people who have no prior history of violence. The popular image of the model citizen who one day goes berserk and kills a family member is largely a media-created myth maintained by newspeople enamored with the dramatic contrast between extremely violent acts and supposedly peaceful backgrounds. For example, in news stories about the Texas Tower killer, Charles Whitman, reporters invariably found a way to mention the fact that Whitman had been a choir boy and an Eagle Scout. Left unsaid, or relegated to the back pages, were the facts that he was raised in a violent home, had repeatedly beaten his wife, and been court-martialed in the Marines for fighting.[23]

The apparently "nonviolent" killer is a rare exception to a rather mundane general rule: People who are seriously violent in the present almost invariably have been seriously violent in the past. While most violent acts escape the attention of authorities and are thus not made a part of official written records, most arrested killers have committed enough violent acts in the past to have been previously arrested or convicted. Data reviewed by Kleck and Bordua indicate that perhaps 70 to 75 percent of domestic homicide offenders have been previously arrested and about half previously convicted.[24] An even more meaningful measure of previous violence indicated that 90 percent of domestic homicides in Kansas City had been preceded by previous police "disturbance calls" at the same address, with a median of five calls per address. Rather than being isolated outbursts, violent acts are almost always part of a continuing pattern of violent behavior, whether the violence is spouse or child abuse[25] or armed robbery committed by "hardened criminals."[26]

The most obvious policy implication of these facts is that reducing gun availability among "ordinary people" will do almost nothing to reduce violent crime. At best, it will act indirectly to reduce the availability of guns to criminals who might steal or otherwise obtain them from legal owners. Unfortunately, "blunderbuss" measures would inevitably have their greatest effect in reducing gun availability among the law-abiding, since it is, by definition, the law-abiding who are most likely to comply with gun control laws or, for that matter, any other laws. Compliance among criminals, on the other hand, would be low, given previous experience with more limited laws. Among the "hardened criminals" who reported previous gun possession when questioned in a recent prison survey, only 15 percent claimed to have ever even applied for a permit to purchase or carry any of the guns, even though about 91 percent of the sample were imprisoned in states with provision for one or the other permit and 32 percent were in states with both.[27] For the entire prison sample, 82 percent agreed with the statement that "Gun laws affect only law-abiding citizens; criminals will always be able to get guns."[28]

The alternative to the blunderbuss measures is more selective "targeted" measures aimed at high-risk subsets of the population such as those with official records of previous criminal behavior. Laws which either prohibit ownership or possession by such persons or which deny them required licenses or purchase permits are examples of targeted measures. These measures have the advantage of not pointlessly denying guns to people who will never commit a serious violent act in their lives, but the concomitant disadvantage of inevitably permitting legal access to guns among some violent people without prior criminal convictions.

However common previous violent and criminal *behavior* is among the currently violent, many violent people nonetheless have no previous criminal *convictions*. Since a simple arrest would not be adequate to constitutionally deny a person a privilege available to others, this means that guns could not be denied, under selective gun control measures such as permissive licensing laws, to about half of the people who will commit homicides in the near future. This assumes, however, that the percentage of offenders with a prior conviction remains constant. If the necessary resources were committed, there would be nothing to prevent police officers and prosecutors from insuring that a higher number of violent people are convicted of an offense which prevents future legal gun ownership, even if they were then given probation or a suspended sentence. This would require a systematic reform of current practices, where domestic disturbances involving repeatedly violent people are usually treated as minor offenses or private family matters not calling for official processing. Nevertheless, even if the number of violent people with a previous conviction were raised, some would necessarily still remain without such a record, and thus qualify for legal gun acquisition under targeted measures like permissive licensing or permit-to-buy systems.

Under targeted gun control laws, various other groups besides convicted criminals may be prohibited from owning or acquiring guns. Typically excluded from gun possession are alcoholics, mentally ill or mentally retarded persons, illegal aliens, and drug addicts. Most such prohibitions are unjust, of doubtful constitutionality, impractical to apply, and pointless for preventing violent crime. There are no universally accepted medical or psychiatric definitions of mental illness, drug addiction, or alcoholism. Those definitions on which some experts manage to agree are too vague to be useful for legal purposes, making prohibitions based on them unconstitutional. Some states use more precise definitions of the prohibited categories, for instance, denying guns only to persons committed involuntarily to mental institutions. Few states have comprehensive registries of involuntary mental patients, alcoholics, drug addicts, or mentally retarded persons, however, making it difficult or impossible to check for such a status.[29]

Most mentally ill persons have no record of violence. Even among those so seriously ill as to require psychiatric hospitalization, only a minority have an official record of violence in the form of an arrest for a violent crime.[30] Further, this minority is confined to that subset of patients who were identifiable as "high risk" by an arrest prior to hospitalization. One careful study found that among mental patients *without* a preadmission arrest, fewer than four percent were arrested for any crime during a postrelease followup period.[31] Thus, violence potential above the minimal level characterizing the general public is limited to a small, identifiable minority of mentally ill persons. Even within this minority, many are already denied legal access to or possession of a gun by virtue of a criminal conviction. There is therefore little factual basis for a broad legal presumption of risk to the public applied indiscriminantly to the mentally ill population as a whole, with corresponding prohibitions on firearms acquisition or possession. Nevertheless, popular stereotypes about mental illness and its supposed connection to violence are likely to keep former mental patients in the prohibited category. A more reasonable alternative would be to maintain state registries on persons admitted to psychiatric hospitals specifically as a result of violent behavior (a minority of psychiatric admissions), and use this as a basis for denying gun ownership, possession, and acquisition. This group, as well as persons with a prior criminal conviction, fugitives from justice, and persons under the age of eighteen could be denied gun ownership on the basis of specific, constitutionally defensible criteria, using existing or easily established record systems.[32]

FOCUS ON HANDGUNS?
THE SUBSTITUTION OF DEADLIER WEAPONS

In the context of gun control measures aimed at all types of long guns (such as rifles and shotguns) as well as handguns, weapon substitution refers to the possibility that offenders deprived of guns could substitute other, less deadly weapons. When the emphasis shifts to measures aimed exclusively or primarily at handguns, however, the substitution issue changes in a crucial way. An offender who has been blocked only from getting a handgun (or even more narrowly, a Saturday Night Special) is not likely to regard a knife or club as the best available substitute. Rather, his deadliest, most intimidating alternative, either for defensive purposes or for furthering a crime, is a rifle or shotgun. While these weapons are not as concealable as a handgun, concealability is not important to most gun crimes. For those crimes in which it is important, sawed-off shotguns or rifles generally provide sufficient concealability. Further, since the average handgun used in crime is of fairly good quality and correspondingly expensive, many rifles and shotguns are no more expensive than the handguns, making cost no obstacle to substitution.[33]

Long gun substitution is a very undesirable prospect because rifles and shotguns, depending on caliber or gauge and the ammunition used, can be anywhere from one and one-half to ten times as deadly as handguns.[34] It is unlikely that criminals willing to violate the strongest social and legal prohibitions against violence would conscientiously opt for only the least deadly varieties of long guns and ammunition.[35] Unless this occurred, however, the result of an effective handgun-only measure would be an increase in criminal homicide deaths.

The precise extent of this increase would depend on two paramaters: the fraction of assault-prone people, otherwise inclined to use handguns, who would substitute long guns in their assaults (the substitution reaction), and the ratio of the deadliness of the substituted long guns to the deadliness of handguns which otherwise would have been used in the absence of handgun controls (the deadliness ratio). The higher either parameter is, the more likely it would be that the net effect of the measure would be an increase in the number of homicides. . . .

It is difficult to know for sure what type of long guns and ammunition would be substituted by criminals if handguns were not available, so the magnitude of the deadliness ratio is not certain. An estimate of three or four seems reasonable. That is, the substituted long guns would be about three to four times as likely to produce a death as handguns currently used in assaults. As to the size of the substitition fraction, the best estimate comes from the Wright and Rossi prison survey.[36] Inmates were asked what they would do if they wanted to carry a handgun but could not obtain one. Among those prisoners who reported they had committed crimes with a gun "many times," "most of the time," or "all of the time," 72 percent said that they would carry a sawed-off shotgun or rifle instead.[37] Substitution of long guns in *ownership* would almost certainly be higher, since many people would acquire a long gun as a substitute for owning a handgun, but would not carry it as frequently as they would their handgun. Thus, substitution in carrying might be about 72 percent but substitution in ownership could be anywhere from 72 to 100 percent. . . .

Of course, if handgun-only measures do not remove handguns from violence prone people in the first place, the laws would be useless on that basis, there would be no need for substitution, and this whole issue would be moot. But the point is that even if such measures *were* effective in reducing handgun possession, they would almost certainly have the perverse effect of causing more people to die than would have died without the measure. This analysis has the clearest possible policy implication: Under no circumstances should restrictions be placed on access to handguns (or specific types of handguns such as Saturday Night Specials) without equally severe restrictions on access to long guns.[38]

STATE OR FEDERAL CONTROLS?

Because there are so many state laws regulating firearms, gun control opponents often ask why any federal laws are needed. Gun control supporters reply that state laws are often ineffective because they are easily evaded if bordering states do not have equally restrictive controls. The primary justification for federal controls is the interstate "leakage" of firearms. For example, Newton and Zimring stated that "[s]erious efforts at state and local regulation have consistently been frustrated by the flow of firearms from one state to another."[39] Beyond this problem, supporters of federal gun control rarely mention any other justification for national measures.

One would think, then, that the only kind of federal legislation necessary to supplement state controls would be a statute aimed at stopping the interstate flow of firearms to unqualified buyers. Such persons could not, as a result, travel from their own restrictive states and obtain guns in less restrictive states, and residents of lenient states could not otherwise transfer firearms to unqualified recipients residing in restrictive states. Ideally, the federal legislation would give those states with a need for restrictive gun control measures a fighting chance to make them work.

Yet, many advocates of federal controls go far beyond such measures. In their report to the National Violence Commission, Newton and Zimring recommended a federal restrictive licensing standard amounting to a virtual ban on private ownership of handguns.[40] Rather than simply supplementing state measures and thus making it possible for states effectively to apply whatever gun control measures they regard as necessary, such a far-reaching proposal is a *substitute* for state controls, a way of overriding state legislatures' unwillingness to pass more restrictive laws of their own.

There are several good reasons to reject this approach. First, the concept of federalism implies that the states should have as much autonomy as possible in drafting their criminal law and other statutes. Second, federal controls are less satisfactory because traditionally there has been a very limited federal law enforcement apparatus in the area of ordinary crime. The Federal Bureau of Investigation (FBI) regards itself more as an investigatory than a law enforcement agency. Nothing at the federal level corresponds to a street police force, and local police agencies, where most law enforcement personnel are concentrated, have generally been reluctant to devote their limited resources to the enforcement of federal laws. Third, the need for gun control differs sharply from one state to another. Some states have almost no violent crime, with or without guns, while others have a great deal. For example, in 1981 South Dakota had only twelve murders and nonnegligent manslaughters and 122 robberies (1.8 and 17.8 per 100,000 population, respectively), while Nevada, with only 23 percent more people, had 148 homicides and 3,867 robberies (17.5 and 64.9 per 100,000, respectively).[41]

Nevertheless, the Gun Control Act of 1968 (GCA),[42] the only major federal gun legislation in the last forty-five years, was generally limited simply to reinforcing whatever controls each state has by prohibiting out-of-state purchasing by its residents. Unfortunately, a number of loopholes in the GCA render this attempt to stem the interstate flow of firearms between nondealers ineffective. For example, although the Act made it unlawful for licensed dealers to sell "any firearm to any person who the licensee *knows or has reasonable cause to believe* does not reside in . . . the state in which the licensee's place of business is located,"[43] it did not require dealers to verify a buyer's residence by, for example, demanding a driver's license or similar identification.[44] Although some states require dealers to verify residency, dealers elsewhere can sell guns to persons from more restrictive states as long as they do not know or have reason to believe that the buyer is a resident of another state. The GCA also made it generally unlawful for persons not licensed as dealers to buy guns in one state for transport to, and sale in, another state, but did not provide any effective means for enforcing the provision.[45] Further, the act allows almost any adult to receive a federal firearm dealer's license for a ten dollar annual fee, as long as the applicant claims he is going to conduct business from some premises (which presumably could include his home).[46] As a result, there were 157,655 federally licensed firearms "dealers" by January 1, 1981 but probably fewer than 4,000 Treasury inspections over that year.[47] This situation made it very easy for licensed dealers to purchase legally large numbers of guns in less restrictive states and to transport them into more restrictive jurisdictions, where the less reputable among the "dealers" could sell the guns to buyers who would not qualify for legal gun acquisition in the more restrictive states. The GCA also left unlicensed individuals free to sell their guns privately, rather than requiring them to go through licensed dealers, thereby making it very difficult to check on the validity of such sales. Among other things, it is virtually impossible to hold a private citizen liable for selling firearms even to hardened criminals, because it cannot be proven that the seller knew about the criminals' felony records. Consequently, both criminals and ordinary residents who cannot obtain permits in their own restrictive states can rely on guns from out-of-state sources.[48]

Given that there are probably over 160 million guns now circulating in private hands in the United States,[49] it is unclear to what extent federal restrictions on interstate trade can prevent criminals from obtaining guns. Nevertheless, whatever enforcement potential does exist could be maximized by a few straightforward revisions to the GCA. Licensed dealers could be required to verify buyers' in-state residence by examining drivers' licenses or other suitable identification, as is already done in many states. The federal dealer's license fee could be raised to $500, as proposed in the Kennedy-Rodino bill,[50] thereby reducing the number of people who can legally transfer guns across state borders. In addition, private gun sales could be brought under closer control by a requirement that such transactions occur only through a licensed dealer. Beyond controls on interstate trafficking, controls at the state level are about as likely to succeed in keeping guns from criminal users as are federal restrictions.

SUMMARY OF THE POLICY LESSONS

A careful reading of recent gun control research suggests the following tentative conclusions for public policy:

(1) Gun control laws should be aimed at restricting gun possession among persons with prior record of violence rather than among the general public. Otherwise, loss of the deterrent effect on crime exerted by widespread civilian gun ownership could outweigh the benefit of a slight reduction in gun possession among the violence prone.

(2) Gun control restrictions should be applied equally to all types of firearms, not just to handguns or "Saturday Night Specials." An inclusive approach would avoid inadvertently encouraging the substitution of deadlier weapons, a distinct possibility not precluded by marginal differences in concealability between the gun types.

(3) Beyond amending the Gun Control Act of 1968 to make evasion of state gun control laws more difficult, further legislation at the federal level is unnecessary, given the greatly varying need for gun control among the states.

(4) Unless the priority criminal justice system personnel assign to enforcing gun laws changes, any additional enactments must depend primarily on voluntary compliance for their effectiveness. It is doubtful

whether additional resources would be made available for enforcement of gun laws, unless the revenues were somehow specifically attached to specialized gun law enforcement agencies.

(5) Gun control measures must deal with the fact that criminals obtain their guns primarily through private, quasi-legal transfers from private parties such as friends or acquaintances "on the street," rather than from licensed dealers, black-market enterprises, or through theft. Such transfers might be minimized by establishing civil liability for damages resulting from an illegal gun transfer to an ineligible recipient. Transfers of firearms would be channeled through dealers who would be required to examine certain legal documents (driver's license, purchase permit, owner's license) to establish that the recipient was eligible. Persons who transferred guns in any other manner would be liable for damages caused with the gun by any ineligible recipient to whom they transferred the gun.

What sort of gun control measures do these lessons imply? They suggest a moderate measure with many features already enacted in one form or another in many states, although not yet in a single integrated package. What is called for is a law establishing a well-enforced state-level permit-to-purchase or license-to-possess requirement applicable to all types of firearms. The law would forbid possession or acquisition of any firearm by persons with a criminal conviction for a felony or violent misdemeanor in the past seven years or psychiatric institutionalization for a violent act during that period, and by fugitives from justice. A check of whatever criminal and psychiatric records were available would have to be completed before any permit or license could be issued. Persons under the age of eighteen would be forbidden from acquiring firearms or ammunition except from members of their immediate family for use while under adult supervision. Individuals who illegally transferred a gun to a person ineligible for firearms acquisition or possession would be subject to civil liability for damages caused with that gun by the ineligibile recipient.

This set of provisions would not prevent law-abiding citizens from obtaining any type of firearm currently available and would add only slight inconvenience to such acquisitions, which are very infrequent transactions for all but a few citizens. The cost of screening applicants for a license or permit would not be great. For example, Cook and Blose[51] report that a record check for prior convictions or psychiatric institutionalization costs only $1.90 in Illinois, where a completely automated system is already in use. In combination with a tightened-up federal Gun Control Act and improved computer criminal record files, these sorts of state screening systems at least hold the potential for producing modest reductions in gun possession among violence prone persons who are only marginally motivated to acquire guns. It is unlikely that much more than this can be done to reduce violence through gun control laws.

Thinking seriously about violence reduction requires going beyond what currently seems politically easy or "realistic." Orthodox crime control programs devised within the framework of traditional political realities have been failures and similar proposals for the future show no prospects of doing any better. Policies aimed at increasing or redistributing police manpower, imposing long prison sentences, increasing the incapacitative impact of the prison system, reducing due process restraints on police and prosecutors, and generally spending more on criminal justice are all acceptable to most political elites, enjoy widespread public support[52]—and are doomed to failure as a means for producing significant reductions in serious crime.[53] The same seems to be true of gun control laws, although the evidence on this issue is not as strong.[54]

To accomplish a significant reduction in violence will require a return to serious consideration of the fundamental social and economic causes of violent behavior, a course which criminologists have repeatedly advocated for decades. This approach has been derided by some as a search for causes which public policy cannot directly affect.[55] Nothing could be further from the truth. For example, research on domestic violence, surely one of those types of crimes assumed to be incapable of control, through public policy, shows that it is strongly related to family economic conditions. The best study of this subject used interviews with a representative national sample of households and found that "unemployed men are twice as likely to use severe violence on their wives as are men employed full time, and men employed part time have a rate of wife-beating three times the rate of full-time employed men."[56] Given that unemployment is strongly related to violent behavior and that reducing unemployment is a well-established goal of public policy, it is ridiculous to suggest that we must rely on gun control laws, or indeed any strategies using criminal law or the criminal justice system, to reduce violence. While it may logically make sense to use a variety of methods to deal with the problem, the political realities are such that attention paid and resources devoted to one strategy tend to divert attention and resources away from other, possibly more productive, strategies. More expensive alternatives will never be given serious consideration as long as policymakers and the general public continue to believe in the efficiency of the crimnial justice approach.

Nor is it valid to say that gun control and other criminal-justice-system-oriented strategies are the only currently available ways to deal effectively with crime in the short term. Strategies directed at reducing unemployment, poverty, and inequality have every bit as much potential for producing short-term results as criminal justice system strategies. Producing short-term decreases in poverty and unemployment is difficult, not impossible. For instance, recent sophisticated evaluation of the Job Corps, a federal program aimed at the "hard-core" poor, shows that males who completed the program not only were receiving an average of $23.24 more per week during the follow-up period than matched nonparticipants, but also experienced eight fewer arrests per 100 Corpsmembers than the control group.[57] Given the minimal investment in programs of this sort, it is surprising that they achieve any success at all,[58] but they can in fact produce significant results in a short period of time. Therefore, a more promising strategy for reducing violence and crime would be one aimed at reducing the entry of underclass adolescents into criminal careers by:

(1) the creation of jobs for which adolescent and young adult members of the underclass can be trained, and

(2) training the target group for those jobs.

Massive numbers of jobs can be created through federally funded construction projects aimed at a much-needed rebuilding of our nation's infrastructure, especially its crumbling highways, bridges, railroads, and urban transit systems. The Job Corps provides a model for the training component of the program. Sufficient resources are available for the program, without tax increases, through reallocation of federal tax money from the bloated defense budget.

Job creation aimed at the underclass has not been attempted on even a modest social scale. The few small efforts in this regard have been moderate successes, despite the aura of failure generated by hostile publicity. Acknowledging the drastic limitations of criminal justice crime control alternatives must be the first step toward making crime control through underclass job creation a respectable part of the mainstream political agenda.

NOTES

1. Bruce-Briggs, "The Great American Gun War," *Public Interest* 45 (1976): 37.

2. G. Newton and F. Zimring, *Firearms and Violence in American Life* (1969) (staff report to the National Commission on the Causes and Prevention of Violence).

3. See e.g., Kleck and Bordua, "The Factual Foundation for Certain Key Assumptions of Gun Control," *Law and Policy Quarterly* 5 (1983): 271.

4. Ibid., pp. 274–78.

5. Cook, "Reducing Injury and Death Rates in Robbery Policy," *Policy Analysis* 6 (1980): 21, 33.

6. See e.g., J. Conklin, *Robbery and the Criminal Justice System* (New York: Harper & Row, 1972), p. 117; *The Prevention and Control of Robbery,* ed. F. Feeney and A. Weir (1973), p. 77; A. Normandeau, "Trends and Patterns in Crimes of Robbery" (1968) (unpublished Ph.D. dissertation, available at University of Pennsylvania), p. 201.

7. Cook, "The Role of Firearms in Violent Crime," in *Criminal Violence,* ed. M. Wolfgang and N. Weiner (Beverly Hills, Calif.: Sage, 1982), pp. 255–57.

8. Cook, "The Effect of Gun Availability on Robbery and Robbery Murder," *Policy Studies Review Annual* 3 (1979): 743.

9. Cook, "A Strategic Choice Analysis of Robbery," in *Sample Surveys of the Victims of Crime,* ed. W. Skogen (Cambridge, Mass.: Ballinger, 1976) pp. 173, 186 (hereinafter cited as *Sample Surveys*); Cook, *supra* note 5, p. 42.

10. Cook, "A Strategic Choice Analasis of Robbery," in *Sample Surveys, supra* note 9, p. 181; Cook, note 5, p. 43.

11. Newton and Zimring, *supra* note 2, p. 48.

12. Hardy and Stompoly, "Of Arms and the Law," *Chicago-Kent Law Review* 51 (1974): 62, 104.

13. See Kleck and Bordau, *supra* note 3, pp. 272–74.

14. Zimring, "Is Gun Control Likely to Reduce Violent Killings?" *Chicago-Kent Law Review* 35 (1968), p. 721.

15. Ibid. p. 727.

16. See, e.g., Federal Bureau of Investigation, 1980 *Uniform Crime Reports, Crime in the United States* (1981), p. 178 [hereinafter cited as UCR (date) (the FBI has published a number of these reports; the specific publication will be identified by the year of coverage)].

17. These studies are reviewed in Kleck, "The Relationship Between Gun Ownership Levels and Rates of Violence in the United States," in *Firearms and Violence: Issues of Public Policy* (ed. D. Kates, 1984), p. 99 [hereinafter cited as *Firearms and Violence*].

18. Kleck, "Capital Punishment, Gun Ownership, and Homicide," *American Journal of Sociology* 84 (1979): 882; Kleck, *supra* note 17.

19. Kleck, *supra* note 17, pp. 121–22, 131; Kleck, *supra* note 18, pp. 883–84.

20. According to the national victimization survey for 1980, 26.9 percent of rapes involved armed offenders, and 34.1 percent of the attackers used a firearm. U.S. Bureau of Justice Statistics, *Criminal Victimization in the United States* 1982 (1984), pp. 60–61. [.269 x .341 = .09 or nine percent.]

21. G. Newton and F. Zimring, *supra* note 2, p. 62.

22. Vera Institute of Justice, *Felony Arrests* (rev. ed. 1981), p. 115.

23. A. Bandura, *Aggression: A Social Learning Analysis* (P-H Social Learning Series, 1973), p. 180.

24. Kleck and Bordua, *supra* note 3, p. 293.

25. See generally M. Strauss, R. Gelles, and S. Steinmetz, *Behind Closed Doors: Violence in the American Family* (New York: Doubleday, 1980).

26. See generally M. Dietz, *Killing for Profit: The Social Organization of Felony Homicide* (Chicago, Ill: Nelson Hall, 1983).

27. J. Wright and P. Rossi, Codebook for Prison Survey (1983) (marginals for question 114) (unpublished) (this author's computations regarding prisoners in states with various gun laws).

28. Ibid. (marginals for question 89).

29. Cook and Blose, "State Programs for Screening Handgun Buyers," *Annals*, No. 455 (1981): 80.

30. Brown, "Mental Patients as Victimizers and Victims," in *Deviants: Victims or Victimizers?* ed. McNamara and A. Karmen (Beverly Hills, Calif.: Sage, 1983), 1: 199–208.

31. Steadman, Vanderwyst, and Ribner, "Comparing Arrest Rates of Mental Patients and Criminal Offenders," *American Journal of Psychiatry* 135 (1978): 1218–20.

32. See Cook and Blose, *supra* note 29, pp. 878–89 (discussing the feasibility and cost of such systems).

33. Kleck, "Handgun-Only Gun Control: A Policy Disaster in the Making," in *Firearms and Violence, supra* note 17, pp. 167, 187, 192.

34. Ibid., p. 174.

35. The same general point also applies to impulsive domestic homicides among supposedly "law-abiding" citizens. If the guns involved in such attacks are originally obtained from home- and self-defense, it is unlikely that the long guns substituted for handguns would be the less deadly types. Many of the same qualities which make some types of guns desirable as offensive weapons also make them desirable as defensive ones.

36. J. Wright and P. Rossi, *supra* note 27.

37. Telephone conversation with James Wright (July 26, 1983).

38. The same general argument applies to measures aimed at the cheap small-caliber handguns known as "Saturday Night Specials," since such measures encourage substitution of large-caliber, better quality, and therefore deadlier, handguns. There is even less difference in concealability and ease of carrying between Saturday Night Specials and other handguns, however, than there is between handguns and sawed-off long guns, thus allowing substitution in an even higher percentage of assault situations.

39. Newton and Zimring, *supra* note 2, p. 95.

40. Ibid. pp. 143–44.

41. UCR (1982), *supra* note 16, pp. 51, 55.

42. Pub. L. No. 90–618, 82 Stat. 1213 (1968) (codified at 18 U.S.C. §§ 921–928, 26 U.S.C. §§ 5801–5802, 5811–5812, 5821–5822, 5841–5849, 5851–5854, 5871–5872, 6806, 7273 (1982).

43. 18 U.S.C. § 922(b)(3) (1982) (emphasis added).

44. S. Brill, *Firearm Abuse: A Research and Policy Report* (1977), p. 176.

45. 18 U.S.C. § 922(a) (1982).

46. 18 U.S.C. § 923(a)(3)(C), (d)(1) (1982).

47. See P. Shields, *Guns Don't Die—People Do* (New York: Arbor House, 1981), p. 182.

48. See S. Brill, *supra* note 41, pp. 82–93.

49. Kleck, *supra* note 17, p. 127.

50. Handgun Crime Control Act of 1979, H.R. 7148, 96th Congress, First Session (1979).

51. Cook and Blose, *supra* note 29, p. 89.

52. U.S. Bureau of Justice Statistics, *supra* note 20, pp. 220–78.

53. See S. Walker, *Sense and Nonsense About Crime: A Policy Guide* (Pacific Grove, Calif.: Brookes-Cole, 1985), for a wide-ranging debunking of such strategies.

54. J. Wright, P. Rossi, and K. Daly, *Under the Gun: Weapons, Crime, and Violence in America* (New York: Aldine de Gruyter, 1983), pp. 308, 317.

55. E.g., J. Wilson, *Thinking About Crime* (New York: Random House, 1983), pp. 42–57.

56. M. Strauss, R. Gelles, and S. Steinmetz, *supra* note 25, p. 150.

57. J. Thompson, M. Suiridoff, and J. McElroy, *Employment and Crime: A Review of Theories and Research* (1981), pp. 176–83.

58. For example, even in 1972 when it was still funded at a relatively high level, the Job Corps program claimed only $202 million, or 0.09 percent, of the federal budget. That figure represented only 1.7 percent of spending on criminal justice at all levels of government. Indeed, the combined budgets of all federal work and training programs, most of them primarily benefiting middle class persons, claimed funds equalling less than one quarter of total criminal justice spending. *U.S. Bureau of the Census, Statistical Abstract of the United States* 1976, pp. 144, 160.

10

On the Needle-in-the-Haystack and the Deadly Long Gun

Franklin E. Zimring and Gordon Hawkins

The needle-in-the-haystack argument is designed to minimize the potential of gun regulation to reduce firearm-related violence. It is argued that a general reduction in firearms availability would be unlikely to be accompanied by a reduction in the availability of firearms to criminals. This is because it is said that something in excess of 99 percent of all privately owned firearms are never involved in any sort of criminal act, and it is likely that the criminally abused 1 percent would be the last guns to be touched by any sort of restrictive weapons policy.

As Don B. Kates, Jr., has put it in *Firearms and Violence: Issues of Public Policy*:

> The conclusion that gun laws cannot dramatically reduce crime necessarily follows from the [finding] . . . that the vast majority of gun owners are responsible adults who neither misuse nor want to misuse their guns. . . . Even in a very violent society the number of potential misusers is so small that the number

of firearms legally or illegally available to its members will always be ample for their needs regardless of how restrictive gun laws are or how strenuously they are enforced.

Currently there are well over 100 million guns in private hands and some 1 million gun incidents in any given year. Thus, the guns now owned exceed the annual incident count by a factor of over 100. The significance of these figures, according to Wright, Rossi, and Daly, is that the existing stock of guns now in private hands is "adequate to supply all conceivable criminal purposes for at least the entire next century, even if the worldwide manufacture of new guns were halted today and if each presently owned firearm were used criminally once and only once."

In these circumstances it is said that even if a national program of firearms confiscation were embarked on, it would involve confiscating at least 100 guns to get one that in any given year would otherwise have been involved in some sort of firearms incident, and several thousand to get one that in any given year would otherwise have been used to bring about someone's death. Moreover, these estimates are based on the totally unrealistic assumption that criminals would turn in their guns like law-abiding gun owners.

There is some dispute about the extent of the criminal misuse of handguns that is the crux of this argument. Wright, Rossi, and Daly say "it may be taken as *self-evident* that something in excess of 99 percent of all privately-owned firearms are never involved in any sort of criminal act," although they do not see why this assertion should be regarded as evident without need of proof or explanation.

Don B. Kates, Jr., makes this claim look like a gross underestimate. He claims that

> the ratio of handgun criminals to handguns is perhaps 1 to 600 (and of handgun murderers to handguns 1 to 5,400) . . . Thus making the over-optimistic assumption that a complete handgun ban would result in a 90 percent diminution through surrender and confiscation, there would still be 60 handguns left for every handgun criminal and 540 for every murderer.

On the basis of his figures, the existing stock of guns would be adequate for all criminal purposes not merely for a century but for something approaching a millennium.

In short, it is said that the number of firearms presently available in the United States is so great that the time to do anything about them has long since passed. Given the number of privately owned guns already present on the scene, even if some reduction in the general availability of firearms to the private market were achieved, it would have a minimal effect on the availability of firearms to persons wishing to arm themselves for criminal or illicit purposes.

Three points should be made about the statistics employed and the inferences that are drawn from them in the argument. First, the interpretations made are both inconsistent and wrong. For example, the estimates of the extent of criminal misuse of guns cited above are arrived at by dividing an estimate of the total handgun stock by an estimate of the number of criminal incidents occurring *in one year*. Thus, Don B. Kates, Jr., explains that his ratio of handgun murders to handguns "is obtained by dividing the estimated number of handguns (54 million) by 10,000 which, plus or minus, is the figure at which handgun homicide has stood *annually* over the past five years" [emphasis added].

It is thus simply not true that 99 percent of all guns are never involved in crime. Instead, fewer than 1 percent of all guns are involved in criminal misuse *in any given year*, just as less than 1 percent of the American population dies of heart disease in a single year. But that does not make either heart disease or gun-related crimes a small problem cumulatively.

The *career* risk of guns being misused is very much greater. The available evidence suggests that probably more than 10 percent of all handguns are used in crime or serious violence, usually within a decade of first sale. This does not apply to long guns, a much smaller fraction of which are so used.

There is also ample evidence to indicate that the existing stock of civilian guns is nowhere near a century's supply for criminal users. Only by ignoring existing data on the firearms used in crime and also assuming that guns owned by anyone are freely available to all who would misuse them can the extravagant claims about "a century's supply" be given any semblance of a conceptual foundation.

Nevertheless, although the conclusions drawn from statistics on civilian ownership in this argument are fantastic, it is true that any balanced view of the potential of different gun control options must start with data on current ownership and use of guns and how these patterns might be affected by various policy options. Detailed knowledge of gun ownership, the determinants of availability to potential gun misusers, and the effect of controls on gun availability in the middle and long run are vital in assessing the prospects of different proposals for reducing gun violence.

The fallacy involved in the needle-in-the-haystack argument is the assumption that the available information on existing gun ownership and gun uses in crime provides an adequate springboard for an inferential leap to a general conclusion. In fact, it can serve as no more than a starting point for analysis. The attempt to use that information as a basis for sweeping policy appraisals involves a substantial misapprehension of the nature of the problem of devising effective gun control mechanisms.

Another argument that is designed to minimize the potential of gun controls to reduce crime relates to gun control proposals that are focused specifically on the handgun. It is acknowledged that currently the great majority of such crimes are committed with handguns. But it is suggested that a reduction in the availability of handguns could mean that in their absence much of the crime now committed with handguns would be committed with shoulder weapons, which are much more lethal.

Wright, Rossi, and Daly have this to say:

> We would do well to remember that there are already some three or four times more shoulder weapons than handguns in circulation in the United States, and that, on the average, they are much deadlier than handguns. If someone intends to open fire on the authors of this study, our *strong* preference is that they open fire with a handgun. . . . The possibility that even a fraction of the predators who now walk the streets armed with handguns would, in the face of a handgun ban, prowl with sawed-off shotguns instead, causes one to tremble. It can be taken as given that some people will continue shooting at one another as long as there are *any* guns around. This being the case, we have to muster the courage to ask whether we wouldn't be just as happy if they shot at one another with handguns [authors' emphasis].

Although there are other questions the authors might have mustered the courage to ask, or at least raise, they fail to do so. It is notable that they present no data on the death rate from various types of assault with shoulder weapons or sawed-off shotguns. Nor do they present any data on the degree to which rifles and shotguns would or do displace scarce handguns in the United States or any other nation.

Another critic of handgun controls who does not allow the absence of evidence to inhibit him unduly is Professor Gary Kleck, who argues in *Firearms and Violence: Issues of Public Policy* (1984) that if severe limits were imposed on the legal ownership of handguns, then the restricted availability of handguns could result in a higher death rate from attacks if more deadly weapons like rifles and shotguns were substituted.

On the question of displacement or substitution, he asserts that "long guns are eminently substitutable for handguns in virtually all felony killing situations." He treats *a guess* in the literature that the displacement to long guns *would be no more than* one-third as the equivalent of *a finding* that it *would be* a third. With regard to differential deadlines he says that "it would be pointless to compare actual observed assault fatality rates of handguns and long guns in order to determine relative deadliness, even if adequate data were available for such an effort, since the fatality rates are not just the result of the deadliness of the weapons themselves."

In place of deadliness he employs the concept of the relative "stopping power" of guns. Although this appears to represent an ackowledgement of instrumentality effects by one of their critics, the superiority of "stopping power" over the actual death rate is difficult to discern. Indeed, when it is applied to what is known about death rates it yields quite preposterous conclusions.

Thus, the use of this method results in estimates that some guns, such as the 12-gauge shotgun with double-ought cartridges, would produce fatalities in head and chest wounds about 18 times as often as .22-caliber rifles. But the death rate from .22-caliber, single wound attacks with a head or chest injury has been found to be 16 percent. Multiplying this death rate by 18 (the difference in relative "stopping power") produces an estimated death rate of 288 percent for single-wound attacks with 12-gauge shotguns that result in head or chest wounds, or approximately three deaths for every individual attacked! The death rate from multiple-wound .22-caliber attacks has been found to be 28 percent. Multiplying this estimate by 18 produces an estimated death rate for shotgun attacks of 504 percent, or five deaths for every individual attacked!

A critique that involves a comparison of the deadliness of different guns but studiously neglects to consider the use of those guns in actual attacks, and entails death rate estimates of three per wounding, tells us nothing about the potential effectivness of handgun controls. But its bizarre character demonstrates that in regard to this topic, even on the scholarly level, partisanship can engender strange aberrations. It must require a potent combination of wishful thinking, reciprocal noncriticism by peers, and absence of self-examination for this kind of catastrophic error to march into the public debate on guns and gun control.

REFERENCES

Cook, Philip J. "Guns and Crime: The Peril of Long Division," *Journal of Policy Analysis and Management* 81 (1981):120–25.
Kates, Don B., Jr., ed. *Firearms and Violence: Issues of Public Policy.* Cambridge, Mass.: Ballinger, 1984.
Wright, James D., Peter H. Rossi, and Kathleen Daly. *Under the Gun: Weapons, Crime, and Violence in America.* New York: Aldine, 1983.
Zimring, Franklin E. "The Medium Is the Message: Firearms Caliber as a Determinant of Death from Assault," *Journal of Legal Studies* 1 (1972):97–123.

11 •

Firearms and Assault: "Guns Don't Kill People, People Kill People"

Franklin E. Zimring and Gordon Hawkins

One of the major arguments against the theory that gun control would save life is that although two-thirds of all homicides are committed with firearms, firearms controls could have no effect on homicide rates because, "human nature being what it is," homicide would continue unabated. Murderers would use the next most convenient weapon. Only the weapons used would change. If guns were eliminated from the scene, more knives, clubs, axes, pieces of pipe, blocks of wood, brass knuckles, or, for that matter, fists would be used. "Guns don't kill people, people kill people."

The classic statement of this argument may be found in Professor Marvin Wolfgang's *Patterns in Criminal Homicide* (1958):

> More than the availability of a shooting weapon is involved in homicide. Pistols and revolvers are not difficult to purchase. . . . The type of weapon used appears

to be, in part, the culmination of assault intentions or events and is only superficially related to causality. To measure quantitatively the effect of the presence of firearms on the homicide rate would require knowing the number and type of homicides that would not have occurred had not the offender—or, in some cases, the victim—possessed a gun. . . . It is the contention of this observer that few homicides due to shootings could be avoided merely if a firearm were not immediately present, and that the offender would select some other weapon to achieve the same destructive goal. Probably only in those cases where a felon kills a police officer, or vice versa, would homicide be avoided in the absence of a firearm.

A more recent statement of this position can be found in Wright, Rossi, and Daly's *Under the Gun* (1983):

Even if we were somehow able to remove all firearms from civilian possession, it is not at all clear that a substantial reduction in interpersonal violence would follow. Certainly the violence that results from hard-core and predatory criminality would not abate by very much. Even the most ardent proponents of stricter gun laws no longer expect such laws to solve the hard-core crime problem, or even to make much of a dent in it. There is also reason to doubt whether the "soft-core" violence, the so-called crimes of passion, would decline by very much. Stated simply, these crimes occur because some people have come to hate others, and they will continue to occur in one form or another as long as hatred persists . . . if we could solve the problem of interpersonal hatred, it may not matter very much what we did about guns, and *unless* we solve the problem of interpersonal hatred, it may not matter very much what we do about guns. There are simply too many other objects in the world that can serve the purpose of inflicting harm on another human being . . . although it is true that under current conditions the large majority of gun crimes are committed with handguns (on the order, perhaps, of 70–75 percent of them), it definitely does *not* follow that, in the complete absence of handguns, crimes now committted with handguns would not be committed! The more plausible expectation is that they would be committed with other weaponry.

The most forcible statements of the opposing viewpoint may be found in the National Commission on the Causes and Prevention of Violence Task Force Report on Firearms and Violence and two Chicago studies of fatal and nonfatal assaults. It is pointed out that although other weapons are involved in homicide, firearms are not only the most deadly instrument of attack but also the most versatile. Firearms make some attacks possible that simply would not occur without firearms. They permit attacks at greater range and from positions of better concealment than other weapons. They also permit attacks by persons physically or psychologically unable to overpower their victim through violent physical contact. It is because of their capacity to kill instantly and from a distance that firearms are virtually the only weapon used in killing police officers.

TABLE 1

PERCENTAGE OF REPORTED GUN AND KNIFE ATTACKS
RESULTING IN DEATH (CHICAGO, 1965–67)

WEAPONS	DEATH AS PERCENTAGE OF ATTACKS
Knives (16,518 total attacks)	2.4
Guns (6,350 total attacks)	12.2

SOURCE: *Firearms and Violence in American Life* (1969), Table 7-2, p. 41.

In addition to providing greater range for the attacker, it is argued, firearms are more deadly than other weapons. The fatality rate of firearms attacks, the Task Force Report noted, was about five times higher than the fatality rate of attacks with knives, the next most dangerous weapon used in homicide. The illustrative data cited are shown in table 1.

The studies also reveal that there was a substantial overlap in the circumstances involved in fatal and nonfatal assaults with guns and those committed with knives. Four out of five homicides occurred as a result of altercations over such matters as love, money, and domestic problems, and 71 percent involved acquaintances, neighbors, lovers, and family members. In short, the circumstances in which most homicides were committed suggested that they were committed in a moment of rage and were not the result of a single-minded intent to kill. Planned murders involving a single-minded intent, such as gangland killings, were a spectacular but infrequent exception.

Not only did the circumstances of homicide and the relationship of victim and attacker suggest that most homicides did not involve a single-minded determination to kill, but also the choice of a gun did not appear to indicate such intent. The similarity of circumstances in which knives and guns were used suggested that the motive for an attack did not determine the weapon used. Figures obtained from the Chicago Police Department showed the similar circumstances of firearms and knife homicides as shown in table 2.

Further evidence that those who used a gun were no more intent on killing than those who used knives was found in comparing the wound locations and the number of wounds as between those assaults committed with knives and those committed with guns. It was found that a greater percentage of knife attacks than gun attacks resulted in wounds to vital areas of the body—such as the head, neck, chest, abdomen, and back—where wounds were likely to be fatal. Also, many more knife attacks than gun attacks resulted in multiple wounds, suggesting that those who used the knife in those attacks had no great desire to spare the victim's life. Nevertheless, even when the comparison was controlled for the number of wounds and the body location

TABLE 2

CIRCUMSTANCE OF HOMICIDE, BY WEAPON (CHICAGO, 1967)

	GUN (PERCENT)	KNIFE (PERCENT)
Altercations:		
General domestic	21	25
Money	6	7
Liquor	2	8
Sex	1	3
Gambling	2	1
Triangle	5	5
Theft (alleged)	—	—
Children	2	1
Other	41	30
Armed robbery	9	9
Perversion and assault on female	2	7
Gangland	1	—
Other	2	—
Undetermined	6	4
Total	100	100
Number of cases*	265	152

*Another 93 homicides were committed with other weapons.
SOURCE: *Firearms and Violence in American Life* (1969), Table 7-5, p. 43.

of the most serious wound, gun assaults were far more likely to lead to death than knife assaults.

Even so, it might be contended that if gun murderers were deprived of guns they would find a way to kill as often with knives. If this were so, knife attacks in cities where guns were widely used in homicide would be expected to show a low fatality rate, and knife attacks in cities where guns were not so widely used would show a higher fatality rate. But analyses of cities for which the pertinent data were available revealed no such relationship. It appeared that as the number of knife attacks increased in relation to the number of firearms attacks (which presumably happened where guns were less available to assailants), the proportion of knife attacks that were fatal did *not* increase relative to that proportion among gun attacks; if anything, the reverse was the case.

The conclusion that weapon dangerousness independent of any other factors had a substantial impact on the death rate from attack, which has been called the "instrumentality hypothesis," was supported by another study of violent assault in Chicago, which compared low-caliber with high-caliber firearms attacks. This study found that attacks with large-caliber firearms were far more likely to cause death than attacks by small-caliber guns that resulted in the same number of wounds to the same parts of the body.

The authors of *Under the Gun,* cited above, have disputed the conclusions drawn from the evidence presented in the Chicago studies. They dismiss the circumstantial evidence such as the motives of homicide and the frequent involvement of alcohol in killings as inconclusive on whether attacks that cause death are often ambiguously motivated. The similar demographic profiles of fatal and nonfatal attacks are not regarded as evidence that the two groups "are similar in any respect relevant to hypotheses about underlying motivations." The same conclusion apparently was applied to the similarities between victim groups.

The authors never address the possibility that chance elements determine a subsample of fatalities from the universe of those assaulted. The crucial fact that most gun killings, like most nonfatal assaults, involve only one wound is rejected as evidence against a single-minded intent to kill in favor of the conclusion that what distinguishes the hundreds of one-shot killings from thousands of one-shot nonfatal woundings in the same body location by the same sort of people is "a level of marksmanship that one would probably not expect under conditions of outrage and duress." This conclusion is reached without any evidence from the extensive literature on criminal violence.

Indeed, the only evidence offered in support of this hypothesis is drawn from the experience of one of the authors in preparing deer carcasses for home freezers. The relevance of this experience to shooting people in a homicidal situation is explained as follows:

> He is yet to encounter, over a sample of some 15–20 taken deer, even a single deer that was taken with one and only one shot . . . [this] suggests that capable marksmen, armed with highly accurate and efficient weaponry, aiming unambiguously to kill roughly man-sized targets, are seldom able to kill their prey with a single shot. That a much higher proportion of murderers, armed with much less impressive weaponry, kill with a single shot might therefore cause us to wonder just how ambiguous the underlying motives are.

The authors do not consider the possibility that some of the marksmen, even if armed with less accurate and efficient weaponry, might not do better if they could maneuver a few of their deer into the living room. Nor do they consider the alternative hypothesis that many killers are randomly drawn from the larger pool of one-shot assaulters, or discuss why "determined" killers will often stop after one wounding when most guns have a multiple wounding capacity.

It is also curious that the sharp differences in death rates for large-caliber versus small-caliber gun assaults are not considered to be evidence that the objective dangerousness of a weapon has a significant influence on the death rate from assault. The authors briefly examine this data, and they caution that this pattern could also be explained if more determined killers chose larger-caliber guns. The evidence from the weapon caliber study that the pattern holds true even when the attacker probably did not choose the weapon is ignored.

CONCLUSION

The issue of instrumentality effects from guns in deadly assaults is important in its own right. It is also an instructive example of the practical and philosophical differences between the ideological forces in conflict about gun control. This dispute about instrumentality effects is not so much about the nature of the evidence available but about what that evidence means and how great the burden of proof should be.

The parable of the butchered deer carcass mentioned above seems the closest Wright and his colleagues can come to a personal background in research on criminal violence. Instead of grounding their discussion in a coherent vision of violent assault, they put forward rival hypotheses to each strand of circumstantial evidence individually, conclude that none is strict proof of instrumentality effects by itself, and assume that the cumulative impact of multiple strands of evidence is no more persuasive than any of the individual strands.

When the time came to recommend future research, the authors were prisoners of their own standards. In their report to the federal government, no further investigation of these critical issues was proposed. In their book, the authors leave the impression that nothing is known on the question of what difference guns make and nothing can be done to increase knowledge. The tone, and the level of denial, remind one of the Tobacco Institute's valiant struggle against premature conclusions on the relationship between cigarettes and lung cancer.

It should also be said that the assertion that "unless we solve the problem of interpersonal hatred it may not matter very much what we do about guns" is a nice example of the "root causes" fallacy. The essence of this argument is that if crime control measures are to be effective, they must deal with the "root causes" of crime——in this case "interpersonal hatred." Even the most effective regime of gun control would not totally eliminate homicide and on this argument could be criticized for not having dealt with the "root cause" of the problem.

REFERENCES

Newton, George D., Jr., and Franklin E. Zimring. *Firearms and Violence in American Life: A Staff Report Submitted to the National Commission on the Causes and Prevention of Violence.* Washington D.C.: National Commission on the Causes and Prevention of Violence, 1969.

Wolfgang, Marvin. *Patterns in Criminal Homicide.* Philadelphia: University of Pennsylvania Press, 1958.

Wright, James D., Peter H. Rossi, and Kathleen Daly. *Under the Gun: Weapons, Crime, and Violence in America.* New York: Aldine, 1983.

Zimring, Franklin E. "Is Gun Control Likely to Reduce Violent Killings?" *University of Chicago Law Review* 35 (1968):721–37.

———. "The Medium Is the Message: Firearms Caliber as a Determinant of the Death Rate from Assault," *Journal of Legal Studies* 1 (1972):97–123.

12

Handguns in the Twenty-First Century

Franklin E. Zimring

What types of public policy toward handgun ownership and use are likely in the United States of 2010? What are some of the probable consequences of these policies in the United States on our children's adulthood, and what kinds of changes can we anticipate during the transition from present circumstances to particular policy futures? No one of my acquaintance possesses a crystal ball sufficiently unclouded to provide clear answers to such questions, yet using the long-range future as a frame of reference can impose a useful discipline on current debates about firearms control. In the first place, thinking about the future requires more sustained analysis of historical trends than one usually encounters in contemporary discussion of firearms control in America. Quite simply, addressing the issue of where we are going over the course of the next few decades suggests an examination of where we have come from of at least equal length.

The second advantage of "futuristic" examination of handgun policy is that it requires the analyst to coordinate projections of public policy toward handguns with other social, technical, structural, and governmental trends that

Reprinted from *The Annals* of the American Academy of Political and Social Science, No. 455 (May 1981): 1-10. Copyright © 1981. Reprinted by permission of the author and publisher.

will shape the United States 30 years from now. A projected handgun policy must either fit with other anticipated future developments or create a form of intellectual friction in which handgun policy elements or other anticipated future conditions must be reexamined.

This essay sketches two alternative national handgun futures. The first, "historically" derived, is a complex amalgam of federal, state, and local regulations characterized by federal minimum standards of accountability and eligibility for purchase and by wide variation among states and localities in imposing supplemental restrictions on possession and sale of handguns. The second, designed to "fit" with other anticipated future developments, projects much more restrictive federal control on eligibility for handgun ownership. The first section discusses the major elements of the historically derived national handgun policy. The second section sketches a more restrictive federal handgun policy that would be implemented to fit more closely with anticipated social conditions 30 years from now. The third section discusses a few of the more important midterm trends that will determine which of these alternative futures will emerge.

CONTINUING PRESENT TRENDS

If history is an appropriate guide, the next 30 years will bring a national handgun strategy composed of three parts: (1) federally mandated or administered restrictions on handgun transfers that amount to permissive licensing and registration;[1] (2) wide variation in state and municipal handgun possession and transfer regulation, with an increasing number of municipal governments adopting restrictive licensing schemes or "bans" on handgun ownership; and (3) increasing federal law enforcement assistance to states, and more particularly, to cities attempting to enforce more restrictive regimes than the federal minimum. Under such a scheme, federal law will neither set quotas on the number of handguns introduced into civilian markets nor dictate ownership policy to the states. Rather, designated high-risk groups, such as minors, convicted felons, and former mental patients, will be excluded from ownership, as is presently the case.

The two major changes in federal law I anticipate are, first, a registration scheme that will link individual handguns to first owners in a central data bank and will require prior notification before handguns are transferred[2] and second, a federal law prohibiting firearms transfers where the possession of a handgun by the transferee would violate the laws of the municipality in which he resides—current federal protection of this kind is only available if a state law would be violated.[3] Centrally stored ownership data would permit federal law to extend to transfers made by nondealers, and regulations requiring timely prior notice of private transfers through dealers or local officials would be added to existing regulations.[4]

The changes in federal law outlined in the preceding paragraphs would facilitate minimal municipal standards for residents acquiring handguns that could not be frustrated by more lenient state government standards. This new power, and a climate favorable to handgun regulations in the big cities, would produce a much larger list of metropolitan or city governments attempting to impose restrictive licensing or bans on civilian ownership among their populations. Presently existing systems in cities such as New York, Boston, Philadelphia, and Washington, D.C. would be emulated in cities such as San Francisco, Los Angeles, Chicago, and Detroit and in most nonsouthern metropolitan areas. Within the South, municipal or metropolitan governments in areas like Miami and Atlanta might follow suit.

All of this would in turn increase the demand, particularly on the part of cities, for federal law enforcement support to protect city boundaries from in-state guns. Within five years after extension of federal protection to municipal handgun control, the intrastate, rather than interstate, migration of handguns will emerge as a top priority in federal firearms law enforcement.

It is, of course, one thing to make up a scheme of handgun regulation and quite another to argue that it is historically derived. Why is it that federal regulation will expand? What is the basis for suggesting that municipal handgun controls will increase? The answers to such questions are neither easy nor obvious.

National handgun registration is only peculiar in that it has not yet been accomplished. Since 1938, federal law has required most of the essential data for registration, but the records have been decentralized in a way that has effectively guaranteed they cannot be used.[5] Two trends suggest momentum in the coming decades toward effectively centralized weapon ownership information. First, the development of efficient and cheap information processing removes any technical barrier to a national handgun data bank. Whatever the circumstances of 1938, we now face a situation where the marginal cost of creating an accountability system for handguns is minimal and central data files are neither technically nor economically difficult.

The ease and cheapness with which weapons can be first-owner registered suggest a shift in the debate about registration from cost factors to more basic principles. Public opinion seems solidly behind handgun-owner accountability if registration is viewed solely as an accountability system and not as a first step toward confiscation of all the guns linked to registered owners. Registration thus seems inevitable, if its proponents can make a creditable case that a registration scheme will not be used to facilitate a shift from permissive to restrictive licensing policies. This could be achieved by "grandfathering" all guns registered to eligible owners so that any subsequent shift in federal regulatory policy would exempt validly registered guns.

The momentum toward municipal licensing is easier to demonstrate. In the cities, pressure for handgun restriction has increased dramatically in the past 15 years, and those cities that have adopted controls almost never repeal them. The momentum toward further handgun restriction in major metropolitan areas appears substantial in all regions except the South and the Southwest.

However, federal handgun registration and more restrictive municipal handgun control are by no means inevitable. Each initiative carries with it seeds of its own defeat. In the case of registration, the principal potential villain is public and gun-owner perception that accountability measures are merely one further step toward prohibition. The effort to secure prohibition in the name of registration has an old federal pedigree, dating from the National Firearms Act of 1934 and its successful attempt to deal with machine guns, if not sawed-off shotguns.[6] Gun-owner perception that registration means confiscation is widespread. Whether such perceptions can ward off a general trend toward centralization of automatic data processing is questionable.

The momentum toward further municipal handgun control seems unstoppable, but this, too, may be misleading. The key issue here is whether sustained attempts at municipal restriction are viewed as successful. In large part, municipal efforts to create handgun scarcity have failed. Very few cities have experienced either the costs or benefits of tight controls. All this may end as we accumulate a decade of experience with the new Washington, D.C., statute and with those cities that will follow on D.C.'s wake.

Substantial changes in municipal and state regulation of handgun ownership have become the rule rather than the exception in those American jurisdictions that have reconsidered handgun regulation in the last twenty years.[7] This has occurred despite complaints about the power of the gun control lobby.

The trend, viewed historically, is toward a patchwork quilt of federal, state, and local regulation. This is not surprising. Significant variations exist in attitudes toward handguns, and it should only be expected that these attitudinal differences would more quickly lead to a wider spectrum of state and local variation than to a unified national strategy. But will such incremental and differential policies produce adequate public protection three decades hence?

HANDGUN SCARCITY AS FEDERAL POLICY

The principal difficulty associated with evolution of a national handgun policy based on state and local variation is that it might not work. Federal attempts to protect tight-control cities and states would continue to be frustrated by interstate and intrastate movement of handguns; the large civilian inventory of handguns would make efforts at accountability based on registration data both expensive and easy to frustrate at the point of first purchase.

Under such circumstances, growing dependence on public transportation, and increased residential desegregation that spreads the risk of violent crime more evenly across metropolitan areas, may produce a climate where more stringent handgun controls may be demanded. Unless the increased fear associated with interdependence is offset by lower rates of violence, it is unlikely that increased public police expenditure or further increases in imprisonment rates will alone lead to tolerable levels of citizen risk. Progress toward a "cashless society" may reduce the incentive for personal robbery and may redistribute the risk of commercial robbery from cashless to cash-holding institutions. But the coincidence of interdependent urban life and freely available handguns will put pressure on "evolutionary" federal handgun policy.

An alternative federal handgun policy would stress reducing, substantially, the population of handguns and thus reducing general handgun availability. Federal standards would require the states to administer handgun licensing systems that would deny most citizens the opportunity to possess handguns and handgun ammunition. The central features of this scheme are the commitment of federal policy to nationwide handgun scarcity, a policy that would be imposed on states and cities where more permissive approaches were preferred, and a policy shift making continuing possession of handguns by millions of households unlawful. Further, whatever the division of responsibility among federal, state, and local law enforcement, this approach would, unlike others, put the federal government in the standard-setting—and most likely, production-control—business.

What one calls such regulation is a secondary matter. Federal "restrictive licensing" is the equivalent of a "national handgun ban!" Indeed, many "ban" bills would leave more guns in circulation than would restrictive licensing because the exceptions—for example, security guards—are broad. The thrust of such a policy is the transition from a 30-million-handgun society to a 3-million-handgun society. This is no small step.

Even if a national policy of handgun scarcity were wholeheartedly adopted, there are limits on the capacity of federal authorities to implement policy without state and local cooperation. Handgun production quotas and regulations governing the distribution of new weapons could be administered at the federal level. Individual determination of whether citizens who apply for licenses meet 'need" criteria is best left to local officials, however, and removing unlawfuly possessed handguns is a by-product of local police activity.[8] The only way to shift this burden to the federal level is to create a national street police force, a radical departure from current practice that should not be expected or desired. Thus even federal policies that attempt to centralize authority to reduce existing handgun ownership will operate at the mercy of state and local law enforcement.

Still, any such national standard setting would represent two major departures from present federal law. First, the federal government would attempt to limit the supply of handguns nationwide. Second, in order to substantially reduce the handgun population, citizens would be denied the opportunity to own weapons even if they were not part of special high-risk groups and in spite of less restrictive policy preferences at the state and local level where they reside.

This type of plenary federal policy has never been seriously considered in the United States. Early in the New Deal, Attorney General Homer Cummings proposed tight federal handgun controls that received scant congressional attention.[9] In the 1970s, a series of proposals to create federal restrictive licensing were introduced and soundly defeated. The urban experiments with restrictive licensing in New York and Washington, D.C., both involved jurisdictions with small inventories of lawfully possessed handguns and cooperating local law enforcement.

If present trends continue, 30 years from now the majority of American citizens will still live in states with less restrictive handgun policies than the proposed federal standard. Under what conditions, then, would this majority's congressional representatives vote for more stringent regulation than state legislatures would support? A restrictive national handgun policy would represent a turning point in public opinion and legislative climate, a relatively sharp departure from the previous twentieth-century politics of handgun control.

MIDTERM POLICIES AND LONG-RANGE GOALS

The road to patchwork federalism in handgun policy requires different midterm regulatory approaches than if the long-term goal were civilian scarcity. Patchwork federalism can, of course, be achieved through the gradual accretion of actions by cities, states, and the federal government. To the extent that we follow this path, however, it will become increasingly difficult to make a later shift to a national scarcity policy, for three reasons. First, city regulations will have the effect of legitimizing handgun possession for those who obtain their guns legally in the city. Second, the inventory of handguns in circulation is likely to grow rapidly under patchwork federalism. Third, people who registered their guns under a federal registration plan would almost certainly be "grandfathered" when the shift to a national scarcity policy occurs. Each of these problems is discussed in more detail in the following pages.

The Impact of Local Registration

Those states and cities that institute programs of owner registration create a population of handguns registered in good faith. One important consequence of registration is that it confers an explicit legal legitimacy on the continued ownership of the weapon by its owner. If a city adopts a registration scheme and later decides to create further restrictions on handguns, the more restrictive policy will usually exempt those owners with prior registration from additional eligibility requirements as long as they continue to possess their registered weapons.

The impact of this type of "grandfather clause" on the inventory of firearms or the availability of guns for misuse will vary from city to city. In a city with a small number of registered guns, such as New York or Washington, D.C., the effect of a grandfather clause on handgun availability would be small. In Chicago, where the population of registered handguns is several hundreds of thousands, the inevitable result of the grandfather clause is a large pool of guns at risk of theft or illegal transfer for many years after a shift to more restrictive ownership criteria.[10] Most major cities have very large handgun inventories. Registration systems, if effective, would legitimate millions of handguns. And the handgun owner wishing to immunize himself from restrictions on continued ownership is well advised to enter the system.

Grandfathering a large number of registered handguns may put pressure on the principles as well as on the practicality of municipal restrictive licensing. With so many prior registrants legally able to own weapons, it will be more difficult to argue that latecomers should be required to prove a special need for a gun before being eligible to acquire one. Further, the period during which a shift to more restrictive strategies is debated might create a large volume of handgun sales to new purchasers anticipating further restriction.

Inventory Consequences of Continued Federalism

In the 12 years following the Gun Control Act of 1968, more than 20 million handguns were added to the civilian handgun inventory in the United States.[11] This total probably represents more than half the stock of operable handguns in the United States and a larger proportion of the handguns involved in violent crime.[12] Each year of federal indifference to handgun supply adds about two million pistols and revolvers to an inventory of weapons that a restrictive policy would seek to shrink. How much of an additional burden this imposes on future restrictive efforts cannot be estimated because we do not know how long new handguns remain operable and because it is not possible to estimate the impact of government repurchase efforts. But each year of unrestricted aggregate handgun supply makes the transition to national handgun scarcity more difficult and more expensive.

Federal Registration as a National Grandfather Clause

Federal handgun registration would replicate the problems that state and local systems present for restrictive policies on a grand scale. At minimum, gun registration records could not be used as the basis for a recall of handguns once more restrictive policies were put in place. This stricture would almost certainly be inserted into the legislation that would initially enable central storage of handgun ownership information. It is also likely that considerable pressure would be exerted to exempt registered handguns from whatever new ownership restrictions might subsequently be imposed as long as the guns remain in possession of the registrant. This would make the move toward tight eligibility prospective in its effect and gradual in its impact on handgun inventory. How much delay this type of provision would produce is not known because there are no good data on how long handguns are retained in particular households.

"Specter Effects" of Restrictive Control Proposals

Public discussion of handgun restrictions or bans has an important influence on all aspects of the debate over firearms control. As previously mentioned, permissive licensing and registration are frequently opposed because they are regarded as "first steps" toward more restrictive policies. Restrictive proposals for handguns are feared as a step toward restrictions on long gun ownership. And fear about future restriction may play a role in the high level of demand for weapons available now and possibly not available in the future. Further, there is evidence that opposition to restrictive control has increased as the issue has received public attention.[13] From the standpoint of an advocate firmly committed to permissive licensing and registration as ultimate federal law, the policy climate would probably have been better if proposals for restrictive handgun policies had not surfaced in the late 1960s.

What are the prospects now for shelving the debate about handgun restriction in favor of a permanent compromise at the federal level? Any such proposal would probably be regarded as inauthentic at this late date. And doubts about the effectiveness of federal neutrality on handgun ownership policy suggest that any "permanent compromise" of that sort would fail to satisfy those who regard handgun violence as a serious national problem. The issue of national handgun policy is thus unlikely to be resolved with a long-standing compromise despite the manifold impact of restrictive federal handgun proposals.

A Turning Point?

Many factors can influence the direction of future handgun policy. A sharp decline in public fear of crime would decrease demand for handguns; at the same time, if this resulted in reduced violent crime, it would reduce the need for handgun control. An increase in burglary rates or, more significantly, in rates of home-invasion robbery would work the other way.

However, the most important element of future policy is not the crime rate, but social notions of appropriate crime countermeasures. In my view, the "social status" of the household self-defense handgun in our cities and suburbs will emerge as a critical leading indicator of future federal handgun control. Public opinion research has indicated that self-defense in the home is the most important "good reason" given for handgun ownership.[14] If citizens continue to believe that possessing a loaded handgun is a respectable method of defending urban households, handgun demand and opposition to restrictive policy will continue. If owning loaded handguns in the home comes to be viewed more as part of the gun problem than as a respectable practice, the prospects for restrictive control will improve over time. The residual uses of handguns—informal target shooting, collection, and hunting sidearms— are peripheral to the handgun control controversy. Household self-defense is a central issue.

Public attitudes toward handguns for self-defense are related to fear of crime, but there are other factors that bear on the respectability of the urban housegun. One is alternative self-defense measures, such as burglar alarms, silent alarms that trigger police or private security responses, and the urban house dog. Most of these systems are more effective against burglary than handguns, but are less effective against home invaders.

A second influence on attitudes towards handguns in the home is public perceptions about the costs of weapon ownership within the household and in the wider community. Household accidents and guns recycled from homes to street crime are two kinds of loss that may influence public opinion about loaded guns in the home. Gun homicide involving family members may also influence the attitude of non-gun owners, but I suspect that most gun-owning families would believe this kind of loss "can never happen to them."

An increase in the social stigma associated with household defense guns will influence the demand for handguns long before it affects national policy toward handgun supply. In the midterm, increasing stigma should reduce the proportion of households purchasing guns and increase the households that report considering and rejecting a handgun purchase. These indications should first appear in younger age segments of the population, rather than households with older heads and established patterns of handgun ownership. Upper-middle-class families "resettling" in older city neighborhoods might be a particularly interesting group to watch. These families have the economic resources to pursue alternative methods of household security. This segment of the population is well known for its trend-setting influence in other issues of style and consumption.

The early indications of a turning point in attitudes toward handguns will be more a function of attitude than hard data trends in crime rates or aggregate gun ownership. This is, in one sense, appropriate because the distinctive feature of the growth in handguns for self-defense has been more a question of perceived need than statistical risk.[15] Whatever happens will probably happen gradually. Thus the precondition for what might be viewed as a revolutionary shift in public policy is an evolutionary change in public attitude. As is so often the case, any discussion of this kind of shift as a future development must acknowledge that this type of attitude change may already be in progress.

CONCLUSIONS

Speculation about future trends is a high-risk enterprise. The values of discussion of long-range futures are the discipline it can impose on assertions about historical trends and the perspective one gains on present trends by examining the likely impact of their continuation. I hope the preceding pages will stimulate others to undertake similar efforts at constructing handgun policy "futures" consistent with the lessons of our recent history, yet suited to the needs of the social order our children will inherit.

NOTES

1. As used in this essay, the terms "permissive licensing," "restrictive licensing," and "registration" are defined following George D. Newton and Franklin E. Zimring, *Firearms and Violence in American Life*, Staff Report to the National Commission on the Causes and Prevention of Violence, 7:83-84 (1969) (hereafter cited as Newton and Zimring). See also Franklin E. Zimring, "Getting Serious About Guns," *The Nation*, 214 (1972): 457, 459-60.

2. Prior notification of transfer could be instituted without comprehensive handgun registration, as discussed by Newton and Zimring in their description of "transfer notice." See Newton and Zimring, p. 84.

3. See Franklin E. Zimring, "Firearms and Federal Law: The Gun Control Act of 1968," *Journal of Legal Studies* 4 (1975): 133, 149 (hereafter cited as "Firearms and Federal Law").

4. Central storage of ownership data is possible even if records of purchase continue to be maintained by individual dealers. Duplicate forms could be forwarded to automatic data-processing systems probably without any changes in the provisions of the Gun Control Act of 1968. See Franklin E. Zimring, "Firearms and Federal Law," *supra* note 3, pp. 151-54.

5. See Zimring, "Firearms and Federal Law," *supra* note 3, pp. 139-40.

6. See Zimring, "Firearms and Federal Law," *supra* note 3, pp. 138-39.

7. See Edward D. Jones, III, "The District of Columbia's 'Firearms Control Regulations Act of 1975': The Toughest Handgun Control Law in the United States—Or Is It?" in *The Annals* of the American Academy of Political and Social Science, 455 (May 1981): 138-49.

8. See Franklin E. Zimring, "Street Crime and New Guns, Some Implications for Firearms Control," *Journal of Criminal Justice*, 4 (1976): 95, 101-2.

9. See Zimring, "Firearms and Federal Law," *supra* note 3, pp. 138. See also "The Politics of Ineffectiveness: Federal Firearms Legislation, 1919-38," *The Annals* of the American Academy of Political and Social Science, No. 455 (May 1981): 48-62.

10. Richard Greenberg, "Pistols Pour Through Sieve of Unenforceable Handgun Laws," *Chicago Reporter* 10(2) (February 1981): 7.

11. Mark Moore, "Keeping Handguns From Criminal Offenders," *The Annals* of the American Academy of Political and Social Science, 455 (May 1981): 92-109.

12. Zimring, "Firearms and Federal Law," *supra* note 3, pp. 169-70.

13. See Tom Smith, "The 75% Solution," *Journal of Criminal Law and Criminology* 7(13): 314.

14. Newton and Zimring, *supra* note 2, p. 62.

15. Handgun ownership reported in public opinion polls is higher among high-income groups than among low-income groups and as great in small cities as in big cities (Newton and Zimring, *supra* note 2, ch. 2). Crime risks are greater for low-income groups and in larger cities. While the polls show white household ownership in excess of black household ownership, the risk of violent crime victimization is greater among black city residents. See also "Estimated Rates of Victimization," in *Sourcebook of Criminal Justice Statistics* (National Criminal Justice Information and Statistical Service, various years), tables and figures.

13

Comparisons among Nations and Over Time

Don B. Kates, Jr.

Anti-gun crusaders are addicted to comparing the United States to foreign nations, a comparison that probably constitutes the single most pernicious source of misinformation and misunderstanding of gun regulation issues. This misinformation and misunderstanding (both are also involved in comparison across time) result from a grotesque mix of statistical misrepresentation with partisan selection and presentation, and from sheer historical ignorance.

Such comparisons are used to argue that gun ownership causes crime, which supposedly results in the United States having more homicides *per capita* than selected other countries that virtually prohibit gun ownership. In fact, determinants of the relative amounts of violence in nations are sociocultural and institutional. The effects of such basic determinants cannot be offset by any gun control strategy, no matter how well crafted and rigorous. Reducing availability of any other kind of weapon, including guns, cannot radically decrease crime because the number of guns that are illegally available will always suffice for those who are determined to obtain and misuse them.

From "Guns, Murder, and the Constitution: A Realistic Assessment of Gun Control" (February 1990): 36–43. Copyright © 1990 by the Pacific Research Institute for Public Policy. Reprinted by permission of the publisher.

INTERNATIONAL HOMICIDE RATES VERSUS GUN AVAILABILITY AND SOCIOCULTURAL DIFFERENCES

Two sociocultural differences that result in widely different murder rates come immediately to mind. The first is the unknown (to Americans) fact that each year hundreds of men in Japan murder their families and then kill themselves. This tradition is so much a part of Japanese culture that it was not even a crime until fairly recently. Japanese murder rates remain admirably low because they exclude these "family suicides."[1]

The second involves comparing America's high murder rate to Europe's far higher suicide rate. Sociologist Seymour Martin Lipset has suggested that cultural factors cause disturbed Americans to strike out against others whereas disturbed Europeans turn their violence on themselves. This difference helps explain the details of American and European statistics set out in the International Intentional Homicide Table.

INTERNATIONAL INTENTIONAL HOMICIDE TABLE

COUNTRY	SUICIDE	HOMICIDE	TOTAL
RUMANIA	66.20	n.a.	66.20 (1984)
HUNGARY	45.90	n.a.	45.90 (1983)
DENMARK	28.70	0.70	29.40 (1984)
AUSTRIA	26.90	1.50	28.40 (1984)
FINLAND	24.40 (1983)	2.86	27.20
FRANCE	21.80 (1983)	4.36	26.16
SWITZERLAND	24.45	1.13	25.58
BELGIUM	23.15	1.85	25.00
W. GERMANY	20.37	1.48	21.85
JAPAN	20.30	0.90	21.20
UNITED STATES	12.20 (1982)	7.59	19.79
CANADA	13.94	2.60	16.54
NORWAY	14.50	1.16	15.66
N. IRELAND	9.00	6.00	15.00

(Homicide rate may not include "political" homicides)

AUSTRALIA	**11.58**	**1.95**	**13.53**
NEW ZEALAND	9.70	1.60	24.50
ENGLAND/WALES	**8.61**	**0.67**	**9.28**

(Homicide rate does not include "political" homicides)

ISRAEL	6.00	2.00	8.00

NOTE: Table is based on figures from two different sources (as further specified below). Insofar as they are given therein, all figures are from the 1983–86 averages in Killias' Tables 1 & 2.* If Killias does not give figures, those numbers are from the latest year listed for the country in United Nations Demographic Yearbook, 1985 (published 1987). Figures from Killias are in boldface; all other figures are in ordinary type.

In contrast, blaming gun owners explains nothing because that interpretation is flatly inconsistent with international statistical evidence. If gun ownership were a major "cause" of crime and if gun availability were a major factor in the amount of criminal homicide, then first, nations where gun availability is more widespread than in the United States would uniformly have appreciably higher murder rates than the norm for demographically comparable nations.[2] And second, nations that ban or severely restrict gun ownership would have appreciably lower homicide rates than the United States. Yet the International Intentional Homicide Table shows that in nations where gun availability exceeds the United States (e.g., Israel, New Zealand, and Switzerland[3]), the homicide rates are as low as those of the highly gun-restrictive Western European and British Commonwealth countries to which America is frequently and aversely compared. Moreover, the two nations that most severely restrict gun ownership (punishing violation with death), Taiwan and South Africa, both have far higher apolitical murder rates than the United States.

HISTORICAL IGNORANCE AND THE ANTI-GUN CRUSADE

Likewise, historical evidence refutes attributing differential international violence rates to differences in gun laws rather than to socio-institutional and cultural differences. People who attribute low violence rates in Europe to banning guns are apparently unaware that low rates *long preceded* the gun bans.[4] In fact, stringent gun laws first appeared in the United States, not Europe—despite which, high American crime rates persisted and grew.[5] Ever-growing violence in various American states from the 1810s on led those states to pioneer ever more severe gun controls.[6] But in Europe, where violence was falling, or was

*Killias, "Gun Ownership and Violent Crime: The Swiss Experience in International Perspective," a paper presented at the 1989 Annual Meeting of the American Society of Criminology.

not even deemed an important problem, gun controls varied from lax to nonexistent. During the nineteenth century in England, for instance, crime fell from its high in the late 1700s to its idyllic low in the early 1900s—yet the only gun control was that police could not carry guns.[7]

In considering reasons for the historical differences between United States and British homicide, Prof. Monckkonen rejects conventional explanations including gun ownership, remarking:

> Virtually every analysis put forward to explain the [comparatively] very high United States homicide rate has been ahistorical. . . . Had they been propsoed as historical, they would have floundered quickly for the explanatory inadequacy of these "pet" theories becomes immediately apprarent in a historical context.[8]

When most European countries finally began enacting gun laws in the post-World War I period, the motivation was not crime (with which those countries had been little afflicted) but terrorism and political violence from which they have continued to suffer until today far more than the United States.[9] This difference is reflected in a practice that helps to keep official English murder rates so admirably low: English statistics do not include "political" murders (e.g., those by the IRA), whereas American statistics include every kind of murder and manslaughter. The different purposes of European versus American laws are evidenced by their diametrically opposite patterns: many of the "Saturday Night Special" laws that American states enacted to deal with nineteenth-century crime have banned all but standard military-issue revolvers (i.e., the very expensive large, heavy Colt). In stark contrast, such military caliber arms were the first guns banned in post-World War I Europe, the purpose being to disarm restive former soldiers and the paramilitary groups they formed.[10]

Moreover, the claim that greater gun availability causes higher United States crime rates can only explain the rates of violence *with guns*. If gun availability were the explanation for higher crime rates, rather than sociocultural and institutional differences, gun banning countries would have less gun crime than the United States, but roughly the same rates of nonviolence. But, in fact, the rate of United States violence *without guns* is so great it exceeds the rate of violence in other comparable nations, both with and without guns (combined). That comparison applies not just among the United States and gun banning countries, but also among the United States and countries where guns are even more available (such as New Zealand, Switzerland, and Israel). These facts utterly refute the notion that greater gun availability is the major factor in violence differences among the United States and other nations.

England's leading gun control analyst sardonically disposes of the issues with two rhetorical questions. First, how do those who blame "lax American gun laws" for the far higher U.S. rate of gun crime expain the country's also having far more knife crimes? Do they think that Englishmen must get a permit to own a butcher knife? Second, how do those who attribute U.S. gun murders to greater gun availability explain the far higher U.S. rate of stranglings and of victims being kicked to death? Do they think that Americans "have more hands and feet than" Britons? Flatly asserting that, no matter how stringent the gun laws, there will always be enough guns in any society to arm those desiring to obtain and use them illegally, the analyst attributes grossly higher American violence rates "not to the availability of any particular class of weapon" but to sociocultural and institutional factors that dictate

> that American criminals are more willing to use extreme violence; [quoting a report of the British Office of Health Economics]: "One reason often given for the high numbers of murders and manslaughters in the United States is the easy availability of firearms. . . . But the strong correlation with racial and linked socioeconomic variables suggests that the underlying determinants of the homicide rate relate to particular cultural factors."[11]

AMERICAN MURDER RATES IN THE 1960S THROUGH 1980S

If increasing gun ownership caused American murder rates to rise in the 1960s, did it also cause them to stabilize in the 1970s and fall in the 1980s? The theory that widespread gun ownership causes murder seemed plausible to Americans in the 1960s when ever-increasing gun sales went hand in hand with (actually were a reaction to) ever-increasing crime rates. But this interpretation is exploded when the time frame is expanded to include statistics from the 1970s and 1980s. In those decades, handgun ownership continued to rise by about 2 million per year, so that the American handgun stock increased from between 24 and 29 million in 1968 to between 65 and 70 million in 1988. Yet homicide actually fell somewhat, and handgun (and other gun) homicides decreased markedly.[12] The point is even more striking when compared to the English homicide rate: in 1974 the American rate was 40 times the English; 15 years (and 30 million more American handguns) later, the American rate was only ten times greater.[13] Since this change occurred in decades during which English gun law severity increased, both administratively and by added legislative restrictions, the trend cannot be explained by attributing murder to widespread gun availability.

The attribution is further undermined if violent crimes are differentiated by type. Anti-gun academic crusaders do not claim that buying a handgun suddenly turns otherwise law-abiding people to rape, robbery, and burglary. Yet such crimes (and murder, during these crimes) have grown spectacularly since the mid-1960s. In contrast, domestic homicides did not increase as sages theorized. (Indeed, the approximate 100 percent increase in handguns during 1968–79 was followed by a 26.6 percent decrease in domestic homicide from

1984 on—despite adding another 2 million handguns in 1980 and in each succeeding year.[14])

CONCEALMENT OF THE DECLINING AMERICAN MURDER TREND

Anti-gun sages have seized on a new device so they do not have to deal with embarrassing facts. They conceal declining American homicides (particularly gun homicides) by combining suicide and murder statistics, producing an "Intentional Homicide" rate that they then claim to be "caused by widespread gun ownership.[15] Yet these same anti-gun academics continue to compare the American *murder* rate (alone) to the murder rates of specially selected foreign countries—without mentioning that virtually every country they select to compare has an enormously higher suicide rate than the United States. For instance, Prof. Baker, the originator of the combined homicide-suicide approach, compares American and Danish murder rates, placing great emphasis on the fact that the American rate is higher by about 7 per 100,000 population. Yet Baker somehow forgets to mention that making the same comparison of suicide rates would show the Danish have 16.5 more deaths per 100,000 than the Americans. Nor, of course, does Baker mention that when suicide and murder figures are combined, the Danish death rate per 100,000 is almost 50 percent higher than the American.[16]

Despite their reliance on international murder comparisons, none of the anti-gun academics who apply the combined murder-suicide approach (in describing American figures) follow the combined approach when making those international comparisons. Could that omission have anything to do with the facts that emerge from the International Intentional Homicide Table? Of eighteen nations for which figures were available, the United States ranks only eleventh in intentional homicide. The U.S. combined homicide and suicide rate is less than half the suicide rate alone in gun-banning Hungary and less than one-third the suicide rate alone of gun-banning Rumania. New Zealand ranks sixteenth despite a rate of gun ownership that far exceeds the U.S. rate. The lowest rate on the table is for Israel, a country that actually encourages and requires almost universal gun ownership.

The evidence from international comparisons is confirmed by various neutral attempts to determine whether gun ownership causes violence as footnoted earlier and by the most extensive and methodologically sophisticated study. This was Kleck's application of modern, computer-assisted statistical techniques to post-World War II American crime rates. The interactive cause-and-effect result he found contradicts that posited by antigun crusaders. Kleck concludes that from the 1960s on, fear of violent crime caused many more people to buy guns. Increased gun ownership did not itself increase crime (if anything, it dampened it). But an increase in gun ownership, or at least gun use, by criminals helped cause the post-1960 increases in violent crime, including murder.[17]

It may be of interest that Kleck simultaneously investigated the possible effect that the cessation of capital punishment in the 1960s and 1970s had in causing the crime wave. He concludes that increased violence was not attributable to the cessation of capital punishment. Note also that this criminological evidence does not support the gun lobby's myopic oposition to gun controls. On the contrary, Kleck endorses sweeping, strongly enforced laws against possession of any firearm by persons convicted of any kind of felony.[18]

Guns are more lethal than some means of death, though less lethal than others such as hanging, certain poisons, and falls from great heights. Because of their lethality, guns may facilitate murder or suicide among people who are so inclined. On the other hand, guns are the most effective means by which a victim may resist violent attack.

NOTES

1. R. Markman and D. Bosco, *Alone with the Devil* (New York: Doubleday, 1989), pp. 342ff.; indeed, 17 percent of all Japanese homicides consist of children killed by their parents. See also Jameson, "Parent-Child Suicides Frequent in Japan," *Hartford Courant,* March 28, 1981.

2. Likewise studies of geographical areas within the United States should show those areas with higher gun ownership having more murder. Yet the consistent result of studies attempting to link gun ownership to violence rates is either no relationship or a *negative* one (i.e., urban and other areas with higher gun ownership have less violence than demographically comparable areas with fewer gun owners. See for example Murray, "Handguns, Gun Control Law, and Firearm Violence," *Social Problems* 23 (1975): 81; Lizotte & Bordua, "Firearms Ownership for Sport and Protection: Two Not So Divergent Models," *American Sociological Review* 45 (1980) and 46 (1981), and Bordua & Lizotte, "Patterns of Legal Firearms Ownership: A Situational and Cultural Analysis of Illinois Counties," *Law & Policy Quarterly* 2 (1979); Kleck, "The Relationship between Gun Ownership Levels and Rates of Violence in the United States," in D. Kates (ed.), *Firearms and Violence* (San Francisco, Calif.: Pacific Research Institute, 1984); McDowall, "Gun Availability and Robbery Rates: A Panel Study of Large U.S. Cities, 1974–1978," *Law & Policy Quarterly* 8 (1986): 135; Bordua, "Firearms Ownership and Violent Crime: A Comparison of Illinois Counties"; Kleck and Patterson, "The Impact of Gun Control and Gun Ownership Levels on City Violence Rates," a paper presented to the 1989 Annual Meeting of the American Society of Criminology (available from the authors at Florida State U. School of Criminology). See also Eskridge, "Zero-Order Inverse Correlations between Crimes of Violence and Hunting Licenses in the United States," *Sociology & Social Research* 71 (1986): 55.

3. For discussion of U.S., Swiss, and Israeli law and practice, see Kates, "Handgun Prohibition and the Original Meaning of the Second Amendment," *Michigan Law Review* 82: 204 at n. 193 and 264ff.; cf. "Swiss Army: A Privilege of Citizenship," *Los Angeles Times,* October 1, 1980, p. 1; "Israeli Official Urges Firearm in Every Home," *Gun Week,* June 29, 1979; "Order by Israel Puts Even More Guns on the Street," *Los Angeles Times,* July 5, 1978. The anti-self-defense basis of Anglo-American gun control theory is so unusual that it produces profound differences not only in policy and administration from those prevailing in other countries but also in understanding superficially similar gun laws. One such deceptive similarity is that the laws in New York City, England, Switzerland, and Israel all require a permit to own a handgun. Indicative of the profound differences among those requirements is that permit issuance for the purpose of personal defense is routine in Israel and Switzerland, administratively discouraged by New York City, and nonexistent in England. In 1984 an attack on a Jerusalem cafe by three terrorists armed with automatic weapons was terminated when handgun-carrying Israeli civilians shot them down, *The Economist,* April 7, 1984, p. 34.

Equally significant are differences in policy about civilian possession of automatic weapons. Either an ordinary rifle or an assault rifle or any other fully automatic weapon requires a permit in England; since 1934, possession of a fully automatic weapon in the United States has required registration and been subject to a prohibitive tax. As of 1986, purchasing new assault rifles or other fully automatic weapons is totally forbidden in the United States. But in Switzerland and Israel the government *distributes* automatic weapons to the general population by the millions. I was once asked by a puzzled Israeli why Americans think they have to personally own guns: "If they have to live or be in dangerous areas, why don't they just check a handgun or submachine gun out of the police armory?" The idea that American law would seek to prevent law-abiding citizens threatened by violence from arming themselves had never occurred to him and, on explanation, the idea was incomprehensible.

4. See generally Gurr, "Historical Trends in Violent Crime: A Critical Review of the Evidence," in *Annual Review of Crime and Justice* (Beverly Hills, Calif.: Sage, 1981), vol. 3; C. Greenwood, *Firearms Control: A Study of Armed Crime and Firearms Control in England and Wales* (London: Routledge & Kegan Paul, 1971), chaps. 1–3; Morn, "Firearms Use and Police: An Historic Evolution of American Values," *Firearms and Violence, supra,* pp. 496–501.

5. Morn, "Firearms Use and Police"; Kates, "Toward a History of Handgun Prohibition in the United States," in D. B. Kates, Jr. (ed.), *Restricting Handguns: The Liberal Skeptics Speak Out* (Naperville, Ill.: Caroline Hse, 1979), pp. 13–14.

6. For instance, in the South, the U.S. region that from earliest times had the highest murder rates, gun law experimentation included the following: the only state law that completely banned handgun sales (S.C., 1902; repealed 1966); the earliest bans on "Saturday Night Specials" (Tenn., 1870); Ark., 1881; Ala., 1893; Tex., 1907; Va., 1925); the earliest registration laws (Miss., 1906; Ga., 1913; N.C., 1917); and three states in which a permit was required to purchase a handgun (N.C. 1917; Mo., 1919; Ark., 1923).

7. Greenwood, *Firearms Control;* Morn, "Firearms Use and Police."

8. Monckkonen, "Diverging Homicide Rates: England and the United States," in T. Gurr, *Violence in America* (Violence, Cooperation, Peace Series, 1989), 1: 81. He rejects gun ownership as a reason for the homicide differential, citing a point that it made below in greater detail. Even those who see guns as the reason do not contend that their removal could reduce American homicide by more than 50 percent; yet if American homicide were reduced by 50 percent, its rate would still be 500 percent greater than the British rate.

9. Naturally, anti-gun academic crusaders do not credit the availability of guns in the United States for the country's relative lack of violence. They (quite correctly) attribute that lack to sociocultural and institutional differences between the United States and Europe. Yet it does not occur to the anti-gun academic crusaders to attribute international crime differentials to sociocultural and institutional differences rather than to differences in gun ownership.

10. L. Kennett and J. L. Anderson, *The Gun in America: The Origins of a National Dilemma* (Westport, Conn.: Greenwood, 1976), p. 213; M. Josserand, *Les Pistolets, Les Revolvers, et Leurs Munitions* (Paris: Crepin-Leblond & Cie, 1967) [in English transl., with co-authorship and additional material by J. Stevenson, *Pistols, Revolvers, and Ammunition* (New York: Bonanza, 1967)], chap. 9.

11. Greenwood and Magaddino, "Comparative Cross-Cultural Statistics," in *Restricting Handguns;* see also Greenwood, *Firearms Control.*

12. For instance, in 1974, when the total U.S. population was 211 million, handguns were involved in approximately 11,125 murders (54 percent of all murders). By 1988 the total U.S. population was 245 million and handguns were involved in around 8,275 murders (45 percent of all murders), a 27 percent decline in handgun homicide. Homicide by all means had declined almost 10 percent. In the 20-year period from 1966 to 1985, murders with guns declined from 64.8 percent of the total murder rate to 58.7 percent.

13. Compare Monckkonen, "Diverging Homicide Rates," p. 81 to the International Intentional Homicide Table.

14. Browne and Flewelling, "Women as Victims or Perpetrators of Homicide," a paper presented to the 1986 Annual Meeting of the American Society of Criminology (available from the Family Res. Lab., U. of New Hampshire); Straus, "Domestic Violence and Homicide Antecedents," *Bulletin of the N.Y. Academy of Medicine* 62 (1986): 446, 450.

15. See for example, Teret, "Public Health and the Law," *American Journal of Public Health* 76 (1986): 1027, 1028; S. Baker et al., *The Injury Fact Book* (Lexington, Mass.: Lexington Books, 1984), pp. 90–91; Teret and Wintemute, "Handgun Injuries: The Epidemiologic Evidence for Assessing Legal Responsibility," *Hamline Law Review* 6 (1983): 341.

16. Compare Baker, "With Guns Do People Kill People?" *American Journal of Public Health* 75 (1985): 587 (comparing U.S. and Danish murder) to International Intentional Homicide Table.

17. Kleck, "Capital Punishment, Gun Ownership, and Homicide," *American Journal of Sociology* 84 (1979): 882; and Kleck, "The Relationship between Gun Ownership Levels and Rates of Violence in the United States," in D. Kates (ed.), *Firearms and Violence.*

18. "Policy Lessons from Recent Gun Control Research," *Law & Contemporary Problems* 49 (1986).

14

Handgun Regulations, Crime, Assaults, and Homicide: A Tale of Two Cities

John Henry Sloan et al.*

Approximately 20,000 persons are murdered in the United States each year, making homicide the eleventh leading cause of death and the sixth leading cause of the loss of potential years of life before age sixty-five. [1-3] In the United States between 1960 and 1980, the death rate from homicide by means other than firearms increased by 85 percent. In contrast, the death rate from homicide by firearms during this same period increased by 160 percent.[3]

Approximately 60 percent of homicides each year involve firearms. Handguns alone account for three fourths of all gun-related homicides.[4] Most homicides occur as a result of assaults during arguments or altercations; a minority occur during the commission of a robbery or other felony.[2,4] Baker has noted that in cases of assault, people tend to reach for weapons that are readily available.[5] Since attacks with guns more often end in death than attacks with knives, and since handguns are disproportionately involved in

From *The New England Journal of Medicine* 319, no. 19 (November 10, 1988): 1256–1262. Reprinted by permission of the publisher.

*Arthur L. Kellermann, Donald T. Reay, James A. Ferris, Thomas Koepsell, Frederick P. Rivara, Charles Rice, Laurel Gray, and James LoGerfo

intentional shootings, some have argued that restricting access to handguns could substantially reduce our annual rate of homicide.[5-7]

To support this view, advocates of handgun control frequently cite data from countries like Great Britain and Japan, where the rates of both handgun ownership and homicide are substantially lower than those in the United States.[8] Rates of injury due to assault in Denmark are comparable to those in northeastern Ohio, but the Danish rate of homicide is only one fifth as high as Ohio's. [5,6] In Denmark, the private ownership of guns is permitted only for hunting, and access to handguns is tightly restricted.[6]

Opponents of gun control counter with statistics from Israel and Switzerland, where the rates of gun ownership are high but homicides are relatively uncommon.[9] However, the value of comparing data from different countries to support or refute the effectiveness of gun control is severely compromised by the large number of potentially confounding social, behavioral, and economic factors that characterize large national groups. To date, no study has been able to separate the effects of handgun control from differences among populations in terms of socioeconomic status, aggressive behavior, violent crime, and other factors.[7] To clarify the relation between firearm regulations and community rates of homicide, we studied two large cities in the Pacific Northwest: Seattle, Washington, and Vancouver, British Columbia. Although similar in many ways, these two cities have taken decidedly different approaches to handgun control.

METHODS

*   *   *

Firearm Regulations

Although similar in many ways, Seattle and Vancouver differ markedly in their approaches to the regulation of firearms. In Seattle, handguns may be purchased legally for self-defense in the street or at home. After a 30-day waiting period, a permit can be obtained to carry a handgun as a concealed weapon. The recreational use of handguns is minimally restricted.[15]

In Vancouver, self-defense is not considered a valid or legal reason to purchase a handgun. Concealed weapons are not permitted. Recreational uses of handguns (such as target shooting and collecting) are regulated by the province, and the purchase of a handgun requires a restricted-weapons permit. A permit to carry a weapon must also be obtained in order to transport a handgun, and these weapons can be discharged only at a licensed shooting club. Handguns can be transported by car, but only if they are stored in the trunk in a locked box. [16,17]

Although they differ in their approach to firearm regulations, both cities aggressively enforce existing gun laws and regulations, and convictions for gun-related offenses carry similar penalties. For example, the commission of a class A felony (such as murder or robbery) with a firearm in Washington State adds a minimum of two years of confinement to the sentence for the felony.[18] In the Province of British Columbia, the same offense generally results in 1 to 14 years of imprisonment in addition to the felony sentence.[16] Similar percentages of homicides in both communities eventually lead to arrest and police charges. In Washington, under the Sentencing Reform Act of 1981, murder in the first degree carries a minimum sentence of 20 years of confinement.[19] In British Columbia, first-degree murder carries a minimum sentence of 25 years, with a possible judicial parole review after 15 years.[20] Capital punishment was abolished in Canada during the 1970s.[21] In Washington State, the death penalty may be invoked in cases of aggravated first-degree murder, but no one has been executed since 1963.

Rates of Gun Ownership

Because direct surveys of firearm ownership in Seattle and Vancouver have never been conducted, we assessed the rates of gun ownership indirectly by two independent methods. First, we obtained from the Firearm Permit Office of the Vancouver police department a count of the restricted-weapons permits issued in Vancouver between March 1984 and March 1988 and compared this figure with the total number of concealed-weapons permits issued in Seattle during the same period, obtained from the Office of Business and Profession Administration, Department of Licensing, State of Washington. Second, we used Cook's gun prevalence index, a previously validated measure of intercity differences in the prevalence of gun ownership.[14] This index is based on data from 49 cities in the United States and correlates each city's rates of suicide and assaultive homicide involving firearms with survey-based estimates of gun ownership in each city. Both methods indicate that firearms are far more commonly owned in Seattle than in Vancouver.

Identification and Definition of Cases

From police records, we identified all the cases of robbery, burglary, and assault (both simple and aggravated) and all the homicides that occurred in Seattle or Vancouver between January 1, 1980, and December 31, 1986. In defining cases, we followed the guidelines of the U.S. Federal Bureau of Investigation's uniform crime reports (UCR).[22] The UCR guidelines define aggravated assault as an unlawful attack by one person on another for the purpose of inflicting severe or aggravated bodily harm. Usually this type of assault involves the actual or threatened use of a deadly weapon. Simple assault is any case of assault that does not involve the threat or use of a deadly weapon or result in serious or aggravated injuries.

A homicide was defined as the willful killing of one human being by another. This category included cases of premeditated murder, intentional killing, and aggravated assault resulting in death. "Justifiable homicide," as defined by the UCR guidelines, was limited to cases of the killing of a felon by a law-enforcement officer in the line of duty or the killing of a felon by a private citizen during the commission of a felony.[22] Homicides that the police, the prosecuting attorney, or both thought were committed in self-defense were also identified and noted separately.

Statistical Analysis

From both Seattle and Vancouver, we obtained annual and cumulative data on the rates of aggravated assault, simple assault, robbery, and burglary. Cases of aggravated assault were categorized according to the weapon used. Data on homicides were obtained from the files of the medical examiner or coroner in each community and were supplemented by police case files. Each homicide was further categorized according to the age, sex, and race or ethnic group of the victim, as well as the weapon used.

Population-based rates of simple assault, aggravated assault, robbery, burglary, and homicide were then calculated and compared. These rates are expressed as the number per 100,000 persons per year and, when possible, are further adjusted for any differences in the age and sex of the victims. Unadjusted estimates of relative risk and 95 percent confidence intervals were calculated with use of the maximum-likelihood method and are based on Seattle's rate relative to Vancouver's.[23] Age-adjusted relative risks were estimated with use of the Mantel-Haenszel summary odds ratio.[24]

RESULTS

During the seven-year study period, the annual rate of robbery in Seattle was found to be only slightly higher than that in Vancouver (relative risk, 1.09; 95 percent confidence interval, 1.08 to 1.12). Burglaries, on the other hand, occurred at nearly identical rates in the two communities (relative risk, 0.99; 95 percent confidence interval, 0.98 to 1.0). During the study period, 18,925 cases of aggravated assault were reported in Seattle, as compared with 12,034 cases in Vancouver. When the annual rates of assault in the two cities were compared for each year of the study, we found that the two communities had similar rates of assault during the first four years of the study. In 1984, however, reported rates of simple and aggravated assault began to climb sharply in Seattle, whereas the rates of simple and aggravated assault remained relatively constant in Vancouver. This change coincided with the enactment that year of the Domestic Violence Protection Act by the Washington State legislature. Among other provisions, this law required changes in reporting and arrests in cases of domestic violence.[25] It is widely believed that this law and the considerable media attention that followed its passage resulted in dramatic increases in the number of incidents reported and in related enforcement costs in Seattle.[26] Because in Vancouver there was no similar legislative initiative requiring police to change their reporting methods, we restricted our comparison of the data on assaults to the first four years of our study. (1980 through 1983)

During this four-year period, the risk of being a victim of simple assault in Seattle was found to be only slightly higher than that in Vancouver (relative risk, 1.18; 95 percent confidence interval, 1.15 to 1.20) The risk of aggravated assault in Seattle was also only slightly higher than in Vancouver (relative risk, 1.16; 95 percent confidence interval, 1.12 to 1.19). However, when aggravated assaults were subdivided by the type of weapon used and the mechanism of assault, a striking pattern emerged. Although both cities reported almost identical rates of aggravated assault involving knives, other dangerous weapons, or hands, fists, and feet, firearms were far more likely to have been used in cases of assault in Seattle than in Vancouver (Table 1). In fact, all the difference in the relative risk of aggravated assault between these two communities was due to Seattle's 7.7-fold higher rate of assaults involving firearms.

Over the whole seven-year study period, 388 homicides occurred in Seattle (11.3 per 100,000 person-years). In Vancouver, 204 homicides occurred during the same period (6.9 per 100,000 person-years). After adjustment for differences in age and sex between the populations, the relative risk of being a victim of homicide in Seattle, as compared with Vancouver, was found to be 1.63 (95 percent confidence interval, 1.28 to 2.08). This difference is highly unlikely to have occured by chance.

When homicides were subdivided by the mechanism of death, the rate of homicide by knives and other weapons (excluding firearms) in Seattle was found to be almost identical to that in Vancouver (relative risk, 1.08; 95 percent confidence interval, 0.89 to 1.32). Virtually all of the increased risk of death from homicide in Seattle was due to a more than fivefold higher rate of homicide by firearms (Table 1). Handguns, which accounted for roughly 85 percent of the homicides involving firearms in both communities, were 4.8 times more likely to be used in homicides in Seattle than in Vancouver.

To test the hypothesis that the higher rates of homicide in Seattle might be due to more frequent use of firearms for self-protection, we examined all the homicides in both cities that were ruled "legally justifiable" or were determined to have been committed in self-defense. Thirty-two such homicides occurred during the study period, 11 of which involved police intervention. After the exclusion of justifiable homicide by police, 21 cases of homicide by civilians acting in self-defense or in other legally justifiable ways remained, 17 of which occurred in Seattle and 4 of which occurred in Vancouver (relative risk, 3.64; 95 percent confidence interval, 1.32 to 10.06). Thirteen of these

TABLE 1

ANNUAL CRUDE RATES AND RELATIVE RISKS OF AGGRAVATED ASSAULT,
SIMPLE ASSAULT, ROBBERY, BURGLARY, AND HOMICIDE
IN SEATTLE AND VANCOUVER, 1980 THROUGH 1986.*

CRIME	PERIOD	SEATTLE	VANCOUVER	RELATIVE RISK	95% CI
		n./ 100,000			
Robbery	1980–1986	492.2	450.9	1.09	1.08–1.12
Burglary	1980–1986	2952.7	2985.7	0.99	0.98–1.00
Simple assault	1980–1983	902	767.7	1.18	1.15–1.20
Aggravated assault	1980–1983	486.5	420.5	1.16	1.12–1.19
Firearms		87.9	11.4	7.70	6.70–8.70
Knives		78.1	78.9	0.99	0.92–1.07
Other		320.6	330.2	0.97	0.94–1.01
Homicides	1980–1986	11.3	6.9	1.63	1.38–1.93
Firearms		4.8	1.0	5.08	3.54–7.27
Knives		3.1	3.5	0.90	0.69–1.18
Other		3.4	2.5	1.33	0.99–1.78

*CI denotes confidence interval. The "crude rate" for these crimes is the number of events occurring in a given population over a given time period. The relative risks shown are for Seattle in relation to Vancouver.

cases (all of which occurred in Seattle) involved firearms. The exclusion of all 21 cases (which accounted for less than 4 percent of the homicides during the study interval) had little overall effect on the relative risk of homicide in the two communities (age- and sex-adjusted relative risk, 1.57; 95 percent confidence interval, 1.22 to 2.01).

When homicides were stratified by the race or ethnic group of the victim, a complex picture emerged (Table 2). The homicide rates in Table 2 were adjusted for age to match the 1980 U.S. population. This technique permits fairer comparisons among racial and ethnic groups with differing age compositions in each city. The relative risk for each racial or ethnic group, however, was estimated with use of the Mantel-Haenszel summary odds ratio.[24] This method, in effect, uses a different set of weights for the various age strata, depending on the distribution of persons among the age strata for that racial or ethnic group only. Hence, these estimates of relative risk differ slightly from a simple quotient of the age-adjusted rates.

Whereas similar rates of death by homicide were noted for whites in both cities, Asians in Seattle had higher rates of death by homicide than

TABLE 2

ANNUAL AGE-ADJUSTED HOMICIDE RATES AND RELATIVE RISKS OF DEATH
BY HOMICIDE IN SEATTLE AND VANCOUVER, 1980 THROUGH 1986,
ACCORDING TO THE RACE OR ETHNIC GROUP OF THE VICTIM.*

RACE OR ETHNIC GROUP	SEATTLE	VANCOUVER	RELATIVE RISK	95% CI
	no./100,000			
White (non-Hispanic)	6.2	6.4	1	0.8–1.2
Asian	15.0	4.1	3.5	2.1–5.7
Excluding Wah Mee murders	9.5	—	2.3	1.4–4.0
Black	36.6	9.5	2.8	0.4–20.4
Hispanic	26.9	7.9	5	0.7–34.3
Native American	64.9	71.3	0.9	0.5–1.5

*CI denotes confidence interval. The relative risks shown are for Seattle in relation to Vancouver.

their counterparts in Vancouver. This difference persisted even after the exclusion of the 13 persons who died in the Wah Mee gambling club massacre in Seattle in 1983. Blacks and Hispanics in Seattle had higher relative risks of death by homicide than blacks and Hispanics in Vancouver, but the confidence intervals were very wide, given the relatively small size of both minorities in Vancouver. Only one black and one Hispanic were killed in Vancouver during the study period. Native Americans had the highest rates of death by homicide in both cities.

DISCUSSION

Previous studies of the effectiveness of gun control have generally compared rates of homicide in nations with different approaches to the regulation of firearms.[7] Unfortunately, the validity of these studies has been compromised by the large number of confounding factors that characterize national groups. We sought to circumvent this limitation by focusing our analysis on two demographically comparable and physically proximate cities with markedly different approaches to handgun control. In many ways, these two cities have more in common with each other than they do with other major cities in their respective countries. For example, Seattle's homicide rate is consistently half to two thirds that reported in cities such as Chicago, Los Angeles, New York, and Houston,[4] whereas Vancouver experiences annual rates of homicide two to three times higher than those reported in Ottawa, Toronto, and Calgary (Canadian Centre for Justice Statistics, Homicide Program, Ottawa: unpublished data).

In order to exclude the possibility that Seattle's higher homicide rate may be explained by higher levels of criminal activity or aggressiveness in its population, we compared the rates of burglary, robbery, simple assault, and aggravated assault in the two communities. Although we observed a slightly higher rate of simple and aggravated assault in Seattle, these differences were relatively small—the rates in Seattle were 16 to 18 percent higher than those reported in Vancouver during a period of comparable case reporting. Virtually all of the excess risk of aggravated assault in Seattle was explained by a sevenfold higher rate of assaults involving firearms. Despite similar rates of robbery and burglary and only small differences in the rates of simple and aggravated assault, we found that Seattle had substantially higher rates of homicide than Vancouver. Most of the excess mortality was due to an almost fivefold higher rate of murders with handguns in Seattle.

Critics of handgun control have long claimed that limiting access to guns will have little effect on the rates of homicide, because persons who are intent on killing others will only work harder to acquire a gun or will kill by other means.[7, 27] If the rate of homicide in a community were influenced more by the strength of intent than by the availability of weapons, we might have expected the rate of homicides with weapons other than guns to have been higher in Vancouver than in Seattle, in direct proportion to any decrease in Vancouver's rate of firearm homicides. This was not the case. During the study interval, Vancouver's rate of homicides with weapons other than guns was not significantly higher than that in Seattle, suggesting that few would-be assailants switched to homicide by other methods.

Ready access to handguns has been advocated by some as an important way to provide law-abiding citizens with an effective means to defend themselves.[27-29] Were this true, we might have expected that much of Seattle's excess rate of homicides, as compared with Vancouver's, would have been explained by a higher rate of justifiable homicides and killings in self-defense by civilians. Although such homicides did occur at a significanly higher rate in Seattle than in Vancouver, these cases accounted for less than 4 percent of the homicides in both cities during the study period. When we excluded cases of justifiable homicide or killings in self-defense by civilians from our calculation of relative risk, our results were almost the same.

It also appears unlikely that differences in law-enforcement activity accounted for the lower homicide rate in Vancouver. Suspected offenders are arrested and cases are cleared at similar rates in both cities. After arrest and conviction, similar crimes carry similar penalties in the courts in Seattle and Vancouver.

We found substantial differences in the risk of death by homicide according to race and ethnic group in both cities. In the United States, blacks and Hispanics are murdered at substantially higher rates than whites.[2] Although the great majority of homicides in the United States involve assailants of the same race or ethnic group, current evidence suggests that socioeconomic status plays a much greater role in explaining racial and ethnic differences in the rate of homicide than any intrinsic tendency toward violence.[2,30,31] For example, Centerwall has shown that when household crowding is taken into account, the rate of domestic homicide among blacks in Atlanta, Georgia, is no higher than that of whites living in similar conditions.[32] Likewise, a recent study of childhood homicide in Ohio found that once cases were stratified by socioeconomic status, there was little difference in race-specific rates of homicide involving children five to fourteen years of age.[33]

Since low-income populations have higher rates of homicide, socioeconomic status is probably an important confounding factor in our comparison of the rates of homicide for racial and ethnic groups. Although the median income and the overall distribution of household incomes in Seattle and Vancouver are similar, the distribution of household incomes by racial and ethnic group may not be the same in Vancouver as in Seattle. For example, blacks in Vancouver had a slightly higher mean income in 1981 than the rest of Vancouver's population (statistics Canada, 1981 Census Custom Tabulation: unpublished data). In contrast, blacks in Seattle have a substantially lower median income than the rest of Seattle's population.[34] Thus, much of the excess risk of homicide among blacks in Seattle, as compared with blacks in Vancouver, may be explained by their lower socioeconomic status. If, on the other hand, more whites in Vancouver have low incomes that whites in Seattle, the higher risk of homicide expected in this low-income subset may push the rate of homicide among whites in Vancouver higher than that for whites in Seattle. Unfortunately, neither hypothesis can be tested in a quantitative fashion, since detailed information about household incomes according to race is not available for Vancouver.

Three limitations of our study warrant comment. First, our measures of the prevalence of firearm ownership may not precisely reflect the availability of guns in the two communities. Although the two measures we used were derived independently and are consistent with the expected effects of gun control, their validity as indicators of community rates of gun ownership has not been conclusively established. Cook's gun prevalence index has been shown to correlate with data derived from national surveys, but it has not been tested for accuracy in cities outside the United States. Comparisons of concealed-weapons permits in Seattle with restricted-weapons permits in Vancouver are probably of limited validity, since these counts do not include handguns obtained illegally. In fact, the comparison of permit data of this sort probably substantially underestimates the differences between the communities in the rate of handgun ownership, since only a fraction of the handguns in Seattle are purchased for use as concealed weapons, whereas all legal handgun purchases in Vancouver require a restricted-weapons permit. Still, these indirect estimates of gun ownership are consistent with one another, and both agree with prior reports that estimate the rate of handgun ownership in Canada to be about one fourth that in the United States.[35]

Second, although similar in many ways, Seattle and Vancouver may well differ in other aspects that could affect their rates of homicide. For example, differences in the degree of illegal drug-related activity, differences in the rate of illicit gun sales, or other, less readily apparent differences may confound the relation between firearm regulations and the rate of homicide. Although such differences may exist, striking socioeconomic similarities between the cities and the fact that they had similar rates of burglary, robbery, and both simple and aggravated assault during comparable reporting periods make such confounding less likely. Unfortunately, changes in the rules for reporting assault cases in Seattle, mandated by the State of Washington in 1984, precluded a valid comparison of the rates of simple and aggravated assault over the entire seven-year period.

Third, conclusions based on a comparison of two cities in the Pacific Northwest may not be generalizable to other urban areas in North America. Given the complex interaction of individual behavior, environment, and community factors in the pathogenesis of violent death, we cannot predict the precise impact that Canadian-style gun control might have in the United States. Even if such a major change in public policy were to take place, the current high rates of handgun ownership might blunt any effects of tougher handgun regulations for years to come.

Our analysis of the rates of homicide in these two largely similar cities suggests that the modest restriction of citizens' access to firearms (especially handguns) is associated with lower rates of homicide. This association does not appear to be explained by differences between the communities in aggressiveness, criminal behavior, or response to crime. Although our findings should be corroborated in other settings, our results suggest that a more restrictive approach to handgun control may decrease national homicide rates.

We are indebted to Noel Weiss, M.D., for his review of the manuscript; to Mr. Robert Galbraith, chief coroner of the British Columbia Coroner's Service; to Steven Floerchinger, M.D., for his assistance with the collection of the data; to Millicent Morrow, Cheryl Pernack, and Carol Conway for assistance in the preparation of the manuscript; and to the police departments of Seattle and Vancouver for their invaluable cooperation and assistance.

REFERENCES

1. *Homicide Surveillance: 1970–78*. Atlanta: Centers for Disease Control, September, 1983.
2. *Homicide Surveillance: High Risk Racial and Ethnic Groups—Blacks and Hispanics, 1970 to 1983*. Atlanta: Centers for Disease Control, November, 1986.
3. Baker, S. P., B. O'Neill, and R. S. Karpf. *The Injury Fact Book*. Lexington, Mass.: Lexington Books, 1984.

4. Department of Justice, Federal Bureau of Investigation. *Crime in the United States* (Uniform Crime Reports). Washington, D.C.: Government Printing Office, 1986.
5. Baker, S. P. "Without Guns, Do People Kill People?" *American Journal of Public Health* 75 (1985): 587-88.
6. Hedeboe, J., A. V. Charles, J. Nielsen, et al. "Interpersonal Violence: Patterns in a Danish Community." *American Journal of Public Health* 75 (1985): 651-53.
7. Wright, J., P. Rossi, K. Daly, and E. Weber-Burdin. *Weapons, Crime and Violence in America: A Literature Review and Research Agenda.* Washington, D.C.: Department of Justice, National Institute of Justice, 1981.
8. Weiss, J. M. A. "Gun Control: A Question of Public/Mental Health?" *Journal of Operational Psychiatry* 12 (1981): 86-88.
9. Bruce-Briggs, B. "The Great American Gun War." *Public Interest* 45 (1976): 37-62.
10. Bureau of Census. 1980 Census of population, Washington. Washington, D.C.: Government Printing Office, 1981.
11. Statistics Canada: 1981 census of Canada, Vancouver, British Columbia. Ottawa, Ont.: Minister of Supply and Services, 1983.
12. Seattle local market T.V. ratings, 1985-86. (Based on Arbitron television ratings.) Provided by KING TV, Seattle, Washington.
13. Vancouver local market T.V. ratings, 1985-86. Provided by Bureau of Broadcast Measurement, Toronto.
14. Cook, P. J. "The Role of Firearms in Violent Crime." In M. Wolfgang, ed., *Criminal Violence* (Beverly Hills, Calif.: Sage, 1982), pp. 236-90.
15. Revised Code of State of Washington. RCW chapter 9.41.090,9.41.095,9.41.070, 1986.
16. Criminal Code of Canada. Firearms and Other Offensive Weapons, Martin's Criminal Code of Canada, 1982. Part II.1 (Sections 81-016.9, 1982).
17. ———. Restricted Weapons and Firearm Control Regulations Sec. 106.2 (11); Amendment Act, July 18, 1977, 1982.
18. Revised Code of State of Washington, Sentence Reform act Chapter 9 94A. 125.1980.
19. Revised Code of State of Washington. Murder I, 9A.32.040.1984.
20. Criminal Code of Canada. Application for Judicial Review Sentence of Life Imprisonment, 1988 Part XX 669-67,1(1).
21. ———. Act to Amend Criminal Code B.11 C84, 1976.
22. Department of Justice, Federal Bureau of Investigation. *Uniform Crime Reporting Handbook.* Washington, D.C.: Government Printing Office, 1984.
23. Rothman, K. J., and J. D. Boice, Jr. *Epidemiologic Analysis with a Programmable Calculator.* Boston: Epidemiology Resources, 1982.
24. Armitage, P., and G. Berry. *Statistical Methods in Medical Research.* 2d ed. Oxford: Blackwell, 1987.
25. Revised Code of State of Washington. RCW Chapter 10.99.010-.100,1984.
27. Seattle Police Department. Inspectional Service Division Report, Domestic Violence Arrest Costs: 1984-87, Seattle, 1986.
28. Drooz, R. B. "Handguns and Hokum: A Methodological Problem." *JAMA* 238 (1977): 43-45.
29. Copeland, A. R. "The Right to Keep and Bear Arms—A Study of Civilian Homicides Committed against Those Involved in Criminal Acts in Metropolitan Dade County from 1957 to 1982." *Journal of Forensic Science* 29 (1984): 584-90.
30. Kleck, G. "Crime Control through the Private Use of Armed Force." *Social Problems* 35 (1988): 1-21.
31. Loftin, C., and R. H. Hill. "Regional Subculture and Homicide: An Examination of the Gastil-Hackney Thesis." *American Sociology Review* 39 (1974): 714-24.
32. Williams, K. R. "Economic Sources of Homicide: Reestimating the Effects of Poverty and Inequality." *American Sociological Review* 49 (1984): 283-89.
33. Centerwall, B. S. "Race, Socioeconomic Status, and Domestic Homicide, Atlanta, 1971-72." *American Journal of Public Health* 74 (1984): 813-15.
34. Muscat, J. E. "Characteristics of Childhood Homicide in Ohio, 1974-84." *American Journal of Public Health* 78 (1988): 822-24.
35. Seattle City Government. *General Social and Economic Characteristics, City of Seattle: 1970-1980.* Planning Research Bulletin no. 45. Seattle: Department of Community Development, 1983.
36. Newton, G., and F. Zimring. *Firearms and Violence in American Life: A Staff Report to the National Commission on the Causes and Prevention of Violence.* Washington, D.C.: Government Printing Office, 1969.

Selected Bibliography

SYMPOSIA

"Firearms and Firearms Regulation: Old Premises, New Research," *Law and Policy Quarterly* 5, no. 3 (1983).

"Gun Control," *The Annals* of the American Academy of Political and Social Science. 455 (1981).

BOOKS

Anderson, Jarvis. *Guns in American Life*. New York: Random House, 1984.

Block, Irvin. *Gun Control: One Way to Save Lives*. New York: Public Affairs Committee, 1976.

Holmberg, Judith Vandell, and Michael Clancy. *People vs. Handguns: The Campaign to Ban Handguns in Massachusetts*. Washington, D.C.: United States Conference of Mayors, 1977.

Kaplan, John, Don B. Kates, Jr., and Raymond Kessler. *Law-Abiding Criminals: Making Gun Ownership a Victimless Crime*. Bellevue, Wash.: Second Amendment Foundation, 1983.

Kates, Don B. Jr. *Criminological Perspectives on Gun Control and Gun Prohibition Legislation*. San Francisco: N.p., 1982.

———. *Restricting Handguns: The Liberal Skeptics Speak Out*. Croton-on-Hudson, N.Y.: North River Press, 1979.

———, ed. *Firearms and Violence: Issues of Public Policy*. Pacific Studies in Public Policy. Cambridge, Mass.: Ballinger Publishing, 1984.

———, ed. *Firearms and Violence: Issues of Regulation*. Pacific Studies in Public Policy. Cambridge, Mass.: Ballinger Publishing, 1983.

Kennett, Lee, and James LaVerne Anderson. *The Gun in America: The Origins of a National Dilemma.* Westport, Conn.: Greenwood, 1975.

Quigley, Paxton. *Armed and Female.* New York: E. P. Dutton, 1989.

Shields, Pete, and John Greenya. *Guns Don't Die—People Do.* New York: Arbor House, 1981.

Wright, James D., and Peter H. Rossi. *Weapons, Crime, and Violence in America: Executive Summary.* Washington, D.C.: National Institute of Justice, 1981.

Wright, James D., Peter H. Rossi, and Kathleen Daly. *Under the Gun: Weapons, Crime, and Violence in America.* New York: Aldine, 1983.

Wright, James D., Peter H. Rossi, Kathleen Daly, and Eleanor Weber-Burdin. *Weapons, Crime, and Violence in America: A Literature Review and Research Agenda.* Washington, D.C.: National Institute of Justice, 1981.

Zimring, Franklin E., and Gordon Hawkins. *The Citizen's Guide to Gun Control.* New York: Macmillan Publishing, 1987.

CONGRESSIONAL DOCUMENTS

United States Congress Senate Committee on the Judiciary. Subcommittee on Juvenile Delinquency. *Handgun Crime Control: 1975-1976: Hearings to Examine the Adequacy of Federal Firearms Controls in Restricting the Availability of Handguns for Criminal Use.* 94th Congress, 1st Session, 1975.

———. Committee on the Judiciary. Subcommittee on the Constitution. *Gun Control and Constitutional Rights: Hearings on Constitutional Oversight of a Regulatory Agency—the Bureau of Alcohol, Tobacco, and Firearms, Department of the Treasury—on the Enforcement of the Gun Control Act of 1968.* 96th Congress, 2d. Session, 1980.

ARTICLES

Cook, Philip J. "The 'Saturday Night Special': An Assessment of the Alternative Definitions from a Policy Perspective." *Journal of Criminal Law and Criminology* 72 (1981):1735–45.

Cook, Philip, and James Blose. "State Programs for Screening Handgun Buyers." *Annals of the American Academy of Political and Social Science,* no. 455 (1981):80–91.

Cook, Philip, and Karen Hawley. "North Carolina's Pistol Permit Law: An Evaluation." *Popular Government* 46 (Spring 1981):1–4.

Danto, Bruce L. "Firearms and Violence." *International Journal of Offender Therapy and Comparative Criminology* 23 (1979):135–46.

Kaplan, John. "Controlling Firearms." *Cleveland State Law Review* 28 (1979):1–28.

———. "The Wisdom of Gun Prohibition." *Annals* of the American Academy of Political and Social Science, No. 455 (1981): 11–23.

Kates, Don B. Jr. "Firearms and Violence: Old Premises and Current Evidence." In Ted Robert Gurr, ed., *Violence in America: The History of Crime*. London: Sage Publications, 1989, pp. 197–215.

———. "Gun Control Versus Gun Prohibition." *American Bar Association Journal* 68 (1982):1052.

———. "Handgun Banning in Light of the Prohibition Experience." In Don B. Kates, Jr., ed., *Firearms and Violence*. Cambridge, Mass.: Ballinger Publishing, 1984, pp. 139–65.

Kleck, Gary, and David J. Bordua. "The Assumptions of Gun Control." In Don B. Kates, Jr., ed., *Firearms and Violence*. Cambridge, Mass.: Ballinger Publishing, 1984, pp. 23–44.

Kleck, Gary. "Handgun-Only Gun Control: A Policy Disaster in the Making." In Don B. Kates, Jr., ed., *Firearms and Violence*. Cambridge, Mass.: Ballinger Publishing, 1984, pp. 167–99.

Leff, Carol Skalnik, and Mark H. Leff. "The Politics of Ineffectiveness: Federal Firearms Legislation, 1919–38." *Annals* of the American Academy of Political and Social Science, No. 455 (1981):48–62.

Loftin, Colin, and David McDowall. " 'One with a Gun Gets You Two': Mandatory Sentencing and Firearms Violence in Detroit." *Annals* of the American Academy of Political and Social Science, No. 455 (1981):150–67.

Moore, Mark H. "Keeping Handguns from Criminal Offenders." *Annals* of the American Academy of Political and Social Science, No. 455 (1981): 92–109.

Pierce, Glenn L., and William J. Bowers. "The Bartley-Fox Gun Law's Short-Term Impact on Crime in Boston." *Annals* of the American Academy of Political and Social Science, No. 455 (1981):120–37.

"Should Handguns Be Outlawed? Yes: Interview with Michael Beard, Executive Director, National Coalition to Ban Handguns; No: Interview with Neal Knox, Executive Director, Institute for Legislative Action, National Rifle Association of America." *U.S. News and World Report* (22 December 1980):23–24.

Wright, James D. "Public Opinion and Gun Control: A Comparison of Results from Two Recent National Surveys.' *Annals* of the American Academy of Political and Social Science, No. 455 (1981):240–49.

Wright, James D., and Linda L. Marston. "The Ownership of the Means of Destruction: Weapons in the United States." *Social Problems* 23 (1975):93–107.

Part Three

Guns for Self-Defense:
Protection or Menace?

Introduction

A key issue in the contemporary gun control debate concerns ownership of handguns for home or self-defense. As gun control advocate Franklin E. Zimring puts it: "The guns that are used for self-defense in cities are mainly handguns. At the same time the handgun is the criminal's primary firearm and handguns have become the pivotal issue in the current debate about gun control."[1]

Those who advocate restricting public access to handguns try to demonstrate that the costs of handgun ownership for ordinary law-abiding citizens outweigh its benefits as a means of protection against burglary and assault. This cost-benefit-analysis approach is especially important for gun control advocates as doubt continues to mount concerning the efficiency of gun control as a crime control mechanism. That is, the case for restricting access to handguns can be made by using cost-benefit-analysis to show that handgun ownership by the ordinary law-abiding citizens constitutes a real menace not only to the owner personally, but to his family and friends.

Specifically, gun control advocates must prove that handguns for such citizens are an ineffective or unnecessary means of home and self-protection, or that handgun possession by people *representative of the entire class of legal gun owners* constitutes a much more significant menace to relatives, friends, children, and self than does criminal intrusion (Yaeger et al., selection 15). These two claims assume a third: that there is no convincing evidence that public gun ownership deters such crimes as burglary, mugging, and rape.

The first claim—that handguns are an ineffective or unnecessary means of home and self-protection—is especially important to gun control advocates in view of the increasing trend of women arming themselves. The proliferation of single parent, female heads of households and particularly professional and single women working and living in high crime areas, accounts for this trend. Significantly, women have traditionally constituted an important part of the gun control constituency.

The second claim—that the possession of handguns by ordinary law-abiding citizens places the owner as well as his family, relatives, friends, and acquaintances at significant risk—has become central to the gun control movement. Studies from the medical and public health sectors have therefore become mainstays in the case outlined by gun control advocates against handguns. The handgun here is described as a major "public health" menace (Kellerman and Reay, selection 16; Wintemute et al., selections 17, 21).

The third claim—that no convincing evidence exists that public gun ownership deters burglary, robbery, and rape—reinforces the idea that handguns are unnecessary or irrelevant to citizen security (Yeager et al., selection 15).

Don B. Kates, Jr. (selection 18) challenges all of the conclusions reached by Yeager and like-minded gun control advocates concerning the claimed lack of defensive utility and the outright defensive liability of firearms. In selection 19, Kates takes on the claims of Yeager and Wintemute (selections 15 and 17) that people who kill family members and acquaintances are representative of the gun owning public. According to Kates, such people typically have criminal records and violent histories that make them unrepresentative of the typical gun owner. And in selection 22 he challenges the data pertaining to childhood deaths involving firearms.

In Gary Kleck's essay (selection 20) data are offered and studies cited in an effort to support the view that civilian gun ownership is an important deterrent to violent crime; a deterrent whose effectiveness rivals that of the criminal justice system itself. If Kleck is correct, then strict or prohibitionist gun control measures would be a social liability.

The following selections present these claims and their supporting evidence as well as the objections critics raise concerning both the content of the claims and the strength of the data offered in their behalf.

NOTE

1. Franklin E. Zimring and Gordon Hawkins. *The Citizen's Guide to Gun Control* (New York: Macmillan, 1987), p. 29.

15

How Well Does the Handgun Protect You and Your Family?

Matthew G. Yeager
with Joseph D. Alviani and Nancy Loving

United States Conference of Mayors
Policy Statement on Handgun Control

Whereas, over 8,000 Americans were felled by handguns in 1970 and nationally 80 percent of all homicide victims knew killers as a relative or friend; and

Whereas, 95 percent of the policemen killed in the line of duty between 1961 and 1970 were felled by handguns; and

Whereas, gun dealers today sell to the mentally ill, criminals, dope addicts, convicted felons, juveniles, as well as good citizens who kill each other; and

Whereas, those who possess handguns cannot be divided into criminals and qualified gun owners; and

Whereas, handguns are not generally used to sporting or recreational purposes, and such purposes do not require keeping handguns in private homes; and

Whereas, the United States Supreme Court ruled in 1939 that firearms regulation is not unconstitutional unless it impairs the effectiveness of the State militia.

Reprinted by permission of the U.S. Conference of Mayors, 1976, Washington, D.C.

Now therefore be it resolved that the United States Conference of Mayors takes a position of leadership and urges national legislation against the manufacture, importation, sale and private possession of handguns, except for use by law enforcement personnel, military and sportsmen clubs; and

Be it further resolved that the United States Conference of Mayors urges its members to extend every effort to educate the American public to the dangerous and appalling realities resulting from the private possession of handguns and that we urge the Congress to adopt a national handgun registration law; and

Be it further resolved that (i) effective legislation be introduced and approved by the states not having adequate legislation to that effect; (ii) the proposed legislation shall provide for the registration of all firearms; (iii) state legislation shall require all citizens interested in carrying a weapon to obtain a license after showing just cause and good conduct; (iv) federal legislation shall provide, in addition to existing restrictions, that any person not having a state license to carry a firearm shall commit an offense for transporting such in interstate commerce.

Adopted
June 1972

INTRODUCTION

Fear of crime has become so common in American life that many Americans have armed themselves to protect their families and their homes. Recent Gallup surveys have reported that nearly one half of America's householders are afraid to walk in their neighborhoods at night, and one out of every five Americans does not even feel safe at night in his or her own home. The result of this anxiety over crime has been a dramatic upsurge in the number of handgun purchases. Approximately 40 million handguns are currently in private circulation in our country, and this arsenal increases by about 2.5 million handguns each year. Including some 96 million rifles and shotguns in private hands, there are about 65 guns for every 100 men, women, and children in the United States. Moreover, a receant national poll disclosed that of the households in America possessing guns, 66 percent responded that they keep them for self-defense.

The irony of this position, however, is that the possession of a handgun only rarely prevents a burglary or a robbery. The use of firearms for self-protection is more likely to lead to a serious accident or death among family and friends than to the death of an intruder. The *probability of being robbed, raped, or assaulted* is low enough to seriously call into question the need for Americans to keep loaded guns on their persons or about their homes. The statistical data available to date on crime and victimization lead to the following conclusions:

- A gun kept in the home for self-protection is far more likely to cause serious injury or death to family and friends than to an intruder. Children and young adults are most vulnerable to firearms misuse.

- A burglar will more often steal a home defense weapon than be repelled by it. The overwhelming majority of burglaries are committed while no one is at home (90 percent), and if a confrontation does occur, it typically involves a verbal exchange only. Few individuals are ever killed during the course of a burglary.

- A study of robbery victimization in eight American cities shows that in most instances, resort to a self-protective measure is less likely to result in a completed robbery (55 percent) as contrasted to those victims taking no self-defense measure (85 percent). Use of a weapon for self-protection may be the most effective means of resisting a robbery. However, the study of robberies in eight American cities suggests that in only 3.5 percent of the victimizations did the person have the opportunity to use a weapon for self-protection; and, data from Chicago and New York indicate that a victim's weapon (if it is a firearm) is more likely to be stolen than used against the robber, Those who resist with a weapon are just as likely to suffer injury as those not taking any self-defense measure, but are five times more likely to incur serious injury leading to prolonged hospitalization. Of special importance, a study in Chicago revealed that robbery victims who make some attempt at resistance are eight times more likely to be killed than those who put up no defense. It would appear that victims using some measure of self-defense against robberies are trading off a lower robbery completion rate for substantial increases in the probability of serious ingury and death.

- The use of weapons as a means of self-protection against aggravated assault appears to be limited. Most aggravated assaults are not completed, regardless of whether or not the victim takes a self-protective measure. For most of the population, the rate of victimization is low enough to question the desirability of firearms as a means of self-protection. Injuries are infrequent, though more likely to be serious if the victim physically resists the offender. More often than not, the victim lacks the opportunity to use a weapon for self-defense since the vast majority of aggravated assaults occur outside the home and are committed by strangers. The availability of a handgun and the taking of a self-defense measure during an aggravated assault dramatically increased the likelihood of a fatality.

- Two-thirds of all rapes are committed outside the home, and more than three-quarters are committed without a weapon. Given the fact that most victims are taken by surprise, it is extremely unlikely that the use of a handgun will significantly deter rapists.

A HANDGUN IN THE HOME

The handgun is rarely an effective instrument for protecting the home against an intruder. According to the 1969 staff report of the National Commission on the Causes and Prevention of Violence:

> Burglary is the most common type of intrusion of the home and causes the greatest property loss, but it rarely threatens the homeowner's life. The burglar typically seeks to commit his crime without being discovered, if possible by entering a home that is not occupied. Consequently, he is more likely to steal the home-defense firearm than be driven off by it.[1]

Few individuals are injured during a burglary, and the number killed is a small percentage of total homicides. The FBI recorded 20,600 homicides in 1974. Of these homicides, the circumstances of the murder were known in 18,362 cases, or 89 percent. However, all of these deaths, only 169 citizens were killed by felons during the commission of a burglary, equaling 0.8 percent of all homicides, and 0.9 percent of homicides where circumstances are known to the police.[2]

Studies in three of our nation's largest cities confirm the conclusion that the likelihood of injury or death during the course of a burglary is minimal.

- In 1967, 18,000 home burglaries were recorded in the Detroit metropolitan areas, and yet only one burglary victim was killed.[3]

- In the entire decade from 1958 through 1967, 20 burglary victims were killed in New York City, while in 1967 alone more than 150,000 burglaries were reported to the police.[4]

- Records of the Chicago Police Department showed that of a total 7,045 homicides in the years 1965 through 1974, only 41 persons were murdered during the course of a burglary. Although the Chicago police were unable to identify a motive in 25 percent (N = 1785) of these cases, it is apparent that burglary victims are in the small minority of all murder victims. Even if the number of burglary-victim homicides were quadrupled, that figure still represents only 2 percent of all Chicago homicides during the years 1965 to 1974, and only 0.04 percent of all reported burglaries (N = 367,436).[5]

A detailed review of burglary-linked homicides in Cuyahoga County, Ohio (the Greater Cleveland metropolitan area) raises further doubt about the utility of firearms for defense of the home. In 1974, six homicides were linked to burglaries in that country. Of those homicides, two were instances in which the victim was shot by the burglar; one was a situation in which the assailant was allegedly hired by the victim's husband to kill his wife; in another instance, the victim's husband claimed that theft was the assailant's motive (the fact that the victim and assailant were wll acquainted led police to suspect narcotics connections); in one murder a husband and wife shot an alleged burglar (police again noted narcotics connections); and in the last murder, an apartment dweller shot an unarmed drunk he mistook for a burglar when the victim pounded on his door. During all of 1974, only one burglar was shot to death by a homeowner in Cuyahoga County.[6]

Family Death Likely

Statistics on firearms violence corroborate the finding that a gun in the home is far more likely to lead to the death or injury of a family member or friend than to the death of an intruder.

A detailed study of accidental firearm fatalities in Cuyahoga County, Ohio, conducted by the School of Medicine at Case Western Reserve University, indicated that from 1958 to 1973, "only 23 burglars, robbers, or intruders who were not relatives or acquaintances were killed by guns in the hands of persons who were protecting their homes. During the same interval, six times as many fatal accidents occurred in the home."[7]

The Staff Report, *Firearms and Violence in American Life,* of the National Commission on the Causes and Prevention of Violence, found that during 1967, more lives were lost in home firearm accidents in Detroit (25 deaths) than in home robberies and burglaries in the previous four and one-half years (23 deaths).[8]

Adding to the importance of these data is the fact that the victims of accidental firearms deaths are often children. A study conducted at Detroit General Hospital of 131 gunshot wounds in children stated:

- Where the circumstances were known, most children were injured while playing with guns acquired for protection of the home.

- Neither the victim nor the shooter had experience or training in firearms use.

- A dramatic increase in gunshot wounds accompanied the purchase of handguns after the civil disorders of 1967.[9]

The study concluded that for the most part, these children were the innocent victims of gun availability.

With the realization that 72 percent of all murders nationwide in 1974 occurred among family members, friends, and acquaintances (firearms being the preferred weapon in 68 percent of all homicides),[10] a loaded handgun in the home is statistically far more likely to be used against family and friends than as a means to repel strangers. If homeowners have little to fear from a pistol-packing burglar, they should maintain no illusions about frightening or apprehending the intruder. Though few studies exist on the frequency of such events, one analysis in the city and county of Honolulu, Hawaii, showed that from 1970 to 1974, not one felony offender was apprehended by an armed citizen.[11]

One might further hypothesize that if firearms are an effective deterrent against burglary, a larger proportion of nonburglary victims would own guns than victims. Of course, one would be assuming that potential burglars are somehow aware that a particular occupant is armed, and that most burglars anticipate a confrontation with the homeowner. Nevertheless, one interview study of 220 randomly selected victims of residential burglary and 682 non-victims in the Boston metropolitan area found that victims were slightly *more likely* (17 percent) to have weapons as household protective measures than non-victims (10 percent).[12] Another study in Toronto, Canada, of 1665 randomly chosen households in a high crime area disclosed that 18 percent of the burglary victims reported owning a handgun or a rifle compared to 17 percent of the nonburglary victims. . . . [13] Apparently, having a gun in the house makes little difference as to whether that household is victimized by a burglary.

Handguns rarely prevent burglaries because the overwhelming majority of burglars commit their crimes when no one is at home. A study of 1988 police-reported burglaries in Boston concluded that the premises were unoccupied in 92 percent of the cases. Of the 159 burglaries in which the home was occupied, police records note the occupant's state of mind in 82 cases. Of these, the occupants were asleep in 51 percent, unaware of the burglary in 14 percent, and aware of the crime in 35 percent of the cases (less than 2 percent of all the burglarie studied). In those situations in which the occupants of the home were aware of the burglary, the police still classified the incident as a burglary. Although a burglary can escalate into a robbery because of an unexpected encounter between the victim and the intruder, the Boston study projected that no more than one burglary in 90 becomes a residential robbery.[14]

Confrontation with Burglar

The extent of actual confrontation, however, may be under-reported in official statistics. For instance, the survey of burglary victims in Toronto, Canada, reflects a higher percentage of confrontations between the victim and the burglar, but not a single instance of the householder using a gun for self-protection.[15] This study surveyed 1665 households in Toronto, and over a 16 month period 116 households, or 7 percent, had been victimized by burglary. Of those 116 burglaries, only 25 victims, or 21 percent, reported that they had confronted the burglar, while another 27 victims, or 23 percent, said the burglary occurred while the home was occupied. The most serious event that usually occurs during a confrontation is a conversation with the suspect. A typical event is described as follows:

> He said he wanted to sell books. Said he thought he heard me say come in. I spoke to him and asked him who he was and what he was doing here.

In no instance was an offernder seen with a firearm (although three of the alleged burglars were armed, two with knives), and only one household victim received injury equiring hospitalization (total cost approximately $50). Although 15 percent of the burglary victims admitted owning a gun or rifle, the firearms were of no consequence in preventing the burglary. In fact, only one victim among the 25 confrontations possessed a firearm, which was not used. Six of the alleged burglars were later apprehended by either the victim or someone else, but weapons made little difference. In only two of the six apprehensions was the person who caught the offender armed with a weapon— a brick, bat, or the like.

Of no small importance, in the 25 cases where the offender had no consent to enter the dwelling, *he was known to the victim in 52 percent (N = 13) of the confrontations.* Extreme caution must be exercised in interpreting the above data given the small numbers involved, and the lack of any replicated studies to date. Furthermore, we suspect that a large proportion of the alleged confrontations may not have been theft-motivated burglaries since many of the suspects were acquaintances and since the question on the survey asked, "Has anyone entered your home illegally or without you or someone else who lives there giving consent?" If one accepts the study's finding that the average value of stolen property from the sample of victimized households was $345,[16] and given the overwhelming nonviolent nature of most burglaries even when confrontations do occur, the presence of armed weapons as household protective measures appears neither useful nor necessary.

In fact, the household weapon is more likely to be stolen by the burglar than used against him. The FBI's National Crime Information Center (NCIC) advises that some 211,750 guns are entered into the NCIC Stolen Property File each year. The NCIC estimates that approximately 75 percent (N = 158,812) of these are actually stolen guns. According to surveys conducted for the Treasury Department's Bureau of Alcohol, Tobacco, and Firearms, some 41,000 guns are stolen annually from gun manufacturers, interstate carriers, and dealers, and approximately 70 percent of all thefts from interstate shipments involve handguns. Subtracting the above estimates from a projected total leaves over 100,000 guns stolen from private owners, the vast majority of which are probably handguns.[17]

VIOLENT CRIME

As concerned as the American public is about burglary, the crimes most feared by our citizens are violent attacks against people: robbery, assault, and rape. However, the belief that when attacked, one can quickly pull out a pistol and either kill the assailant or protect oneself from injury or property loss bears little relationship to reality. The facts on violent crime and its victims show:

- The chances of encountering a mugger, robber, or rapist—even in the Nation's largest cities—is very remote for the overwhelming majority of citizens.

- Most such encounters, if they occur, take place outside the home. A gun kept in the home would provide no defense.

- An assault, robbery, or rape attack almost always occurs so quickly that the victim is taken by surprise. Even if one were available, the opportunity to use a firearm is minimal.

- Assailants, robbers, and rapists usually do not carry a firearm, but statistics indicate that if a gun is present, on either the attacker or the victim, the result of the confrontation is much more likely to be fatal.

ROBBERY

Robbery is the forceful taking of something of value from a person. Although robberies occur far less frequently than household burglaries, polls indicate that the fear of robbery is one of the dominant aspects of many Americans' lives. These citizens stay home at night, go out less frequently, and pray for tranquility. Understanding the nature of robbery demonstrates, however, that for the vast majority of Americans, the probability of being robbed in any given year is relatively small.

A U.S. Census survey of approximately 60,000 households for the year 1973 reveals a national victimization rate for robbery of approximately 6.9 victims per 1,000 population age 12 and over. The victimization rate for robbery and attempted robbery *with injury* is approximately 2.4 per 1,000 population age 12 and over.[18] Among the nation's five largest cities—Chicago, New York, Los Angeles, Detroit, and Philadelphia—victimization rates jump to an average of 6.6 per 1,000 for robbery with injury, and 19 per 1,000 for robbery without injury.[19] Nevertheless, in any given year, the vast majority of people will never be robbed.

This same survey indicates that only 12 percent of robberies take place inside a home, motel, or hotel room, while 60 percent take place on a street, park, or field.[20] Hence, unless a person is prepared to carry a loaded handgun on his or her person at all times, the chance of preventing 88 percent of the robberies that occur outside the home is negligible.

Paradoxically, a robbery where the offender used a firearm is less likely to result in injury than other robberies. For example, one study of reported robberies in Philadelphia from 1960 to 1966 concluded that while firearms were used to intimidate the victim in 33 percent of the cases, victims were acutally harmed by firearms in only 1.3 percent of the robberies. The majority of victims suffering injury are harmed by physical means (fists or shoes).[21] Another sample of robberies in 17 major U.S. cities revealed that victims were rarely injured by firearms.[22]

Finally, the national victimization survey conducted by the U.S. Bureau of the Census indicates that for 1973, robberies involving a gun and injury comprised only 3.4 percent of all robbery incidents (includes attempted robbery) among the U.S. population age 12 and older, and only 9.3 percent of all robberies where injury occurred. Although 36 percent of all robbery incidents result in injury to the victim, whether or not the offender uses a weapon seems to make little difference. However, when we break down weapon use by gun, knife, and other weapon, most injuries occur when the offender uses no weapon, a knife, or "other" weapon. Of those robberies where the offender used a gun, only 19 percent resulted in injury as compared with 37 percent no weapon used, 34 percent knife used, and 58 percent other weapon used. As we shall later see, much of the likelihood of being seriously injured during a robbery is directly related to taking a measure of self-protection.[23]

In conjunction with this study of handguns and self-protection, access was obtained to U.S. Census victimization surveys in eight American cities—Atlanta, Baltimore, Cleveland, Dallas, Denver, Newark, Portland, and St. Louis. In each city, a probability smaple of approximately 9,700 households was drawn (some 21,000 persons age 12 and over). The U.S. Bureau of the Census interviewed each member of the household about victimizations he or she may have suffered during the period commencing from the middle of 1971 to the late summer of 1972.[24] Detailed questions, covering the personal crimes of rape, robberry, assault, and personal larceny, were asked of those persons who were victimized.[25] These questions included the amount of loss, the extent and types of injury, the use of a weapon, reporting to the police, and so forth. The results were then aggregated for the entire eight cities, and each victimization was multiplied by a constant (depending on the age, sex, and race of the victim) in order to approximate the total number of personal crimes occurring in the population.[26]

Self-Protection Studied

For all robberies, respondents were asked whether they did anything to protect themselves or their property, and if so, what type of self-protective measure was employed. The self-protective measures included hitting or kicking the offender, use of a weapon, holding on to one's property, yelling for help, reasoning with the offender, running away, and other behaviors.

More than 45 percent of all robbery victims took some self-protective measure. Nonetheless, of those who used a self-protective measure, 55 percent of the victimizations resulted in a completed robbery. Of those not taking any self-protective measure, 85 percent of the robberies were completed. Those victims who hit or kicked the offender, yelled for help, held onto their property, or engaged in some other self-defense measure were the least successful in thwarting a completed robbery. On the other hand, victims who used a weapon, reasoned with the offender, or ran away more often than not maintained possession of their property.[27]

Of those victims who used a weapon, 63 percent of the robberies were attempted as compared with 37 percent which were completed.[28] On its face, this finding might appear to support those who favor arming citizens with firearms for self-protection. Unfortunately, this finding is subject to several limitations. Due to defects in the survey questionnaire,[29] we were unable to determine how many individuals actually used a firearm as a means of self-protection. Undoubtedly, a sizeable number of those persons who "used a weapon" for self-protection did so with a knife or some other sharp or blunt object. Second, from a total of 66,151 robberies, only 3.5 percent of the victims had the opportunity to use a weapon for self-protection, and of those who took some self-protective measure, only 7.7 percent used a weapon alone or in combination with some other measure. These data strongly support the belief that in the vast majority of cases, the victim is taken by surprise and has little time to use a weapon. Thus, most of the self-protection measures taken by victims are those *not* involving the use of a weapon. In addition, when compared to using a weapon, running away or reasoning with the offender are almost as effective in thwarting a robbery, and as we shall later see, less likely to result in injury to the victim.

When the offender is unarmed and the victim used some type of self-protection, 55 percent of the robberies are completed. Even when the offender is armed with a weapon, the percentage of those using a self-protective measure that resulted in a completed robbery remains the same (55 percent). Likewise, whether or not the offender is armed, 63 percent of the robbery victimizations are attempted when the victim uses a weapon as a means of self-protection. However, an extremely small number of cases are involved.

Since 91 percent (N = 60.239) of the robberies occur among strangers, the overall percentage differences between completed/attempted robbery and self-protection are not substantially affected. However, robberies among acquaintances are more likely to be completed when the victim takes a self-protective measure, 32 percent attempted versus 68 percent completed.

If we examine injury occurring during a robbery by measures of self-protection, we find that 34 percent of those victims using any measure of self-protection were injured as compared to 25 percent of those not taking a self-protective measure. In general, a robbery victim is most likely to be injured when he or she physically attacks the robber, yells, or holds onto the property. A victim who uses a weapon for self-protection is just as likely to be injured (26 percent) as those persons who do not attempt to resist the robbery (25 percent); victims who attempt to reason with the offender or run away are slightly less likely to be injured than those taking no self-protective measure.

These results clearly suggest that *victims who use self-protective measure are more likely to be injured than victims not utilizing such measures.* Unfortunately, an additional defect in the survey instrument raises some doubt about the data on self-protection and injury. The questionnaire used in these eight cities does not provide any information about the sequence of events.[30] Some victims may have resorted to a self–protective measure only after having been successfully robbed or attacked while other victims may precipitate the offender to attack by using self-protective measures. Hence, until more detailed information can be gathered, it is impossible with this data to make causal inferences about the relationships among the use of self-protective measures, injury to the victim, and the outcome of a robbery.

Paradoxically, a robbery victim who uses a self-protective measure is slightly more likely *not* to have reported it to the police (52 percent). More than half (51 percent) of those using a weapon felt no compelling need to report the victimization to the police, and this percentage remains the same whether taking into consideration attempted or completed robberies.

Chicago Robberies in 1975

In order to verify the findings obtained from an examination of the victimization surveys, we examined data on 1,222 robberies reported to the Chicago police in 1975.[31] Ninety-two percent (N = 1126) of the robberies resulted in completion compared to 8 percent that were attempted. Of the 1,220 robberies where circumstances are known, the victim took no resistance measure in 75 percent of the reported cases. In only 25 percent of the incidents did the victim offer resistance, most of the time with physical force, yelling, the verbal denial of goods, or flight. In less than one percent of the robberies did the victim have the opportunity to resist with a weapon of any kind. This would tend to corroborate the finding in the victimization survey that robbery victims only rarely have the opportunity to resist with weapons.

Of those victims *not* engaging in any form of resistance, 98 percent of the robberies were completed, compared to a 75 percent (N = 209/280) completion rate among those who took some form of self-protection. There was no difference in completion rates by location of the robbery. However, of the six robberies where the victim used a handgun to resist the offender, four took place inside a home or motel room. Of these, one was completed and three resulted in an attempted robbery.

In addition, the Chicago study reveals one facet not available in the victimization survey. Among the 1,220 robberies where circumstances are known, 29 robberies resulted in a firearm being stolen from the victim; this includes one of the victims who attempted to use a handgun for self-defense. Most such victims put up no resistance.

Perpetrators used handguns in 41 percent of all the robberies, and firearms of any kind were utilized in 50 percent of the reported robberies. No weapons were used in 35 percent of the cases, and knives or other weapons were used in 15 percent of the robberies.

While victims who put up no resistance are more likely to be successfully robbed of their property, victims who resist experience much higher rates of fatality and injury. Among the 1,222 robberies, 48, or 4 percent, resulted in death to the robbery victim. Of those victims taking no resistance measures, the probability of death was 7.67 per 1,000 robbery incidents, while the death rate among those taking self-protection measures was 64.29 per 1,000 robbery incidents.[32] Based on this sample of Chicago robberies, *a victim is more than eight times as likely to be killed when using a self-protective measure than not.*

Injury rates were examined using the same methodology and it was discovered that of those victims offering no resistance, 144.6 robbery incidents per 1,000 resulted in injury to some victim. The injury rate among those taking a self-protective measure was 439.3 per 1,000 robbery incidents. It would thus appear that *a victim is three times more likely to be injured when taking a self-proteciton measure than not.* Finally, of the six incidents where a victim used a handgun in self-defense, two incidents resulted in injury to the victim (one of which was completed) and a third incident also became a completed robbery. The remaining three incidents were attempted robberies in which the offender was identified and arrested in two and identified only in the remaining incident.

Clearly, robbery victims who use self-protective measures in the Chicago sample of robberies are trading off a slightly lower robbery completion rate for substantial increases in the probability of injury and death.

Seriousness of Injury to Victim

In order to measure the seriousness of injury among those victims using a self-protection measure, we again consulted the U.S. Census victimization survey for the entire domestic population (1973).[33] All personal violent crimes with and without theft were aggregated for the analysis, with both simple and aggravated assault accounting for the vast bulk of violent personal crimes.

Among the total U.S. population age 12 and older, an estimated 11.7 percent of those victims subject to a violent crime required medical attention. Twenty-three percent of those taking no self-protective measures were hospitalized overnight compared with 15 percent of those taking some measure of resistance—a difference due largely to the overwhelming number of assaults. Nevertheless, those taking a self-protective measure accounted for 58 percent of the emergency room treatments and their injuries were twice as serious, as judged by the mean days of hospitalization. While the probability of hospitalization for those needing medical attention because of a violent encounter was the same for both victims who used a weapon (23 percent) and those who undertook no resistance (23 percent), the seriousness of the injury was five times as great for those victims using a weapon for self-protection. No other type of self-protective measure has such a high degree of serious injury except for the category of "running away." Even so, only seven percent of these victims who ran away were hospitalized as compared to 23 percent among victims who used a weapon for self-defense.

The seriousness of gunshot and knife wounds among injured victims is underscored by a number of studies showing the high cost and mortality of violence by weapons.[34] One study of 251 consecutive knife and gunshot patients who were treated at the Detroit General Hospital between December 1971 and May 1972 showed that 21 deaths resulted (an eight percent mortality) and another 14 persons were permanently or seriously disabled. One hundred and fifty persons required hospitalization and treatment at an estimated cost of $3,500 per patient.[35]

A staff report to the National Commission on the Causes and Prevention of Violence concluded that the possession of firearms by businesspersons "entails less risk of accidents, homicides, and suicide than firearms in the home."[36] Nevertheless, that same report was unable to determine whether the possession of firearms by businesspersons deters robberies. According to an early victimization survey conducted by the Small Business Administration (SBA) in 1968:

> Because of the sudden, almost violent action of robbery, the victims are often taken by surprise and off their guard. The typical robbery occurs in a very short period of time, less than a minute. Almost invariably, police departments counsel against the victim of the robbery taking any action which might antagonize the robber. Instead, he or she is cautioned to cooperate fully with the robber's wishes . . . The typical business person is neither adequately trained nor prepared mentally to face up to the robber.[37]

The SBA study also discovered that approximately three percent of retail businesses with and without firearms were victimized by robbery.

Though for the moment it is not known whether guns protect businesses, the robbery victimization rate for all types of business establishments, nationally, was approximately 39 per 1,000 establishments in 1973.[38] Among the five largest U.S. cities, the victimization rate per 1,000 businesses ranges from 47 to 179, with the average being 97.[39] Variations do occur among types of commercial establishments, with retail businesses far outnumbering wholesale, service, and other industries in victimization; nonetheless, most firms in any given year do not become the targets of robbery.

Two additional studies raise further doubts about the utility of a handgun for self-protection. A New York City Police Department study of the 170 pistol license holders who were victims of a robbery in 1974 indicated that 65 percent (N = 110) of the pistol holders had their guns stolen during the robbery. Of the remaining 60 cases in which the license holder used a firearm to resist the robbery, 13 offenders, three bystanders, and eight license holders were injured.[40] In a study of 89 robbery-motivated homicides occuring in Detroit during 1972, robbers killed their victims in 66 percent (N = 59) of the cases and were killed by their intended victim in the remaining 34 percent (N = 30) of the robbery homicides.[41]

In the 1967 study of violent crimes among 17 major U.S. cities, only 8.8 percent of the homicides cleared by arrest involved robbery as a motive.[42] Recently, however, this percentage has increased dramatically. In New York City, the percentage of known robbery homicides to total homicides was 14.8 percent in 1973 and 18.7 percent in 1974.[43] In Chicago, data for the same years was 19.2 percent and 21.6 percent respectively.[44] Nonetheless, neither the probability of being victimized by a robbery, nor the rate of homicide victimization in the United States (9.7 per 100,000 population in 1974)[45] justifies the wholesale arming of all business establishments.

ASSAULT

Assault is the most frequent crime of violence, occurring almost four times more often than robbery, and 23 times more often than rape.[46] Generally characterized as an unlawful physical attack upon the victim, "aggravated" assaults refer to an attack in which the victim suffers serious injury (inflicted with or without a weapon) or the threat to do harm with a weapon, but with no actual injury to the victim. Simple assaults, on the other hand, involve no weapon and result in minor injuries, if any. Although assaults stemming from domestic quarrels are probably underreported in victimization surveys, some of the fear of assault arises from the fact that approximately 60 percent of all assaults involve strangers.[47]

In order to assess the utility of guns as instruments of self-defense against assault, one ought to ask what is the probability of being assaulted or injured, the likelihood of weapon use, and the rate of fatalities that result.

Nationally, the chance of being victimized by an assault or attempted assault is approximately 26.0 victimizations per 1,000 population, age 12 or older (data for the entire year, 1973).[48] In the nation's five largest cities, survey data for 1972 show a slightly lower victimization rate of 22 per 1,000.[49] Of all assaults, only 30 percent end in some injury to the victim, occurring at a nationwide rate of approximatley 6.2 per 1,000.[50] Here again, among the nation's five largest cities, only 10 percent of all assault victims require some hospital care, mostly in the emergency room. Only 35 percent of all offenders in assault are armed with weapons (11 percent by firearms), corresponding to a rate of approximately 7.7 weapon assaults per 1,000 population age 12 or older.[51]

Thus, the chance of being assaulted in a given year, of being assaulted with a weapon, or of sustaining injuries is statistically neglegible for the U.S. population as a whole. This is not to argue that differing social strata, age groups, or races experience the same victimization rate; nor the victimization rates remain static according to location, such as the inner city versus rural areas. Nonetheless, one could hardly interpret this as compelling evidence for arming the entire population with handguns for self-protection.

As in the case with robberies, most assaults occur outside the home. Victimization surveys for 1973 reveal that only 21 percent of all assaults take place inside or near a home.[52] Here again, unless a person intends to carry a loaded handgun about his or her person at all times, the chances of using a gun for self-defense are slim.

The U.S. Census victimization survey for the eight American cities was again consulted to examine the outcome of aggravated assaults among those victims taking some means of self-protection. For the eight impact cities there were an estimated 49,601 personal victimizations during the survey period, commencing from approximately the middle of 1971 to the late summer of 1972. Ninety-six percent (N = 47,720) of the aggravated assault victimizations involved an offender with a weapon. Thus, of the total number of victimizations, 38.2 percent (N = 18,933) occurred with the offender possessing a gun, 25.2 percent (N = 12,486) with a knife, and 35 percent (N = 17,348) with some other type of weapon. Victims were threatened or assaulted by strangers in 69 percent (N = 34,158) of the personal victimizations, and by acquaintances in 31 percent (N = 15,443).[53]

Sixty-five percent (N = 32,403) of the victimizations resulted in an attempted aggravated assault; the remaining 17,198 victimizations (35 percent) were completed. Nevertheless, whether or not the victim takes a self-protection measure makes little difference in the outcome. Among those aggravated assaults where the victim engages in some type of self-defense, 66 percent were attempted as compared with 63 percent among those victims taking *no* self-protection measure. While over 62 percent of the victims took some self-protective measure, only seven percent (N = 3,486) of the total number of victims had an opportunity to use a weapon for self-protection. Among this select group, 68 percent of the victimizations were attempted. By far, the most successful means of self-protection is running away, with 83 percent of the victimizations resulting in an attempted aggravated assault. The least successful self-protective measures were hitting or kicking the offender, followed by yelling for help. Here again, a victim may have used one or more self-protective measures in combination; consequently, these measures do not sum up to the total number of victims taking some type of self-defense measure. Moreover, the large number of victims who reported hitting or kicking the offender might be explained by the possibility that an attack was already in progress when the victim began resisting.

Whether or not the offender is a stranger seems to make little difference in the outcome.[54] Among strangers, 70 percent of the victims taking a self-protective measure were successful in thwarting a completed aggravated assault, as contrasted with 64 percent of those victims not taking any measure of self-protection. Seventy percent of those victims resisting with a weapon were likewise successful. Among acquaintances, 59 percent of the victimizations involving an aggravated assault were attempted for those victims taking some measure of self-protection. Victims offering no resistance successfully thwarted the aggravated assault in 63 percent of the victimizations; and 64 percent of those who used a weapon for self-defense were also successful.

Type of Weapon Critical

What affects the nature of aggravated assault in the type of weapon used by the offender. When the offender had a gun, only 17 percent of the victimizations resulted in completion. Twenty-nine percent of the victimizations were completed when the offender was armed with a knife, and 53 percent were completed when the offender used some "other" type of weapon. In general these attempted-completed percentages remain the same, regardless of whether or not the victim takes some measure of self-protection. It would thus appear that offenders are cognizant of the possibility of inflicting serious injury with the use of certain weapons and are making adjustments accordingly.[55]

Overall, 35 percent of the victims of aggravated assault in the eight cities suffered injury. But whether or not the victim took some measure of self-protection makes little difference in the probability of injury.[56] Thirty-seven percent of the victims who offered no resistance were injured compared to 34 percent who took some measure of self-protection. Moreover, 32 percent of those victims using a weapon were injured as opposed to 64 percent of those who hit or kicked the offender in self-defense. Again, the safest response is to run away. Only 17 percent of those victims who chose to run away were injured.

Because of defects in the survey instrument, we are again unable to make any causal statements about the effectiveness of using a weapon for protection against assaults. Nonetheless, the evidence suggests that one is almost just as likely to be injured when using a weapon for self-defense than he or she is when taking no resistance measures whatever against aggravated assault. Moreover, it would appear that using a weapon for self-protection is significantly less effective in thwarting an aggravated assault than reasoning with the offender or running away, and only slightly more effective than not taking any self-protective measures at all.

Of the 49,601 victims of aggravated assault in the victimization study, only 50 percent reported the incident to the police. Not only does this percentage remain relatively constant regardless of whether or not the victim takes a self-protective measure, but only 57 percent of these who use a weapon for self-defense reported the matter to law enforcement authorities.

We have observed that victims taking some measure of self-protection, or using a weapon for self-defense, were significantly more likely to suffer serious injury at the hands of an offender. In order to examine the probability of death resulting from an aggravated assault, we obtained access to a sample of 2,176 aggravated assaults reported to the Chicago police in 1975.[57]

Among the 2,176 reported aggravated assaults, whites were victims in 21 percent (N = 454) of the cases, blacks in 67 percent (N = 1,458), and Spanish-surnamed victims in 11 percent (N = 233) of the incidents. The remaining cases were composed of other ethnic groups and unknown victims. Relative to the relationship between the victim and the offender, 23 percent (N = 500) of the incidents involved relatives or lovers, 35.9 percent (N = 782) involved acquaintances, 21.3 percent (N = 463) occurred among strangers, and 19.8 percent (N = 431) of the cases were unknown.

Contrary to popular belief, both the offender and the victim had been drinking in 11 percent (N = 243) of the aggravated assaults, only the victim had been drinking in another 23 percent (N = 499) of the cases, and the offender had been the only one drinking in 2.5 percent (N = 54) of the incidents. Thus, in only 36.6 percent of the incidents had anyone been drinking.

Handguns Most Fatal Weapon

If the offender used a handgun, the probability that the victim died as a result of the aggravated assault was 14.06 deaths per 100 handgun attacks. If a long gun was utilized, the fatality rate dropped to 4.69 deaths per 100 longgun attacks. On the other hand, the mortality rate per 100 knife attacks was 3.57 and the rate per 100 blunt instrument attacks was 0.85. Consequently, the Chicago data indicate that when the offender uses a handgun, the victim's chance of being killed is three times more likely than when a long gun is used, four times more likely than a knife attack, and sixteen times more probable

TABLE 1

HOSPITALIZATION OF VICTIMS OF AGGRAVATED ASSAULTS REPORTED
TO THE CHICAGO POLICE DEPARTMENT DURING 1975,
BY WEAPON USED TO INFLICT MOST SERIOUS WOUND

TYPE OF WEAPON	NO	YES- CONFINED	YES-TREATED & RELEASED	YES- UNCLEAR	YES- DIED	TOTAL
			VICTIMS HOSPITALIZED			
Handguns	94 (20.1%)	158 (35.3%)	66 (14.7%)	67 (15.0%)	63 (14.1%)	448 (100%) 21.0%
Long guns	52 (27.1%)	43 (22.4%)	54 (28.1%)	34 (17.7%)	9 (4.7%)	192 (100%) 9.0%
Sharp Instrument	72 (11.2%)	107 (16.6%)	301 (46.7%)	141 (21.9%)	23 (3.6%)	644 (100%) 30.1%
Blunt Instrument	94 (16.0%)	61 (10.4%)	320 (54.4%)	108 (18.4%)	5 (0.8%)	588 (100%) 27.5%
Body	27 (20.3%)	25 (18.8%)	53 (39.8%)	25 (18.8%)	3 (2.3%)	133 (100%) 6.2%
Other	13 (15.9%)	8 (9.8%)	33 (40.2%)	21 (25.6%)	7 (8.5%)	82 (100)% 3.8%
Unknown	14 (27.4%)	5 (9.8%)	17 (33.3%)	15 (29.4%)	0	51 (100%) 2.4%
TOTAL	366 (17.1%)	407 (19.0%)	844 (39.5%)	411 (19.2%)	110 (5.1%)	2138 (100%)

NOTE: The column and row percentages may not total 100% due to rounding. Thirty-eight (38) unknown hospitalization cases were deleted from a total of 2176 aggravated assaults.

than when the offender uses a blunt instrument. In his study of assaults and homicides in Chicago, Professor Franklin Zimring found that the rate of gun deaths per 100 reported gun assaults was five times the knife fatality rate per 100 reported knife attacks.[58] The results presented in Table 1 tend to confirm Zimring's finding and suggest that handguns dramatically increase the probability of death resulting from a conflict.

TABLE 2

HOSPITALIZATION OF VICTIMS OF AGGRAVATED ASSAULT REPORTED TO THE
CHICAGO POLICE DEPARTMENT DURING 1975, BY TYPE OF VICTIM RESISTANCE

| TYPE OF VICTIM RESISTANCE | VICTIMS HOSPITALIZED | | | | | |
	NO	YES-CONFINED	YES-TREATED & RELEASED	YES-UNCLEAR	YES-DIED	TOTAL
Unprovoked	86 (17.7%)	105 (21.6%)	193 (39.6%)	92 (18.9%)	11 (2.3%)	487 (100%) 22.8%
Physical Force	53 (12.7%)	85 (45.2%)	166 (39.9%)	79 (19.0%)	33 (7.9%)	416 (100%) 19.5%
Flight	5 (25.0%)	4 (20.0%)	7 (35.0%)	4 (20.0%)	0	20 (100%) 0.9%
Verbal	157 (18.4%)	139 (16.3%)	363 (42.5%)	163 (19.1%)	33 (3.9%)	855 (100%) 40.1%
Unknown	65 (18.3%)	72 (20.3%)	113 (31.8%)	73 (20.6%)	32 (9.0%)	355 (100%)
TOTAL	366 (17.2%)	405 (19.0%)	842 (39.5%)	411 (19.3%)	109 (5.1%)	2133 (100%)

NOTE: The column and row percentages may not total 100% due to rounding. Forty-three (43) miscellaneous, missing, and unknown hospitalization cases were deleted from a total of 2176 aggravated assaults.

The probability of death resulting from an incident which began as an aggravated assault is also strongly related to taking a self-protection measure (see Table 2). The death rate for an unprovoked attack stands at approximately 2.26 per 100 unprovoked attacks. When the victim used force to resist the assault, the death rate increases to 7.93 per 100 attacks. Among those who verbally accosted the offender, the death rate is 3.86 per 100 attacks. But, if one controls for the type of victim resistance, the relationship between handguns and fatalities becomes even more apparent. In all categories, handgun deaths are substantially more likely to take place than knife deaths (see Table 3). It would appear that the probability of death resulting from an aggravated assault is strongly related to the type of weapon used by the offender and the nature of victim resistance.

TABLE 3

DEATH RATE OF VICTIMS OF AGGRAVATED ASSAULTS REPORTED TO THE CHICAGO POLICE DEPARTMENT DURING 1975, BY TYPE OF VICTIM RESISTANCE

	DEATH RATE OF VICTIMS (PER 100 ATTACKS)	
TYPE OF VICTIM RESISTANCE	BY HANDGUN	BY KNIFE
Unprovoked	5.93	0.00
Physical Force	26.25	6.54
Flight	0.00	0.00
Verbal	13.04	2.21
Unknown	18.92	5.61

TABLE 4

TYPE OF WEAPONS USED IN HOMICIDES AND AGGRAVATED ASSAULTS DURING 1973, BY PERCENT[60]

WEAPON TYPE	HOMICIDE	AGGRAVATED ASSAULT
Firearm	67%	29%
Handgun	53%	
Rifle	6%	
Shotgun	8%	
Knife, cutting instrument	18%	27%
Other Weapon: Club, hammer	7%	36%
Personal Weapons (hands, feet)	9%	—
Not ascertained	—	8%
TOTAL	100% (N = 19.509)	100% (N = 1.313.180)

NOTE: Percentages may not sum to 100% due to rounding.

The importance of firearms is further underscored by the correspondence between homicides and assaults. One study of the circumstances surrounding homicides and aggravated assaults in 17 American cities suggests that the motives for homicide and aggravated assault are more *similar* than different.[59]

Research such as that above supports the inference that aggravated assault and homicide arise from the same types of interpersonal conflicts, one major difference being the nature of the weapon used. Table 4 illustrates the lethal nature of firearms in criminal violence by comparing weapons used for both homicide and aggravated assault.

In summary, the use of weapons as a means of self-defense against aggravated assault appears to be limited. For most of the population, the rate of victimization from assault is low enough to question the desirability of firearms as a means of self-protection. Injuries are infrequent, though more likely to be serious if the victim physically resists the offender. More often than not, the victim lacks the opportunity to use a weapon for self-defense since the vast majority of aggravated assaults occur outside the home and are committed by strangers. Since the availability of guns dramatically increases the probability of a homicide resulting from a conflict, one must seriously question the benefits of carrying a loaded firearm for self-defense.

RAPE

Clearly one of the most frightening personal crimes of violence, rape is only beginning to receive proper attention from criminal justice and health agencies. It is difficult to estimate how frequently rape occurs and to assess the need for various degrees of self-protection needed by potential victims. Rape has traditionally been the most underreported crime and represents the smallest category of offenses of all serious offenses. Estimates of the actual number of rapes range from five to twenty times as frequent as the number of rapes reported to the police.

The 1973 national victimization survey conducted by the census bureau determined that the rape victimization rate per 1,000 potential victims (females age 12 and over) was 1.8, including forcible rapes and attempted rapes. This rate, however, is probably conservative due to victim reluctance to report rape.

Approximately 75 percent of all rapes involve strangers, and most rapes occur without a weapon (66 percent).[61] The 1973 victimization survey for the entire country also revealed that only about 11 percent of all rapes involve a gun, and in 6 percent of all rapes the perpetrator is armed with a knife. Like assault, most rapes take place outside the home; only 33 percent of all rapes in 1973 occurred inside or near a residence.[62] When the offender is armed with a firearm, the probability of serious injury (physical harm in addition to the sex act) to the victim is low. According to a 1967 survey of police-reported rapes in 17 American cities, only 1.4 percent of rape cases cleared by arrest and only 0.5 percent of uncleared cases resulted in the victim being seriously injured with a firearm. On the other hand, 17.7 percent of cleared cases and 18.9 percent of uncleared cases resulted in serious injury being inflicted through bodily means.[63]

A study of reported rapes in Denver during 1973 indicated that the presence of a weapon on the offender only slightly contributed to the completion of a rape.[64] In 59 percent of the completed forcible rapes the offender was armed, but so were 48.2 percent of the offenders involved in attempted rapes. Moreover, no weapon was used by the offender in 41 percent of the completed rapes and in 51.8 percent of the attempted rapes.[65]

A study of Denver rapes that occurred from July 1970 to July 1972[66] raises questions about the efficacy of using a handgun for self-protection against rapists. The greatest proportion of these rapes occurred during midnight and 4 A.M. and while the victim was asleep in her bedroom.[67] In the 35 percent of the cases where the rape was interrupted or aborted, the most successful methods used by the victim were flight, yelling, or physical resistance.[68]

The Denver study also found that in 68.5 percent of the reported rapes there was no security device, such as a dog, locking device, or security patrol present.[68] This figure indicates that preventative measures taken against potential intruders may be the best weapon against rape in one's home.

Since rape is an act of personal violence involving forced sexual intercourse, the presence of a weapon is often used to intimidate the victim into passive nonresistance. In two-thirds of the reported Denver rapes, the victim was not physically injured; of the victims who were injured, the most frequent source of injury was the offender's hands and feet.[70]

Using a handgun to protect oneself against rape is questionable due to the surprise nature of the attack and the effectiveness of other means of resistance, such as verbal and physical resistance.

CONCLUSION

Ownership of handguns by private citizens for self-protection against crime appears to provide more of a psychological belief in safety than actual deterrence to criminal behavior. Indeed, when the final irony occurs and a citizen's handgun is either stolen or used against him or her in the commission of a crime, the source of the victim's security is instantly transformed into the source of his or her terror. And possible death.

The data presented in this report indicate that private handgun ownership provides no significant deterrent to burglary and violent crime. It may, in fact, escalate the severity of the violence if offenders believe they must be more heavily armed than the citizenry. The use of a weapon in resistance to a criminal attack usually results in a greater probability of bodily injury or death to the victim. Other methods of resistance, such as flight or verbal resistance, are usually more effective in aborting the crime and they have less probability of causing harm or death to the victim. In circumstances where the offender is armed, nonresistance will most likely result in the minimum amount of harm to the victim.

Because of the surprise nature of most violent crime and since it is likely to occur between strangers, the belief that one is going to have sufficient time to retrieve, load, and draw a handgun on an assailant is ludicrous. The alternative, always carrying a loaded handgun on one's person, is illegal in most states, except for specially licensed individuals.

Burglary and rape are two offenses for which handgun ownership provides the least amount of protection. Most burglaries occur when no one is present in the home, and a significant portion of rapes occur when the victim has been asleep prior to the assault.

Robbery and aggravated assault victims may indeed ward off their assailants by a weapon but they are risking a greater chance of bodily harm or death if they do so. If a handgun is involved, the probability of either the victim or offender being killed is significantly higher than any other type of weapon.

Thus, while armed individual citizens occasionally thwart a criminal offense, they represent a minority of victims. Handgun ownership raises the risks of escalating the violence of the crime, of accidents and suicides among family members, and, finally, of gross harm or death for the citizen.

It is time that the risks involved in civilian ownership of handguns for self-protection are presented to the American people and their elected officials. Through this technical report we have attempted to report the facts related to these risks as clearly as possible. It is our hope that these facts lead to constructive actions and that citizens adopt preventative measures against crime that are less dangerous and more effective than handgun ownership.

NOTES

1. Franklin E. Zimring and George D. Newton, Jr., *Firearms and Violence in American Life, A Staff Report to the National Commission on the Causes and Prevention of Violence* (Washington, D.C.: U.S. Government Printing Office, 1970), p. 62.

2. Data supplied courtesy of the Uniform Crime Reports Section, Federal Bureau of Investigation, via telephone interview, February 17, 1976.

3. Zimring and Newton, *Firearms and Violence,* p. 62.

4. Ibid.

5. Data on Chicago homicides supplied courtesy of the Chicago Police Department and Dr. Richard Block of the Center for Studies in Criminal Justice, University of Chicago, February 1976.

Data on the total number of burglaries for Chicago, 1965 to 1974, were compiled from the Uniform Crime Reports, *Crime in the United States, 1965,* Annually to 1974, (Washington, D.C.: U.S. Government Printing Office).

6. Jeffrey E. Spiegler and John J. Sweeney, *Gun Abuse in Ohio* (Cleveland, Ohio: Administration of Justice Committee, June 1975), p. 41.

7. Hirsh, Rushforth, Ford, and Adleson, "Accidental Firearm Fatalities in a Metropolitan County," *American Journal of Epidemiology* 100 (1975): 504, No. 6. Emphasis supplied.

8. Zimring and Newton, *Firearms and Violence.* p. 64.

9. Marilyn Heins, R. Kahn, and J. Bjordnal, "Gunshot Wounds in Children," *American Journal of Public Health* 64, no. 4 (April 1974): 326–30.

10. Kelley, *Crime in the United States—1974* (Washington, D.C.: U.S. Government Printing Office, November 1975), p. 19.

11. Testimony of John W. McKay, on behalf of the City and County of Honolulu, before the Senate Judiciary Committee, Hawaii State Legislature, March 1974.

12. Thomas A. Reppetto, *Residential Crime* (Cambridge, Mass.: Ballinger, 1974), p. 150.

13. These data come from a study of burglary victims conducted by Dr. J. Irvin Waller and his research associate Norman Okihiro. A stratified sample of 2,483 households in a high crime neighborhood of Toronto, Canada, was selected, focusing on adults aged 18 years or older. Of the 2,483 original cases, 1,665 responses were obtained, representing a 67 percent completion rate. This somewhat low response rate is at least partially explained by the high rate of apartment dwellers in the sampling frame. Residents were asked to recall burglary victimizations during the period commencing January 1, 1973 through April 1974.

We are especially grateful to Dr. Waller for granting us permission to publish material from his monograph *Burglary and the Public* (Unpub. MS Centre of Criminology, University of Toronto, 1974). Norman Okihiro performed the computer analysis.

14. Reppetto, *Residential Crime,* pp. 5, 17.

15. See note 13, *supra.*

16. Ibid. Randomized surveys of crime victims in the Nation's five largest cities show that over 20% of household burglaries apparently do not result in any monetary loss or damage, and that another 52% result in losses under $250. The FBI reports that for 1973, the average dollar loss per officially-reported burglary was $337.

See *Criminal Victimization Surveys in the Nation's Five Largest Cities, National Crime Panel Surveys of Chicago, Detroit, Los Angeles, New York, and Philadelphia,* Law Enforcement Assistance Administration, U.S. Department of Justice (Washington, D.C.: U.S. Government Printing Office, April 1975), pp. 44, 51–55; See also Kelley, *Crime in the United States—1973* (Washington, D.C.: U.S. Government Printing Office, September 1974), p. 22.

17. See testimony of Rex D. Davis, Director, Bureau of Alcohol, Tobacco, and Firearms, Department of the Treasury, in *Hearings on Firearms Legislation before the Subcommittee on Crime, Committee on the Judiciary, House of Representatives, 94th Congress, 1st Session, Part 1,* March 20, 1975, pp. 255, 290; additional data can be found in the Subcommittee's files, attached as an explanation for the diagram appearing on page 254 of the record. See also "The Escalating Rate of firearms Crime," in *Hearings on Firearms Legislation before the Subcommittee on Juvenile Delinquency, Committee on the Judiciary, Senate, 94th Congress, 1st Session,* Stenographic transcripts, April 23, 1975, Vol. 1, pp. 128–29.

18. *Criminal Victimization in the United States, 1973 Advance Report, A National Crime Panel Survey Report for* the *Law Enforcement Assistance Administration. U.S. Department of Justice* (Washington, D.C.: U.S. Government Printing Office, May 1975), Vol. 1, p. 12.

19. *Criminal Victimization Surveys in the Nation's Five Largest Cities,* pp. 69–72. For the population figures per each city, see p. 43.

20. Michael J. Hindelang et al., *Sourcebook of Criminal Justice Statistics—1974* (Washington, D.C.: U.S. Government Printing Office, July 1975), Table 3.22, p. 238.

21. Andre Normandeau, "Trends and Patterns in Crimes of Robbery (with special reference to Philadelphia, Pennsylvania, 1960 to 1966)" (Philadelphia: University of Pennsylvania Ph.D. dissertation, 1968); compare John E. Conklin, *Robbery and the Criminal Justice System* (Philadelphia: Lippincott, 1972), pp. 102–22.

22. Lynn Alan Curtis, "Criminal Violence: Inquiries into National Patterns and Behavior" (Philadelphia: University of Pennsylvania Ph.D. dissertation, 1972), p. 648. See also Lynn A. Curtis, *Criminal Violence* (Lexington, Mass.: Lexington Books, 1974).

23. From Table 3.23, *Sourcebook of Criminal Justice Statistics—1974.* p. 238.

24. See *Crime in Eight American Cities, National Crime Panel Surveys of Atlanta, Baltimore, Cleveland, Dallas, Denver, Newark, Portland, and St. Louis.* Law Enforcement Assistance Administration, U.S. Department of Justice (Washington, D.C.: LEAA, July 1974). Advance Report, p. iii.

25. For definitions, see ibid., p. 7–8. See also Appendix 1.

26. Because we are interested in the question of self-protection, a word of warning is appropriate. This victimization survey is based on a sample of the population. Consequently, we can expect some degree of sampling error in making inferences to the total population. In many instances, the sampling error is small due to the large number of cases. However, as we proceed to analyze the various types of self-protective measures used, we encountered, time and time again, projections based on a very small number of cases. Because sampling error increases as the number of cases diminishes, many of the findings to be reported may lack substance. Hence, the percentages differences and comparisons must be treated cautiously.

27. *National Crime Panel Victimization Survey.*

28. Ibid.

29. The survey questionnaire asked "Did you do anything to protect yourself or your property during the incident?" If the person responded "Yes," he or she was then asked "What did you do?" A box was available for "Used/brandished a Weapon." Unfortunately, we are unable to determine how many guns, knives, and "other" instruments are encompassed under the term "Weapon."

30. Michael Gottfredson and Michael Hindelang, "The Nature and Correlates of Physical Injury Suffered by Victims of Personal Crimes," in Wesley Skogan (ed.), *Sample Surveys of Victims of Crime* (Cambridge, Mass.: Ballinger Press, 1976).

31. A sample of Chicago robberies occurring between March 5, 1975 and June 24, 1975 was selected for study by Dr. Richard Block and his associates at the Center for Studies in Criminal Justice, University of Chicago. Within this time frame, all robberies taking place every fifth day (interval sample) were coded for analysis. Robbery is considered to be the taking or attempt to take something of value from a person by force or the threat of force. Assault to commit robbery and attempts are included.

32. 7 deaths/913 no resistance attempts (x) 1000 = 7.67; 18 deaths/280 resistance attempts (x) 1000 = 64.29. The rates of injury were calculated in the same fashion.

33. Zimring and Newton, *Firearms and Violence,* p. 67.

34. John R. Kirkpatrick and Alexander J. Walt, "The High Cost of Gunshot and Stab Wounds," *Journal of Surgical Research* 14 (1973): 260–64. See also the testimony of Clyde W. Phillips, M.D., Robert L. Replogle, M.D., and Peter Rosen, M.D., in *Hearings on Firearms Legislation before the Subcommittee on Crime, Committee on the Judiciary, House of Representatives, 94th Congress, 1st Session, Part 2,* April 15, 1975, pp. 610–36.

35. Kirkpartick and Walt, "The High Cost of Gunshot and Stab Wounds," p. 262.

36. See note 32, *supra.*

37. Zimring and Newton, *Firearms and Violence,* p. 66.

38. *Criminal Victimization in the United States—1973,* p. 23.

39. *Criminal Victimization Surveys in the Nation's Five Largest Cities,* pp. 115–119.

40. See the testimony of Deputy Inspector Peter J. Maloney, Commanding Officer of the License Division, New York City Police Department, in *Hearings on Firearms Legislation before the Subcommittee on Crime, Committee on the Judiciary, House of Representatives, 94th Congress,* July 25, 1975.

41. Data especially prepared for this study by G. Marie Wilt, Ph.D., from her dissertation "Towards an Understanding of the Social Realities of Participants in Homicides" (Wayne State University, Detroit, Mich., 1975).

42. Curtis, *Criminal Violence,* p. 66.

43. See Selwyn Raab, "Felony Murder Rose 15.7% Here Last Year," *New York Times,* 23 March 1975, p. 1.

44. See the Chicago Police Department, "Five Year Murder Analysis, 1965–1969," and "Murder Analysis" for the years 1970, 1971, 1972, 1973, and 1974, respectively (mimeo).

45. Kelley, *Crime in the United States—1974,* p. 15.

46. Calculated from Table 3.23, *Sourcebook of Criminal Justice Statistics—1974,* p. 238.

47. *Criminal Victimization in the United States—1973.* p. 3.

48. Ibid, p. 12.

49. *Criminal Victimization Surveys in the Nation's Five Largest Cities,* pp. 68–72.

50. Calculated from Table 3.23, *Sourcebook of Criminal Justice Statistics—1974,* p. 238.

51. Ibid.

52. See Table 3.22, *Sourcebook of Criminal justice Statistics—1974,* p. 238.

53. *National Crime Panel Victimization Survey.*

54. Ibid.

55. Ibid.

56. Ibid.

57. A sample of all aggravated assaults occurring in Chicago between March 5, 1975 and June 24, 1975 was selected for study by Dr. Richard Block and his associates at the Center for Studies in Criminal Justice, University of Chicago. Aggravated assault is usually defined as an attack or attempt to attack a person for the purpose of inflicting severe injury usually accompanied by the use of a weapon.

58. Franklin E. Zimring, "Is Gun Control Likely to Reduce Violent Killings?" *University of Chicago Law Review* 35 (1968): 721–37.

59. Curtis, *Criminal Violence,* p. 66.

60. Kelley, *Crime in the United States—1973,* p. 9; and *Sourcebook of Criminal Justice Statistics—1974,* p. 238.

61. *Criminal Victimization in the United States—1973,* p. 3.

62. See Table 3.22, *Sourcebook of Criminal Justice Statistics—1974,* p. 238.

63. Curtis, "Criminal Violence: Inquiries into National Patterns," p. 648.

64. Data supplied courtesy of Frank Javorek of Denver General Hospital.

65. Ibid.

66. Thomas Giacinti, "Forcible Rape: The Offender and His Victim" (Carbondale: University of Southern Illinois Masters Thesis, 1973).
    67. Ibid., pp. 37 and 43.
    68. Ibid., p. 120.
    69. Ibid., p. 125.
    70. Ibid., p. 123.

APPENDIX 1

The following are definitions of those personal crimes utilized by the U.S. Bureau of the Census for the National Crime Panel surveys of eight American cities (Atlanta, Baltimore, Cleveland, Dallas, Denver, Newark, Portland, and St. Louis):

Attempted robbery—An attempt to steal or take something without permission, by force or threat of force, with or without the offender using a weapon. The victim may have been attacked in some fashion but he or she suffered no injuries.

Completed robbery—(1) Something was stolen or taken without permission *or* an attempt was made to steal or take something without permission, and the offender was either armed with a weapon or not, *and* the victim suffered injury; (2) Something was stolen or taken without permission and the offender was either armed or not armed with a weapon. the victim may have been attacked (i.e., knocked down) in some fashion, but he or she suffered no injureis.

Attempted aggravated assault—Nothing was stolen or taken without permission, nor was there an attempt to steal or take something. The offender had a weapon and the victim was threatened or attacked in some fashion but suffered no injuries.

Completed aggravated assault—Nothing was stolen or taken without permission, nor was there an attempt to steal or take something. The offender had a weapon and the victim was injured *or* the offender was unarmed *and* the victim was injured *or* hospitalized.

Attempted larceny with contact—An attempt was made to steal or take a purse and the offender was not armed. The victim was not threatened with harm or actually attacked.

Completed larceny with contact—Cash, a purse, or a wallet was taken or stolen without permission by an unarmed offender, and the victim was not threatened or attacked.

Injury—Knife or gunshot wounds, broken bones, or teeth knocked out, internal injuries, knocked unconscious, bruises, black eye, cuts, scratches, and the like, including injury that required hospitalization.

16

Protection or Peril?

An Analysis of Firearm-Related Deaths in the Home

Arthur L. Kellermann and Donald T. Reay

There are approximately 120 million guns in private hands in the United States.[1,2] About half of all the homes in America contain one or more firearms.[1-8] Although most persons who own guns keep them primarily for hunting or sport, three-quarters of gun owners keep them at least partly for protection.[1-4] One-fifth of gun owners identify "self-defense at home" as their most important reason for having a gun.[5]

Keeping firearms in the home carries associated risks.[1,9] These include injury or death from unintentional gunshot wounds, homicide during domestic quarrels, and the ready availability of an immediate, highly lethal means of suicide. To understand better the epidemiology of firearm-related deaths in the home, we studied all the gunshot deaths that occurred in King County, Washington, between 1978 and 1983. We were especially interested in characterizing the gunshot deaths that occurred in the residence where the firearm involved was kept.

From *The New England Journal of Medicine* 314, no. 24 (June 12, 1986): 1557-60. Reprinted by permission of the publisher.

METHODS

King County, Washington (1980 census population 1,270,000), contains the cities of Seattle (population 494,000) and Bellevue (population 74,000), as well as a number of smaller communities.[10] The county population is predominantly urban (92 percent) and white (88.4 percent), with smaller black (4.4 percent) and Asian (4.3 percent) minorities. All violent deaths in King County are investigated by the office of the medical examiner.

We systematically reviewed the medical examiner's case files to identify every firearm-related death that occurred in the county between January 1, 1978, and December 31, 1983. In addition to general demographic information, we obtained specific data regarding the manner of death, the scene of the incident, the circumstances, the relationship of the suspect to the victim, the type of firearm involved, and the blood alcohol level of the victim at the time of autopsy. When records were incomplete, corroborating information was obtained from police case files and direct interviews with the original investigating officers.

Gunshot deaths involving the intentional shooting of one person by another were considered homicides. Self-protection homicides were considered "justifiable" if they involved the killing of a felon during the commission of a crime; they were considered "self-defense" if that was the determination of the investigating police department and the King County prosecutor's office.[11] All homicides resulting in criminal charges and all unsolved homicides were considered criminal homicides.

The circumstances of all homicides were also noted. Homicides committed in association with another felony (e.g., robbery) were identified as "felony homicides." Homicides committed during an argument or fight were considered "altercation homicides." Those committed in the absence of either set of circumstances were termed "primary homicides."

Deaths from self-inflicted gunshot wounds were considered suicides if they were officially certified as such by one of us (D. T. R.), who is the medical examiner. Unintentional self-inflicted gunshot wounds were classified as accidental. Although the medical examiner's office considers deaths involving the unintentional shooting of one person by another as homicide, we classified these deaths as accidental for our analysis. Deaths in which there was uncertainty about the circumstances or motive were identified as "undetermined."

RESULTS

Over the six-year interval, the medical examiner's office investigated 743 deaths from firearms (9.75 deaths per 100,000 person-years). This total represented

22.7 percent of all violent deaths occurring in King County during this period, excluding traffic deaths. Firearms were involved in 45 percent of all homicides and 49 percent of all suicides in King County—proportions lower than the national averages of 61 and 57 percent, respectively.[12,13] Guns accounted for less than 1 percent of accidental deaths and 5.7 percent of deaths in which the circumstances were undetermined.

Of the 743 deaths from firearms noted during this six-year period, 473 (63.7 percent) occurred inside a house or dwelling, and 398 (53.6 percent) occurred in the home where the firearm involved was kept. Of these 398 firearm deaths, 333 (83.7 percent) were suicides, 50 (12.6 percent) were homicides, and 12 (3 percent) were accidental gunshot deaths. The precise manner of death was undetermined in three additional cases involving self-inflicted gunshot wounds.

In 265 of the 333 cases of suicide (80 percent), the victim was male. A blood ethanol test was positive in 86 of the 245 suicide victims tested (35 percent) and showed a blood ethanol level of 100 mg per deciliter or more in 60 of the 245 (24.5 percent). Sixty-eight percent of the suicides involved handguns. In eight cases, the medical examiner's case files specifically noted that the victim had acquired the firearm within two days of committing suicide.

The victim was male in 30 of the 50 homicide deaths (60 percent). A blood ethanol test was positive in 27 of 47 homicide victims tested (5 percent) and showed a blood ethanol level of 100 mg per deciliter or more in 10 of the victims (21 percent). Handguns were involved in 34 of these deaths (68 percent).

Forty-two homicides (84 percent) occurred during altercations in the home, including seven that were later determined to have been committed in self-defense. Two additional homicides involving the shooting of burglars by residents were considered legally "justifiable."[11] Forty-one homicides (82 percent) resulted in criminal charges against a resident of the house or apartment in which the shooting occurred.

Four of the 12 accidental deaths involved self-inflicted gunshot wounds. All 12 victims were male. A blood ethanol test in the victims was positive in only two cases. Eleven of these accidental deaths involved handguns.

Excluding firearm-related suicides, 65 deaths occurred in the house where the firearm involved was kept. In two of these cases, the victim was a stranger to the persons living in the house, whereas in 24 cases (37 percent), the victim was an acquaintance or friend. Thirty-six gunshot victims (55 percent) were residents of the house in which the shooting occurred, including 29 who were victims of homicide. Residents were most often shot by a relative or family member (11 cases), their spouse (9 cases), a roommate (6 cases), or themselves (7 cases).

Guns kept in King County homes were involved in the deaths of friends or acquaintances 12 times as often as in those of strangers. Even after the exclusion of firearm-related suicides, guns kept at home were involved in the death of a member of the household 18 times more often than in the death of a stranger. For every time a gun in the home was involved in a "self-protection" homicide, we noted 1.3 accidental gunshot deaths, 4.6 criminal homicides, and 37 firearm-related suicides.

DISCUSSION

We found the home to be a common location for deaths related to firearms. During our study period, almost two-thirds of the gunshot deaths in King County occurred inside a house or other dwelling. Over half these incidents occurred in the residence in which the firearm involved was kept. Few involved acts of self-protection.

Less than 2 percent of homicides nationally are considered legally justifiable.[11,13] Although justifiable homicides do not include homicides committed in self-defense, the combined total of both in our study was still less than one-fourth the number of criminal homicides involving a gun kept in the home. A majority of these homicide victims were residents of the house or apartment in which the shooting occurred.

Over 80 percent of the homicides noted during our study occurred during arguments or altercations. Baker has observed that in cases of assault, people tend to reach for the most lethal weapon readily available.[14] Easy access to firearms may therefore be particularly dangerous in households prone to domestic violence.

We found the most common form of firearm-related death in the home to be suicide. Although previous authors have correlated regional suicide rates with estimates of firearm density,[15,16] the precise nature of the relation between gun availability and suicide is unclear.[1,17] the choice of a gun for suicide may involve a combination of impulse and the close proximity of a firearm. Conversely, the choice of a gun may simply reflect the seriousness of a person's intent. If suicides involving firearms are more a product of the easy availability of weapons than of the strength of intent, limiting access to firearms will decrease the rate of suicide. If the opposite is true, suicidal persons will only work harder to acquire a gun or kill themselves by other means. For example, although the elimination of toxic coal gas from domestic gas supplies in Great Britain resulted in a decrease in successful suicide attempts,[18] a similar measure in Australia was associated with increasing rates of suicide by other methods.[19]

A recent study of 30 survivors of attempts to commit suicide with firearms suggests that many of them acted on impulse.[20] Whether this observation applies to nonsurvivors as well is unknown. The recent acquisition of a firearm was noted in only eight of our cases, and we do not know how long before death any suicide victim planned his or her attempt. However, given the high case-fatality rate associated with suicide attempts involving firearms, it seems likely that easy access to guns increases the probability that an impulsive suicide attempt will end in death.[21]

Detectable concentrations of ethanol were found in the blood of a substantial proportion of the victims tested. This suggests that ethanol may be an independent risk factor for gunshot death.[22-25] Although this hypothesis is compatible with the known behavioral and physiologic effect of ethanol, the strength of this association remains to be defined.[25]

There are many reasons that people own guns. Unfortunately, our case files rarely identified why the firearm involved had been kept in the home. We cannot determine, therefore, whether guns kept for protection were more or less hazardous than guns kept for other reasons.

We did note, however, that handguns were far more commonly involved in gunshot deaths in the home than shotguns or rifles. The single most common reason for keeping firearms given by owners of handguns, unlike owners of shoulder weapons, is "self-defense at home."[1,4] About 45 percent of the gun-owning households nationally own handguns.[1] If the proportion of homes containing handguns in King County is similar to this national average, then these weapons were 2.6 times more likely to be involved in a gunshot death in the home than were shotguns and rifles combined.

Several limitations of this type of analysis must be recognized.[1,26] Our observations are based on a largely urban population and may not be applicable to more rural communities. Also, various rates of suicide and homicide have been noted in other metropolitan counties.[27] These differences may reflect variations in social and demographic composition as well as different patterns of firearm ownership.

Mortality studies such as ours do not include cases in which burglars or intruders are wounded or frightened away by the use or display of a firearm. Cases in which would-be intruders may have purposely avoided a house known to be armed are also not identified. We did not report the total number or extent of nonlethal firearm injuries involving guns kept in the home. A complete determination of firearm risks versus benefits would require that these figures be known.

The home can be a dangerous place. We noted 43 suicides, criminal homicides, or accidental gunshot deaths involving a gun kept in the home for every case of homicide for self-protection. In the light of these findings, it may reasonably be asked whether keeping firearms in the home increases a family's protection or places it in greater danger. Given the unique status of firearms in American society and the national toll of gunshot deaths, it is imperative that we answer this question.

REFERENCES

1. Wright, J. D., P. Rossi, K. Daly, and E. Weber-Burdin. *Weapons, Crime, and Violence in America: A Literature Review and Research Agenda.* Washington, D.C.: Government Printing Office, 1981.
2. Wright, J. D., and P. Rossi. *Weapons, Crime, and Violence in America: Executive Summary.* Washington, D.C.: Government Printing Office, 1981.
3. Wright, J. D. "Public Opinion and Gun Control: A Comparison of Results from Two Recent National Surveys." *Annals* of the American Academy of Political and Social Science, No. 455 (1981):24–39.
4. *An Analysis of Public Attitudes Towards Handgun Control.* Cambridge, Mass.: Cambridge Reports, 1978.
5. *Attitudes of the American Electorate Toward Gun Control.* Santa Anna, Calif.: Decision Making Institute, 1978.
6. Newton, G. D., and F. E. Zimring. *Firearms and Violence in American Life: Task Force Report on Firearms.* Washington, D.C.: Government Printing Office, 1969.
7. Davis, J. A. *General Social Surveys, 1972–1978: Cumulative Codebook.* Chicago: National Opinion Research Center, University of Chicago (1978):172.
8. Alexander, G. R., et al. "Firearm-Related Fatalities: An Epidemiologic Assessment of Violent Death." *American Journal of Public Health* 75(1985):165–68.
9. Yeager, M., J. D. Alviani, and N. Loving. *How Well Does that Handgun Protect You and Your Family?* Technical Report No. 2. United States Conference of Mayors, Washington, D.C., 1976.
10. Bureau of Census. *1980 Census of Population, Washington.* Washington, D.C.: Government Printing Office, 1981.
11. *Uniform Crime Reporting Handbook.* Washington, D.C.: Federal Bureau of Investigation, United States Department of Justice, 1984.
12. Centers for Disease Control. *Suicide Surveillance, 1970–1980.* April 1985.
13. *Crime in the United States 1983: Crime Reports for the United States.* Washington, D.C.: Federal Bureau of Investigation, United States Department of Justice, 1984.
14. Baker, S. P. "Without Guns, Do People Kill People?" *American Journal of Public Health* 75(1985):587–88.
15. Cook, P. J. *The Effect of Gun Availability on Robbery and Robbery Murder: A Cross-Section Study of 50 Cities.* In: Hearings Before the Subcommittee on Crime of the Committee on the Judiciary, House of Representatives, Washington, D.C.: Government Printing Office, 1978.
16. Markush, R. E., and A. A. Bartolucci. "Firearms and Suicide in the United States." *American Journal of Public Health* (1984) 74:123–27.
17. Westemeyer, J. "Firearms, Legislation, and Suicide Prevention." *American Journal of Public Health* 74(1984):108.
18. Brown, J. H. "Suicide in Britain: More Attempts, Fewer Deaths, Lessons for Public Policy." *Archives of General Psychiatry* 36(1979):1119–24.
19. Burvill, P., W. "Changing Patterns of Suicide in Australia, 1910–1977." *Acta Psychiatr. Scand,* 62(1980):258–68.
20. Peterson, L. G., et al. "Self-Inflicted Gunshot Wounds: Lethality of Method Versus Intent." *American Journal of Psychiatry* 142(1985):228–31.
21. Baker, S. P., B. O'Neill, and R. S. Karpf. *The Injury Fact Book.* Lexington, Mass.: Lexington Books, 1984.
22. Tinklenberg, J. R. "Alcohol and Violence." In *Alcoholism: Progress in Research and Treatment,* edited by P. G. Bourne and R. Rox, pp. 195–210. New York: Academic Press, 1973.
23. "Alcohol and Violent Death—Erie County, New York 1973–1983." *MMWR* 33(1984):226–27.
24. Hedeboe, J., et al. "Interpersonal Violence: Patterns in a Danish Community." *American Journal of Public Health* 75(1985):651–53.
25. Goodman, R. A., et al. "Alcohol Use and Interpersonal Violence: Alcohol Detected in Homicide Victims." *American Journal of Public Health* 765(1986):144–49.
26. Drooz, R. B. "Handguns and Hokum: A Methodological Problem." *Journal of the American Medical Association* 238(1977):43–45.
27. Ray, D., and J. Tapp. Annual Report 1980: Division of the King County Medical Examiner, Department of Public Health. Seattle: King County, 1981.

17

The Epidemiology of Firearm Deaths Among Residents of California

Garen J. Wintemute, Stephen P. Teret, and Jess F. Kraus

Firearms are a leading cause of death and disability in the United States. Each year more than 30,000 Americans die as a result of gunfire. More than 100,000 injuries have been estimated to occur annually from unintentional shootings alone.[1] With few exceptions[2-4] epidemiologic analyses of firearm mortality have considered only one aspect of the problem, separating murders from suicides from unintentional deaths.

This essay analyzes the 26,422 firearm deaths that occurred to California residents from 1977 through 1983. It focuses on the vehicle common to these deaths—the gun—in an effort to provide a clearer estimate of the impact of firearms on the public's health. By de-emphasizing the behavioral aspects of firearm deaths, this unifying approach also promotes the consideration of prevention strategies beyond those addressing the behavior of persons actually involved in shootings. It may well be that here, as elsewhere in medicine and public health, the most effective preventive measures do not attempt to modify the behavior of those to be protected.

Reprinted by permission of the *Western Journal of Medicine* 146, no. 3 (March 1987): 374–77.

METHODS

Data from death certificates for all deaths occurring to California residents from 1977 through 1983 were obtained by a computerized search of the California Master Mortality File. The 1980 census data for California were used for a mid-interval population; intercensal estimates were obtained from the Population Research Unit, California State Department of Finance. . . .

The leading causes of death for Californians* were reranked, listing firearms separately and excluding firearm deaths from those categories in which they would otherwise be found. Nonfirearm suicides and homicides were combined into a "nonfirearm intentional death" category. Standardized mortality ratios were used as a summary measure of the evenness of distribution of firearm deaths across race and gender groups. Years of potential life lost were calculated using the method employed by the Centers for Disease Control.[5]

Three limitations resulting from this study's reliance on death certificate data should be noted. While diagnostic accuracy for firearm deaths should be high, as virtually all these death certificates were signed by a coroner following an investigation and autopsy, accuracy for nonfirearm causes of death may be lower.[6] Second, this essay does not report separate results for Hispanics. California vital statistics do not categorize Hispanics separately, but classify them as white unless a different racial origin is noted on the death certificate. Finally, separate results for handguns, rifles, shotguns, and other firearms are not presented, as the type of firearm involved was reported in only 20 percent of firearm deaths.

RESULTS

Firearms caused 26,442 deaths among California residents during the years 1977 to 1983—2 percent of all deaths in that population. The mean annual crude firearm mortality rate was 16.0 per 100,000 population. Rates for individual years ranged from 14.4 per 100,000 population in 1983 to 17.2 per 100,000 population in 1980; no consistent trend was observed.

Males accounted for 84 percent of firearm deaths, and had a mortality rate of 27.1 per 100,000 population; the rate for all females was 5.1 per 100,000 population. A bimodal pattern in risk existed for males. Men 75 years old and older had the highest firearm mortality rate, followed by young adult men aged 25 to 34 years. For women, a single peak in the 25- to 34-year

---

*The definitions employed were those of the California State Center for Health Statistics, which are virtually identical to those used by the National Center for Health Statistics.

age group occurred. Rates for both boys and girls younger than 15 were substantially lower than those for all other age groups.

. . . The mortality rate for blacks was as much as ten times that for some other racial groups. Blacks suffered nearly 2.5 times as many firearm deaths (an excess of 415 deaths each year) as would have been seen if their age-specific firearm mortality rates had equaled those for all Californians combined.

Age- and race-specific rates for males: Black men aged 25 to 34 had a mortality rate of 135 per 100,000 population, more than three times that for the group at next highest risk and more than eight times that for the state as a whole. Rates were highest for blacks in all age groups except those over 75; the finding that the rate for all male Californians combined was highest over age 75 derived from the increased mortality in that age group among whites. Mortality rates for other races tended to be maximal in young adulthood and decline or remain relatively stable thereafter. (Firearm mortality rates for Asian, Native American, and "other" boys aged 5 to 14 and for "other" boys under age 5 were all less than 1.0 per 100,000 population. No firearm deaths occurred among Asian or Native American boys under age 5, or among Native American men aged 75 and older.)

Among female Californians, firearm mortality rates were greatest for blacks in all age groups. Black women aged 25 to 34 had the highest female rate observed, 17.4 per 100,000 population. Rates for females of all races were highest for ages 15 to 34 and declined thereafter.

Firearms and the Causes of Violent Death

Firearms were the leading cause of intentional death in the state, accounting for 54 percent of all suicides and homicides combined. Firearms were used in 59 percent of all California homicides. Among persons aged 15 to 34, the high-risk group for homicides in California, 65 percent of these deaths were attributable to firearms. Of all suicides, 49 percent were firearm-related; this percentage remained relatively stable across all age groups.

A plurality of firearm deaths were suicides. Suicides accounted for 12,798 deaths over the study period, or 48 percent of all firearm deaths. Homicide ranked second with 12,329 deaths, 47 percent of the total. Unintentional shootings accounted for only 688 deaths, 3 percent of all firearm deaths. There were 2 percent classified as undetermined.

The percentage of all firearm deaths attributable to homicide, suicide, or unintentional shootings was related to age. . . . Under age 1, a total of 89 percent of all firearm deaths were homicides. The percentage contribution of firearm homicide to overall firearm mortality dropped steadily thereafter except during young adulthood. Among persons aged 75 and older, 90 percent of firearm deaths were suicides. Unintentional firearm deaths were most prominent among children and young adults; 61 percent of these deaths occurred to persons aged 1 to 24 years.

The distribution of firearm deaths by cause was related to race as well. Among whites, firearm suicides outnumbered homicides by almost 50 percent; there were 11,863 firearm suicides and 8,041 firearm homicides in this group. For every other racial group, homicides were more frequent. Among blacks there were 3,884 firearm homicides and 702 firearm suicides, a more than fivefold difference.

As a result of these effects, the relative contribution of firearm homicide, suicide, and unintentional death varied among the groups at highest risk for a firearm death. For black men aged 25 to 34, a total of 80 percent of firearm deaths were homicides; only 12 percent were suicides. Yet for white men that same age, suicides outnumbered homicides and accounted for 48 percent of all firearm deaths. Among men 75 years old and above, 93 percent of all firearm deaths were suicides.

Firearms Among Other Causes of Death

Firearms ranked as the eighth leading cause of death for California residents as a whole, sixth for males, second for all persons aged 15 to 34 and first for black males aged 15 to 34 and black females aged 15 to 24. . . . Firearms accounted for 43 percent of all deaths among young black men aged 15 to 24 and 19 percent of deaths in that age group for the state as a whole.

Firearm deaths among black males resulted in 139,866 years of potential life lost over the study period. By this measure, firearms were the leading cause of premature death for black men and boys. Firearms ranked fourth among causes of premature death for all California residents combined, accounting for 746,705 years of potential life lost. If the firearm mortality rates observed in this study were to remain unchanged indefinitely, 1 in 22 black and 1 in 43 white males born between 1977 and 1983 would suffer a firearm-related death by age 75.

DISCUSSION

The central hypothesis of this study was that examining firearm deaths in aggregate would lead to a clearer picture of the effect of firearms on the public's heath. Firearms emerge as a major public health problem. They are the number one cause of death for some segments of the population of California and are among the top ten causes of death for the state as a whole. California is not atypical in this regard; its rates for firearm homicide, suicide, and unintentional death are all close to the median for the fifty states.[7]

It was further hypothesized that this approach might yield useful insights into our current efforts to prevent firearm deaths and injuries and suggest directions for the future. This has also occurred.

Suicide was the leading mode of firearm death in this study. It may therefore be inappropriate to rely primarily on criminal justice approaches to firearm deaths and injuries. In fact, such approaches may be inherently limited in their effectiveness against criminal shootings as well. The Federal Bureau of Investigation has underscored this point, stating that "it has long been recognized that murder is primarily a societal problem over which law enforcement has little or no control."[8]

Only 3 percent of the firearm deaths in this study were unintentional. In 1982 unintentional shootings accounted for only 6 percent of firearm deaths nationally (National Center for Health Statistics, unpublished data, June 1984). Therefore, it is unlikely that expanded educational efforts to promote the safe use of firearms will lead to significant future reductions in firearm deaths.

There are multiple high-risk groups for a firearm death. These groups differ from one another not only in age, race, and gender, but in the types of firearm death for which they are particularly at risk. Prevention strategies targeted specifically at high-risk groups will need to include all these factors.

Such findings support preventive measures directed against firearms themselves. All firearm deaths, however they may otherwise be classified, are by definition associated with a common vehicle of transmission. By analogy, control of many infectious diseases has been dependent upon control of an associated vector. Motor vehicle-related deaths and injuries were substantially reduced by improvements in the design of motor vehicles, rather than efforts to change the behavior of persons using them.[9]

Restricting the availability of firearms, and particularly handguns, is one such measure. In a major study prepared for Congress, the General Accounting Office cited handgun availability as a major determinant of rising firearm homicide rates.[10] A subsequent special study of firearm suicide[11] has yielded supportive results.

Attention to the design of firearms themselves may be beneficial. The Maryland Court of Appeals found in 1985 that a Saturday Night Special—the highly concealable handgun that was a special target of the Gun Control Act of 1968—constitutes an unreasonably dangerous product. Its manufacturer and distributors may therefore he held liable for harm resulting from its use.[12]

Physicians and other health professionals are uniquely able to bring information on the health effects of firearms to their patients and the public. The dangers inherent in having firearms in the home can be made clear to patients as a part of basic health education. When a major family conflict arises or a patient is seriously depressed, a special effort can be made to ascertain whether there are firearms in the home and to have them removed.

Health professionals can have their greatest effect by initiating community wide efforts and legislative action. Widespread public support for greater control of firearms has been documented repeatedly.[13,14] The lack of a stable, visible constituency for change has often prevented this support from being translated into public policy.

By emphasizing that firearms are a major public health problem, concerned health professionals can reverse this trend. Through research such as that presented here, they can bring to light the full impact of firearms on health and guide the evolution of public policy in this area. They can promote widespread public awareness at the local level through coalitions with other community leaders. They can educate their local, state, and national legislators. They can encourage their state medical societies and similar organizations to become active advocates for measures to minimize the health problem created by firearms. And they can create a new professional association to promote and coordinate all these efforts.

Few health issues in our recent history have engendered as complex and lasting a controversy as that surrounding the prevention of firearm deaths and injuries. Through individual and collective action, health professionals can become a potent force to control this epidemic of modern times.

REFERENCES

1. Iskrant, A. P., and P. V. Joliet. *Accidents and Homicide.* Cambridge, Mass.: Harvard University Press, 1968.
2. Alexander, G. R., et al. "Firearm-Related Fatalities: An Epidemiologic Assessment of Violent Death." *American Journal of Public Health* 75(February 1985):165–68.
3. Mahler, A. J., and J. E. Fielding. "Firearms and Gun Control: A Public Health Concern." *New England Journal of Medicine* 297(September 1977):556–58.
4. Fatteh, A., and D. Troxler. "The Gun and Its Victims: A Study of 1024 Firearm Fatalities in North Carolina During 1970." *North Carolina Medical Journal* 32(December 1971):489–95.
5. Centers for Disease Control. *MMWR* 35(January 17, 1986):27.
6. Kircher, T., J. Nelson, and H. Burdo. "The Autopsy as a Measure of Accuracy of the Death Certificate." *New England Journal of Medicine* 313(November 1985):1263–69.
7. Baker, S. P., B. O'Neill, and R. S. Karpf. *The Injury Fact Book.* Lexington, Mass.: D. C. Health, 1984.
8. *Uniform Crime Reports 1983.* Washington, D.C.: Federal Bureau of Investigation, 1984.
9. Robertson, L. *Injuries.* Lexington, Mass.: D. C. Heath, 1983.
10. *Handgun Control: Effectiveness and Costs.* GAO publication No. PAD-78-4. Washington, D.C.: Government Printing Office, 1978.
11. Markush, R. E., and A. A. Bartolucci. "Firearms and Suicide in the United States." *American Journal of Public Health* 74(February 1984):123–27.
12. *Kelley et al. v. RG Industries Inc. et al.* Maryland Court of Appeals, 1985.
13. Alviani, J. D., and W. R. Drake. *Handgun Control: Issues and Alternatives.* Washington, D.C.: U.S. Conference of Mayors, 1975.
14. Brown, E. J., T. J. Flanagan, and M. McLeod. *Sourcebook of Criminal Justice Statistics—1983.* Washington, D.C.: Bureau of Justice Statistics, U.S. Department of Justice, 1984 (Publication No. NCJ-91534).

18

Defensive Gun Ownership as a Response to Crime

Don B. Kates, Jr.

The impossibility of the police preventing endemic crime, or protecting every victim, has become tragically evident over the past quarter century. The issues are illustrated by the ongoing phenomenon of pathological violence against women by their mates or former mates[1]:

> **Baltimore, Md.** Daonna Barnes was forced into hiding with her children because, since making threats is not a crime, police could not arrest her former boyfriend for his threats to kill her. On August 11, 1989, he discovered the location of her new apartment, broke in, and shot and stabbed her and her new boyfriend. Released on bail while awaiting trial on charges of attempted murder, the former boyfriend continues to harass Ms. Barnes, who says: "I feel like there is nobody out there to help me. It's as if [I'll have to wait until he kills me] for anyone to take this seriously. . . ."

From "Guns, Murders, and the Constitution: A Realistic Assessment of Gun Control" (February 1990): 17–36. Copyright © 1990 by the Pacific Research Institute for Public Policy. Reprinted by permission of the publisher.

Mishawaka, Ind. Finally convicted of kidnapping and battery against Lisa Bianco, her husband was sentenced to 7 years imprisonment. On March 4, 1989, he took advantage of release on an 8-hour pass to break into her house and beat her to death.

Los Angeles, Calif. On August 27, 1989, Maria Navarro called the sheriff's office to report that her former husband was again threatening to kill her, despite a restraining order she had obtained against him. The dispatcher instructed her, "If he comes over, don't let him in. Then call us." Fifteen minutes later he burst in on her twenty-seventh birthday party and shot her and three others dead. Noting that Ms. Navarro's call was part of a perennial overload of 2,000 or more 911 calls that the sheriff's office receives daily, a spokesman frankly admitted, "Faced with the same situation again, in all probability, the response would be the same."

Denver, Colo. On February 16, 1989, a mere 9 days after she filed for divorce, Lois Lende's husband broke into her home, beat and stabbed her to death, and then shot himself to death.

Connecticut. Late last year Anthony "Porky" Young was sentenced to a year in prison for stripping his girlfriend naked and beating her senseless in front of her 4-year-old son. "He says next time he's going to make my kids watch while he kills me," she says. Despite scores of death threats he has written to her while in prison, the prison authorities will have to release him when his year is up.

Literally dozens of such newspaper stories appear each week around the United States. Even extreme anti-gun advocates must wonder if a society that cannot protect its innocent victims should not leave them free to choose to own a handgun for defense.[2] Here I analyze the arguments offered for denying that choice.

POLICE PROTECTION VERSUS THE CAPACITY TO DEFEND ONESELF

Perhaps the single most common argument against freedom of choice is that personal self-defense has been rendered obsolete by the existence of a professional police force.[3] For decades, anti-gun officials in Chicago, San Francisco, New York, and Washington, D.C., have admonished the citizenry that they don't need guns for self-defense because the police will defend them. This advice is mendacious: when those cities are sued for failure to provide police protection, those same officials send forth their city attorneys to invoke

> [the] fundamental principle of American law that a government and its agents are under no general duty to provide public services, such as police protection, to any individual citizen.[4]

Even as a matter of theory (much less in fact), the police do NOT exist to protect the individual citizen. Rather their function is *to deter crime in general* by patrol activities and by apprehension after the crime has occurred. If circumstances permit, the police should and will protect a citizen in distress. But they are not legally duty bound even to do that nor to provide any direct protection—no matter how urgent a distress call they may receive. *A fortiori* the police have no duty to, and do not, protect citizens who are under death threat (e.g., women theatened by former boyfriends or husbands).

An illustrative case is *Warren* v. *District of Columbia* in which three rape victims sued the city under the following facts. Two of the victims were upstairs when they heard the other being attacked by men who had broken in downstairs. Half an hour having passed and their roommate's screams having ceased, they assumed the police must have arrived in response to their repeated phone calls. In fact, their calls had somehow been lost in the shuffle while the roommate was being beaten into silent acquiescence. When the roommates went downstairs to see to her, as the court's opinion graphically describes it, "For the next fourteen hours the women were held captive, raped, robbed, beaten, forced to commit sexual acts upon each other, and made to submit to the sexual demands" of their attackers.

Having set out these facts, the District of Columbia's highest court exonerated the District and its police, because it is "fundamental [in] American law" that the police do not exist to provide personal protection to individual citizens.[5] In addition to the case law I have cited, this principle has been expressly enunciated over and over again in statute law.[6]

The fundamental principle that the police have no duty to protect individuals derives equally from practical necessity and from legal history. Hiistorically, there were no police, even in large American or English cities, before the mid-nineteenth century. Citizens were not only expected to protect themselves (and each other), but also legally required in response to the hue and cry to chase down and apprehend criminals. The very idea of a police was anathema, American and English liberalism viewing any such force as a form of the dreaded "standing army."[7] This view yielded only grudgingly to the fact that citizens were unwilling to spend their leisure hours patrolling miles of city streets and were incapable even of chasing fleeing criminals down on crowded city streets—much less tracing and apprehending them or detecting surreptitious crimes.

Eventually, police forces were established to *augment* citizen self-protection by systematic patrol to deter crime and to detect and apprehend criminals if a crime should occur. Historically, there was no thought of the police displacing the citizen's right of self-protection. Nor, as a practical matter, is that displacement remotely feasible in light of the demands a high-crime society makes on the limited resources available to police it. Even if all 500,000 American police officers were assigned to patrol, they could not protect 240 million citizens from upwards of 10 million criminals who enjoy the luxury of deciding when and where to strike. But we have nothing like 500,000 patrol officers: to determine how many police are actually available for any one shift, we must divide the 500,000 by four (three shifts per day, plus officers who have days off, are on sick leave, etc.). The resulting number must be cut in half to account for officers assigned to investigations, juvenile, records, laboratory, traffic, etc., rather than patrol.[8]

Doubtless the deterrent effect of the police helps ensure that many Americans will never be so unfortunate as to live in circumstances requiring personal protection. But for those who do need such protection, police do not and cannot function as bodyguards for ordinary citizens (though in New York and other major cities police may perform bodyguard services for the mayor and other prominent officials). Consider just the number of New York City women who each year seek police help, reporting threats by ex-husbands, ex-boyfriends, etc. To bodyguard just those women would exhaust the resources of the nation's largest police department, leaving no officers available for street patrol, traffic control, crime detection, apprehension of perpetrators, responses to emergency calls, and so forth.[9]

Given what New York courts have called "the crushing nature of the burden,"[10] the police cannot be expected to protect the individual citizen. Individuals remain responsible for their own personal safety, with police providing only an auxiliary general deterrent. The issue is whether those individuals should be free to choose gun ownership as a means of protecting themselves, their homes, and their families.

THE DEFENSIVE UTILITY OF FIREARMS OWNERSHIP—PRE-1980S ANALYSIS

Until recently a combination of problematic data, lacunae, and legerdemain allowed anti-gun advocates to claim "the handgun owner seldom even gets the *chance* to use his gun" and "guns purchased for protection are rarely used for that purpose."[11] The evidence to support this view came from a selective and manipulative rendition of pre-1980s city-level figures on the number of violent felons whom civilians lawfully kill. Because of a lack of any better data, these lawful homicide data were the best available before the 1980s. But anti-gun discussions should have mentioned the major defect in judging how many defense uses there were on the basis of defensive killings alone. That excludes as much as 96 percent of all defensive gun uses which did not involve killing criminals but only scaring them off or capturing them without death. This omission speciously minimizes the extent of civilian defensive gun use. Data now available show that gun-armed civilians capture or rout upwards of 30 times more criminals than they kill.[12]

Exacerbating the minimization problem was the highly misleading way opponents of handgun ownership selected and presented pre–1980s lawful homicide data. Some big cities had kept lawful homicide data since the 1910s. Naturally, many more felons were killed by victims in high crime eras like the 1970s and 1980s, or the 1920s and 1930s (when victims tended to buy and keep guns loaded and ready), than in the low crime era of 1945–65. For instance, Chicago figures starting in the 1920s show that lawful civilian homicide constituted 31.4 percent of all homicides (including fatal automobile accidents), that for decades the number of felons killed by civilians roughly equaled those killed by police, and that by the 1970s civilians were lawfully killing about three times as many felons as were police. Yet no mention of Chicago or these data (or comparable Washington, D.C., figures) are found in the anti-gun literature.[13]

Instead, that literature concentrates on Detroit. Even so, the data somehow omit these pertinent facts. In the 1920s, felons killed by civilians constituted 26.6 percent of all homicides in Detroit.[14] As crime rose after 1965, civilian killings of felons rose 1,305 percent (by 1971) and continued rising so that, by the late 1970s, twice as many felons were being lawfully killed by civilians than by police.[15]

Without mentioning any of this, even the most scrupulous of the anti-gun analysts, George Newton and Franklin Zimring, advanced the highly misleading claim that in the 5 years 1964–68 only "seven *residential* burglars were shot and killed by" Detroit householders, and there were only "three cases of the victim killing a *home* robber."[16] This claim is highly misleading because Newton and Zimring have truncated the lawful homicide data without informing readers that they are omitting the two situations in which most lawful defensive homicides occur: robbers killed by shopkeepers, and the homicidal assailant shot by his victim (e.g., the abusive husband shot by the wife he is strangling). Had these two categories not been surreptitiously omitted, Newton and Zimring's Detroit figure of lawful civilian homicide would have been 27 times greater—not 10 deaths, but rather 270 in the 1964–68 period.[17]

1980S DATA ON THE DEFENSIVE EFFICACY OF HANDGUNS

All pre-1980s work has been eclipsed by more recent data, which allow estimation not only of how many felons are killed annually by armed citizens but also of those captured or scared off. This evidence derives from private national surveys on gun issues. Though sponsored by pro- or anti-gun groups, the polls were conducted by reputable independent polling organizations and have all been accorded credibility by social scientists analyzing gun issues.[18] Further evidence of the polls' accuracy is that their results are consistent (particularly their results on defensive gun use), regardless of their sponsorship.[19]

Moreover, because the different surveys' data are mutually consistent, any suspicion of bias or falsification may be precluded by simply not using data from NRA-sponsored polls.

Therefore, on the basis of only anti-gun polls, it is now clear that handguns are used as or more often in repelling crimes annually as in committing them, approximately 645,000 defense uses annually versus about 580,000 criminal misuses.[20] Handguns are used another 215,000 times annually to defend against dangerous snakes and animals. As to their effectiveness, handguns work equally well for criminals and victims: in about 83 percent of the cases in which a victim faces a handgun, he (or she) submits; in 83 percent of the cases in which a victim with a handgun confronts a criminal, the criminal flees or surrenders.

These victim survey data are confirmed by complementary data from a survey among felons in state prisons across the country. Conducted under the auspices of the National Institute of Justice, the survey found that 34 percent of the felons said that

> they had been "scared off, shot at, wounded, or captured by an armed victim," [quoting the actual question asked] and about two-thirds (69 percent) had at least one acquaintance who had had this experience.[21]

In response to two other questions, 34 percent of the felons said that in contemplating a crime they either "often" or "regularly" worried that they "might get shot at by the victim," and 57 percent agreed that "most criminals are more worried about meeting an armed victim than they are about running into the police."[22]

In sum, the claim that "guns purchased for protection are rarely used for that purpose" could not have been maintained by a full and accurate rendition of pre-1980s data; that claim is definitively refuted by the comprehensive data collected in the 1980s under the auspices of the National Institute of Justice and both pro- and anti-gun groups.

ANTI-GUN OBLIVIOUSNESS TO WOMEN'S DEFENSIVE NEEDS: THE CASE OF DOMESTIC AND SPOUSAL HOMICIDE

My point is not that opponents of precautionary handgun ownership are oblivious to domestic homicide, but only that they are oblivious (or worse) to the situation of women in such homicides. That obliviousness is epitomized by the failure to differentiate men from women in the ubiquitous anti-gun admonition that "the use of firearms for self-protection is more likely to lead to . . . *death among family and friends* than to the death of an intruder."[23] This admonition misportrays domestic homicide as if it were all murder and ignores the fact that around 50 percent of interspousal homicides are committed by abused wives.[24] To understand domestic homicide, we must distinguish unprovoked murder from lawful self-defense against homicidal attack —a distinction that happens in these cases to correlate closely with the distinction between husband and wife.

Not surprisingly when we look at *criminal* violence between spouses, we find that "91 percent were *victimizations of women* by their husbands or ex-husbands. . . ."[25] Thus, the 50 percent of interspousal homcides in which husband kills wife are real murders—but in the overwhelming majority of cases where wife kills husband, she is defending herself or the children.[26] In Detroit, for instance, husbands are killed by wives more often than *vice versa*, yet men are far more often convicted for killing a spouse—because three-quarters of wives who killed were not even charged, prosecutors having found their acts lawful and necessary to preserve their lives or their children's.[27]

When a woman kills a man, she requires a weapon (most often a handgun) to do so. Eliminating handguns from American life would not decrease the total number of killings between spouses. (If anything, the number would increase because, as we have seen, gun-armed victims may ward off attacks without killing 25–30 times more often than the few times they have to kill). To eliminate handguns would only change the sex of the decedents by ensuring that, in virtually every case, it would be the abused wife, not the murderous husband. After all, a gun is far more useful to the victim than her attacker. "Husbands, due to size and strength advantages, do not need weapons to kill."[28] Having a gun is not necessary to attack a

> victim who is unarmed, alone, small, frail . . . [But] even in the hands of a weak and unskilled assailant a gun can be used . . . without much risk of effective counterattack . . . [and] because everyone knows that a gun has these attributes, the mere display of a gun communicates a highly effective threat.[29]

Of course, it is tragic when an abused woman has to kill a current or former mate. But such killings cannot be counted as if they were *costs* of precautionary handgun ownership; rather they are palpable benefits from society's and the woman's point of view, if not from the attacker's. Thus, it is misleading (to the point of willful falsehood) for critics of handgun ownership to misrepresent such lawful defensive killings as what they prevented—domestic murder.

A final, tangential, but significant, point emerges from statistics on using guns in domestic self-defense: those statistics strongly support the defensive efficacy of firearms. As noted above, "men who batter [wives] average 45 pounds heavier and 4 to 5 inches taller than" their victim.[30] If guns were not effective for defense, a homicidal attack by a husband upon his wife would almost invariably end in the wife's death rather than in his about 50 percent of the time.

ANTI-GUN OBLIVIOUSNESS TO WOMEN'S DEFENSIVE NEEDS: ATTACKS BY MALE ACQUAINTANCES

In arguing against precautionary handgun ownership, anti-gun authors purport to comprehensively refute the defensive value of guns (i.e., to every kind of victim). Yet, *without exception* (and without mentioning the omission), those authors omit any mention of the acquaintance crime to which women are most often subjected. The empirical evidence establishes that "women are more likely to be assaulted, more likely to be injured, more likely to be raped, and more likely to be killed by a male partner than by any other type of assailant."[31] Yet, to a man (and, invariably, they are men), anti-gun authors treat self-defense in terms of the gun owner's fears "that a hostile *stranger* will invade *his* home."[32]

Only by turning a blind eye to acquaintance crime could the Chairman of Handgun Control Inc., claim that "the handgun owner rarely even gets the *chance* to use his gun." That assertion restates the argument of Newton and Zimring and the Handgun Control Staff. They emphasized the unexpectedness of stranger attacks—from which they characterized it as "ludicrous" to think a victim "will have sufficient time to retrieve" her handgun.[33]

As discussed above, even in cases of crime by strangers, this view is supported only by Newton and Zimring's inaccurate and misleading rendition of pre-1980s data, which is further discredited by the data available today. Moreover, in relation to violence against women, the assertion that women would invariably be too surprised by violent attack to use a handgun in self-defense is insupportable. On the contrary, in most instances, the man who beats or murders a women (often even the rapist) is an acquaintance who has previously assaulted her on one or two occasions.[34] Such crimes commonly occur after a protracted and bellicose argument over a long-simmering dispute. The women's defensive homicide literature shows that such a victim is almost uniquely positioned for self-defense. Knowing the mannerisms and circumstances that triggered or preceded her attacker's earlier attacks, she has

> "a hypervigilance to cues of any kind of impending violence. . . . [She is] a little bit more responsive to situations than somebody who has not been battered might be." A woman who has [previously] been battered and then is threatened with more abuse is more likely to perceive the danger involved faster than one who has not been abused.[35]

In this connection consider a point that anti-gun crusaders take in another context but ignore in this one. They (rightly) warn victims that a defense gun may be of little use if a person is attacked by a robber who is himself using a gun. The fact is that a gun is so dangerous a weapon that it is extremely risky for a victim to resist—even if the victim has a gun. A basic dictum of police and martial arts training is that even a trained professional should never attack a gun-armed assailant unless convinced that the assailant is about to shoot (in which case there is nothing to lose).[36]

This strong point about the overwhelming power of the person wielding a gun should have provoked academic anti-gun crusaders into at least considering a correlative question: where does the balance of power lie between a victim who has a gun and an attacker armed only with a knife or some lesser weapon? Under those circumstances the victim will usually have the clear advantage (remember Kleck's finding that in 83 percent of cases in which a victim has a handgun, the criminal surrenders or flees). But anti-gun crusaders avoid the embarrassment of admitting that a victim with a gun might have an advantage over a lesser-armed attacker; they either ignore the issue or assume it away. Anti-gun analyses that expressly deal with a situation in which a victim tries to use a gun against an attacker wantonly assumes that the attacker will also have a gun.[37] In fact, however, in 89.6 percent of the violent crimes directed against women during the 10 years of 1973–82, the offender did not have a gun;[38] only 10 percent of rapists used guns,[39] and only 25 percent of nonstrangers who attacked victims (whether male or female) had any weapon whatever.[40] In sum, the same strong arguments that anti-gun analysts offer against the wisdom of a victim resisting a gun-armed attacker suggest that women with handguns will have the advantage because most rapists and other attackers do not have guns.[41]

At this point it may be appropriate to address the old bugaboo that a woman who seeks to resist a male attacker will have her gun taken away and used against her. I emphasize that this is only a *theoretical* bugaboo: the rape literature contains no example of such an occurrence.[42] Moreover, police instructors and firearms experts strongly reject its likelihood. Not only do they aver that women are capable of gun-armed self-defense,[43] they find women much easier to properly train than men, because women lack the masculine ego problems that cause men to stubbornly resist accepting instruction. Thus, a police academy instructor who simultaneously trained a male police academy class and a class of civilian women "most of [whom] had never held a revolver, much less fired one" found that after one hour on the range and two hours of classroom instruction in the Chattanooga Police Academy's combat pistol course, the women consistently outshot police cadets who had just received eight times as much formal instruction and practice.[44]

ANTI-GUN OBLIVIOUSNESS TO WOMEN'S
DEFENSIVE NEEDS: RAPE

Antigun academics necessarily neglect analyzing the gun's value in defending against rape because they eschew any mention of rape.[45] This surprising omission cannot be explained as a mere side effect of ignoring acquaintance crimes. After all, many rapists are strangers rather than acquaintances; indeed, many rapes are committed in the course of crimes that anti-gun literature does address, such as robbery and burglary.[46] But, almost invariably, the "intruder" whom anti-gun authors discuss is not a rapist but a "robber" whom they represent as "confront[ing] too swiftly" for rape or a "burglar" whom they represent as only breaking into unoccupied homes.[47]

This obliviousness to women's self-defense in general, and to rape in particular, leaves anti-gun authors free to deprecate the defensive utility of guns on grounds that don't apply to most circumstances in which women use guns defensively. Anti-gun writings correctly stress that it is illegal to shoot to prevent mere car theft, shoplifting, or trespass that does not involve entry into the home itself.[48] In contrast, the law allows a woman to shoot a rapist or homicidal attacker.[49] Also, in some cases a man attacked by another man of comparable size and strength may be hard put to justify his need to shoot, which is far less of a problem for a female victim of male attack.[50]

In short, to the extent academic anti-gun crusaders have made valid points about armed self-defense, these points do not apply to women. The anti-gun crusaders avoid acknowledging attacks on women by the simple device of never mentioning rape, or women's armed self-defense, at all. One anti-gun writer, Robert Drinan, did discuss rape, albeit not entirely voluntarily; he was responding to an article in which I highlighted the issue as justifying women's freedom to choose guns for self-defense. Drinan responded, in essence, that women detest guns and don't want to own them for self-defense.[51] This response is both factually and conceptually erroneous. It is factually erroneous because evidence shows that currently (though not necessarily when Drinan wrote) women constitute one-half of purely precautionary gun owners. It is conceptually erroneous because freedom of choice is a residual value even for things that many or most people do not now—and may not ever—want to choose.

Newton and Zimring's chapter on self-defense dismisses women's concerns about rape (or, presumably, other kind of attack) in one contemptuous sentence to the effect that "women generally are less capable of self-defense [than men] and less knowledgeable about guns."[52] Feminist outrage about this derisive comment may account for the fact that Prof. Zimring's subsequent writings, including his self-defense chapter in a 1987 book, prudently eschew any attempt to deal with women's rights to, or capacity for, self-defense with guns.[53]

Other anti-gun treatments do not specifically address rape beyond their general position that victims should always submit to criminals unless flight is possible: the best way to "keep you alive [is to] put up no defense—give them what they want or run" advises Handgun Control Inc.[54] However unacceptable that advice may be to feminists, at least it avoids the confusion that marks the discussion of gun-armed defense against rape in a pamphlet by the Handgun Control Staff of the U.S. Conference of Mayors. For the first 31 of its 36 pages, the pamphlet harps on the prohibitive dangers of any physical resistance to crime. Throughout, the Handgun Control Staff's argument against precautionary gun ownership consists of warning against handguns or *any other* form of physical resistance—the risk of *any kind* of physical resistance is so high that victims should always submit to attackers.[55]

But when they finally got to rape, the Staff offers a startling *volte face* —all the more startling because the pamphlet lacks an explanation, much less a justification, of its contradicting all that preceded it. The Handgun Control Staff blithely announces that women don't need handguns because of "the effectiveness of other means of resistance such as verbal and physical resistance."[56] Yet, if the authors believe their own prior warnings, "physical resistance" is prohibitively dangerous. For example, the pamphlet twice repeated its point (each time in italics) that *"a victim is more than eight times as likely to be killed when using a self-protective measure"* of any kind,[57] and it contained a more general admonition (again in italics) that *"victims who resist experience much higher rates of fatality and injury."*[58]

The Handgun Control Staff's pamphlet also points out that many rapes do not occur in the victim's home but in places where she presumably would not be legally entitled to carry a gun. However, this highlights the fact that most rapes *do* occur in the victim's home where she is entitled to have a gun (in all but a few jurisdictions like Washington, D.C., where victims are not permitted guns for self-defense). In short, most rapes occur where a woman may legally have a gun, and the empirical evidence is that in 83 percent of the cases it will protect her from being raped.

INCIDENCE OF INJURY TO HANDGUN-ARMED VICTIMS WHO RESIST CRIMINAL ATTACK

Some readers may object that the preceding section of this study shirks the crucial issue of victim injury by veering onto the side issue of intellectual honesty. Yes (they may say), the Handgun Control Staff's discussion of rape is inconsistent to the point of dishonesty; nevertheless, the pamphlet does marshall impressive data that victims who resist are often seriously hurt or killed.[59] Do those data not validate Zimring, Hawkins, and Handgun Control Inc. in teaching that victims ought to submit to rapists, robbers, or other violent criminals: the best way to "keep you alive [is to] put up no defense—give them what they want or run."[60]

The short answer is the Handgun Control Staff's pamphlet presents data that are irrelevant to the risk of injury to victims who resist with a handgun. The pre–1980s data do not deal with guns specifically. The information gives only a conglomerate figure for the percentage of victims injured or killed when resisting physically in any way. This conglomerate figure includes some few victims who resisted with a gun; many more who used knives, clubs, or some makeshift weapon; and many who resisted totally unarmed. It is crucial to distinguish resistance with a gun from all other kinds of resistance, because a gun differs *qualitatively* in its defensive value. Criminals generally select victims who are weaker than themselves. Only a gun gives weaker, older, less aggressive victims equal or better chances against a stronger attacker. As even Zimring and Hawkins state, guns empower "persons [who are] physically or psychologically unable to overpower [another] through violent physical contact."[61]

The difference is evident in post-1978 National Crime Survey data, which do allow us to distinguish victim injury in cases of gun-armed resistance from victim injury in cases where resistance was with lesser weapons, and from victim injury in cases of nonresistance. Ironically, the results validate the anti-gun critics' danger-of-injury concerns for every form of resistance *except* a gun. The gun-armed resister was actually much less likely to be injured than the nonresister who was, in turn, much less likely to be injured than those who resisted without a gun. Only 12 to 17 percent of gun-armed resisters were injured. Those who submitted to the felons' demands were twice as likely to be injured (gratuitously). Those resisting without guns were three times as likely to be injured as those with guns.[62]

I emphasize that these results do *not* mean that a gun allows victims to resist regardless of circumstances. In many cases submission will be the wiser course. Indeed, what the victim survey data suggest differs startlingly from both pro- and anti-gun stereotypes: keeping a gun for defense may induce sober consideration of the dangers of reckless resistance. The low injury rate of these victims may show that gun owners are not only better able to resist, but to evaluate *when* to submit, than are nonowners who, having never seriously contemplated those choices, must suddenly decide between them.

THE "SUBMISSION" POSITION ADVOCATED BY WHITE, MALE ACADEMIA

By the "submission position, I mean, of course, the view embraced by various anti-gun scholars that victims should submit to felons rather than offering forcible resistance *of any kind*. If an attacker cannot be "talked out" of his crime, the victim should comply to avoid injury.[63] Not insignificantly, academic proponents of the submission position are all white males.[64]

This white male's viewpoint is significant insofar as the submission position is conditioned by the relative immunity to crime that its proponents enjoy because of their racial, sexual, and economic circumstances. In general, the submission position literature does not even mention rape. Equally significant, it treats robbery as the once-in-a-lifetime danger it is for a salaried, white, male academic. His risk of meeting a robber is so low that he is unlikely to keep a gun ready for that eventuality. Moreover, submitting once in a lifetime to losing the money in his wallet may well be "the better part of valor" for a victim who can replace that money at his bank's automatic teller machine and can minimize the loss by taking it off his taxes. A very different calculus of costs and benefits of resisting may apply either to

> an elderly Chicano whom the *San Francisco Examiner* reports has held onto his grocery by outshooting fifteen armed robbers [while] nearby stores have closed because thugs have either bankrupted them or have casually executed their unresisting proprietors . . . [or to] welfare recipients whom robbers target, knowing when their checks come and where they cash them . . . [or to] the elderly trapped in deteriorating neighborhoods (such as the Manhattan couple who in 1976 hanged themselves in despair over repeatedly losing their pension checks and furnishings to robbers).[65]

Regrettably, for many victims, crime is not the isolated happenstance it is for white male academics.[66] Let us imagine a black shopkeeper, perhaps a retired Marine master sergeant who has invested his life savings in the only store he can afford following his "20-years-and-out" career. Not coincidentally, the store is in an area where robbery insurance is prohibitively high or unobtainable at any price. In deciding whether to submit to robbery or resist, he and others who live or work in such areas must weigh a factor that finds no place in the submission position literature: that to survive they may have to establish a reputation for not being easily victimized.[67] The submission position literature is equally oblivious to special factors that are important to rape victims; even one rape—much less several—may cause catastrophic psychological injury that may be worsened by submission and may be mitigated by even an unsuccessful attempt at resistance.[68]

By no means am I arguing that resistance with guns (or without) optimum for crime victims in any or all situations. I am just adding factors that really ought to be considered by well-salaried, white, male intellectuals who presume (as I certainly would not) to tell people who are most often crime victims what is best for them. Scholars, however learned, are presumptuous to pontificate on what is best for a victim whose values and situation they may not share. Consider the reflections of a woman who (without a gun) successfully resisted rape:

> I believed he would kill me if I resisted. But the other part was that I would try to kill him first because I guess that for me, at that time in my life, it would have been better to have died resisting rape than to have been raped. I decided I wasn't going to die. It seemed a waste to die on the floor of my apartment so I decided to fight.[69]

NOTES

1. As exemplified in the examples given in the text, I use the terms "husband," "wife," "mate," and "spousal" to include not only actual, ongoing, and legal marriages, but also "common law" marriage (which is legal in some states, but not others) and "boyfriend-girlfriend," as well as estranged and former versions of all these relationships.

2. All discussion of gun-armed self-defense in this study is directed to handguns because they are infinitely more efficacious for defense than rifles or shotguns. In contrast to the unwieldy long gun, the short-barrelled handgun is much easier to bring into play at close quarters and much harder for an assailant to wrest away. Consider the situation of a woman holding an intruder at bay while trying to dial the police. With a rifle, this is difficult and hazardous at best. Given only the two-inch barrel of a snub-nosed handgun to grasp, not even the strongest man can lever it from a woman's grip before she shoots him. M. Ayoob, *The Truth About Self-Protection* (New York: Bantam, 1983) pp. 332-33, 341-42, 345-55.

3. Thus Ramsey Clark denounces precautionary gun ownership as an atavistic insult to American government: "A state in which a citizen needs a gun to protect himself from crime has failed to perform its first purpose"; it is "anarchy, not order under law—a jungle where each relies on himself for survival," R. Clark, *Crime in America* (1971), p. 88. For similar views, see also Wills, "Handguns that Kill," *Washington Star*, January 18, 1981; "John Lennon's War," *Chicago Sun Times*, December 12, 1980; and "Or Worldwide Gun Control," *Philadelphia Inquirer*, May 17, 1981; editorial: "Guns and the Civilizing Process," *Washington Post*, September 26, 1972.

4. *Warren* v. *District of Columbia*, 444 A.2d 1 (D.C. Ct. of Ap. 1981). For similar cases from New York and Chicago, see *Riss* v. *City of New York*, 22 N.Y. 2d 579, 293 NYS2d 897, 240 N.E. 2d 860 (N.Y. Ct. of Ap. 1958); *Keane* v. *City of Chicago*, 98 Ill. App.2d 460, 240 N.E.2d 321 (1968). See also the cases cited in the next two footnotes and *Bowers* v. *DeVito*, 686 F.2d 61 (7 Cir. 1982) (no federal constitutional requirement that states or local agencies provide sufficient police protection).

5. 444 A.2d at 6; see also *Morgan* v. *District of Columbia*, 468 A.2d 1306 (D.C. Ct. of Ap. 1983). To the same effect, see *Calogrides* v. *City of Mobile*, 475 So. 2d 560 (S. Ct. Ala. 1985); *Morris* v. *Musser*, 478 A.2d 937 (1984); *Davidson* v. *City of Westminster*, 32 C.3d 197, 185 Cal. Rptr. 252, 649 P.2d 894 (S. Ct. Cal. 1982); *Chapman* v. *City of Philadelphia*, 434 A.2d 753 (Sup. Ct. Penn. 1981); *Weutrich* v. *Delia*, 155 N.J. Super. 324, 326, 382 A.2d 929,930 (1978); *Sapp* v. *City of Tallahassee*, 348 So.2d 363 (Fla. Ct. of Ap. 1977); *Simpson's Food Fair* v. *Evansville*, 272 N.E. 2d 871 (Ind. Ct. of Ap.); *Silver* v. *City of Minneapolis*, 170 N.W.2d 206 (S. Ct. Minn. 1969); and the other authorities cited in the footnotes preceding and following this one.

6. See Cal. Govt. Code §§ 821, 845, 846, and 85 Ill. Rev. Stat. 4-102, construed in *Stone* v. *State*, 106 C.A.3d 924, 165 Cal. Rptr. 339 (Cal. Ct. of Ap. 1980); and *Jamison* v. *Chicago*, 48 Ill. App. 567 (Ill. Ct. of Ap. 1977) respectively; see generally 18 *McQuillen on Municipal Corporations*, sec. 53.80.

7. See generally *Michigan Law Review* 82:214-16, and F. Morn, "Firearms Use and the Police: A Historic Evolution of American Values," in D. Kates (ed.), *Firearms and Violence: Issues of Public Policy* (PRIPP 1984).

8. See the extended discussion in Bowman, "An Open Letter," *Police Marksman*, July–August 1986.

9. Silver and Kates, "Handgun Ownership, Self-Defense and the Independence of Women in a Violent, Sexist Society," in D. Kates (ed.), *Restricting Handguns: The Liberal Skeptics* (Naperville, Ill.: Caroline Hse., 1979), pp. 144-47. Prof. Leddy, formerly a New York officer, cites personal experience:

The ability of the state to protect us from personal violence is limited by resources and personnel shortages [in addition to which] the state is usually unable to know that we need protection until it is too late. By the time that the police can be notified and then arrive at the scene, the violent criminal has ample opportunity to do serious harm. *I once waited 20 minutes for the New York City Police to respond to an "officer needs assistance" call which has their highest priority.* On the other hand, a gun provides immediate protection. Even where the police are prompt and efficient, the gun is speedier.

From "The Ownership and Carrying of Personal Firearms," *International Journal of Victimology* (Emphasis added). Cf. the Riss and Silver cases cited above, as well as *Wong v. City of Miami*, 237 So.2d 132 (Fla., 1970). All emphasize the need for judicial deference to administrators' allocation of scarce police resources as a reason for denying liability for failure to protect.

10. *Wiener v. Metropolitan Transit Authority*, 433 N.E. 2d 124, 127, 55 N.Y. 2d 175, 498 N.Y.S. 2d 141 (N.Y. App. Div. 1982).

11. The first quotation is from a book by Nelson "Pete" Shields, the founder of Handgun Control, Inc., *Guns Don't Die, People Do* (New York: Arbor House 1981), p. 49 (emphasis in original); the second is from Meredith, "The Murder Epidemic," *Science* (December 1986): 46. The point appears as a *leitmotif* throughout the Handgun Control Staff pamphlet. To the same effect, please see Newton and Zimring, *Firearms and Violence in American Life* (1969), p. 68, and F. Zimring and G. Hawkins, *The Citizen's Guide to Gun Control* (New York: Macmillan, 1987) (hereinafter Zimring and Hawkins, 1987), p. 31.

12. In 68–75 percent of instances, the attacker is scared off without being shot at all. See Kleck, "Guns and Self-Defense: Crime Control through the Use of Force in the Private Sector," *Social Problems* 35(1988):4 (hereinafter cited as *Social Problems*); J. Wright and P. Rossi, *Armed and Dangerous: A Survey of Felons and their Firearms* (New York: Aldine, 1986), p. 146. See results reported and analyzed in Hardy, "Firearms Ownership and Regulation: Tackling an Old Problem with Renewed Vigor," *William & Mary Law Review* 20(1978):235. See generally "Policy Lessons," *Law and Contemporary Problems* 49:44. Even where attackers are shot, in more than five out of six instances they are wounded rather than killed. Ibid.; Cook, "The Case of the Missing Victims: Gunshot Wounds in the National Crime Survey," *Journal of Quantitative Criminology* 91: 94–96.

13. For the civilian-police comparisons, Silver and Kates, "Handgun Ownership, Self-Defense and the Independence of Women in a Violent, Sexist Society," in D. Kates (ed.), *Restricting Handguns* (1979), p. 156. Robin, "Justifiable Homicide by Police Officers," p. 295, n. 3, of M. Wolfgang, *Studies in Homicide* (1967) notes that 1920s justifiable civilian homicides composed 26.6 percent and 31.4 percent of all homicides in Detroit and Chicago, respectively, and 32 percent of the total homicides in Washington, D.C, in the period 1914–18.

14. Zahn, "Homicide in the 20th Century," in T. Gurr (ed.), *Violence in America* (Violence, Cooperation, Peace Ser., 1989), 1:221–22.

15. M. Dietz, *Killing for Profit: The Social Organization of Felony Homicide* (Chicago: Nelson-Hall, 1983), Table A.1, pp. 202–203.

16. Newton and Zimring above, p. 63 (my emphasis).

17. Computation from the yearly Detroit homicide figures for "Excusable" and "Justifiable: Civilian" homicides in Dietz above. Because about 10 percent of excusable homicides are nonculpable accidental killings, in computing from the excusable column I have reduced its total by 10 percent. See discussion of justifiable and excusable homicide in "Policy Lessons" above, p. 44.

18. See for example, *Social Problems*. pp. 7–9; Wright, "Public Opinion and Gun Control: A Comparison of Results from Two Recent National Surveys," *Annals* of the American Academy of Politics and Social Science, No. 455(1981):24; Hardy above and Bordua, "Adversary Polling and the Construction of Social Meaning," *Law & Policy Quarterly* 5(1983):345.

19. *Social Problems*, pp. 7–9.

20. Ibid.

21. The survey was released by the National Institute of Justice in summary form only. The entire survey with exhaustive analysis has been privately published by Aldine de Guyter Press as J. Wright and P. Rossi, *Armed and Considered Dangerous: A Survey of Felons and Their Firearms* (1986). The survey question and results cited appear at 154.

22. Ibid., p. 145 and Table 7.2.

23. Emphasis added. This particular wording derives from the Handgun Control Staff pamphlet, p. 1 and from the other Handgun Control Staff publication Alviani and Drake, *Handgun Control: Issues and Alternatives*, p. 8. But the same theme, often expressed in virtually identical language, will be found in almost all critical treatments of precautionary gun ownership. See, for example, Rushforth et al., "Violent Death in a Metropolitan County," *New England Journal of Medicine* 297 (1977): 531, 533; Drinan, "Gun Control: The Good Outweighs the Evil," *Civil Liberties Review* 3 (1976): 43, 49; and Shields above, pp. 49–53 and 124–25.

24. U.S. Bureau of Justice Statistics release "Family Violence" (April 1984), Table 1. See generally Straus, "Domestic Violence and Homicide Antecedents," *Bulletin of the N.Y. Academy of Medicine* 52 (1986): 446; Kates, "Firearms and Violence: Old Premises, Current Evidence," in T. Gurr (ed.), *Violence in America* (Violence, Cooperation, Peace Ser., 1989), 1: 203–204.

25. Figures reported for the period 1973–81 in U.S. Bureau of Justice Statistics release "Family Violence" (April 1984), p. 4 (emphasis added).

26. See for example, Straus, above Saunders,"When Battered Women Use Violence: Husband Abuse or Self-Defense?" *Violence and Victims* 1(1986):47, 49 (hereinafter cited as Saunders-1; Barnard et al., "Till Death Do Us Part: A Study of Spouse Murder," *Bulletin of the American Academy of Psychology and Law* 10(1982):271; D. Lunde, *Murder and Madness* (San Francisco: Stanford Portable Ser., 1976), p. 10 (in 85 percent of cases of decedent-precipitated interspousal homicides, the wife is the killer and the husband precipitated his own death by abusing her); M. Daly and M. Wilson, *Homicide* (New York: Aldine, 1988), p. 278 ("when women kill, their victims are . . . most typically men who have assaulted them"); E. Benedek, "Women and Homicide," in B. Danto et al., *The Human Side of Homicide* (New York: Columbia, 1982).

It must be noted, however, that not all female defensive killings of husbands are legal. The legality depends on whether the wife reasonably anticipated that the husband's beating would cause her death or great bodily harm. Even where the statutes classify wife beating as a felony her proper resort is to seek prosecution; unless she was in imminent danger of death or great bodily harm, she must submit to beating rather than resist with deadly force. *People* v. *Jones*, 191 C.A.2d 478 (Cal. Ct. of Ap., 1961); see generally Kates and Engberg, "Deadly Force Self-Defense Against Rape," *U.C.-Davis Law Review* 15(1982):873, 876–77. When a wife kills only after surviving numerous prior beatings, it may be particularly difficult to convince police or jury that she reasonably believed this time was different—even though the pattern of men who eventually kill their wives is generally one of progressively more severe beatings until the final one. See Howard above.

27. Daly and Wilson above, p. 15 and Table 9.1, p. 200.

28. Howard above, pp. 82–83; see also Saunders-1, above: "Men who batter [wives] average 45 pounds heavier and 4 to 5 inches taller than" their victims.

29. Cook, "The Role of Firearms in Violent Crime: An Interpretative Review of the Literature," in M. Wolfgang and N. Weiler (ed.), *Criminal Violence* 269 (1982):247; Wright, "Second Thoughts About Gun Control," *The Public Interest* 91 (1988): 3, 32 ("Analysis of the family homicide data reveals an interesting pattern. When women kill men, they often use a gun. When men kill women, they usually do it in some more degrading or brutalizing way—such as strangulation or knifing"); and Saunders, "Who Hits First and Who Suffers Most? Evidence for the Greater Victimization of Women in Intimate Relationships," a paper presented at the 1989 Annual Meeting of the American Society of Criminology (available from Daniel Saunders, M.D., Department of Psychiatry, U. of Wisconsin).

30. Saunders-1 above, p. 94.

31. Browne and Williams "Resource Availability for Women at Risk: Its Relationship to Rates of Female-Perpetrated Partner Homicide," a paper presented at the 1987 annual meeting of the American Society of Criminology (available from the authors at the Family Research Laboratory, U. of New Hampshire).

32. Zimring and Hawkins (1987), p. 32 (emphasis added); Rushforth, Hirsch, Ford, and Adelson, "Accidental Firearm Fatalities in a Metropolitan County (1958–73)," *American Journal of Epidemiology* 100(1975): 499, 502 (deprecating value of gun-armed self-defense, based only on analysis expressly limited to shootings of "burglars, robbers, or intruders *who were not relatives or acquaintances*"—emphasis added); Conklin & Seiden, "Gun Deaths: Biting the Bullet on Effective Control," *Public Affairs Report* 22 (U. Cal. Inst. of Govt. Studies, 1981): 1, 4 (same: "burglars or thieves" entering home); J. Spiegler and J. Sweeney, *Gun Abuse in Ohio;* p. 41 (same: "burglars, robbers, or intruders"). See also two publications by the National Coalition to Ban Handguns: its undated, unpaginated pamphlet, "A Shooting Gallery Called America," and Fields, "Handgun Prohibition and Social Necessity," *St. Louis University Law Journal* 23(1979):35, 39, 42; Handgun Control Staff (Alviani and Drake, above, pp. 5–7, considering defense only against the "robber or burglar"); and Shields, *Guns Don't Die, People Do,* as well as Teret and Wintemute, "Handgun Injuries: The Epidemiologic Evidence for Assessing Legal Responsibility," *Hamline Law Review* 6(1983):341, 349–50; Riley, "Shooting to Kill the Handgun: Time to Martyr Another American 'Hero'," *Journal of Urban Law* 51(1974):491, 497–99; I. Block, *Gun Control: One Way to Save Lives,* pp. 10–12 (pamph. issued by Public Affairs Committee, 1976); and Drinan above.

33. Handgun Control Staff pamphlet, p. 35 and Alviani and Drake above, p. 6 (paraphrasing almost identically Newton and Zimring, p. 68):

The handgun is rarely an effective instrument for protecting the home against either the *burglar* or the *robber* because the former avoids confrontation [by striking only unoccupied premises] and the latter confronts too swiftly [for the victim to get his gun.]

Compare Zimring and Hawkins (1987), p. 31 (emphasis added): "it is rare indeed that a household handgun actually stops the *burglar* [because he strikes when the home is unoccupied], or the home *robber* who counts on surprise and a weapon of his own." See also Riley and I. Block above.

34. Saunders-1, pp. 51, 56; Benedek, "Women and Homicide," pp. 155–56, 162; Browne and Williams; Browne and Flewelling; and sources there cited.

35. *People* v. *Aris*, C.A.3d [89 Cal. Daily Op. Serv. 8505, 8509 (Cal. Ct. of Ap., Nov. 17, 1989)] (citing and adopting the testimony of expert witness, Dr. Lenore Walker, the leading American authority on battererd wife syndrome). See also *State* v. *Kelly*, 478 A.2d 364, 378 (1984); Schneider, "Describing and Changing: Women's Self-Defense Work and the Problem of Expert Testimony on Battering," *Women's Rights Law Review* 9(1986):195; and authorities there cited.

36. This is particularly true against a handgun whose short barrel makes it both much harder to wrest away than a long gun and much easier to bring it into play at close quarters. See note 2 above.

37. For instance, although fewer than 10 percent of burglars carry guns, Riley conceptualizes what will ensue if householders with guns confront burglars in terms of " 'bedroom shootouts' [which will be] won by alert desperadoes with drawn guns rather than the usually unwarned, sleepy-eyed residents," "Shooting to Kill the Handgun: Time to Martyr Another American 'Hero',", *Journal of Urban Law* 51(1974):491, 497–98; see also Zimring and Hawkins (1987) p. 31; I. Block, *Gun Control: One Way to Save Lives*, pp. 10–12 (pamph. issued by Public Affairs Committee, 1976). Neither these nor any other anti-gun treatment ever consider the possibility of a victim with a gun being attacked by a felon without a gun.

38. U.S. Bureau of Justice Statistics release "The Use of Weapons in Committing Offenses" (January 1986), Table 6.

39. U.S. Bureau of Justice Statistics release "The Crime of Rape" (March 1985).

40. U.S. Bureau of Justice Statistics release "Violent Crime by Stranger and Non-Strangers" (January 1987). Note that this is a different sample (covering the period 1982–84) and that the figure for armed victimizations applies to all victims, not just women.

41. Kleck and Bordua, "The Factual Foundation for Certain Key Assumptions of Gun Control," *Law & Policy Quarterly* 5(1983):271, 290.

42. Silver and Kates above, pp. 159–61.

43. P. Quigley, *Armed and Female* (New York: Dutton, 1988); M. Ayoob, *In the Gravest Extreme* (New York: Dutton), p. 38. Cf. J. Carmichael, *The Women's Guide to Handguns* (New York: Bobbs-Merrill, 1982), pp. 3–4: ". . . when it comes to shooting, women are not the weaker sex," noting that the leading woman's score equalled the leading man's in recent Olympic handgun competition and that in college shooting where "no distinction is made between men and women," women are coming more and more to dominate . . . because women have certain physical and mental characteristics that give them an edge over men"—viz. patience, "excellent hand-eye coordination," and the concentration to perform delicate motor functions time after time.

44. Hicks, "Point Gun, Pull Trigger," *Police Chief*, May 1975. See also Quigley, Carmichael, and Ayoob above.

45. See for example Riley, "Shooting to Kill the Handgun," pp. 491, 497–99; Fields, "Handgun Prohibition," *St. Louis University Law Journal* 23(1979):35, 39–42; Teret and Wintemute, "Handgun Injuries: The Epidemiologic Evidence for Assessing Legal Responsibility," pp. 341, 349–50.

46. See generally the U.S. Bureau of Criminal Justice releases "The Crime of Rape'" (March 1985), "Robbery Victims" (April 1987), and "Household Burglary" (January 1985).

47. Handgun Control Staff pamphlet, p. 35; and Alviani and Drake above, p. 6 (paraphrasing almost identically Newton and Zimring, p. 68):

> The handgun is rarely an effective instrument for protecting the home against either the *burglar* or the *robber* because the former avoids confrontation [by only striking unoccupied premises] and the latter confronts too swiftly [for the victim to get his gun].

Compare Zimring and Hawkins (1987), p. 31.

48. Newton and Zimring, p. 68.

49. Cf. Kates and Engberg, "Deadly Force Self-Defense Against Rape," pp. 873, 877–78ff.

50. Ibid., pp. 879 and 890–94. See also Saunders, pp. 47, 49: "men who batter [their mates] average 45 pounds heavier and 4 to 5 inches taller than" the victim.

51. Drinan, "Gun Control: The Good Outweighs the Evil."

52. Newton and Zimring, p. 64.

53. Zimring and Hawkins (1987), chap. 4.

54. Shields, *Guns Don't Die, People Do*, pp. 124–25. To the same effect see Riley, "Shooting to Kill the Handgun," pp. 497–98; Zimring and Hawkins (1987); Newton and Zimring; and the Handgun Control Staff pamphlet above.

55. As discussed *infra*, the primary problem with the Handgun Control Staff pamphlet is that the evidence, upon which it posits the rate of injury to gun-armed resisters, is fundamentally flawed because it applies to resistance with all kinds of weapons and does not break out gun-armed resistance.

56. Handgun Control Staff pamphlet, p. 33. The pamphlet cites no statistics to show that rapists are less likely than robbers or burglars to injure or kill victims who resist, nor could they be since rapist, robber, and burglar are often one and the same. See for example, Bureau of Justice Statistics releases *Household Burglary* (January 1985) and *Robbery Victims* (1987).

57. Handgun Control Staff pamphlet, p. 18; also at p. 2 (also in italics).

58. Handgun Control Staff pamphlet, p. 17. See also pp. 16 and 18, respectively, for the admonitions (again in original italics) that *"victims who take self-protective measures are more likely to be injured than victims not using such measures"* and that *"a victim is three times more likely to be injured when taking a self-protection measure than when not."* See also p. 11 ("the likelihood of being seriously injured during a robbery is directly related to taking a measure of self-protection" rather than submitting); p. 14 ("running away or reasoning with the offender . . . [is] less likely to result in injury to the victim"); p. 19 ("those taking a self-protective measure accounted for 58 percent of the emergency room treatments and their injuries were twice as serious, judged by the mean days of hospitalization"); and again on p. 19 (of victims hospitalized after rape, mugging, or assault, compared to nonresisters, "the seriousness of injury was five times as great for those using a weapon for self-protection"); and p. 30 (injuries in aggravated assault are "more likely to be serious if the victim physically resists the offender").

59. A point that the pamphlet never makes—but that emerges quite forcefully from neutral evaluations of the evidence—is that submission does not ensure that the victim will escape injury or death. Felons may injure victims at the outset to ensure compliance with the demands and to foreclose resistance, or felons may execute victims gratuitously. See for example, Cook, "The Relationshp Between Victim Resistance and Injury in Noncommercial Robbery," *Journal of Legal Studies* 15(1986):405, 406.

60. To avoid confusion, we should note that (a) Handgun Control Inc., currently the most important organization in the anti-gun lobby, has no direct link to the Handgun Control Staff, a nonlobbying "research" organization that fell into desuetude in the 1970s, and that (b) Professors Zimring and Hawkins are academic gun control advocates with no direct link to either organization. The "give them what they want" language is from Shields, *Guns Don't Die, People Do*, pp. 124–25, which relies heavily on the Handgun Control Staff's research. Zimring, Hawkins, and Newton take the same position; see also Riley, "Shooting to Kill the Handgun," pp. 491, 497–98.

61. Zimring and Hawkins (1987) above, p. 15. Curiously, they make this point in discussing how guns aid weaker people to victimize stronger ones—a crime pattern that is comparatively rare, to say the very least. The point is unaccountably missing from their later chapter on "Guns for Self Defense" to which it is far more relevant.

62. *Social Problems*, pp. 7–9. The National Crime Surveys are conducted under auspices of the National Institute of Justice (NIJ). Census Bureau interviewers contact a nationally representative sample of about 60,000 households every 6 months and record information from personal interviews concerning the crime victimization experience of all household members aged 12 or older. Cook, "The Relationship between Victim Resistance and Victim Resistance and Injury in Noncommercial Robbery," pp. 405, 406.

63. The preeminent submission exponents include Zimring and Zuehl, "Victim Injury and Death in Urban Robbery: A Chicago Study," *Journal of Legal Studies* 15(1986):1; Skogan and Block, "Resistance and Injury in Nonfatal Assaultive Violence," *Victimology* 81(1983):215; and Wolfgang, "Victim Intimidation, Resistance, and Injury: A Study of Robbery" (paper presented at the Fourth International Symposium on Victimology, Tokyo, 1982). Prof. Wolfgang's ethically based support for banning guns is detailed in Benenson, "A Controlled Look at Gun Controls," *N.Y. Law Forum* 14(1968):718, 723. As to Prof. Zimring's pragmatically based anti-gun views (which Prof. Block shares), see generally Newton, Zimring, and Zuehl, pp. 37–38.

64. Their views have been strongly criticized by a female criminologist (who is, nevertheless, *not pro-gun*) on the ground that for victims to submit encourages crime. Ziegenhagen and Brosnan, "Victim Responses to Robbery and Crime Control Policy," *Criminology* 23(1985):675, 677–78.

65. "Gun Control," *The Public Interest* 84:45–46.

66. A recent U.S. Department of Justice study concludes that, over their lifetimes, 83 percent of American children now aged 12 will be victims of some kind of violent felony, 52 percent will suffer two or more such offenses, and 87 percent will have property stolen on three or more occasions. In all these crime categories, blacks will be much more frequently victimized than whites. *New York Times*, March 9, 1987, n. above 13. Cf. Sherman, "Free Police from the Shackles of 911," *Wall Street Journal*, March 20, 1987. Minneapolis police records show that in 1986 "23 percent of all the robberies, 15 percent of all the rapes, and 19 percent of all the assaults and disturbances" occurred repeatedly at only .3 percent of the city's commercial and residential addresses; "a mere 5 percent of all the addresses . . . produced 64 percent of all the calls for police service." Needless to say, it is unlikely that any of those who have to live or work at those repeatedly victimized addresses are white male academics.

67. See for example, " 'There's This Place in the Queens It's Not Such a Good Idea to Rob'," *Wall Street Journal*, October 20, 1971 (Puerto Rican shopkeeper reported to have shot more violent criminals in a year than had any New York City police officer in an entire career).

68. Kates and Engberg, "Deadly Force Self-Defense Against Rape," pp. 873, 879–90, n. 20, and 898ff..

69. Quoted in Silver and Kates above, p. 139.

19

The Law-Abiding Gun Owner as Domestic and Acquaintance Murderer

Don B. Kates, Jr.

Conceding that banning handguns would not disarm terrorists, or assassins, the anti-gun argument portrays those people as exceptions to the generality, which is *"previously law-abiding citizens* committing impulsive gun murders while engaged in arguments with family members or acquaintances."[1] The anti-gun crusaders claim most murders result from gun ownership among ordinary citizens: "That gun in the closet to protect against burglars will most likely be used to shoot a spouse in a moment of rage. . . . *The problem is you and me—law-abiding folks.*"[2]

If this portrayal of murderers were true, a gun ban might drastically reduce murder because the primary perpetrators (law-abiding citizens) might give up guns even though hardened criminals, terrorists, and assassins would not. Unfortunately for this appealingly simple nostrum, every national and local study of homicide reveals that murderers are not ordinary citizens—nor are they people who are likely to comply with gun laws. Murderers (and fatal

From "Guns, Murders, and the Constitution: A Realistic Assessment of Gun Control" (February 1990): 45–49. Copyright © 1990 by the Pacific Research Institute for Public Policy. Reprinted by permission of the publisher.

gun accident perpetrators) are atypical, highly aberrant individuals whose spectacular indifference to human life, including their own, is evidenced by life histories of substance abuse, automobile accident, felony, and attacks on relatives and acquaintances.[3]

PRIOR FELONY RECORD OF MURDERERS

The FBI's annual crime reports do not regularly compile data on the prior criminal records of murderers, and no such data are otherwise available on a national basis. But in a special data run for the Eisenhower Commission, the FBI found that 74.7 percent of murder arrestees nationally over a four-year period had prior arrests for violent felony or burglary.[4] In another one-year period 77.9 percent of murder arrestees had priors.[5] Over yet another five-year period nationally, arrested murderers had *adult* criminal records showing an average prior criminal career of at least six years duration, including four major felony arrests; 57.1 percent of these murder arrestees had been convicted of at least one prior adult felony; and 64 percent of a national sample of convicted murderers who had been released were rearrested within four years.[6]

These data have been confirmed by numerous local studies over the past forty years.[7] For instance, a profile showed that a typical murderer in Washington, D.C., had six prior arrests, including two for felonies, one for a violent felony.[8] Note that these data do not begin to reflect the full extent of murderers' prior criminal careers—and thus cannot illustrate how different murderers are from the ordinary law-abiding person. Much serious crime goes unreported. Of those crimes that are reported, a large number are never cleared by arrest; of those so cleared, many are juvenile arrests that are not included in the data recounted above. At the same time we know that most juvenile, unsolved, or unreported serious crimes are concentrated in the relatively small number of people who have been arrested for other crimes.[9]

PRIOR VIOLENCE HISTORY OF WIFE MURDERERS

Intrafamily murderers are especially likely to have engaged in far more previous violent crimes than show up in their arrest records. But because these attacks were on spouses or other family members, they will rarely have resulted in an arrest.[10] So domestic murderers' official records tend not to show their full prior violence, but only their adult arrests for attacking people outside their families. Therefore, only about "70 to 75 percent of domestic homicide offenders have been previously arrested and about half previously convicted."[11] As to how many crimes they perpetrate *within the family,* even in a relatively short time, "review of police records in Detroit and Kansas City" shows that in

> 90 percent of the cases of domestic homicide, police had responded at least once to a disturbance call at the home during the two-year period prior to the fatal incident, and in over half (54 percent) of the cases, they had been called five or more times.[12]

A leading authority on domestic homicide notes: "The day-to-day reality is that most family murders are preceded by a long history of assaults . . . . " Studies (including those just cited) "indicate that intrafamily homicide is typically just one episode in a long-standing syndrome of violence."[13] Nor is "acquaintance homicide" accurately conceptualized as a phenomenon of previously law-abiding people killing each other in neighborhood arguments. The term "acquaintance homicide" covers, and far more typically is exemplified by, examples such as a drug addict killing his dealer in the course of robbing him; a loan shark or bookie killing a nonpaying customer; or gang members, drug dealers, and members of organized crime "families" killing each other.[14]

NON SEQUITUR AND FABRICATION IN LABELING MURDERERS AS ORDINARY CITIZENS

In contrast to these evaluations, neither of the data sets, which are cited as supporting claims that murderers "are good citizens who kill each other," is persuasive. The National Coalition to Ban Handguns' assertion that "most murders are committed by a relative or close acquaintance of the victim"[15] is conceptually unpersuasive because it is a *non sequitur:* it simply does not follow that because a murderer knows or is related to his victims, he must be an ordinary citizen rather than a long-time criminal. The conclusion would make sense only if ordinary citizens differed from criminals by neither knowing anyone nor being related to anyone.

The other data set that supposedly shows murderers as ordinary citizens is Lindsay's assertion that "most murderers (73 percent in 1972) are committed by previously law-abiding citizens committing impulsive gun murders while engaged in arguments with family members or acquaintances."[16] While there is nothing *conceptually* wrong with this statement, it is *empirically* unpersuasive because it is simply a fabrication. Lindsay claims his figures are from the FBI 1972 *Uniform Crime Report.* But that report offers no such statistic; rather it and other FBI data diametrically contradict the statement. Far from showing that 73 percent of murderers nationally were "previously law-abiding citizens," the report shows that 74.7 percent of persons arrested for murder had prior arrests for a violent felony or burglary.[17]

As the abstract to the National Institute of Justice Evaluation concludes:

> It is commonly hypothesized that much criminal violence, especially homicide, occurs simply because the means of lethal violence (firearms) are readily at hand and, thus, that much homicide would not occur were firearms generally less available. *There is no persuasive evidence that supports this view.*[18]

I emphasize that this statement does NOT refute the case for gun control, including rationally tailored gun bans. The fact that murderers are "real criminals" with life histories of violence, felony, substance abuse, and auto accident highlights the danger in such people having handguns—or guns of any kind![19] But it is very misleading when homicide statistics that are idiosyncratic to gun misusers are presented as arguing for banning guns from the whole populace. Idiosyncratic statistics provide no basis for the claim that precautionary gun ownership by average citizens seriously endangers their friends or relatives.

NOTES

1. Lindsay, "The Case for Federal Firearms Control" (1973), p. 22 (emphasis added). Citing Lindsay, the National Coalition to Ban Handguns pamphlet, "A Shooting Gallery Called America," asserts that "each year" thousands of "gun murders [are] done by law-abiding citizens who might have *stayed* law-abiding if they had not possessed firearms" (emphasis in original); and "that most murders are committed by previously law-abiding citizens where the killer and the victim are related or acquainted." See also Edwards, "Murder and Gun Control," *Wayne State University Law Review* 18(1972):1335.

2. Kairys, "A Carnage in the Name of Freedom," *Philadelphia Inquirer,* September 12, 1988 (emphasis added). Mr. Kairys is a lawyer and part-time teacher of sociology.

3. See discussion below and Lane, "On the Social Meaning of Homicide Trends in America," In T. Gurr, *Violence in America,* (Violence, Cooperation, Peace Ser., 1989), 1:59 (". . . the psychological profile of the accident-prone suggests the same kind of aggressiveness shown by most murderers").

4. Set out in tabular form in D. Mulvihill et al., *Crimes of Violence: Report of the Task Force on Individual Acts of Violence* (Washington, D.C.: Govt. Print. Off., 1969), p. 532.

5. FBI, *Uniform Crime Report, 1971,* p. 38.

6. FBI, *Uniform Crime Report, 1975,* pp. 42ff.

7. In addition to the studies reviewed in Kleck and Bordua, "The Factual Foundation for Certain Key Assumptions of Gun Control," *Law & Policy Quarterly* 5(1983):271, 292ff; and Kleck, "Capital Punishment, Gun Ownership, and Homicide," *American Journal of Sociology* 84(1979):882, 893. See for example, R. Narloch, *Criminal Homicide in California* (Cal. Bur. of Crim. Stats., 1973), pp. 53–54; A. Swersey and E. Enloe, *Homicide in Harlem* (Rand, 1975), p. 17 ("We estimate that the great majority of both perpetrators and victims of assaults and murders had previous arrests, probably over 80 percent or more").

8. Data reported to the Senate Sub-committee to Investigate Juvenile Delinquency, 19th Congress; see *Hearings, Second Session,* pp. 75–76.

9. J. Wright and P. Rossi, *Armed and Dangerous: A Survey of Felons and their Firearms* (New York: Aldine, 1986), chap. 3; J. and M. Chaiken, *Varieties of Criminal Behavior* (1982); M. Wolfgang et al., *Delinquency in a Birth Cohort* (1972).

10. Police have traditionally been loath to arrest in such situations; moreover, in upwards of 50 percent of relatively serious cases, the police have no opportunity to make an arrest because the victim fails to report the matter (out of belief that the matter is a private affair, or that the police will not take action, or out of fear of retaliation). See the U.S. Bureau of Justice Statistics releases, "Family Violence" (April 1984); "Preventing Domestic Violence Against Women" (August 1986); and "Violent Crime by Strangers and Non-Strangers" (January 1987), all based on survey responses rather than reports to police.

11. "Policy Lessons," *Law and Contemporary Problems* 49:40–41, emphasis added.

12. Browne and Williams, "Resource Availability for Women at Risk: Its Relationship to Rates of

Female-Perpetrated Partner Homicide," a paper presented at the 1987 annual meeting of the American Society of Criminology (available from the authors at the Family Research Laboratory, U. of New Hampshire).

13. Straus, "Domestic Violence and Homicide Antecedents," *Bulletin of the N.Y. Academy of Medicine* 62(1986):446, 454, 457; and Straus, "Medical Care Costs of Intrafamily Assault and Homicide," *Bulletin of the N.Y. Academy of Medicine* 62(1986):556, 557 fn. For a detailed review of relevant studies, see Browne and Flewelling, "Women as Victims or Perpetrators of Homicide," a paper presented at the 1986 annual meeting of the American Society of Criminology (available from the authors at the Family Research Laboratory, U. of New Hampshire).

14. Current Research in T. Gurr, *Violence in America,* 1:203.

15. Both this and the preceding quote are from the National Coalition to Ban Handguns, undated, unpaginated pamphlet, "A Shooting Gallery Called America."

16. Lindsay, *The Case for Federal Firearms Control* (1973), p. 22.

17. Cf. the FBI 4-year national homicide data set out in Mulvihill et al. above, p. 532. Lindsay's reference gives no specific page citation for the 1972 *Uniform Crime Report*. His 73 percent figure is directly contradicted by the special "Careers in Crime" data appearing at pp. 35–38 of that *Report* and the other FBI data discussed above. Please note, incidentally, that neither the 1972 *Report* nor any other FBI publication gives figures for the percentage of family and/or acquaintance murders that are committed with guns. The 1972 *Report* does contain a figure for the overall number of murders in which a gun was used, but it is 65 percent, not Mayor Lindsay's 73 percent.

18. Emphasis added. The language quoted is from the abstract to J. Wright, P. Rossi, and K. Daly, *Weapons, Crime and Violence in America: Executive Summary* (Washington, D.C.: Gov. Print. Off., 1981), published as a separate document accompanying the main NIJ Evaluation. It does not appear in *haec verba* in the revised commercially published version *(Under the Gun),* but see pp. 192–94 and 321–22 thereof.

19. See for example, "Policy Lessons," pp. 40–41, 59–60 (gun policy should focus on such high-risk owners, outlawing their possession of all guns, not just handguns).

20

Crime Control Through the Private Use of Armed Force

Gary Kleck

In his 1972 Presidential Address to the American Sociological Association, William Goode argued that because sociologists share a humanistic tradition that denies the importance of physical coercion, they have failed to accurately assess the degree to which social systems rest on force. While affirming his personal dislike for the use of force, Goode urged social analysts to put aside their "kindly bias" against the effectiveness of threats and punishment and recognize the degree to which force is a crucial element in the social structure, in democracies as well as tyrannies, in peacetime as well as in war. He stated that "in any civil society . . . everyone is subject to force. All are engaged in it daily, not alone as victims but as perpetrators as well . . . . We are all potentially dangerous to one another" (Goode, 1972:510). This study addresses the social control effects of private citizens' uses of guns in response to predatory criminal behavior, particularly violent crime and residential burglary.

The prevalence and defensive use of guns in America are important topics for many research questions, yet they have been almost entirely ignored. For example, the "routine activities" approach to crime sees criminal incidents as the result of the convergence of "likely offenders and suitable targets in the absence of capable guardians" (Cohen and Felson, 1979:590). While this view has broadened criminologists' interests beyond the supply of "likely offenders," it ignores the extent to which being armed with a deadly weapon would seem to be an important element of capable guardianship. Given that about half of U.S. households and a quarter of retail businesses keep firearms (Crocker, 1982; U.S. Small Business Administration, 1969), gun ownership must surely be considered a very routine aspect of American life and of obvious relevance to the activities of criminals.

Victimology is concerned with, among other things, the response of victims to their victimization. Yet, despite evidence that people buy guns to defend against becoming victims of crimes (Kleck, 1984), victimology scholars have largely ignored victim gun ownership and use. Similarly, the recent wave of interest in private crime control has been largely limited to either the "privatization" of police and corrections services and the use of commercial security services by businesses and other large institutions (e.g., Cunningham and Taylor, 1985) or to nonforceful private crime control efforts like neighborhood watch activities (Greenberg et al., 1984). Finally, nearly all of the considerable literature on deterrence of criminal behavior focuses on the effect of public criminal justice agencies. Conventional definitions of deterrence are often limited to the crime preventive effects of legal punishment, arrest, and prosecution (e.g., Gibbs, 1975). This precludes considering private ownership and use of firearms as a deterrent to crime. That victim gun use may be one of the most serious risks a criminal faces is only beginning to be recognized (Wright and Rossi, 1986).

Without denying the possible criminogenic effects of gun ownership, I want to establish as plausible and worthy of research the hypothesis that when citizens own and use guns to defend themselves, the amount of violent crime is reduced to a degree that could rival the effect of the criminal justice system. Toward that end I consider three kinds of evidence: the frequency and nature of private citizens' defensive uses of firearms against criminals, the effectiveness and risks of such actions, and the potential deterrent impact on crime of defensive gun ownership and use. Finally, I discuss the implications of this evidence for crime control policy (see also, Kleck, 1987).

THE FREQUENCY AND TYPES OF DEFENSIVE GUN USE

Overall Use, Including Display and Firing

At least six national and state-wide surveys have asked probability samples of the adult population about defensive gun use. The most informative of the surveys is the 1981 Hart poll of 1,228 registered voters. It is the only survey to cover a national population, ask about defensive uses in a specific, limited time period, ask the question of all respondents, distinguish civilian use from police and military uses, and distinguish uses against humans from uses against animals. Note, however, that the five other national and state surveys, while not as satisfactory as the Hart poll, yield results that are compatible with the results of that survey. These results as reported here have never been published; they were obtained privately from Peter D. Hart Research Associates, Inc. (Garin, 1986).[1] In this survey, 6 percent of the adults interviewed replied yes to the question: "Within the past five years, have you yourself or another member of your household used a handgun, even if it was not fired, for self-protection or for the protection of property at home, work, or elsewhere, excluding military service or police work?" Those who replied yes were then asked "Was this to protect against an animal or a person?" Of the total sample, 2 percent replied "animal," 3 percent "person," and 1 percent "both." Therefore, 4 percent of the sample reported gun use against a person by someone in their household.

Like crime victimization prevalence figures, the defensive gun use percentages are small. They represent, however, large numbers of actual uses. In 1980 there were 80,622,000 U.S. households (U.S. Bureau of the Census, 1982). Extrapolating from the 4 percent Hart figure yields an estimate of 3,224,880 households with at least one person who used a handgun defensively during the period 1976-1981. Conservatively assuming only one use per household and dividing by five (the number of years covered), I estimate there were about 645,000 defensive uses of handguns against persons per year, excluding police or military uses.[2]

The Hart sample was of registered voters, who are older and wealthier than the general public. This implies a population less frequently victimized by crime, especially by violent crime, and thus less likely to have used a gun defensively. Since gun ownership increases with income (Wright et al., 1983:107–8), however, there should be more gun owners in a sample of registered voters. It is unclear what the net effects of these sample biases might be on the estimate of defensive uses.

The Hart survey asked only about handgun use, ignoring defensive uses of the far more numerous long guns (rifles and shotguns). And the DMI (Decision-Making-Incorporated) surveys, which did ask about all gun types, did not ask about a specific time period. The best all-guns estimate is based on an extrapolation of the Hart survey handgun results. According to the December, 1978 DMIb survey, 45 percent of respondents in handgun-owning households reported handguns were owned primarily for "self-defense and protection at home," while the corresponding figure for all gun types combined was 21 percent. It was estimated that at the end of 1978, the total private stock of handguns in the United States was about 47 million and the stock of all guns was about 156 million (Kleck, 1984:112). Combining these figures, there were about 21 million handguns and 33 million guns of all types, including handguns, owned primarily for protection or defense in December, 1978. If among guns owned primarily for defense, we assume both types of guns are equally likely to be so used, we can multiply the handguns defensive uses figure of 645,000 by the ratio 33:21 to very roughly estimate that guns of all types are used for defensive purposes about one million times a year.

The magnitude of these figures can be judged by comparison with an estimate of the total number of crimes in which guns were somehow used in 1980, based on the Uniform Crime Reports (UCR) count of homicides and National Crime Survey (NCS) victimization survey estimates of assaults, robberies, and rapes. Including minor assaults in which the gun was not fired and including both crimes reported to the police and unreported crimes, the total for handguns was about 580,000, while the corresponding figure for all gun types was about 810,000 (Kleck, 1986b:307). Thus the best available evidence suggests that handguns may be used about as often for defensive purposes as for criminal purposes, and guns of all types are used substantially more often defensively than criminally.

EFFECTIVENESS AND RISKS OF
ARMED RESISTANCE TO CRIMINALS

It has been argued that resistance by crime victims, especially forceful resistance, is generally useless and even dangerous to the victim (Block, 1977; Yeager et al., 1976). Evidence is moderately consistent with this position as it applies to some forms of resistance. However, the evidence does not support the claim as it pertains to resistance with a gun.

Preventing Completion of the Crime

The figures in Table 1 are from analysis of the 1979–1985 incident-level files of the National Crime Survey (NCS) public use computer tapes (ICPSR, 1987b). They contain information on over 180,000 sample crime incidents reported by nationally representative samples of noninstitutionalized persons aged 12 and over. The surveys asked respondents if they had been victims of crimes. Those who reported crimes involving personal contact with the offender were asked if they used any form of self-protection, if they were attacked, if they suffered injury, and if the crimes were completed. For assaults, "completion" means injury was inflicted; thus completion data convey nothing beyond what injury data convey. For robberies, "completion" refers to whether the robber took property from the victim. The figures show that victims who resisted robbers with guns or with weapons other than guns or knives were less likely to lose their property than victims who used any other means of resistance or who did nothing.

TABLE 1

ATTACK, INJURY, AND CRIME COMPLETION RATES IN ROBBERY AND ASSAULT INCIDENTS, BY SELF-PROTECTION METHOD, U.S., 1979–1985[a]

METHOD OF SELF-PROTECTION	ROBBERY				ASSAULT		
	(1) PERCENT COMPLETED	(2) PERCENT ATTACKED	(3) PERCENT INJURED	(4)[a] PERCENT TIMES USED	(5) PERCENT ATTACKED	(6) PERCENT INJURED	(7)[b] PERCENT TIMES USED
Used gun	30.9%	25.2%	17.4%	89,009	23.2%	12.1%	386,083
Used knife	35.2	55.6	40.3	59,813	46.4	29.5	123,062
Used other weapon	28.9	41.5	22.0	104,700	41.4	25.1	454,570
Used physical force	50.1	75.6	50.8	1,653,880	82.8	52.1	6,618,823
Tried to get help or frighten offender	63.9	73.5	48.9	1,561,141	55.2	40.1	4,383,117
Threatened or reasoned with offender	53.7	48.1	30.7	955,398	40.0	24.7	5,743,008
Nonviolent resistance, including evasion	50.8	54.7	34.9	1,539,895	40.0	25.5	8,935,738
Other measures	48.5	47.3	26.5	284,423	36.1	20.7	1,451,103
Any self-protection	52.1	60.8	38.2	4,603,671	49.5	30.7	21,801,957
No self-protection	88.5	41.5	24.7	2,686,960	39.9	27.3	6,154,763
Total	65.4	53.7	33.2	7,290,631	47.3	29.9	27,956,719

SOURCES: Analysis of incident files of 1979–1985 National Crime Survey public use computer tapes (ICPSR, 1987b).
NOTES: a. See U.S. Bureau of Justice Statistics (1982) for exact question wordings, definitions, and other details of the surveys. b. Separate frequencies in columns (4) and (7) do add to totals in "Any self-protection" row since a single crime incident can involve more than one self-protection method.

Avoiding Injury

For both robbery and assault, victims who used guns for protection were less likely either to be attacked or injured than victims who responded any other way, including those who did not resist at all. Only 12 percent of gun resisters in assault and 17 percent in robberies suffered any kind of injury.

After gun resistance, the course of action least likely to be associated with injury is doing nothing at all, i.e., not resisting. However, passivity is not a completely safe course either since 25 percent of robbery victims and 27 percent of assault victims who did not resist were injured anyway.

Finally, using guns for protection in robberies and assaults is considerably less common than milder, less forceful methods not requiring weapons. This presumably is at least partly due to the fact that so many crimes occur in circumstances where victims do not have effective access to their guns.

Some analysts of robbery data have assumed that where crimes involve victims who resisted and were also injured, resistance somehow caused the injury by provoking the offender into an attack (e.g., Yeager et al., 1976). Although the NCS does not yet routinely ask questions about the sequence of attack and self-protection acts by the victim, such questions were included in a special Victim Risk Supplement questionnaire administered to 14,258 households as part of the regular NCS in February of 1984. In only 9.8 percent of assaults involving both forceful self-protection actions and attack did the actions occur before the attack. For assaults involving nonforceful self-protective actions, only 5.7 percent of the actions preceded the attack. For cases involving both robbery and attack, forceful self-protective actions never preceded attack, while in only 22 percent of similar incidents involving nonforceful self-protective actions did the actions precede the attack. Thus, even among the minority of cases where forceful self-protective acts were accompanied by attacks on the victim, few incidents support the contention that the victim's defensive action provoked the attack.

CRIME CONTROL EFFECTS OF CIVILIAN GUN OWNERSHIP AND USE

When victims use guns to resist crimes, the crimes usually are disrupted and the victims are not injured. This does not necessarily imply that such resistance has any general deterrent effect on crimes. Whether criminals are deterred by the prospect of armed resistance is an issue separate from how effective defensive gun use is for victims who resist. In this section, I consider the kinds of crimes most likely to involve victim defensive gun use and the kinds of crimes most likely to be deterred by such use. I also consider evidence on the deterrent effect of civilian gun ownership and on the effects of possible confrontation by a gun-wielding citizen on burglars and burglaries in occupied homes.

Crimes Involving Defensive Gun Use

What crimes are defensive gun users defending against? Evidence from NCP surveys suggests that about 64,000 rapes, robberies, and assaults involved a victim using a gun for self-protection in 1983 (U.S. Bureau of Justice Statistics, 1985c:12,69,70). However, this figure is unreliable since it is well established that victim surveys seriously underestimate violent crime among nonstrangers (Gove et al., 1985:464–65). Because such crimes are especially likely to occur in the home, where guns are available to their owners, the victim surveys must also underestimate victim defensive uses of guns. Further, commercial robberies are no longer covered in these surveys, and the doubts victims may have about the legality of their gun uses may further contribute to an under-reporting of defensive uses. Finally, since crimes involving victim gun use usually involve neither property loss nor victim injury, victims are especially likely to forget or otherwise fail to report them to interviewers, just as they fail to report them to police.

There are no published data on the number of defensive gun uses in burglary. The best that can be done is to estimate the number of opportunities for victim gun use. NCS data indicate that about 12.7 percent of residental burglaries occur while a household member is present (U.S. Bureau of Justice Statistics, 1985a:4) and that there were an estimated 6,817,000 household burglaries in 1980 (U.S. Bureau of Justice Statistics, 1982:22). Averaging the results of two national surveys in 1980, I estimate that about 46 percent of U.S. households have at least one gun (Crocker 1982:255). If it is assumed that gun ownership is at least as high in burglarized homes as in homes in general, about 400,000 residential burglaries occurred in gun-owning house-holds while a household member was present. . . .

If all of the opportunities for victims to use guns during burglaries were actually taken, they would constitute about 40 percent of the estimated one million annual defensive gun uses. However, two very different sources of information suggest that burglary-related uses are less numerous than that and that assaults at home are the most common crimes involving victim gun use. Table 2 displays the results of the 1976 Field poll of California (Field Institute, 1976) and data from medical examiner records concerning civilian justifiable homicides committed in Dade County in 1980 (compiled from Wilbanks, 1984:190–374). The Field poll addresses only handgun use and indicates locations of gun uses, while the medical data cover all gun types but do not usually indicate the location of homicides. Nevertheless, the results are consistent concerning the crimes with which defensive gun uses are associated.

The California survey data indicate that 62 percent of uses are connected to assault or rape. The medical examiner data indicate a figure of 65 percent for these offenses, while also showing that nearly all of these uses are connected to assault rather than rape. "Theft at home" in the California survey

TABLE 2
CRIMES ASSOCIATED WITH DEFENSIVE USES
OF GUNS, FREQUENCY AND PERCENT

1976 SURVEY OF CALIFORNIA ADULTS[a]			1980 DADE COUNTY (MIAMI)[b]		
CRIME	FREQUENCY	PERCENT	CRIME	FREQUENCY	PERCENT
Assault or rape at home	40	41	Assault	46	64
Assault Elsewhere	20	21	Rape	1	1
Theft at home	19	20	Burglary	6	8
Theft elsewhere	11	11	Robbery	19	26
All other reasons for use	7	7			
Total	97	100%	Total	72	100%

SOURCES: California survey, Field Institute (1976); Dade County justifiable homicides compiled from a short narrative description in Wilbanks (1984:190–374).

NOTES: a. Handgun use only b. Civilian justifiable homicides

includes burglary, and the justifiable homicide data suggest that burglary accounts for most of the cases in this category. "Theft elsewhere" in the California survey includes retail store robberies, and the robbery category among justifiable homicides may consist largely of uses linked to such crimes. This interpretation is supported by information on the locations of civilian justifiable homicides in California in 1982, 86 percent of which involved guns. Police records showed that 32 percent occurred in the killer's residence, 23 percent in a business location (especially in robbery-prone businesses like liquor stores and bars), 14 percent on the street or sidewalk and 30 percent elsewhere (California 1983:67). This set of California homicides excludes pure self-defense homicides (i.e., killings not involving any other felonies besides an assault on the defender) and thus is not strictly comparable with the Dade County defensive homicides, most of which are pure self-defense killings. This at least partially accounts for the smaller share of California homicides occurring in the home, since it means that cases like those involving women defending themselves against abusive husbands or boyfriends would ordinarily be excluded. Therefore the California data do not undercut the conclusion that most defensive gun uses occur in the home and involve defense against assaults. Home defenses against burglars and retail store defenses against robbers each account for substantial minorities of the uses.

Gun Deterrable Crimes

If there is a deterrent effect of defensive gun use, it would depend on a criminal being able to realistically anticipate a potential victim using a gun to disrupt the crime. The types of crimes most likely to be influenced by this possibility are crimes occurring in homes—where victims might have access to a gun—and in the kinds of business establishments where proprietors keep guns, i.e., crimes such as residential burglary, assault in the home and retail store robbery. About one in eight residential burglaries occurs while a household member is present (U.S. Bureau of Justice Statistics, 1985a:4), and, by definition, all robberies, rapes, assaults, and homicides involve direct contact between a victim and an offender. In many of these incidents the offender has the initiative, often taking the victim by surprise. Further, the situations often develop too quickly for victims to get to their guns. The most common single location for violent crimes, especially homicides and assaults between intimates, is in or near the home of the victim or the home of both victim and offender (U.S. Bureau of Justice Statistics, 1980:22; Curtis, 1974:176).

Strategic attributes of some crime types make them better than average candidates for disruption by armed victims. For example, violent acts between intimates are typically part of a persistent, ongoing pattern of violence (Wilt et al., 1977). While prospective victims of such violence may not ordinarily be able to predict the exact time of the next violent episode, they often are able to recognize the usual precursors of repetitive violence. Wives and girlfriends of violent men, for example, may understand well the significance of their husband/boyfriend getting drunk and verbally abusive. This implies a distinct tactical difference between violence among intimates and other crimes. Victims of intimate violence can take advantage of behavioral cues which serve as advance warning signs and ready themselves accordingly. In the most threatening situations, advance preparations could include securing a weapon.

Deterrence Effects

Demonstrating deterrent effects of criminal justice system punishment has proven difficult (e.g., Blumstein et al., 1978) and the same must certainly be true for the private use of force, which is even less well measured than the risk-generating activities of the criminal justice system. Therefore, the following evidence should be regarded only as suggestive. Nevertheless, while more limited in quantity, this evidence is quite diverse, consistent and in some ways as compelling as evidence cited in favor of the deterrence thesis for criminal justice system activity.

Results from deterrence research have been highly mixed and often negative. Why should we expect deterrence from the armed citizenry when the criminal justice system appears to have so little impact? The deterrence doctrine states that punishment deters as its certainty, severity, and celerity (promptness) increase (Gibbs, 1975). One obvious difference between the risk from criminal justice activity and that from civilian gun use for the criminal is that the maximum potential severity of citizen self-help is far greater than legal system responses to crime. The maximum legal penalty a burglar, robber, or even a murderer is likely to face is a few years in prison; only 20 persons were legally executed, all for murders, between mid-1967 and mid-1984 (U.S. Bureau of Justice Statistics, 1984). Since thousands of criminals are killed by gun-wielding private citizens every year, criminals, following a "minimax" strategy (i.e., acting to minimize their chances of experiencing the maximum potential negative consequence of their actions) should be influenced more by the risks of civilian gun use than by risks from the legal system. How many criminals are guided by such a strategy is unknown.

The frequency of defensive gun uses roughly equals the total number of U.S. arrests for violent crime and burglary, which numbered about 988,000 in 1980 (U.S. FBI, 1981:190). Being threatened or shot at by a gun-wielding victim is about as probable as arrest and substantially more probable than conviction or incarceration. This is not surprising since there are only about 600,000 police officers in the United States, fewer than a quarter of whom are on duty at any one time (U.S. Bureau of the Census, 1982:184). There are, on the other hand, tens of millions of civilians with immediate access to firearms, obviously well motivated to deter or disrupt crimes directed at themselves, their families, or their property.

Finally, victims almost always use guns defensively within minutes of the attempted crime. In contrast, when an arrest occurs, it can follow the crime by days or even weeks. At the very quickest, it comes after the minutes it takes a patrol car to respond to a citizen's call. In any case, the average celerity of even arrest is much lower than for citizen gun use, while the celerity of conviction and punishment is lower still.

Evidence from Surveys of Criminals. There is direct, albeit not conclusive, evidence on the deterrent effects of victim gun use from surveys of apprehended criminals. Wright and Rossi (1986) interviewed 1,874 felons in prisons in ten states and asked about their encounters with armed victims and their attitudes towards the risks of such encounters. Among felons who reported ever committing a violent crime or a burglary, 42 percent said they had run into a victim who was armed with a gun, 38 percent reported they had been scared off, shot at, wounded, or captured by an armed victim (these were combined in the original survey question), and 43 percent said they had at some time in their lives decided not to do a crime because they knew or believed the victim was carrying a gun (my tabulations from ICPSR, 1986).

Concerning the felons' attitudes towards armed victims, 56 percent agreed with the statement that "most criminals are more worried about meeting an armed victim than they are about running into the police," 58 percent agreed that "a store owner who is known to keep a gun on the premises is not going to get robbed very often," and 52 percent agreed that "a criminal is not going to mess around with a victim he knows is armed with a gun." Only 27 percent agreed that "committing a crime against an armed victim is an exciting challenge" (my tabulations from ICPSR, 1986). Further, 45 percent of those who had encountered an armed victim reported that they thought regularly or often about the possibility of getting shot by their victims. Even among those without such an encounter the figure was 28 percent (Wright and Rossi, 1986:149). These results agree with earlier findings from less sophisticated surveys of prisoners (Firman, 1975; Link, 1982).

Many objections to prison survey research on deterrence concern flaws the correction of which would tend to strengthen conclusions that there are deterrent effects. For example, Zimring and Hawkins (1973:31–32) discuss the "Warden's Survey fallacy" whereby wardens concluded that the death penalty could not deter murder since all the killers on death row to whom they spoke said the penalty had not deterred them. Clearly, prisoners are biased samples of criminals and prospective criminals since their presence in prison itself indicates that deterrence was not completely effective with them. However, prison survey results supporting a deterrence hypothesis are all the more impressive in light of this bias. Such doubts about the validity of pris- oners' responses to surveys are discussed throughout the Wright and Rossi book (1986, but especially 32–38). Given that being "scared off" by a victim is not the sort of thing a violent criminal is likely to want to admit, inci- dents of this nature may well have been underreported, if misreported at all. Even more significantly, the most deterrable prospective criminals and those deterred from crime altogether will not be included in prison samples. These results therefore, may reflect a minimal baseline picture of the deterrent poten- tial of victim gun use.

Quasi-Experimental Evidence. Increases in actual gun ownership are ordinarily fairly gradual, making interrupted time series analyses of such in- creases impractical. However, highly publicized programs to train citizens in gun use amount to "gun awareness" programs that could conceivably produce sharp changes in prospective criminals' *awareness* of gun ownership among potential victims. The impact of these programs can be assessed because they have specific times of onset and specific spans of operation which make it easier to say when they might be most likely to affect crime.

From October, 1966 to March, 1967 the Orlando Police Department trained more than 2,500 women to use guns (Krug, 1968). Organized in response to demands from citizens worried about a recent sharp increase in rape, this was an unusually large and highly publicized program. It received several front page stories in the local daily newspaper, the *Orlando Sentinel,* a co- sponsor of the program. An interrupted time series analysis of Orlando crime trends showed that the rape rate decreased by 88 percent in 1967, compared to 1966, a decrease far larger than in any previous one-year period. The rape rate remained constant in the rest of Florida and in the United States. Interestingly, the only other crime to show a substantial drop was burglary. Thus, the crime targeted, rape, decreased, and the offense most likely to occur where victims have access to guns, burglary, also decreased (Kleck and Bordua, 1983:282–88).

Green (1987:75) has interpreted the results of the Orlando study as indicating a partial "spillover" or displacement of rape from the city to nearby areas, i.e., a mixture of absolute deterrence of some rapes and a shifting in location of others. Unfortunately, this possibility of displacement can never be eliminated when considering any location-specific crime control effort, be it a local job training program, an increase in police manpower or patrol frequency, or a gun training program.

Green also suggests that the apparent rape decrease might have been due to allegedly irregular crime recording practices of the Orlando city police department, without, however, presenting any evidence of police reporting changes over time beyond the sharp changes in the rape rates themselves. Although largely speculative, Green's comments point to potential problems that could affect interpretation of this sort of quasi-experimental evidence.

A much smaller training program was conducted with only 138 persons from September through November, 1967 by the Kansas City Metropolitan Police in response to retail businessmen's concerns about store robberies (U.S. Small Business Administration, 1969:253–56). . . . While the frequency of robbery increased from 1967 to 1968 by 35 percent in the rest of Missouri, by 20 percent in the West North Central (WNC) region, and by 30 percent in the United States, it essentially levelled off in Kansas City and declined by 13 percent in surrounding areas. Robberies had been increasing in the five years prior to the training program and continued to increase again in 1968. Thus, the upward trend was distinctly interrupted in the year immediately following the gun training program. This cannot be attributed to some general improvement in the social conditions generating robbery rates in the nation, region, or state, given the upward trends in robbery elsewhere. Nor can the effect be attributed to improvements in conditions producing violent crime in general in Kansas City, since robbery was the only violent crime to level off. Something occurred in the Kansas City area in the 1967–1968 period which caused an upward trend in reported robberies to level off, something not generally occurring elsewhere and something not related to other violent crime categories. Interestingly, Kansas City also experienced a levelling off in its sharply upward trend in burglary, suggesting a possible "by-product" deterrent effect much like the one indicated by the Orlando data.

The results of these natural quasi-experiments are not cited for the narrow purpose of demonstrating the short-term deterrent effects of gun training programs. Indeed, there is no evidence as to whether citizens used the training in any significant number of real-life defensive situations and no solid evidence that gun ownership increased in the program areas. These results however, do support the argument that routine gun ownership and defensive use by civilians has an ongoing impact on crime, with or without such pro grams, an impact which is intensified at times when prospective criminals' awareness of potential victims' gun possession is dramatically increased. Gun training programs are just one source of increased awareness; publicity surrounding citizen gun use against criminals would be another, as would general stories in the news media about gun ownership and increases in gun sales. The two examples cited resemble instances of crime drops following gun training programs elsewhere, including decreases in grocery robberies in Detroit after a grocer's organization began gun clinics and decreases in retail store robberies in Highland Park, Michigan, attributed to "gun-toting merchants" (Krug, 1968:H571).

After "subway vigilante" Bernhard Goetz used a handgun to wound four robbers on a New York City subway train on December 22, 1984, subway robberies decreased by 43 percent in the next week, compared to the two weeks prior to the incident, and decreased in the following two months by 19 percent, compared to the same period in the previous year, even though nonrobbery subway crime increased and subway robberies had been increasing prior to the shootings (*Tallahassee Democrat,* 1985; *New York Times,* 1985a, 1985b). However, because New York City transit police also greatly increased manpower on the subway trains immediately after the shootings, any impact uniquely attributable to the Goetz gun use was confounded with potential effects of the manpower increase. (There were no correspondingly large increases in police manpower in Orlando in 1966–1967 or in Kansas City in 1967–1968. See U.S. FBI, 1967–1969).

Finally, the deterrent effect of civilian gun ownership is supported by the experience of Kennesaw, Georgia, a suburb of Atlanta with a 1980 population of 5,095 (U.S. Bureau of the Census, 1983:832). To demonstrate their disapproval of a ban on handgun ownership passed in Morton Grove, Illinois, the Kennesaw City council passed a city ordinance requiring heads of households to keep at least one firearm in their homes. In the seven months following passage of the ordinance (March 15, 1982 to October 31, 1982), there were only five reported residential burglaries, compared to 45 in the same period in the previous year, an 89 percent decrease (Benenson, 1982). This drop was far in excess of the modest 10.4 percent decrease in the burglary rate experienced by Georgia as a whole from 1981 to 1982, the 6.8 percent decrease for South Atlantic states, the 9.6 percent decrease for the United States, and the 7.1 percent decrease for cities under 10,000 population (U.S. FBI, 1983:45–47, 143).

Guns and Displacement of Burglars from Occupied Homes

Residential burglars devote considerable thought, time, and effort to locating homes that are unoccupied. In interviews with burglars in a Pennsylvania prison, Rengert and Wasilchick (1985) found that nearly all the two hours spent on the average suburban burglary was devoted to locating an appropriate target, casing the house, and making sure no one was home. There are at least two reasons why burglars make this considerable investment of time and effort: to avoid arrest and to avoid getting shot. Several burglars in this study reported that they avoided late night burglaries because it was too difficult to tell if anyone was home, explaining, "That's the way to get shot" (Rengert and Wasilchick, 1985:30). Burglars also stated they avoided neighborhoods occupied largely by persons of a different race because "You'll get shot if you're caught there" (Rengert and Wasilchick, 1985:62). Giving weight to these opinions, one of the 31 burglars admitted to having been shot on the job (Rengert and Wasilchick, 1985:98). In the Wright Rossi survey, 73 percent of felons who had committed a burglary or violent crime agreed that "one reason burglars avoid houses when people are at home is that they fear being shot" (unpublished tabulations from ICPSR, 1986).

The nonconfrontational nature of most burglaries at least partly accounts for the infrequency of associated deaths and injuries. Don Kates (1983:269) has argued that because victim gun ownership is partly responsible for the nonconfrontational nature of burglary, it is therefore to be credited with reducing deaths and injuries by its deterrent effects. The benefit is enjoyed by all potential burglary victims, not just those who own guns, since burglars are rarely in a position to know exactly which households have guns and thus must attempt to avoid confrontations in all their burglaries.

Under hypothetical no-guns circumstances, the worst a burglar would ordinarily have to fear is having to break off a burglary attempt if confronted by a householder who managed to call the police. A typical strong, young burglar would have little reason to fear attack or apprehension by unarmed victims, especially if the victim confronted was a woman, a smaller male, or an elderly person. Further, there would be positive advantages to burglary of occupied premises since this would give the burglar a much better chance to get the cash in victims' purses or wallets.

Even under no-guns conditions, many burglars would continue to seek out unoccupied residences simply because contact with a victim would increase their chances of capture by the police. Others may have chosen to do burglaries rather than robberies because they were emotionally unable or unwilling to confront their victims and thus would avoid occupied premises for this reason. However, this certainly does not seem to be true of all burglars. Prison surveys indicate that few criminals specialize in one crime type, and most imprisoned burglars report having also committed robberies. In the Wright and Rossi survey, of those who reported ever committing a burglary, 62 percent also reported committing robberies (my secondary analysis of their dataset, ICPSR, 1986). Thus, most of these burglars are temperamentally capable of confronting victims, even though they clearly prefer to avoid them when committing a burglary.

Results from victimization surveys in at least three nations indicate that in countries with lower rates of gun ownership than the United States, residential burglars are much more likely to enter occupied homes, where confrontation with a victim is possible. In the 1982 British Crime Survey, 59 percent of attempted burglaries and 26 percent of completed burglaries were committed with someone at home (Mayhew, 1987). A 1977 survey in the Netherlands found an occupancy rate of 48 percent for all burglaries, compared to 9 percent in the United States the previous year (Block, 1984:26). And Waller and Okihiro (1978:31) reported that 44 percent of burglarized Toronto residences were occupied during the burglaries, with 21 percent of the burglaries resulting in confrontations between victim and offender. The differences between the United States and Great Britain and Canada cannot be explained by differences in legal threats since the probability of arrest and imprisonment and the severity of sentences served for common crimes are at least as high in the latter nations as in the United States (Wilson, 1976:1819; U.S. Bureau of Justice Statistics, 1987).

IMPLICATIONS FOR CRIME CONTROL POLICY

I have argued that gun use by private citizens against violent criminals and burglars is common and about as frequent as arrests, is a more prompt negative consequence of crime than legal punishment, and is more severe, at its most serious, than legal system punishments. Victim gun use in crime incidents is associated with lower rates of crime completion and of victim injury than any other defensive response, including doing nothing to resist. Serious predatory criminals say they perceive a risk from victim gun use which is roughly comparable to that of criminal justice system actions, and this perception appears to influence their criminal behavior in socially desirable ways.

The evidence presented here is, of course, subject to multiple differing interpretations. I believe, however, that the simplest and most plausible interpretation is that the civilian ownership and defensive use of guns has a deterrent and social control effect on violent crime and burglary. None of the foregoing can establish exactly how many crimes are deterred by the civilian possession and use of firearms. We cannot precisely calculate the social control impact of gun use and ownership any more than we can do so for the operations of the legal system. However, available evidence is compatible with the hypothesis that gun ownership among potential crime victims may exert as much effect on violent crime and burglary as do criminal justice system activities.

The paucity of scholarly attention to civilian use of guns for defense may be partially due to the very limited visibility of such acts. No criminology text reports estimates of the frequency of defensive uses of guns. Published police-based crime statistics like those found in the Uniform Crime Reports do not cover the subject, and such incidents are rarely reported in the national news media, the Bernhard Goetz case notwithstanding. It is also possible that scholars feel shooting or threatening to shoot another person, even in self-defense, is so morally wrong that it is preferable not to address the subject at all (Goode, 1972; see also Tonso, 1984 on scholars' attitudes towards firearms). It could even be argued that to study the matter seriously might imply some endorsement and encourage the indiscriminant spread of the behavior.

Nevertheless, much social order in America may precariously depend on the fact that millions of people are armed and dangerous to each other. The availability of deadly weapons to the violence-prone probably contributes to violence by increasing the probability of a fatal outcome of combat (but see Wright et al., 1983:189–212). However, it may also be that this very fact raises the stakes in disputes to the point where only the most incensed or intoxicated disputants resort to physical conflict, the risks of armed retaliation deterring attack and coercing minimal courtesy among otherwise hostile parties. Likewise, rates of commercial robbery and residential burglary might be far higher than their already high levels were it not for the dangerousness of the prospective victims. Gun ownership among prospective victims may even have as large a crime-*inhibiting* effect as the crime-*generating* effects of gun possession among prospective criminals. This would account for the failure of researchers to find a significant net relationship between rates of crime like homicide and robbery and those measures of gun ownership which do not distinguish between gun availability among criminals and availability in the largely noncriminal general public (e.g., Cook, 1979; Kleck, 1984). The two effects may roughly cancel each other out (see also Bordua, 1986).

Guns are potentially lethal weapons whether wielded by criminals or crime victims. They are frightening and intimidating to those they are pointed at, whether these be predators or the preyed-upon. Guns thereby empower both those who would use them to victimize and those who would use them to prevent their victimization. Consequently, they are a source of both social order and disorder, depending on who uses them, just as is true of the use of force in general. The failure to fully recognize this can lead to grave errors in devising public policy to minimize violence through gun control.

Some gun laws are intended to reduce gun possession only among relatively limited "high-risk" groups such as convicted felons, e.g., laws licensing gun owners or requiring permits to purchase guns. However, other laws are aimed at reducing gun possession in all segments of the civilian population, both criminal and noncriminal. Examples would be the aforementioned Morton Grove handgun possession ban, near approximations of such bans (as in New York City), prohibitions of handgun sales (such as those in Chicago and Washington, D.C.), and most laws restricting the carrying of concealed weapons. By definition, laws are most likely to be obeyed by the law-abiding, and gun laws are no different. Therefore, measures applying equally to criminals and noncriminals are almost certain to reduce gun possession more among the latter than the former. Because very little serious violent crime is committed by persons without previous records of serious violence (Kleck and Bordua, 1983), there would be little direct crime control benefit to be gained by reductions in gun possession among noncriminals, although even marginal reductions in gun possession among criminals could have crime-reducing effects. Consequently one has to take seriously the possibility that "across-the-board" gun control measures could decrease the crime-control effects of noncriminal gun ownership more than they decreased the crime-causing effects of criminal gun ownership. For this reason, more narrowly targeted gun control measures like gun owner licensing and purchase-to-permit systems seem advisable (see Kleck, 1986a for an extended discussion).

Having an armed victim population is obviously not without risks. Some victims are also offenders, and their possession of guns may embolden them to commit assaults and other crimes they otherwise would not have attempted. And the use of guns in assaults instead of likely substitutes such as knives or fists probably increases the fraction of assaults which result in death. However, evidence gathered to date on these questions has been very mixed and is no more conclusive than the evidence presented here concerning defensive effects of guns (see Wright et al., 1983, esp. 129–38, 189–212; Kleck, 1986a). Similarly ambiguous conclusions apply to evidence concerning gun involvement in suicides and accidental deaths. The number of gun suicides which would not have occurred in the absence of guns appears to be fairly small (Kleck, 1986c). And gun accidents appear to be less a by-product of routine gun ownership and use by ordinary citizens than the result of unusually hazardous activities with guns by a small, extremely reckless minority of gun owners. For example, insurance company studies indicate that many gun accidents occur when the shooter handles a gun while intoxicated, "plays" Russian roulette with a revolver, or points a loaded gun at another person "in fun." And examination of police and traffic records indicates that accidental shooters have histories of arrests for violent acts, alcohol-related arrests, traffic citations, and highway crashes far in excess of those of matched controls (Kleck, 1986d).

REFERENCES

Benenson, Mark K. Memorandum recording telephone conversation with Kennesaw, Ga., Police Chief Ruble, November 4, 1982.

Bensing, Robert C., and Oliver Schroeder. *Homicide in an Urban Community*. Springfield, Ill.: Charles Thomas, 1960.

Block, Richard. *Violent Crime*. Lexington, Mass.: Lexington, 1977.

———. "The Impact of Victimization, Rates and Patterns: A Comparison of the Netherlands and the United States." Pp. 23–28 in Richard Block (ed.), *Victimization and Fear of Crime: World Perspectives*. Bureau of Justice Statistics. Washington, D.C.: U.S. Government Printing Office, 1984.

Blumstein, Alfred, Jacqueline Cohen, and Daniel Nagin (eds.). *Deterrence and Incapacitation: Estimating the Effects of Criminal Sanctions on Crime Rates*. Washington, D.C.: National Academy of Sciences, 1978.

Bordua, David J. "Firearms Ownership and Violent Crime: A Study Comparing Illinois Counties." Working Papers in Criminology, CR8501, Department of Sociology, University of Illinois: Urbana, Ill., 1986.

California. *Homicide in California, 1982.* Sacramento, Calif.: Bureau of Criminal Statistics and Special Services, 1983.

Cambridge Reports. *An Analysis of Public Attitudes Towards Handgun Control.* Cambridge, Mass.: Cambridge Reports, Inc., 1978.

Cohen, Lawrence E., and Marcus Felson. "Social Change and Crime Rate Trends: A Routine Activities Approach." *American Sociological Review* 44(1979):588–608.

Cook, Philip. "The Effect of Gun Availability on Robbery and Murder." Pp. 743–81 in Robert Haveman and B. Bruce Zellner (eds.), *Policy Studies Review Annual*, volume 3. Beverly Hills, Calif.: Sage, 1979.

Cook, Philip J. "The Case of the Missing Victims: Gunshot Woundings in the National Crime Survey." *Journal of Quantitative Criminology* 1(1985):91–102.

Crocker, Royce. "Attitudes Toward Gun Control: A Survey." Pp. 229–67 in Harry L. Hogan (ed.), *Federal Regulation of Firearms*. Washington, D.C.: U.S. Government Printing Office, 1982.

Cunningham, William C., and Todd H. Taylor. *Crime and Protection in America: A Study of Private Security and Law Enforcement Resources and Relationships*. National Institute of Justice, Washington, D.C.: U.S. Government Printing Office, 1985.

Curtis, Lynn A. *Criminal Violence: National Patterns and Behavior.* Lexington, Mass.: Lexington, 1974.

DMI (Decision/Making/Information). *Attitudes of the American Electorate Toward Gun Control.* Santa Ana, Calif.: DMI, 1978.

Field Institute. *Tabulations of the Findings of a Survey of Handgun Ownership and Access Among a Cross Section of the California Adult Public.* San Francisco: Field Institute, 1976.

Firman, Gordon R. "In Prison Gun Survey the Pros Are the Cons." *The American Rifleman* 23 (November 1975):13.

Garin, Geoffrey. Telephone Conversation with Geoffrey Garin of Peter D. Hart Research Associates, Inc. Washington, D.C., April 30, 1986.

Gibbs, Jack P. *Crime, Punishment, and Deterrence.* New York: Elsevier, 1975.

Goode, William J. "Presidential Address: The Place of Force in Human Society." *American Sociological Review* 37(1985):507–19.

Gove, Walter R., Michael Hughes, and Michael Gerrken. "Are Uniform Crime Reports a Valid Indicator of the Index Crimes? An Affirmative Answer with Minor Qualifications." *Criminology* 23(1985):451–501.

Green, Gary S. "Citizen Gun Ownership and Criminal Deterrence: Theory, Research, and Policy." *Criminology* 25(1987):63–82.

Greenberg, Stephanie W., William M. Rohe, and J. R. Williams. *Informal Citizen Action and Crime Prevention at the Neighborhood Level: Synthesis and Assessment of the Research.* National Institute of Justice. Washington, D.C.: Government Printing Office, 1984.

ICPSR (Inter-University Consortium for Political and Social Research). Codebook for ICPSR Study 9028. *Uniform Crime Reports, 1980–1982: Supplementary Homicide Report.* Ann Arbor, Mich.: ICPSR, 1984.

———. Codebook for ICPSR Study 8437. *Armed Criminals in America: A Survey of Incarcerated Felons.* Ann Arbor, Mich.: ICPSR, 1986.

———. Codebook for ICPSR Study 8316. *National Crime Surveys: Victim Risk Supplement, 1983.* Ann Arbor, Mich.: ICPSR, 1987a.

———. Codebook for ICPSR Study 8608. *National Crime Surveys: National Sample, 1979–1985* (Revised Questionnaire). Ann Arbor, Mich.: ICPSR, 1987b.

Kates, Don B., Jr. "Handgun Prohibition and the Original Meaning of the Second Amendment." *Michigan Law Review* 82 (1983):204–73.

Kleck, Gary. "The Relationship between Gun Ownership Levels and Rates of Violence in the United States. Pp. 99–135 in Don B. Kates, Jr. (ed.). *Firearms and Violence: Issues of Public Policy*. Cambridge, Mass.: Ballinger, 1989.

———. "Policy Lessons from Recent Gun Control Research." *Law and Contemporary Problems* 49 (1986a): 35–62.

———. "Evidence that 'Saturday Night Specials' Not Very Important for Crime." *Sociology and Social Research* 70 (1986b): 803–807.

———. "Suicide, Firearms, and Gun Control." Unpublished manuscript, 1986c.

———. "Firearms Accidents." Unpublished manuscript, 1986d.

———. "Guns and Self-Defense: Crime Control through the Use of Armed Force in the Private Sector." Unpublished manuscript, 1987.

Kleck, Gary, and David J. Bordua. "The Factual Foundations for Certain Key Assumptions of Gun Control," *Law & Policy Quarterly* 5 (1983): 271–98.

Krug, Alan S. "The Relationship between Firearms Ownership and Crime Rates: A Statistical Analysis." *The Congressional Record* (January 30, 1968): H570-2.

Link, Mitchell. "No Handguns in Morton Grove—Big Deal!" *Menard Times* (prison newspaper of Menard, Ill. Federal Penitentiary) 33 (1982): 1.

Lundsgaarde, Henry P. *Murder in Space City: A Cultural Analysis of Houston Homicide Patterns.* New York: Oxford University Press, 1977.

Mayhew, Pat. *Residential Burglary: A Comparison of the United States, Canada and England and Wales* National Institute of Justice. Washington, D.C.: U.S. Government Printing Office, 1987.

"22% Drop Reported in Crime on Subways." *New York Times,* March 22, 1985a, B4.

"Subway Felonies Reportedly Down." *New York Times,* April 18, 1985b, 87.

Ohio Statistical Analysis Center. *Ohio Citizen Attitudes Concerning Crime and Criminal Justice.* Columbus, Ohio: Ohio Department of Development, 1982.

Rengert, George, and John Wasilchick. *Suburban Burglary: A Time and Place for Everything.* Springfield, Ill.: Charles Thomas, 1985.

Rushforth, Norman B., et al. "Violent Death in a Metropolitan County: Changing Patterns in Homicide (1958–74)." *New England Journal of Medicine* 297 (1977): 531–38.

Sherman, Lawrence W., and Robert H. Langworthy. "Measuring Homicide by Police Officers." *Journal of Criminal Law and Criminology* 70 (1979): 54–60.

Shields, Pete. *Guns Don't Die—People Do.* New York: Arbor House, 1981.

"Subway Robberies Drop." *Tallahassee Democrat,* January 25, 1985, A1.

Tonso, William R. "Social Problems and Sagecraft: Gun Control as a Case in Point." Pp. 71–92 in Don B. Kates, Jr. (ed.), *Firearms and Violence: Issues of Public Policy.* Cambridge, Mass.: Ballinger, 1984.

U.S. Bureau of the Census. *Statistical Abstract of the United States, 1982–83.* Washington, D.C.: U.S. Government Printing Office, 1982.

———. *County and City Data Book 1983.* Washington, D.C.: U.S. Government Printing Office, 1983.

U.S. Bureau of Justice Statistics. *Intimate Victims: A Study of Violence Among Friends and Relatives.* Washington, D.C.: U.S. Government Printing Office, 1980.

———. *Criminal Victimization in the United States 1980.* Washington, D.C.: U.S. Government Printing Office, 1982.

———. *Capital Punishment 1983.* BJS Bulletin. Washington, D.C.: U.S. Government Printing Office, 1984.

———. *Household Burglary.* BJS Bulletin. Washington, D.C.: U.S. Government Printing Office, 1985a.

———. *The Risk of Violent Crime.* BJS Special Report. Washington, D.C.: U.S. Government Printing Office, 1985b.

———. *Criminal Victimization in the United States 1983.* Washington, D.C.: U.S. Government Printing Office, 1985c.

———. *Imprisonment in Four Countries.* BJS Special Report. Washington, D.C.: U.S. Government Printing Office, 1987.

U.S. Federal Bureau of Investigation (FBI). *Crime in the United States: Uniform Crime.* Washington, D.C.: U.S. Government Printing Office, 1962–75; 1980, 1982.

———. *Crime in the United States.* Washington, D.C.: U.S. Government Printing Office, 1981.

———. *Crime in the United States.* Washington, D.C.: U.S. Government Printing Office, 1983.

———. *Law Enforcement Officers Killed and Assaulted* [covering single years 1977 to 1983]. Washington, D.C.: U.S. Government Printing Office, 1984.

U.S. Library of Congress. *Gun Control Laws in Foreign Countries.* Law Library. Washington, D.C.: U.S. Government Printing Office, 1981.

U.S. National Center for Health Statistics (NCHS). *Public Use Data Tape Documentation: Mortality Detail 1980 Data.* Hyattsville, Md.: U.S. Public Health Service, 1983.

U.S. Small Business Administration. *Crime Against Small Business.* Senate Document No. 91-14, Washington, D.C.: U.S. Government Printing Office, 1969.

Waller Irvin, and Norman Okihiro. *Burglary: The Victim and the Public.* Toronto: University of Toronto Press, 1978.

Wilbanks, William. *Murder in Miami.* Laham, Md.: University Press, 1984.

Wilson, James Q. "Crime and Punishment in England." *The Public Interest* 43 (1976): 3–26.

Wilt, G. Marie, et al. *Domestic Violence and the Police: Studies in Detroit and Kansas City.* Washington, D.C.: U.S. Government Printing Office, 1977.

Wolfgang, Marvin E. *Patterns in Criminal Homicide.* Philadelphia: University of pennsylvania Press, 1958.

Wright James D., Peter H. Rossi, and Kathleen Daly. *Under the Gun: Weapons, Crime, and Violence in America.* Hawthorne, N.Y.: Aldine, 1983.

Wright, James D., and Peter H. Rossi. *The Armed Criminal in America: A Survey of Incarcerated Felons.* Hawthorne, N.Y.: Aldine, 1986.

Yeager, Matthew G., Joseph D. Alviani, and Nancy Loving. *How Well Does the Handgun Protect You and Your Family?* Handgun Control Staff Technical Report 2. Washington, D.C.: United States Conference of Mayors, 1976.

Zimring, Franklin F., and Gordon J. Hawkins. *Deterrence: The Legal Threat in Crime Control.* Chicago: University of Chicago Press, 1973.

21

When Children Shoot Children

Garen J. Wintemute, Stephen P. Teret, Jess F. Kraus,
Mona A. Wright, and Gretchen Bradfield

Firearms rank among the United States' ten leading causes of death, accounting for more than 30,000 deaths annually.[1,2] Unintentional firearm deaths are most common among children and young adults.[3,4] Such deaths may be susceptible to preventive measures beyond those available for youthful firearm sucide and homicide. This study describes the 88 unintentional firearm deaths in which *both* the shooter and the victim were California children 14 years of age or younger, occurring during the years 1977 through 1983.

METHODS

The California Master Mortality File yielded death certificate records for 137 firearm deaths of California residents aged 0 through 14 years, occurring during 1977 through 1983, that were classified as unintentional (*International Classification of Diseases* code E 922). Using coroner or medical examiner

From *JAMA* 257, no. 22 (June 12, 1987): 3107-3109. Copyright © 1987, American Medical Association. Reprinted by permission of the publisher.

reports and supplemental information from local police agencies, we identified 88 cases in which the shooter was also under 15 years of age. Cases in which one child shot another and self-inflicted shootings were both included.

These cases were classified as unintentional by county medical examiners or coroners, based on investigations conducted by their own staffs and local police authorities. Studies of suicide among latency-age children (aged 6 through 12 years) have not reported suicide by firearm.[5] It is nonetheless possible that some self-inflicted shooting deaths, particularly among children aged 10 through 14 years, were intentional.[6]

Mortality rates are averages for the seven-year study period; midinterval population data were obtained from the 1980 California census. Denominators used in rate calculations are age, race, and gender, specific as appropriate. Years of potential life lost were calculated using the method developed by the Centers for Disease Control.[7]

RESULTS

Case Reports

Several case prototypes emerged, characterized by the following case summaries. (The frequencies cited for each prototype are conservative, reflecting the fact that full case descriptions were often not available.)

Firearm owners' perceived need for protection was associated with at least nine cases. In case 1, a 5-year-old boy shot himself in the head with a .38-caliber revolver. The child had found the loaded revolver under an older family member's pillow. The gun was usually stored out of view 6 feet above the floor but was placed under the pillow at night. The older family member had left the bedroom for a few minutes to watch television. In case 2, an 11-year-old boy was shot in the head by his 12-year-old brother with a 10-gauge shotgun owned by the boys' father. The boys were playing with the gun and did not know it was loaded. Ordinarily, the gun was kept unloaded. The previous night a prowler had been seen; the father loaded the gun at that time. In case 3, a 6-year-old boy shot himself in the head with a .38-caliber revolver. He had found the gun in the purse of a houseguest.

In at least three cases the shooter thought the gun was a toy. In case 4, a 2-year-old girl was shot in the head with a .22-caliber rifle. The shooter, her 4-year-old brother, thought the gun was a toy. He had found it under their parents' bed, pointed it at her, and pulled the trigger. In case 5, a 7-year-old boy was shot in the chest with a .22-caliber pistol by his 8-year-old brother. The brother had retrieved the loaded gun from a drawer in their parents' bedroom. Thinking it a toy, he aimed it at his younger brother and pulled the trigger.

Defective weapons were involved in at least seven cases. In case 6, a 2-year-old boy shot himself in the head with a .38-caliber revolver, which was stored with other weapons in his parents' bedroom. The criminalist technician found the revolver had an abnormally light trigger pull. In case 7, an 8-year-old girl was shot in the head by a 7-year-old playmate with a .38-caliber handgun. The loaded gun had been left under the couch by the victim's parents, who slept in the living room. The safety catch was broken.

Epidemiologic Profile

. . . The risk of involvement as a victim or shooter in other-inflicted deaths rose with age. Self-inflicted deaths did not follow this pattern and were the most common type of unintentional firearm death among children 0 through 4 years of age.

The mortality rate for boys was 4.3 per 1 million children per year and that for girls 0.5 per 1 million children per year. Mortality rates by race were as follows: white non-Hispanic, 4.1; black, 3.8; and Hispanic, 1.4 (all per 1 million children per year). The 88 deaths resulted in 5,016 years of potential life lost.

Thirty-five deaths (40 percent) were self-inflicted. The shooter was another family member, usually a sibling, in 21 cases (24 percent), a playmate in 31 (35 percent), and unspecified in one case. A boy aged 10 to 14 years was the shooter in 58 (70 percent) of the 83 cases in which the shooter's age and gender were recorded.

The shooting occurred at a residence in 82 cases (93 percent). In at least 35 cases (40 percent), the gun involved was kept in the room where the shooting occurred. . . . The most common case history was of children playing with a gun that had been stored loaded unlocked, and out of view; the shooting often occurred in the room where the gun was stored.

Handguns were involved in 51 cases (58 percent), rifles in 24 cases (27 percent), and shotguns in 13 cases (15 percent). At least 39 (76 percent) of the handguns were revolvers. Seven weapons (five handguns and two shotguns) were reported as malfunctioning at the time of the shooting.

In 21 cases, the shooter stated he did not know the gun was loaded. In 16 (76 percent) of these, the shooter was 10 years old or older. Nine (43 percent) of these cases involved handguns; rifles and shotguns each accounted for six cases (29 percent).

Sixty-one children (69 percent) were shot in the head or neck. Wounds to the thorax (19, or 22 percent) and abdomen (seven, or 8 percent) accounted for most of the remainder. Reflecting the severity of these injuries, 33 children (38 percent) were dead either at the shooting site or on initial arrival at the hospital, and an additional 23 (26 percent) were pronounced dead while still in the emergency department. Forty-one children (47 percent) were dead within one hour of being shot; only 16 (18 percent) survived for more than six hours.

Blood alcohol levels were measured in 48 percent of the victims and in 72 percent of those aged 10 to 14 years. All results were normal.

Comment

The cases reported constituted 64 percent of the unintentional firearm deaths and 19 percent of all the firearm deaths that occurred among California children 0 through 14 years of age during the years studied. The total number of such shootings, fatal and nonfatal alike, must be substantially higher; an earlier review of unintentional shootings in Vermont found that only 6 percent were fatal.[8]

Serious long-term effects are not limited to those killed or injured. At least 52 of the 53 shooters in deaths inflicted by others were family members or friends of the children who were shot. They are almost certainly at increased risk for acute and chronic emotional and behavioral disturbance; to our knowledge, this hypothesis has not yet been evaluated.

Contributing factors that are susceptible to intervention exist. Easy access to firearms is chief among these. In at least 48 percent of residential shootings, children gained access to firearms that were stored loaded—but never locked away—in the house where the shooting occurred. Cases in which children knowingly made use of loaded firearms, such as while hunting or playing Russian roulette, were unusual.

The belief that, on balance, firearms provide personal or household protection was directly involved in a number of deaths. Previous studies have established that this belief may be incorrect; unintentional fatal shootings of friends and family members in the home are as much as six times as common as fatal shootings of criminals.[9-11]

Defects in current firearm design are important. It should be possible, for example, to design firearms so that users can easily determine whether they are loaded. In 36 percent of cases the record contained a clear statement that the child shooter did not know the gun was loaded or did not know it was real, or the shooter's age was such (younger than 5 years) that he/she would be unlikely to make such determinations reliably, given current design practices. This confusion involved both handguns and long guns and was not restricted to young children.

Likewise, firearm safety catches should be designed so that they are automatically and always engaged unless held in a disengaged position by the user. With such an alteration, small children in particular would be much less likely to discharge a firearm inadvertently. The malfunctioning of individual firearms appeared to be less important than these general design shortcomings.

Those firearms that figure most commonly in firearm homicide were also commonly involved in these shootings. Handguns were involved in 59 percent of cases, but they constituted only 43 percent of national firearm production during the study period.[12] Revolvers of .22 caliber were used in 35 percent of handgun shootings but constituted only 17 percent of national handgun production during this period.[12] The ready availability of handguns in the home appears to contribute to their involvement in both unintentional shootings and homicide.[13] Therefore, efforts to reduce firearm availability might best be focused on handguns.

Within the year, handguns made largely of plastic may be widely available at a relatively low cost.[14,15] Children are likely to encounter these handguns, which are promoted by their manufacturers as "dishwasher safe"[16] and by others as "particularly attractive for women to use as a self-defense weapon."[17] Because of their composition and light weight, these firearms may resemble toys even more closely than do those now on the market. Before they are introduced, their unique potential for aggravating the problem we have described should be considered.

REFERENCES

1. Baker, S. P., B. O'Neill, and R. Karpf. *The Injury Fact Book.* Lexington, Mass.: D. C. Heath, 1984.
2. Wintemute, G. J. "Firearms as a Cause of Death in the United States, 1920–1982." *Journal of Trauma* 27(1987):532–36.
3. Morrow, P. L., and P. Hudson. "Accidental Firearm Fatalities in North Carolina, 1976–1980." *American Journal of Public Health* 76(1966):1120–23.
4. Wintemute, G. J., S. P. Teret, and J. Kraus. "The Epidemiology of Firearm Deaths Among Residents of California." *Western Journal of Medicine* 146(1987):374–77.
5. Pfeffer, C. R. "The Distinctive Features of Children Who Threaten or Complete Suicide." In C. F. Wells and I. R. Stuart (eds.), *Self-Destructive Behavior in Children and Adolescents.* New York: Van Nostrand Reinhold Co., 1981, pp. 106–20.
6. Jobes, D. A., A. L. Berman, and A. R. Josselson. "The Impact of Psychological Autopsies on Medical Examiners' Determination of Manner of Death." *Journal of Forensic Science* 31(1986):177–89.
7. "Table V: Estimated Years of Potential Life Lost Before Age 65 and Cause-Specific Mortality, by Cause of Death—United States, 1984." *MMWR* 35(1986):27.
8. Waller, J. A., and E. B. Whorton. "Unintentional Shootings, Highway Crashes and Acts of Violence: A Behavior Paradigm." *Accident Analysis and Prevention* 5(1973):351–56.
9. Kellerman, A. L., and D. T. Reay. "Protection or Peril? An Analysis of Firearm-Related Deaths in the Home." *New England Journal of Medicine* 314(1986):1557–60.
10. Heins, M., R. Kahn, and J. Biordnal. "Gunshot Wounds in Children." *American Journal of Public Health* 64(1974):326–30.
11. Rushforth, N. B., et al. "Accidental Firearm Fatalities in a Metropolitan County (1958–1973)." *American Journal of Epidemiology* 110(1975):499–505.
12. *Consolidated Annual Firearms Manufacturing and Exportation Report.* Washington, D.C.: Bureau of Alcohol, Tobacco, and Firearms, 1977–1983 editions.
13. Teret, S. P., and G. J. Wintemute. "Handgun Injuries: The Epidemiologic Evidence for Assessing Legal Responsibility." *Hamline Law Review* 6(1983):341–50.
14. *Technical Questions Regarding Plastic Firearms.* Washington, D.C.: Office of Technology Assessment, 1986.
15. Byron, D. "Undetectable Guns?" Transcript of the "MacNeil/Lehrer News Hour." New York: Journal Graphics Inc., May 26, 1986, pp. 7–11.
16. *Hearings Before the Subcommittee on Crime of the House of Representatives Committee on the Judiciary,* 99th Cong., 2nd sess. (May 15, 1986) (testimony of Mary Ellen McDonald Burns).

17. *Hearings Before the Subcommittee on Crime of the House of Representatives Committee on the Judiciary,* 99th Cong., 2nd sess. (May 15, 1986) (testimony of Lawrence D. Pratt, executive director, Gun Owners of America).

22

Gun Accidents

Don B. Kates, Jr.

FATALITIES AMONG CHILDREN

To emphasize accidental handgun fatalities among children, Handgun Control Inc. runs a national advertisement that pictures an infant playing with a pistol. An academic-produced video for schools and libraries solemnly asserts that "a child is acidentally killed by a handgun every day" (i.e., 365 per year).[1] Two academic anti-gun crusaders put the accidental death toll at "almost 1,000 children" per year.[2]

Fortunately, these assertions are grotesque exaggerations. In fact, the National Safety Council's figures of identifiable accidental fatalities from handguns average only 246 people of *all ages* per year.[3] For children alone, the identifiable handgun average was 10–15 accidental fatalities per year for children under age five and 50–55 yearly for children under age fifteen.[4]

From "Guns, Murders, and the Constitution: A Realistic Assessment of Gun Control" (February 1990): 50–52. Copyright © 1990 by the Pacific Research Institute for Public Policy. Reprinted by permission of the publisher.

Obviously, it is a terrible tragedy when a child dies in an accident, whether from a handgun or otherwise. But that does not justify falsifying statistics to concoct an argument for banning handguns. . . . Fatal gun accidents (including those involving children) are largely attributable to gun possession among the same kinds of irresponsible aberrant adults who commit murders. Some feasible proposals for controls to reduce child (and other) accidental deaths from firearms are offered in my conclusion. As to the advisability of going beyond controls to banning handguns, the 13 children under age five who died in handgun accidents may be compared to the 381 children who drowned in swimming pools in 1980. Yet nobody would demand a ban on new swimming pools—much less demand that all those who currently own pools be required to fill them in.

Anti-gun fanatics are wont to exclaim that even if a gun ban saves only one life, it is worth it. That statement has special appeal if the lives being saved are those of very young children. But if anti-gun advocates feel prohibiting or confiscating upward of 70 million handguns is justified to save 13 young children's lives (and confiscating upward of 200 million guns of all types to save 34 children), why does saving 381 annually not justify banning swimmig pools, or at least prohibiting their proliferation? Is it possible that anti-gun fanatics are motivated more by hatred of guns and their owners than by saving lives? Of course, handguns and swimming pools are very different things that may merit very different policy responses. Among the relevant differences are that, unlike handguns, pools are not used to defend against approximately 645,000 crimes each year and do not save thousands of innocent lives.

This disparity is even more striking in regard to fatalities caused by cigarettes. Compare the 10–15 children under age five who die in handgun accidents annually to the 432 who die in residential fires caused by adults who fall asleep while smoking.[5] Not only do we not forbid smoking in the home, the federal government actually pays tobacco farmers subsidies to grow their crops. Yet cigarettes, which have absolutely no social utility (except perhaps for the subjective pleasure they give smokers), take hundreds of times more lives than do handguns in accidents, murders, and suicides combined. In that connection, note that we do not ban alcoholic beverages, though people under their influence commit more murders and suicides than occur with handguns—and alcohol causes hundreds of times more fatal accidents and non-fatal violent crimes than involve handguns.[6] (If it be suggested that we repealed Prohibition only because it proved unenforceable, the short answer is that a handgun ban is even less enforceable.[7])

ABERRANCE OF GUN ACCIDENT PERPETRATORS

My reason for limiting the preceding discussion primarily to children is because the issues that arise with adults who perpetrate serious accidents are much the same as with murderers. This kind of person is just as atypical as the murderer; indeed, he closely resembles the murderer in attitudes and life history of singular irresponsibility and indifference to human life and welfare.[8] This similarity is marked in perpetrators of fatal gun accidents. When compared to cars (which take 190 times as many lives[9]), handguns are simple mechanisms that are entirely safe for any owner who is responsible enough to observe elementary precautions. Empirical studies show that "a gun becomes involved in a fatal accident through misuse." Unlike the average gun owner, those "who cause such accidents are disproportionately involved in other accidents, violent crime, and heavy drinking."[10] If we examine their backgrounds of serious felonies, substance abuse, automobile and other dangerous accidents, frequently irrational assaults on families, and the like, the question about these reckless or irresponsible people is not *whether* they will kill themselves or others, but *when*.[11] Indeed, a large portion of child gun accidents may be attributable to these irresponsible people who leave loaded guns unsecured.

NOTES

1. "Violence: Kids with Guns," produced by Films for the Humanities and Sciences, Inc., Princeton, N.J., 1989.

2. Teret, S. P., and G. J. Wintemute, "Handgun Injuries: The Epidemiologic Evidence for Assessing Legal Responsibility," *Hamline Law Review* 6(1983):346.

3. The National Safety Council began breaking handgun accidents out of the total number of accidental gun fatalities only in 1979. The 246 figure given in the text represents the average for identifiable handgun accidents for 1979 and succeeding years.

4. Kleck, untitled MS to be published by Aldine Press in 1991 (hereinafter Kleck-Aldine), Table 7.5 (figures for 1980 derived from Prof. Kleck's review of the Public Health Service's computerized detail tapes). Compare the Center for Disease Control's figure that accidents with handguns and long guns *combined* killed 34 children under age 5 in 1984. "Mortality and Morbidity Weekly Report," March 11, 1988, p. 145. It should be noted that, while the number of accidental long gun fatalities is clearly substantially higher, the figures given for handgun deaths may understate the phenomenon since many figures of accidental gun fatalities do not determine whether the weapon was a handgun or a long gun.

5. See the Centers for Disease Control, "Mortality and Morbidity Weekly Report," March 11, 1988, pp. 144–45.

6. U.S. Public Health Service, *Alcohol and Health* (1978), p. 4; see discussion and citations in Kates, "Handgun Banning and the Prohibition Experience," in Don B. Kates (ed.), *Firearms and Violence: Issues of Public Policy* (Cambridge, Mass.: Ballinger, 1984), pp. 143–44.

7. Analyzing enforceability requires considering two sub-issues: the likelihood of voluntary compliance, and the ease with which a handgun ban can be enforced against the noncompliant. As to the first sub-issue, massive resistance can be expected since people believe (whether rightly or not is irrelevant) that they urgently need a handgun for their family's defense and that a handgun ban would be illegal because it is against the constitutional right to arms. In contrast, no one but alcoholics "need" liquor and Prohibition was clearly legal, having been enacted as a constitutional amendment. As to enforcement against the noncompliant, liquor is consumed; therefore, continuing to use it required violators to take relatively high viability steps to buy more liquor. In contrast, to find and confiscate upwards of 70 million extant handguns would require unconstitutional house-to-house searches. For those who do not already own one, buying a handgun requires only one purchase—and if handguns were smuggled in at the rate marijuana is estimated to be, 20 million new handguns would be available for purchase each year. See discussion in "Handgun Banning and the Prohibition Experience," in *Firearms and Violence*, pp. 144–66.

8. ". . . the psychological profile of the accident-prone suggests the same kind of aggressiveness shown by most murderers." Lane, "On the Social Meaning of Homicide Trends in America," in T. Gurr, *Violence in America* (Violence Cooperation Peace Ser., 1989), p. 59. See also J. Wilson and R. Hernstein, *Crime*

and Human Nature (Austin, Texas: TX S&S Press, 1985): "Young men who drive recklessly and have many accidents tend to be similar to those who commit crimes."

9. "Motor vehicle crashes in 1986 resulted in 46,056 deaths." Center for Disease Control, *Mortality and Morbidity Weekly Report,* March 11, 1988.

10. Cook, "The Role of Firearms in Violent Crime: An Interpretative Review of the Literature," in M. Wolfgang and N. Weiler (ed.), *Criminal Violence* (1982), p. 369.

11. Kleck-Aldine above, chap. 7. For further evidence that fatal gun accident perpetrators and murders differ "rather dramatically" from the general population, see Cook above, pp. 270–71 and Danto, "Firearms and Violence," *International Journal of Offender Therapy* 5(1979):135.

Selected Bibliography

BOOKS

Cruit, Ronald L. *Intruder in Your Home: How to Defend Yourself Legally with a Firearm.* New York: Stein and Day, 1983.

Kennett, Lee, and James LaVerne Anderson. *The Gun in America: The Origins of a National Dilemma.* Westport, Conn.: Greenwood Press, 1975.

Quigley, Paxton. *Armed and Female.* New York: E. P. Dutton, 1989.

Shields, Pete, and John Grenya. *Guns Don't Die—People Do.* New York: Arbor House, 1981.

Zimring, Franklin E., and George Hawkins. *The Citizens Guide to Gun Control.* New York: Macmillan, 1987.

ARTICLES

Benson, Bruce L. "Guns for Protection and Other Private Sector Responses to the Fear of Rising Crime." In Don B. Kates, Jr., ed., *Firearms and Violence.* Cambridge, Mass.: Ballinger Publishers, 1984, pp. 329–56.

Lizotte, Alan J., David J. Bordua, and Carolyn S. White. "Firearms Ownership for Sport and Protection: Two Not So Divergent Models." *American Sociological Review* 46 (1981):499–503.

Silver, Carol Ruth, and Don B. Kates, Jr. "Self-Defense, Handgun Ownership, and the Independence of Women in a Violent Sexist Society." In Don B. Kates, Jr., ed., *Restricting Handguns: The Liberal Skeptics Speak Out.* Croton-on-Hudson, N.Y.: North River Press, 1979, pp. 139–69.

Wright, James D. "The Ownership of Firearms for Reasons of Self-Defense." In Don B. Kates, Jr., ed., *Firearms and Violence*. Cambridge, Mass.: Ballinger Publishers, 1984, pp. 301–327.

————. "Public Opinion and Gun Control: A Comparison of Results from Two Recent National Surveys." *Annals of the American Academy of Political and Social Science*, no. 455 (1981):24–39.

Wright, James D., and Linda Marston. "The Ownership and the Means of Destruction: Weapons in the United States." *Social Problems* 23 (1975):93–107.

Part Four

Interpreting the
Second Amendment:
Culture Conflict Revealed

Introduction

"A well regulated Militia, being necessary to the security of a Free State, the right of the people to keep and bear Arms, shall not be infringed."

Second Amendment
U.S. Constitution

What does this sentence mean? The reader will by now suspect that its meaning is determined by the value that members of society place on firearms. Defenders of public firearm ownership may experience a rush of exhilaration, tingles down the spine, a feeling of real gratitude toward a nation that so values firearms that citizen ownership is specifically protected in its most hallowed and important document.

Those who voice concern about firearms and easy public access to weaponry undoubtedly experience very different emotions: distrust, annoyance, puzzlement, aversion, and the urge to minimize the importance of such a disturbing anachronism.

Consider the following facts: most serious contemporary scholars of the Constitution have simply chosen to ignore the Second Amendment in professional publications. A few scholars, to the extent they bother to address the amendment, for the most part interpret it as aiming only at protecting the existence of state militias in light of the possibility that the federal government might establish the then dreaded "standing army." This interpretation means that since the militia issue is irrelevant for our day and age, the Second Amendment is irrelevant as well. Second, since the amendment is interpreted to focus only on militias, it does not support an individual right to own and use firearms.

A few scholars have granted that *the people* might refer to the individual armed citizen. For the most part, however, they have argued that with the development of powerful modern armies and armed police forces the "right to bear arms" is, in contemporary terms, anachronistic and dangerous.

Scholars constitute a well-educated class who have mostly urban backgrounds and are in the main politically liberal. However, large segments of the general population, especially those committed to gun ownership, believe the Second Amendment to be among the most important if not *the* most important feature of the Bill of Rights. Together with a small group of constitutional scholars, they believe that the Second Amendment guarantees protection against confiscation or restricted ownership of legally obtainable firearms.

In light of these facts, readers can now consider whether interpretations of the Second Amendment, scholarly or popular, are connected to the *emotions* stirred by the amendment—in other words, emotions that are the outgrowth of culturally influenced attitudes toward and values placed on firearms.

The selections that follow, therefore, are included not only to provide an understanding of the substantive issues in this debate but also to consider whether such a connection exists. The connection, if it does exist, would of course strengthen the reliability of the idea raised in earlier parts of this volume (e.g., Bruce-Briggs and Tonso): that the gun control debate must be understood as both symptomatic of and heavily influenced by a larger ongoing cultural debate between urban liberals and the more traditional political conservatives concerning a number of complex political, social, and moral issues. As noted in the Introduction to this volume, however, the truth concerning any substantive or empirical questions is independent of its cultural context.

The first selection, a discussion by Sanford Levinson, will be of special interest to readers not only because it is lively and provocative but also because of its author's affiliation. Levinson is a member of the American Civil Liberties Union, which is fiercely committed to the First Amendment and its support of freedom of expression and the free exchange of ideas. These freedoms can be very dangerous, as those who seek to limit them constantly attest. The ACLU nevertheless views them as central to the meaning and value of the American democratic experiment. The organization, however, has had very different attitudes toward the value of free public access to firearms and the importance of the Second Amendment. Levinson's discussion of why this is so—the influence of these attitudes and their advocates on Second Amendment scholarship and his assessment of the various interpretations offered—is made even more noteworthy when we consider that he remains a supporter of stricter gun control. He seeks to bridge the gap between the contending parties of the debate by both acknowledging biases and distinguishing them from the facts of the case. Levinson is one who recognizes that the possibility of finding intelligent and politically acceptable solutions to gun control problems will require that both parties accept each other's legitimate fears and interests. The second selection, a rejoinder by feminist scholar Wendy Brown, illustrates the difficulty of this task in the ongoing gun control debate in America.

23

The Embarrassing Second Amendment

Sanford Levinson

One of the best known pieces of American popular art in this century is the *New Yorker* cover by Saul Steinberg presenting a map of the United States as seen by a New Yorker. As most readers can no doubt recall, Manhattan dominates the map; everything west of the Hudson is more or less collapsed together and minimally displayed to the viewer. Steinberg's great cover depends for its force on the reality of what social psychologists call "cognitive maps." If one asks inhabitants ostensibly of the same cities to draw maps of that city, one will quickly discover that the images carried around in people's minds will vary by race, social class, and the like. What is true of maps of places—that they differ according to the perpectives of the map-makers—is certainly true of all conceptual maps.

To continue the map analogy, consider in this context the Bill of Rights: Is there an agreed upon "projection" of the concept? Is there even a canonical text of the Bill of Rights? Does it include the first eight, nine, or ten Amendments to the Constitution?[1] Imagine two individuals who are asked to draw a "map" of the Bill or Rights. One is a (stereo-) typical member of the American

Reprinted by permission of the Yale Law Journal Company and Fred B. Rothman & Company from *The Yale Law Journal* 99 (December 1989):637–59.

Civil Liberties Union (of which I am a card-carrying member); the other is an equally (stereo-) typical member of the "New Right." The first, I suggest, would feature the First Amendment[2] as Main Street, dominating the map, though more, one suspects, in its role as protector of speech and prohibitor of established religion than as guardian of the rights of of religious believers. The other principal avenues would be the criminal procedure aspects of the Constitution drawn from the Fourth,[3] Fifth,[4] Sixth,[5] and Eighth[6] Amendments. Also depicted prominently would be the Ninth Amendment,[7] although perhaps as in the process of construction. I am confident that the ACLU map would exclude any display of the just compensation clause of the Fifth Amendment[8] or the Tenth Amendment.[9]

The second map, drawn by the New Rightist, would highlight the free exercise clause of the First Amendment,[10] the just compensation clause of the Fifth Amendment,[11] and the Tenth Amendment.[12] Perhaps the most notable difference between the two maps, though, would be in regard to the Second Amendment: "A well regulated Militia being necessary to the security of a free State, the right of the people to keep and bear Arms shall not be infringed." What would be at most only a blind alley for the ACLU mapmaker would, I am confident, be a major boulevard in the map drawn by the New Right adherent. It is this last anomaly that I want to explore in this essay.

THE POLITICS OF INTERPRETING THE SECOND AMENDMENT

To put it mildly, the Second Amendment is not at the forefront of constitutional discussion, at least as registered in what the academy regards as the venues for such discussion—law reviews,[13] casebooks,[14] and other scholarly legal publications. As Professor Larue has recently written, "the second amendment is not taken seriously by most scholars."[15]

Both Laurence Tribe[16] and the Illinois team of Nowak, Rotunda, and Young[17] at least acknowledge the existence of the Second Amendment in their respective treatises on constitutional law, perhaps because the treatise genre demands more encyclopedic coverage than does the casebook. Neither, however, pays it the compliment of extended analysis. Both marginalize the Amendment by relegating it to footnotes; it becomes what a deconstructionist might call a "supplement" to the ostensibly "real" Constitution that is privileged by discussion in the text.[18] Professor Tribe's footnote appears as part of a general discussion of congressional power. He asserts that the history of the Amendment "indicate[s] that the central concern of [its] framers was to prevent such federal interferences with the state militia as would permit the establishment of a standing national army and the consequent destruction of local autonomy."[19] He does note, however, that "the debates surrounding congressional approval of the Second Amendment do contain references to individual self-protection as well as to states' rights," but he argues that the presence of the preamble to the Amendment, as well as the qualifying phrase " 'well regulated' makes any invocation of the amendment as a restriction on state or local gun control measures extremely problematic."[20] Nowak, Rotunda, and Young mention the Amendment in the context of the incorporation controversy, though they discuss its meaning at slightly greater length.[21] They state that "[t]he Supreme Court has not determined, at least not with any clarity, whether the amendment protects only a right of state governments against federal interference with state militia and police forces . . . or a right of individuals against the federal and state government[s]."[22]

Clearly the Second Amendment is not the only ignored patch of text in our constitutional conversations. One will find extraordinarily little discussion about another one of the initial Bill of Rights, the Third Amendment: "No Soldier shall, in time of peace be quartered in any house, without the consent of the Owner, nor in time of war, but in a manner to be prescribed by law." Nor does one hear much about letters of marque and reprisal[23] or the granting of titles of nobility.[24] There are, however, some differences that are worth noting.

The Third Amendment, to take the easiest case, is ignored because it is in fact of no current importance whatsoever (although it did, for obvious reasons, have importance at the time of the founding). It has never, for a single instance, been viewed by any body of modern lawyers or groups of laity as highly relevant to their legal or political concerns. For this reason, there is almost no caselaw on the Amendment.[25] I suspect that few among even the highly sophisticated readers of this [volume] can summon up the Amendment without the aid of the text.

The Second Amendment, though, is radically different from these other pieces of constitutional text just mentioned, which all share the attribute of being basically irrelevant to any ongoing political struggles. To grasp the difference, one might simply begin by noting that it is not at all unusual for the Second Amendment to show up in letters to the editors of newspapers and magazines.[26] That judges and academic lawyers, including the ones who write casebooks, ignore it is most certainly not evidence for the proposition that no one cares about it. The National Rifle Association, to name the most obvious example, cares deeply about the Amendment, and an apparently serious Senator of the United States averred that the right to keep and bear arms is the "right most valued by free men."[27] Campaigns for Congress in both political parties, and even presidential campaigns, may turn on the apparent commitment of the candidates to a particular view of the Second Amendment. This reality of the political process reflects the fact that millions of Americans, even if (or perhaps *especially* if) they are not academics, can quote the Amendment and would disdain any presentation of the Bill of Rights that did not give it a place of pride.

I cannot help but suspect that the best explanation for the absence of the Second Amendment from the legal consciousness of the elite bar, including that component found in the legal academy,[28] is derived from a mixture of sheer opposition to the idea of private ownership of guns and the perhaps subconscious fear that altogether plausible, perhaps even "winning," interpretations of the Second Amendment would present real hurdles to those of us supporting prohibitory regulation. Thus the title of this essay—"The Embarrassing Second Amendment"—for I want to suggest that the Amendment may be profoundly embarrassing to many who both support such regulation and view themselves as committed to zealous adherence to the Bill of Rights (such as most members of the ACLU). Indeed, one sometimes discovers members of the NRA who are equally committed members of the ACLU, differing with the latter only on the issue of the Second Amendment but otherwise genuinely sharing the libertarian viewpoint of the ACLU.

It is not my style to offer "correct" or "incorrect" interpretations of the Constitution.[29] My major interest is in delineating the rhetorical structures of American constitutional argument and elaborating what is sometimes called the "politics of interpretation," that is, the factors that explain why one or another approach will appeal to certain analysts at certain times, while other analysts, or times, will favor quite different approaches. Thus my general tendency to regard as wholly untenable any approach to the Constitution that describes itself as obviously correct and condemns its opposition as simply wrong holds for the Second Amendment as well. In some contexts, this would lead me to label as tendentious the certainty of NRA advocates that the Amendment means precisely what they assert it does. In this particular context—i.e., the pages of a [volume] whose audience is much more likely to be drawn from an elite, liberal portion of the public—I will instead be suggesting that the skepticism should run in the other direction. That is, we might consider the possibility that "our" views of the Amendment, perhaps best reflected in Professor Tribe's offhand treatment of it, might themselves be equally deserving of the "tendentious" label.

THE RHETORICAL STRUCTURES OF THE RIGHT TO BEAR ARMS

My colleague Philip Bobbitt has, in his book *Constitutional Fate*,[30] spelled out six approaches—or "modalities," as he terms them—of constitutional argument. These approaches, he argues, comprise what might be termed our legal grammar. They are the rhetorical structures within which "law-talk" as a recognizable form of conversation is carried on. The six are as follows:

(1) textual argument—appeals to the unadorned language fo the text;[31]

(2) historical argument—appeals to the historical background of the provision being considered, whether the history considered be general, such as background but clearly crucial events (such as the American Revolution), or specific appeals to the so-called intentions of the framers;[32]

(3) structural argument—analyses inferred from the particular structures established by the Constitution, including the tripartite division of the national government; the separate existence of both state and nation as political entities; and the structured role of citizens within the political order;[35]

(4) doctrinal argument—emphasis on the implications of prior cases decided by the Supreme Court;[34]

(5) prudential argument—emphasis on the consequences of adopting a proferred decision in any given case;[35] and, finally

(6) ethical argument—reliance on the overall "ethos" of limited government as centrally constituting American political culture.[36]

I want to frame my consideration of the Second Amendment within the first five of Bobbitt's categories; they are all richly present in consideration of what the Amendment might mean. The sixth, which emphasizes the ethos of limited government, does not play a significant role in the debate of the Second Amendment.[37]

Text

I begin with the appeal to text. Recall the Second Amendment: "A well regulated Militia, being necessary to the security of a free State, the right of the people to keep and bear Arms, shall not be infringed." No one has ever described the Constitution as a marvel of clarity, and the Second Amendment is perhaps one of the worst drafted of all its provisions. What is special about the Amendment is the inclusion of an opening clause—a preamble, if you will—that seems to set out its purpose. No similar clause is a part of any other Amendment,[38] though that does not, of course, mean that we do not ascribe purposes to them. It would be impossible to make sense of the Constitution if we did not engage in the ascription of purpose. Indeed, the major debates about the First Amendment arise precisely when one tries to discern a purpose, given that "literalism" is a hopelessly failing approach to interpreting it. We usually do not even recognize punishment of fraud—a classic speech act—as a free speech problem because we so sensibly assume that the purpose of the First Amendment could not have been, for example, to protect the circulation of patently deceptive information to potential investors in commercial enterprises. The sharp differences that distinguish those who would limit the reach of the First Amendment to "political" speech from those who would extend it much further, encompassing nondeceptive commercial speech, are all derived from different readings of the purpose that underlies the raw text.[39]

A standard move of those legal analysts who wish to limit the Second Amendment's force is to focus on its "preamble" as setting out a restrictive purpose. Recall Laurence Tribe's assertion that the purpose was to allow the states to keep their militias and to protect them against the possibility that the new national government will use its power to establish a powerful standing army and eliminate the state militias. This purposive reading quickly disposes of any notion that there is an "individual" right to keep and bear arms. The right, if such it be, is only a state's right. The consequence of this reading is obvious: the national government has the power to regulate—to the point of prohibition—private ownership of guns, since that has, by stipulation, nothing to do with preserving state militias. This is, indeed, the position of the ACLU, which reads the Amendment as protecting only the right of "maintaining an effective state militia. . . . [T]he individual's right to bear arms applies only to the preservation or efficiency of a well-regulated [state] militia. Except for lawful police and military purposes, the possession of weapons by individuals is not constitutionally protected."[40]

This is not a wholly implausible reading, but one might ask why the Framers did not simply say something like "Congress shall have no power to prohibit state-organized and directed militias." Perhaps they in fact meant to do something else. Moreover, we might ask if ordinary readers of late eighteenth century legal prose would have interpreted it as meaning something else. The text at best provides only a starting point for a conversation. In this specific instance, it does not come close to resolving the questions posed by federal regulation of arms. Even if we accept the preamble as significant, we must still try to figure out what might be suggested by guaranteeing to "the people the right to keep and bear arms"; moreover, as we shall see presently, even the preamble presents unexpected difficulties in interpretation.

History

One might argue (and some have) that the substantive right is one pertaining to a collective body—"the people"—rather than to individuals. Professor Cress, for example, argues that state constitutions regularly used the words "man" or "person" in regard to "individual rights such as freedom of conscience," whereas the use in those constitutions of the term "the people" in regard to a right to bear arms is intended to refer to the "sovereign citizenry" collectively organized.[41] Such an argument founders, however, upon examination of the text of the federal Bill of Rights itself and the usage there of the term "the people" in the First, Fourth, Ninth, and Tenth Amendments.

Consider that the Fourth Amendment protects "[t]he right of the people to be secure in their persons," or that the First Amendment refers to the "right of the people peaceably to assemble, and to petition the Government for a redress of grievances." It is difficult to know how one might plausibly read the Fourth Amendment as other than a protection of individual rights, and it would approach the frivolous to read the assembly and petition clause as referring only to the right of state legislatures to meet and pass a remonstrance directed to Congress or the President against some governmental act. The Tenth Amendment is trickier, though it does explicitly differentiate between "states" and "the people" in terms of retained rights.[42] Concededly, it would be possible to read the Tenth Amendment as suggesting only an ultimate right of revolution by the collective people should the "states" stray too far from their designated role of protecting the rights of the people. This reading follows directly from the social contract theory of the state. (But, of course, many of these rights are held by individuals.)

Although the record is suitably complicated, it seems tendentious to reject out of hand the argument that one purpose of the Amendment was to recognize and individual's right to engage in armed self-defense against criminal conduct.[43] Historian Robert E. Shalhope supports this view, arguing in his article "The Ideological Origins of the Second Amendment"[44] that the Amendment guarantees individuals the right "to possess arms for their own personal defense."[45] It would be especially unsurprising if this were the case, given the fact that the development of a professional police force (even within large American cities) was still at least a half century away at the end of the colonial period.[46] I shall return later in this essay to this individualist notion of the Amendment, particularly in regard to the argument that "changing circumstances," including the development of a professional police force, have deprived it of any continuing plausibility. But I want now to explore a second possible purpose of the Amendment, which as a sometime political theorist I find considerably more interesting.

Assume, as Professor Cress has argued, that the Second Amendment refers to a communitarian, rather than an individual, right.[47] We are still left the task of defining the relationship between the community and the state apparatus. It is this fascinating problem to which I now turn.

Consider once more the preamble and its reference to the importance of a well-regulated militia. Is the meaning of the term obvious? Perhaps we should make some effort to find out what the term "militia" meant to eighteenth-century readers and writers, rather than assume that it refers only to Dan Quayle's Indiana National Guard and the like. By no means am I arguing that the discovery of that meaning is dispositive as to the general meaning of the Constitution for us today. But it seems foolhardy to be entirely uninterested in the historical philology behind the Second Amendment.

I, for one, have been persuaded that the term "militia" did not have the limited reference that Professor Cress and many modern legal analysts assign to it. There is strong evidence that "militia" refers to all of the people, or at least all of those treated as full citizens of the community. Consider, for example, the question asked by George Mason, one of the Virginians who refused to sign the Constitution because of its lack of a Bill of Rights: "Who are the Militia? They consist now of the whole people."[48] Similarly, the *Federal Farmer,* one of the most important Anti-Federalist opponents of the Constitution, referred to a "militia, when properly formed, [as] in fact the people themselves."[49] We have, of course, moved now from text to history. And this history is most interesting, especially when we look at the development of notions of popular sovereignty. It has become almost a cliche of contemporary American historiography to link the development of American political thought, including its constitutional aspects, to republican thought in England, the "country" critique of the powerful "court" centered in London.

One of this school's important writers, of course, was James Harrington, who not only was influential at the time but also has recently been given a certain pride of place by one of the most prominent of contemporary "neo-republicans," Professor Frank Michelman.[50] One historian describes Harrington as having made "the most significant contribution to English libertarian attitudes toward arms, the individual, and society."[51] He was a central figure in the development of the ideas of popular sovereignty and republicanism.[52] For Harrington, preservation of republican liberty requires independence, which rests primarily on possesion of adequate property to make men free from coercion by employers or landlords. But widespread ownership of land is not sufficient. These independent yeomen should also bear arms. As Professor Morgan puts it, "[T]hese independent yeomen, armed and embodied in a militia, are also a popular government's best protection against its enemies, whether they be aggressive foreign monarchs or scheming demagogues within the nation itself."[53]

A central fear of Harrington and of all future republicans was a standing army, composed of professional soldiers. Harrington and his fellow republicans viewed a standing army as a threat to freedom, to be avoided at almost all costs. Thus, says Morgan, "A militia is the only safe form of military power that a popular government can employ; and because it is composed of the armed yeomanry, it will prevail over the mercenary professionals who man the armies of neighboring monarchs."[54]

Scholars of the First Amendment have made us aware of the importance of John Trenchard and Thomas Gordon, whose *Cato's Letters* were central to the formation of the American notion of freedom of the press. That notion includes what Vincent Blasi would come to call the "checking value" of a free press, which stands as a sturdy exposer of governmental misdeeds.[55] Consider the possibility, though, that the ultimate "checking value" in a republican polity is the ability of an armed populace, presumptively motivated by a shared commitment to the common good, to resist government tyranny.[56] Indeed, one of Cato's letters refers to "the Exercise of despotick Power [as] the unrelenting war of an armed Tyrant upon his unarmed Subjects. . . ."[57]

Cress persuasively shows that no one defended universal possession of arms. New Hampshire had no objection to disarming those who "are or have been in actual rebellion," just as Smauel Adams stressed that only "peaceable citizens" should be protected in their right of "keeping their own arms."[58] All these points can be conceded, however, without conceding as well that Congress—or, for that matter, the States—had the power to disarm these "peaceable citizens."

Surely one of the foundations of American political thought of the period was the well-justified concern about political corruption and consequent governmental tyranny. Even the Federalists, fending off their opponents who accused them of foisting an oppressive new scheme upon the American people, were careful to acknowledge the risks of tyranny. James Madison, for example, speaks in *Federalist* Number Forty-Six of "the advantage of being armed, which the Americans possess over the people of almost every other nation."[59] The advantage in question was not merely the defense of American borders; a standing army might well accomplish that. Rather, an armed public was advantageous in protecting political liberty. It is therefore no surprise that the Federal Farmer, the nom de plume of an anti-federalist critic of the new Constitution and its absence of a Bill of Rights, could write that "to preserve liberty, it is essential that the whole body of the people always possess arms, and be taught alike, especially when young, how to use them. . . ."[60] On this matter, at least, there was no cleavage between the proratification Madison and his opponent.

In his influential *Commentaries on the Constitution*, Joseph Story, certainly no friend of anti-Federalism, emphasized the "importance" of the Second Amendment.[61] He went on to describe the militia as "the natural defence of a free country" not only "against sudden foreign invasions" and "domestic insurrections," with which one might well expect a Federalist to be concerned, but also against "domestic usurpations of power by rulers."[62] The right of the citizens to keep and bear arms has justly been considered," Story wrote, "as the palladium of the liberties of a republic; since it offers a strong moral check against the usurpation and arbitrary power of rulers; and will generally, even if these are successful in the first instance, enable the people to resist and triumph over them."[63]

We also see this blending of individualist and collective accounts of the right to bear arms in remarks by Judge Thomas Cooley, one of the most influential nineteenth-century constitutional commentators. Noting that the state might call into its official militia only "a small number" of the eligible citizenry, Cooley wrote that "if the right [to keep and bear arms] were lim-

ited to those enrolled, the purpose of this guaranty might be defeated altogether by the action or neglect to act of the government it was meant to
hold in check."[64] Finally, it is worth noting the remarks of Theodore Schroeder, one of the most important developers of the theory of freedom of speech
early in this century.[65] "[T]he obvious import [of the constitutional guarantee to carry arms]," he argues, "is to promote a state of preparedness for
self-defense even against the invasions of government, because only governments have ever disarmed any considerable class of people as a means toward
their enslavement."[66]

Such analyses provide the basis for Edward Abbey's revision of a common bumper sticker, "If guns are outlawed, only the government will have
guns."[67] One of the things this slogan has helped me to understand is the
political tilt contained within the Weberian definition of the state—i.e., the
repository of a monopoly of the legitimate means of violence[68]—that is so
commonly used by political scientists. It is a profoundly statist definition,
the product of a specifically German tradition of the (strong) state rather
than of a strikingly different American political tradition that is fundamentally mistrustful of state power and vigilant about maintaining ultimate power,
including the power of arms, in the populace.

We thus seek what I think is one of the most interesting points in regard
to the new historiography of the Second Amendment—its linkage to concep-
tions of republican political order. Contemporary admirers of republican theory use it as a source both of critiques of more individualist liberal theory
and of positive insight into the way we today might reorder our political
lives.[69] One point of emphasis for neo-republicans is the value of participation in government, as contrasted to mere representation by a distant leadership, even if formally elected. But the implications of republicanism might
push us in unexpected, even embarrassing, directions: just as ordinary citizens
should participate actively in governmental decision-making through offering their own deliberative insights, rather than be confined to casting ballots
once every two or four years for those very few individuals who will actually
make decisions, so should ordinary citizens participate in the process of law
enforcement and defense of liberty rather than rely on professionalized peace-
keepers, whether we call them standing armies or police.

Structure

We have also passed imperceptibly into a form of structural argument, for
we see that one aspect of the structure of checks and balances within the
purview of eighteenth-century thought was the armed citizen. That is, those
who would limit the meaning of the Second Amendment to the constitutional protection of state-controlled militias agree that such protection rests
on the perception that militarily competent states were viewed as a potential

protection against a tyrannical national government. Indeed, in 1801 several governors threatened to call out state militias if the Federalists in Congress refused to elect Thomas Jefferson president.[70] But this argument assumes that there are only two basic components in the vertical structure of the American polity—the national government and the states. It ignores the implication that might be drawn from the Second, Ninth, and Tenth Amendments: the citizenry itself can be viewed as an important third component of republican governance insofar as it stands ready to defend republican liberty against the depredations of the other two structures, however futile that might appear as a practical matter.

One implication of this republican rationale for the Second Amendment is that it calls into question the ability of a state to disarm its citizenry. That is, the strongest version of the republican argument would hold it to be a "privilege and immunity of United States citizenship"—of membership in a liberty-enhancing political order—to keep arms that could be taken up against tyranny wherever found, including, obviously, state government. Ironically, the principal citation supporting this argument is to be Chief Justice Taney's egregious opinion in *Dred Scott*,[71] where he suggested that an uncontroversial attribute of citizenship, in addition to the right to migrate from one state to another, was the right to possess arms. The logic of Taney's argument at this point seems to be that, because it was inconceivable that the Framers could have genuinely imagined blacks having the right to possess arms, it follows that they could not have envisioned them as being citizens, since citizenship entailed that right. Taney's seeming recognition of a right to arms is much relied on by opponents of gun control.[72] Indeed, recall Madison's critique, in *Federalist* Numbers Ten and Fourteen, of republicanism's traditional emphasis on the desirability of small states as preservers of republican liberty. He transformed this debate by arguing that the states would be less likely to preserve liberty because they could so easily fall under the sway of a local dominant faction, whereas an extended republic would guard against this danger. Anyone who accepts the Madisonian argument could scarcely be happy enhancing the powers of the states over their own citizens; indeed, this has been one of the great themes of American constitutional history, as the nationalization of the Bill of Rights has been deemed necessary in order to protect popular liberty against state depredation.

Doctrine

Inevitably, one must at least mention, even though there is not space to discuss fully, the so-called incorporation controversy regarding the application of the Bill of Rights to the states through the Fourteenth Amendment. It should be no surprise that the opponents of gun control appear to take a "full incorporationist" view of that Amendment.[73] They view the privileges and immunities clause, which was eviscerated in the *Slaughterhouse Cases*,[74] as designed to require the states to honor the rights that had been held, by Justice Marshal in *Barron* v. *Baltimore* in 1833,[75] to restrict only the national government. In 1875 the Court stated, in *United States* v. *Cruikshank*,[76] that the Second Amendment, insofar as it grants any right at all, "means no more than that it shall not be infringed by Congress. This is one of the amendments that has no other effect than to restrict the powers of the national government. . . . " Lest there be any remaining doubt on this point, the Court specifically cited the *Cruikshank* language eleven years later in *Presser* v. *Ilinois*,[77] in rejecting the claim that the Second Amendment served to invalidate an Illinois statute that prohibited "any body of men whatever, other than the regular organized volunteer militia of this State, and the troops of the United States . . . to drill or parade with arms in any city, or town, of this State, without the license of the Governor thereof. . . ."[78]

The first "incorporation decision," *Chicago, B. & Q. R. Co.* v. *Chicago*,[79] was not delivered until eleven years after *Presser*; one therefore cannot know if the judges in *Cruikshank* and *Presser* were willing to concede that *any* of the amendments comprising the Bill of Rights were anything more than limitations on congressional or other national power. The obvious question, given the modern legal reality of the incorporation of almost all of the rights protected by the First, Fourth, Fifth, Sixth, and Eighth Amendments, is what exactly justifies treating the Second Amendment of the great exception. Why, that is, should *Cruikshank* and *Presser* be regarded as binding precedent any more than any of the other "pre-incorporation decisions refusing to apply given aspects of the Bill of Rights against the states?

If one agrees with Professor Tribe that the Amendment is simply a federalist protection of state rights, then presumably there is nothing to incorporate.[80] If, however, one accepts the Amendment as a serious substantive limitation on the ability of the national government to regulate the private possession of arms based on either the "individualist" or "neo-republican" theories sketched above, then why not follow the "incorporationist" logic applied to other amendments and limit the states as well in their powers to regulate (and especially to prohibit) such possession? The Supreme Court has almost shamelessly refused to discuss the issue,[81] but that need not stop the rest of us.

Returning, though, to the question of Congress' power to regulate the keeping and bearing of arms, one notes that there is, basically, only one modern case that discusses the issue, *United States* v. *Miller*,[82] decided in 1939. Jack Miller was charged with moving a sawed-off shotgun in interstate commerce in violation of the National Firearms Act of 1934. Among other things, Miller and a compatriot had not registered the firearm, as required by the Act. The court below had dismissed the charge, accepting Miller's argument that the Act violated the Second Amendment.

The Supreme Court reversed unanimously, with the arch-conservative Justice McReynolds writing the opinion.[83] Interesting enough, he emphasized that there was no evidence showing that a sawed-off shotgun "at this time has some reasonable relationship to the preservation of efficiency of a well regulated militia."[84] And "[c]ertainly it is not within judicial notice that this weapon is any part of the ordinary military equipment or that its use could contribute to the common defense."[85] *Miller* might have had a tenable argument had he been able to show that he was keeping or bearing a weapon that clearly had a potential military use.[86]

Justice McReynolds went on to describe the purpose of the Second Amendment as "assur[ing] the continuation and render[ing] possible the effectiveness of [the Militia]."[87] He contrasted the Militia with troops of a standing army, which the Constitution indeed forbade the states to keep without the explicit consent of Congress. "The sentiment of the time strongly disfavored standing armies; the common view was that adequate defense of country and laws could be secured through the Militia—civilians primarily, soldiers on occasion."[88] McReynolds noted further that "the debates in the Convention, the history and legislation of Colonies and States, and the writings of approved commentators [all] [s]how plainly enough that the Militia comprised all males physically capable of acting in concert for the common defense."[89]

It is difficult to read *Miller* as rendering the Second Amendment meaningless as a control on Congress. Ironically, *Miller* can be read to support some of the most extreme anti-gun control arguments, e.g., that the individual citizen has a right to keep and bear bazookas, rocket launchers, and other armaments that are clearly relevant to modern warfare, including, of course, assault weapons. Arguments about the constitutional legitimacy of a prohibition by Congress of private ownership of handguns or, what is much more likely, assault rifles, might turn on the usefulness of such guns in military settings.

Prudentialism

We have looked at four of Bobbitt's categories—text, history, structure, and caselaw doctrine—and have seen, at the very least, that the arguments on behalf of a "strong" Second Amendment are stronger than many of us might wish were the case. This, then, brings us to the fifth category, prudentialism, or an attentiveness to practical consequences, which is clearly of great importance in any debates about gun control. The standard argument in favor of strict control and, ultimately, prohibition of private ownership focuses on the extensive social costs of widespread distribution of firearms. Consider, for example, a recent speech given by former Justice Lewis Powell to the American Bar Association. He noted that over 40,000 murders were committed in the United States in 1986 and 1987, and that fully sixty percent of them were committed with firearms. England and Wales, however, saw only 662 homicides in 1986, less than eight percent of which were committed with firearms.[90] Justice Powell indicated that, "[w]ith respect to handguns," in contrast "to sporting rifles and shotguns[,] it is not easy to understand why the Second Amendment, or the notion of liberty, should be viewed as creating a right to own and carry a weapon that contributes so directly to the shocking number of murders in our society."[91]

It is hard to disagree with Justice Powell; it appears almost crazy to protect as a constititional right something that so clearly results in extraordinary social costs with little, if any, compensating social advantage. Indeed, since Justice Powell's talk, the subject of assault rifles has become a staple of national discussion, and the opponents of regulation of such weapons have deservedly drawn the censure even of conservative leaders like William Bennett. It is almost impossible to imagine that the judiciary would strike down a determination by Congress that the possession of assault weapons should be denied to private citizens.

Even if one accepts the historical plausibility of the arguments advanced above, the overriding temptation is to say that times and circumstances have changed and that there is simply no reason to continue enforcing an outmoded, and indeed dangerous, understanding of private rights against public order. This criticism is clearest in regard to the so-called individualist argument, for one can argue that the rise of a professional police force to enforce the law has made irrelevant, and perhaps even counterproductive, the continuation of a strong notion of self-help as the remedy for crime.[92]

I am not unsympathetic to such arguments. It is no purpose of this essay to solicit membership for the National Rifle Association or to express any sympathy for what even Don Kates, a strong critic of the conventional dismissal of the Second Amendment, describes as "the gun lobby's obnoxious habit of assailing all forms of regulation on 2nd Amendment grounds."[98] And yet . . . .

Circumstances may well have changed in regard to individual defense, although we ignore at our political peril the good-faith belief of many Americans that they cannot rely on the police for protection against a variety of criminals. Still, let us assume that the individualist reading of the Amendment has been vitiated by changing circumstances. Are we quite so confident that circumstances are equally different in regard to the republican rationale outlined earlier?

One would, of course, like to believe that the state, whether at the local or national level, presents no threat to important political values, including liberty. But our propensity to believe that this is the case may be little more than a sign of how truly different we are from our radical forbearers. I do not want to argue that the state is necessarily tyrannical; I am not an anarchist. But it seems foolhardy to assume that the armed state will necessarily be benevolent. The American political tradition is, for good or ill, based in large measure on a healthy mistrust of the state. The development of widespread suffrage and greater majoritarianism in our polity is itself no sure protection, at least within republican theory. The republican theory is predicated on the stark contrast between mere democracy, where people are motivated by selfish personal interest, and a republic, where civic virtue, both in citizens and leadership, tames selfishness on behalf of the common good. In any event, it is hard for me to see how one can argue that circumstances have so changed as to make mass disarmament constitutionally unproblematic.[94]

Indeed, only in recent months have we seen the brutal suppression of the Chinese student demonstrations in Tianamen Square. It should not surprise us that some NRA sympathizers have presented that situation as an object lesson to those who unthinkingly support the prohibition of private gun ownership. "[I]f all Chinese citizens kept arms, their rulers would hardly have dared to massacre the demonstrators. . . . The private keeping of hand-held personal firearms is within the constitutional design for a counter to government run amok. . . . As the Tianamen Square tragedy showed so graphically, AK-47s fall into that category of weapons, and that is why they are protected by the Second Amendment."[95] It is simply silly to respond that small arms are irrelevant against nuclear-armed states: Witness contemporary Northern Ireland and the territories occupied by Israel, where the sophisticated weaponry of Great Britain and Israel have proved almost totally beside the point. The fact that these may not be pleasant examples does not affect the principal point, that a state facing a totally disarmed population is in a far better position, for good or for ill, to suppress popular demonstrations and uprisings than one that must calculate the possibilities of its soldiers and officials being injured or killed.[96]

TAKING THE SECOND AMENDMENT SERIOUSLY

There is one further problem of no small import: If one does accept the plausibility of any of the arguments on behalf of a strong reading of the Second Amendment, but, nevertheless, rejects them in the name of social prudence and the present-day consequences produced by finicky adherence to early understandings, why do we not apply such consequentialist criteria to each and every part of the Bill of Rights?[97] As Ronald Dworkin has argued, what it means to take rights seriously is that one will honor them even when there is significant social cost in doing so. If protecting freedom of speech, the rights of criminal defendants, or any other part of the Bill of Rights were always (or even most of the time) clearly costless to the society as a whole, it would truly be impossible to understand why they would be as controversial as they are. The very fact that there are often significant costs—criminals going free, oppressed groups having to hear viciously racist speech and so on—helps to account for the observed fact that those who view themselves as defenders of the Bill of Rights are generally antagonistic to prudential arguments. Most often, one finds them embracing versions of textual, historical, or doctrinal argument that dimiss as almost crass and vulgar any insistence that times might have changed and made too "expensive" the continued adherence to a given view. "Cost-benefit" analysis, rightly or wrongly, has come to be viewed as a "conservative" weapon to attack liberal rights.[98] Yet one finds that the tables are strikingly turned when the Second Amendment comes into play. Here it is "conservatives" who argue in effect that social costs are irrelevant and "liberals" who argue for a notion of the "Living Constitution" and "changed circumstances" that would have the practical consequence of removing any real bite from the Second Amendment.

As Fred Donaldson of Austin, Texas, wrote, commenting on those who defended the Supreme Court's decision upholding flag-burning as compelled by a proper (and decidedly non-prudential) understanding of the First Amendment, "[I]t seems inconsistent for [defenders of the decision] to scream so loudly" at the prospect of limiting the protection given expression "while you smile complacently at the Second torn and bleeding. If the Second Amendment is not worth the paper it is written on, what price the First?"[99] The fact that Mr. Donaldson is an ordinary citizen rather than an eminent law professor does not make his question any less pointed or its answer less difficult.

For too long, most members of the legal academy have treated the Second Amendment as the equivalent of an embarrassing relative, whose mention brings a quick change of subject to other, more respectable family members. That will no longer do. It is time for the Second Amendment to enter full scale into the consciousness of the legal academy. Those of us who agree with Martha Minow's emphasis on the desirability of encouraging different "voices" in the legal conversation[100] should be especially aware of the importance of recognizing the attempts of Mr. Donaldson and his millions of colleagues to join the conversation. To be sure, it is unlikely that Professor Minow had those too often peremptorily dismissed as "gun nuts" in mind as possible providers of "insight and growth," but surely the call for sensitivity to different or excluded voices cannot extend only to those groups "we" already, perhaps "complacent[ly]," believe have a lot to tell "us."[101] I am not so naïve as to believe that conversation will overcome the chasm that now separates the sensibility of, say, Senator Hatch and myself as to what constitutes the "right[s] most valued by free men [and women]."[102] It is important to remember that one will still need to join up sides and engage in vigorous political struggle. But it might at least help to make the political sides appear more human to one another. Perhaps "we" might be led to stop referring casually to "gun nuts" just as, maybe, members of the NRA could be brought to understand the real fear that the currently almost uncontrolled system of gun ownership sparks in the minds of many whom they casually dismiss as "bleeding-heart liberals." Is not, after all, the possibility of serious, engaged discussion about political issues at the heart of what is most attractive in both liberal *and* republican versions of politics?

NOTES

1. It is not irrelevant that the Bill of Rights submitted to the states in 1789 included not only what are now the first ten Amendments, but also two others. Indeed, what we call the First Amendment was only the third one of the list submitted to the states. The initial "first amendment" in fact concerned the future size of the House of Representatives, a topic of no small importance to the Anti-Federalists, who were appalled by the smallness of the House seemingly envisioned by the Philadelphia framers. The second prohibited any pay raise voted by members of Congress to themselves from taking effect until an election "shall have intervened." See J. Goebel, *The Oliver Wendell Holmes Devise History of the Supreme Court of the United States: Antecedents and Beginnings to 1801* (1971), 1:442, n. 162. Had all of the initial twelve proposals been ratified, we would, it is possible, have a dramatically different cognitive map of the Bill of Rights. At the very least, one would neither hear defenses of the "preferred" status of freedom of speech framed in terms of the "firstness" of (what we know as) the First Amendment, nor the wholly invalid inference drawn from that "firstness" of some special intention of the Framers to safeguard the particular rights laid out there.

2. "Congress shall make no law respecting an establishment of religion . . . or abridging the freedom of speech, or of the press; or the right of the people peaceably to assemble, and to petition the Government for a redress of grievances." U.S. Const. amend. I.

3. "The right of the people to be secure in their persons, houses, papers, and effects, against unreasonable searches and seizures, shall not be violated; and no Warrants shall issue but upon probable cause, supported by Oath or affirmation, and particularly describing the place to be searched, and the person or things to be seized." U.S. Const. amend. IV.

4. "No person shall be held to answer for a capital, or otherwise infamous crime, unless on a presentment of indictment of a Grand Jury, except in cases arising in the land or naval forces, or in the Militia, when in actual service in time of War or public danger; nor shall any person be subject for the same offence to be twice put in jeopardy of life or limb; nor shall be compelled in any criminal case to be a witness against himself, or be deprived of life, liberty, or property, without due proces of law . . . ." U.S. Const. amend. V.

5. "In all criminal prosecutions, the accused shall enjoy the right to a speedy and public trial, by an impartial jury of the State and district wherein the crime shall have been committed, which district shall have been previously ascertained by law, and to be informed of the nature and cause of the accusation; to be confronted with the witnesses against him; to have compulsory process for obtaining witnesses in his favor, and to have the Assistance of Counsel for his defense." U.S. Const. amend. VI.

6. "Excessive bail shall not be required, nor excessive fines imposed, or cruel and unusual punishment inflicted." U.S. Const. amend. VIII.

7. "The enumeration in the Constitution, of certain rights, shall not be construed to deny or disparage others retained by the people." U.S. Const. amend. IX.

8. "[N]or shall private property be taken for public use, without just compensation." U.S. Const. amend. IV.

9. "The powers not delegated to the United States by the Constitution, nor prohibited by it to the States, are reserved to the States respectively, or to the people." U.S. Const. amend. X.

10. "Congress shall make no law . . . prohibiting the free exercise thereof [religion]. . . ." U.S. Const. amend. I.

11. See *supra* note 8.

12. See *supra* note 9.

13. There are several law review articles discussing the Amendment. See, e.g., Nelson Lund, "The Second Amendment, Political Liberty, and the Right to Self-Preservation," *Alabama Law Review* 103 (1987) (see note 7), and the articles cited in Dowlut and Knoop, "State Constitutions and the Right to Keep and Bear Arms," *Oklahoma City University Law Review* 7 (1982): 177, 178, n. 3. See also the valuable symposium on Gun Control, edited by Don Kates, in *Law & Contemporary Problems* 49 (1986): 1–267, including articles by Shalhope, "The Armed Citizen in the Early Republic," p. 125; Kates, "The Second Amendment: A Dialogue," p. 143; Halbrook, "What the Framers Intended: A Linguistic Analysis of the Right to "Bear Arms," p. 151. The symposium also includes a valuable bibliography of published materials on gun control, including Second Amendment considerations, pp. 251–67. The most important single article is almost undoubtedly Kates, "Handgun Prohibition and the Original Meaning of the Second Amendment," *Michigan*

Law Review 82 (1983):204. Not the least significant aspect of Kates's article is that it is basically the only one to have appeared in an "elite" law review. However, like many of the authors of other Second Amendment pieces, Kates is a practicing lawyer rather than a legal academic. I think it is accurate to say that no one recognized by the legal academy as a "major" writer on constitutional law has deigned to turn his or her talents to a full consideration of the Amendment. But see Larue, "Constitutional Law and Constitutional History," *Buffalo Law Review* 36(1988): 373, 375-78, briefly discussing Second Amendment). Akhil Reed Amar's reconsideration of the foundations of the Constitution also promises to delve more deeply into the implications of the Amendment. See Amar, "Of Sovereignty and Federalism," *Yale Law Journal* 96(1987):1425, 1495-1500. Finally, there is one book that provides more in-depth treatment of the Second Amendment: S. Halbrook, *That Every Man Be Armed, the Evolution of a Constitutional Right* (Albuquerque: University of New Mexico Press, 1984).

George Fletcher, in his study of the Bernhard Goetz case, also suggests that Second Amendment analysis is not frivolous, though he does not elaborate the point. G. Fletcher, *A Crime of Self-Defense* (New York: Free Press, 1988), pp. 156-58, 210-11.

One might well find this overt reference to "elite" law reviews and "major" writers objectionable, but it is foolish to believe that these distinctions do not exist within the academy or, more importantly, that we cannot learn about the sociology of academic discourse through taking them into account. No one can plausibly believe that the debates that define particular periods of academic discourse are a simple reflection of "natural" interest in the topic. Nothing helps an issue so much as its being taken up as an obsession by a distinguished professor from, say, Harvard or Yale.

14. One will search the "leading" casebooks in vain for any mention of the Second Amendment. Other than its being included in the text of the Constitution that all of the casebooks reprint, a reader would have no reason to believe that the Amendment exists or could possibly be of interest to the constitutional analyst. I must include, alas, P. Brest and S. Levinson, *Processes of Constitutional Decisionmaking*, 2d ed. (Boston, Mass.: Little, Brown & Co., 1983), within this critique, though I have every reason to believe that this will not be true of the forthcoming third edition.

15. Larue, *supra* note 13, p. 375.

16. L. Tribe, *American Constitutional Law*, 2d ed. (1988).

17. J. Nowak, R. Rotunda, and J. Young, *Constitutional Law*, 3d ed. (1986).

18. For a brilliant and playful meditation on the way the legal world treats footnotes and other marginal phenomena, see Balking, "The Footnote," *Northwestern University Law Review* 83(1989):275, 276-81.

19. Tribe, *supra* note 16, p. 299, n. 6.

20. Ibid.; see also J. Ely, *Democracy and Distrust: A Theory of Judicial Review* (Cambridge, Mass.: Harvard University Press, 1980) ("[T]he framers and ratifiers . . . opted against leaving to the future the attribution of [other] purposes, choosing instead explicitly to legislate the goal in terms of which the provision was to be interpreted."). As shall be seen below, see *infra* text accompanying note 38, the preamble may be less plain in meaning than Tribe's (and Ely's) confident argument suggests.

21. J. Nowak, R. Rotunda, and J. Young, *supra* note 17, p. 316, n. 4. They do go on to cite a spate of articles by scholars who have debated the issue.

22. Ibid.

23. U.S. Const. art. I, § 10.

24. U.S. Const. art. I, § 9, cl. 8.

25. See, e.g., Legislative Reference Serv., Library of Congress, *The Constitution of the United States of America: Analysis and Interpretation* (1964), p. 923, which quotes the Amendment and then a comment from Miller, *The Constitution* (1893), p. 646: "This amendment seems to have been thought necessary. It does not appear to have been the subject of judicial exposition; and it is so thoroughly in accord with our ideas, that further comment is unnecessary." Cf. *Engblom* v. *Carey*, 724 F.2d 28 (2d Cir. 1983), *aff'g* 572 F. Supp. 44 (S.D.N.Y. 1983). *Engblom* grew out of a "statewide strike of correction officers, when they were evicted from their facility-residences . . . and members of the National Guard were housed in their residences without their consent." The district court had initially granted summary judgment for the defendants in a suit brought by the officers claiming a deprivation of their rights under the Third Amendment. The Second Circuit, however, reversed on the ground that it could not "say that as a matter of law appellants were not entitled to the protection of the Third Amendment." *Engblom* v. *Carey*, 677 F.2d 957, 964 (2d Cir. 1982). The District Court on remand held that, as the Third Amendment Rights had not been clearly established at the time of the strike, the defendants were protected by a qualified immunity, and it is this opinion that was upheld by the Second Circuit. I am grateful to Mark Tushnet for bringing this case to my attention.

26. See, e.g., "The Firearms the Second Amendment Protects," *New York Times,* June 9, 1988, p. A22, col. 3 (three letters); "Second Amendment and Gun Control," *Los Angeles Times,* March 11, 1989, Part II, p. 9, col. 1 (nine letters); "What 'Right to Bear Arms'?" *New York Times,* July 20, 1989, p. A23, col. 1 (national ed.) (op. ed. essay by Daniel Abrams); see also "We Rebelled To Protect Our Gun Rights," *Washington Times,* July 20, 1989, p. F2, col. 4.

27. See Subcommittee on the Constitution of the Comm. of the Judiciary, *The Right to Keep and Bear Arms*, 97th Cong., 2d Sess. viii (1982) (preface by Senator Orrin Hatch) [hereinafter *The Right to Keep and Bear Arms*].

28. Ibid., notes 13–14.

29. See Levinson, "Constitutional Rhetoric and the Ninth Amendment," *Chicago-Kent Law Review* 64 (1988): 131.

30. P. Bobbitt, *Constitutional Fate* (1982).

31. Ibid., pp. 25–38.

32. Ibid., pp. 9–24.

33. Ibid., pp. 74–92.

34. Ibid., pp. 39–58.

35. Ibid., pp. 59–73.

36. Ibid., pp. 93–119.

37. For the record, I should note that Bobbitt disagrees with this statement, making an eloquent appeal (in conversation) on behalf of the classic American value of self-reliance for the defense of oneself and, perhaps more importantly, one's family. I certainly do not doubt the possibility of constructing an "ethical" rationale for timing the state's power to prohibit private gun ownership. Nevertheless, I would claim that no one unpersuaded by any of the arguments derived from the first five modes would suddenly change his or her mind upon being presented with an "ethical" argument.

38. Cf., e.g., the patents and copyrights clause, which sets out the power of Congress "[t]o promote the Progress of Science and useful Arts, by securing for limited Times to Authors and Inventors the exclusive Right in their respective Writings and Discoverise." U.S. Const. art. 1., § 8.

39. For examples of this, see F. Schauer, *Freedom of Speech: A Philosophical Enquiry* (1982); Levinson, "First Amendment, Freedom of Speech, Freedom of Expression: Does It Matter What We Call It?" *Northwestern University Law Review* 80(1985):767 (reviewing M. Redish, *Freedom of Expression: A Critical Analysis* [Charlottesville, Va.: Michie Co., 1984]).

40. ACLU Policy #47. I am grateful to Joan Mahoney, a member of the national board of the ACLU, for providing me with a text of the ACLU's current policy on gun control.

41. Cress, "An Armed Community: The Origins and Meaning of the Right to Bear Arms," *Journal of American History* 71(1984):22, 31.

42. *See* U.S. Const. amend. X.

43. For a full articulation of the individualist view of the Second Amendment, see Kates, "Handgun Prohibition and the Original Meaning of the Second Amendment," *Michigan Law Review* 82(1983):204. One can also find an efficient presentation of this view in Lund, *supra*, p. 117.

44. Shalhope, "The Ideological Origins of the Second Amendment," *Journal of American History* 69(1982):599.

45. Ibid., 614.

46. See Daniel Boorstein's laconic comment that "the requirements for self-defense and food-gathering had put firearms in the hands of nearly everyone," "Colonial America," in D. Boorstein, *The Americans— The Colonial Experience* (1958), p. 353. The beginnings of a professional police force in Boston are traced in R. Lane, *Policing The City: Boston 1822–1855* (1967). Lane argues that as of the earlier of his two dates, "all the major eastern cities . . . had several kinds of officials serving various police functions, all of them haphazardly inherited from the British and colonial past. These agents were gradually drawn into better defined and more coherent organizations." (p. 1). However, as Oscar Handlin points out in his introduction to the book, "to bring into being a professional police force was to create precisely the kind of hireling body considered dangerous by conventional political theory (p. vii).

47. See Cress, *supra* note 1.

48. J. Elliot, *Debates in the General State Conventions*, 3d ed. (1937), p. 3 (statement of George Mason, June 14, 1788), reprinted in Kates, *supra* note 13, p. 216, n. 51.

49. *Letters from the Federal Farmer to the Republican*, ed. W. Bennett (University of Alabama Press, 1978), p. 123 (ascribed to Richard Henry Lee), reprinted in Kates, *supra* note 13, p. 216, n. 51.

50. Michelman, "The Supreme Court 1985 Term—Foreword: Traces of Self-Government," *Harvard Law Review* 100(1986):4,39 (Harrington is "pivotal figure in the history of the 'Atlantic' branch of republicanism that would find its way to America").

51. Shalhope, *supra* note 44, p. 602.

52. Edmund Morgan discusses Harrington in his recent book, *Inventing the People* (New York: Norton, 1989), pp. 85–87.

53. Ibid., p. 156.

54. Ibid., p. 157. Morgan argues, incidentally, that the armed yeomanry was neither effective as a fighting force nor particularly protective of popular liberty, but that is another matter. For our purposes, the ideological perceptions are surely more important than the "reality" accompanying them (pp. 160–65).

55. Blasi, "The Checking Value in First Amendment Theory," *American B. Foundation Research Journal* (1977):521.

56. See Lund, *supra*, pp. 111-16.

57. Shalhope, *supra*, p. 603, note 44 (quoting 1755 edition of *Cato's Letters*).

Shalhope also quotes from James Burgh, another English writer well known to American revolutionaries:

> The possession of arms is the distinction between a freeman and a slave. He, who has nothing, and who himself belongs to another, must be defended by him, whose property he is, and needs no arms. But he, who thinks he is his own master, and has what he can call his own, ought to have arms to defend himself, and what he possesses; else he lives precariously, and at discretion (p. 604).

To be sure, Burgh also wrote that only men of property should in fact comprise the militia: "A militia consisting of any others than the men of *property* in a country, is no militia; but a mungrel army." Cress, *supra*, p. 27, note 41 (emphasis in original) (quoting J. Burgh, *Political Disquisitions: or, An Enquiry into Public Errors, Defects, and Abuses* (1774-75), p. 2. Presumably, though, the widespread distribution of property would bring with it equally widespread access to arms and membership in the militia.

58. *See* Cress, *supra*, p. 34, note 41.

59. *The Federalist* No. 46, at 299 (J. Madison) (C. Rossiter ed. 1961).

60. *Letters From the Federal Farmer to the Republican* 124 (W. Bennett ed., 1978).

61. J. Story, "Commentaries" § 1890 (1833), p.3, quoted in *The Founders' Constitution*, ed. P. Kurland and R. Lerner (Chicago, Ill.: University of Chicago Press, 1987), p. 214.

62. Ibid.

63. Ibid. Lawrence Cress, despite his forceful critique of Shalhope's individualist rendering of the Second Amendment, nonetheless himself notes that "[t]he danger posed by manipulating demagogues, *ambitious rulers*, and foreign invaders to free institutions required the vigilance of citizen-soldiers cognizant of the common good." Cress, *supra*, p. 41, note 41 (emphasis added).

64. T. Cooley, *The General Principles of Constitutional Law in the United States of America*, 3d ed., (1898), p. 298.

> The right of the people to bear arms in their own defence, and to form and drill military organizations in defence of the State, may not be very important in this country, but it is significant as having been reserved by the people as a possible and necessary resort for the protection of self-government against usurpation, and against any attempt on the part of those who may for the time be in possession of State authority or resources to set aside the constitution and substitute their own rule for that of the people. Should the contingency ever arise when it would be necessary for the people to make use of the arms in their hands for the protection of constitutional liberty, the proceeding, so far from being revolutionary, would be in strict accord with popular right and duty.

Cooley advanced this same idea in "The Abnegation of Self-Government," *Princeton Review* 12(1883):213-14.

65. See Rabban, "The First Amendment in Its Forgotten Years," *Yale Law Journal* 90 (1981):514,560. ("Prodigious theoretical writings of Theodore Schroeder . . . were the most extensive and libertarian treatments of freedom of speech in the prewar period"), see also Graeber, "Transforming Free Speech" (manuscript at 4-12; on file with author).

66. T. Schroeder, *Free Speech For Radicals* (1916; reprint 1969). p. 104.

67. Shalhope, *supra*, p. 45, note 44.

68. See M. Weber,. *The Theory of Social and Economic Organization*, ed. T. Parsons (New York: Free Press 1947), p. 156, where he lists among "[t]he primary formal characteristics of the modern state" the fact that:

> to-day, the use of force is regarded as legitimate only so far as it is either permitted by the state or prescribed by it . . . . The claim of the modern state to monopolize the use of force is as essenteial to it as its character of compulsory jurisdiction and of continuous organization.

69. See, e.g., "Symposium: The Republican Civil Tradition," *Yale Law Journal* 97(1988):1493-1723.

70. See D. Malone, *Jefferson and His Times: Jefferson the President, First Term, 1801-1805* (1970), p. 4 (republican leaders ready to use state militias to resist should lame duck Congress attempt to violate clear dictates of Article II by designating someone other than Thomas Jefferson as President in 1801).

71. *Scott* v. *Sanford*, 60 U.S. (19 How.) 393, 417 (1857).

72. See, e.g., Featherstone, Gardiner, and Dowlut, "The Second Amendment to the United States Constitution Guarantees an Individual Right to Keep and Bear Arms," in *The Right to Keep and Bear Arms, supra*, p. 100, note 27.

73. See, e.g., Halbrook, "The Fourteenth Amendment and the Right to Keep and Bear Arms: The Intent of the Framers," in *The Right to Keep and Bear Arms, supra* note 27, p. 79. Not the least of the ironies observed in the debate about the Second Amendment is that NRA-oriented conservatives like

Senator Hatch could scarcely have been happy with the wholesale attack leveled by former Attorney General Meese on the incorporation doctrine, for here is one area where some "conservatives" may in fact be more zealous adherents of that doctrine than are most liberals, who, at least where the Second Amendment is concerned, have a considerably more selective view of incorporation.

74. 83 U.S. 36 (1873).

75. 32 U.S. (7 Pet.) 243 (1833).

76. 92 U.S. 542, 553 (1875).

77. 116 U.S. 252, 267 (1886). For a fascinating discussion of *Presser*, see Larue, *supra* pp. 386–90, note 13.

78. U.S. at 253. There is good reason to believe this statute, passed by the Illinois legislature in 1879, was part of an effort to control (and, indeed, suppress) widespread labor unrest linked to the economic troubles of the time. For the background of the Illinois statute, see P. Avrich, *The Haymarket Tragedy* (Princeton, N.J.: Princeton University Press, 1984), p. 45:

> As early as 1875, a small group of Chicago socialists, most of them German immigrants, had formed an armed club to protect the workers against police and military assaults, as well as against physical intimidation at the polls. In the eyes of its supporters . . . the need for such a group was amply demonstrated by the behavior of the police and [state-controlled] militia during the Great Strike of 1877, a national protest by labor triggered by a ten percent cut in wages by the Baltimore and Ohio Railroad, which included the breaking up of workers' meetings, [and] the use of club, pistol, and bayonet against strikers and their supporters . . . . Workers . . . were resolved never again to be shot and beaten without resistance. Nor would they stand idly by while their meeting places were invaded or their wives and children assaulted. They were determined, as Albert Parsons [a leader of the anarchist movement in Chicago] expressed it, to defend both "their persons and their rights."

79. 166 U.S. 226 (1897) (protecting rights of property owners by requiring compensation for takings of property).

80. My colleague Douglas Laycock has reminded me that a similar argument was made by some conservatives in regard to the establishment clause of the First Amendment. Thus, Justice Brennan noted that "[i]t has been suggested, with some support in history, that absorption of the First Amendment's ban against congressional legislation 'respecting an establishment of religion' is conceptually impossible because the Framers meant the Establishment Clause also to foreclose any attempt by Congress to *disestablish* the existing official state churches." *Abington School Dist.* v. *Schempp*, 374 U.S. 203, 254 (1963) (Brennan, J., concurring) (emphasis added). According to this reading, it would be illogical to apply the establishment clause against the states "because that clause is not one of the provisions of the Bill of Rights which in terms protects a 'freedom' of the individual" (p. 256), inasmuch as it is only a federalist protection of states against a national establishment (or disestablishment). "The fallacy in this contention," responds Brennan, "is that it underestimates the role of the Establishment Clause as a co-guarantor, with the Free Exercise Clause, of religious liberty" (p. 256). Whatever the sometimes bitter debates about the precise meaning of "establishment," it is surely the case that Justice Brennan, even as he almost cheerfully concedes that at one point in our history the "states-right" reading of the establishment clause would have been thoroughly plausible, expresses what has become the generally accepted view as to the establishment clause being some kind of limitation on the state as well as on the national government. One may wonder whether the interpretive history of the establishment clause might have any lessons for the interpretation of the Second Amendment.

81. It refused, for example, to review the most important modern gun control case, *Quilici* v. *Village of Morton Grove*, 695 F.2d 261 (7th Cir. 1982), *cert. denied*, 464 U.S. 863 (1983), where the Seventh Circuit Court of Appeals upheld a local ordinance in Morton Grove, Illinois, prohibiting the possession of handguns within its borders.

82. 307 U.S. 174 (1939).

83. Justice Douglas, however, did not participate in the case.

84. *Miller*, 37 U.S., p. 178.

85. Ibid., p. 1788 (citation omitted).

86. Lund notes that "commentators have since demonstrated that sawed-off or short-barreled shotguns are commonly used as military weapons." Lund, *supra*, p. 109.

87. 307 U.S., p. 178.

88. Ibid., p. 179.

89. Ibid.

90. L. Powell, "Capital Punishment," Remarks Delivered to the Criminal Justice Section, ABA 10 (August 7, 1988).

91. Ibid., p. 11.

92. This point is presumably demonstrated by the increasing public opposition of police officials to private possession of handguns (not to mention assault rifles).

93. D. Kates, "Minimalist Interpretation of the Second Amendment" (draft September 29, 1986) (unpublished manuscript available from author), p. 2.

94. *See* Lund, *supra,* p. 116.

95. Wimmershoff-Caplan, "The Founders and the AK-47," *Washington Post,* July 6, 1989, p. A18, col. 4, reprinted as "Price of Gun Deaths Small Compared to Price of Liberty," *Austin American-Statesman,* July 11, 1989, p. A11. Ms. Wimmershoff-Caplan is identified as a "lawyer in New York" who is "a member of the National Board of the National Rifle Association." One of the first such arguments in regard to the events at Tianamen Square was made by William A. Black in a letter, "Citizens Without Guns," *New York Times,* June 18, 1989, p. D26, col. 6. Though describing himself as "find[ing] no glory in guns [and] a very profound anti-hunter," he nonetheless "stand[s]" with those who would protect our right to keep and bear arms" and cited for support the fact that "none [of the Chinese soldiers] feared bullets: the citizens of China were long ago disarmed by the Communists." "Who knows," he asks, "what the leaders and the military and the police of our America will be up to at some point in the future? We need an armed citizenry to protect our liberty."

As one might expect, such arguments draw heated responses. See Rudlin, "The Founders and the AK-47 (Cont'd)," *Washington Post,* July 20, 1989, p. A22, col 3. Jonathan Rudlin accused Ms. Wimmershoff-Caplan of engaging in Swiftian satire, as no one could "take such brilliant burlesque seriously." Neal Knox, however, endorsed her essay in full, adding the Holocaust to the list of examples: "Could the Holocaust have occurred if Europe's Jews had owned thousands of then-modern military Mauser bolt action rifles?" See also *Washington Post,* July 12, 1989, p. A22, for other letters.

96. See Lund, *supra,* p. 115:

> The decision to use military force is not determined solely by whether the contemplated benefits can be successfully obtained through the use of available forces, but rather is determined by the *ratio* of those benefits to the expected costs. It follows that any factor increasing the anticipated cost of a military operation makes the conduct of that operation incrementally more unlikely. This explains why a relatively poorly armed nation with a small population recently prevailed in a war against the United States, and it explains why governments bent on the oppression of their people almost always disarm the civilian population before undertaking more drastically oppressive measures.

97. *See* D. Kates, *supra* note 93, p. 24–25, for a discussion of this point.

98. See, e.g., Justice Marshall's dissent, joined by Justice Brennan, in *Skinner* v. *Railway Labor Executive Ass'n.,* 109 S. Ct. 1402 (1989), upholding the government's right to require drug tests of railroad employees following accidents. It begins with his chastising the majority for "ignor[ing] the text and doctrinal history of the Fourth Amendment, which require that highly intrusive searches of this type be based on probable cause, not on the evanescent cost-benefit calculations of agencies or judges," p. 1423, and continues by arguing that "[t]he majority's concern with the railroad safety problems caused by drug and alcohol abuse is laudable; its cavalier disregard for the Constitution is not. There is no drug exception to the Constitution, any more than there is a communism exception or an exception for other real or imagined sources of domestic unrest" (p. 1426).

99. Donaldson, Letter to the Editor, *Austin American-Statesman,* July 8, 1989, p. A19, col. 4.

100. *See* Minow, "The Supreme Court 1986 Term—Foreword: Justice Engendered," *Harvard Law Reveiw* 101(1987):10, 74–90. "We need settings in which to engage in the clash of realities that breaks us out of settled and complacent meanings and creates opportunities for insight and growth," ibid., p. 95; see also Getman, "Voices," *Texas Law Review* 66(1988):577.

101. And, perhaps, more to the point, "you" who insufficiently listen to "us" and to "our" favored groups.

102. See *supra* note 27 and accompanying text.

24

Guns, Cowboys, Philadelphia Mayors, and Civic Republicanism:
On Sanford Levinson's
The Embarrassing Second Amendment

Wendy Brown

Sanford Levinson's reading of the Second Amendment deftly parlays a strategy of historical interpretation into an opening move in a much needed contemporary political conversation about guns, individual rights, popular sovereignty, and state power.[1] This reading suggests an intriguing recovery of the Amendment's origins in republican antistatism and, in the same gesture, potentially retrieves the political value of the Amendment for those who ordinarily have little in common with its stickiest adherents. Historically situated in the republican concern with popular power, the Second Amendment might be less the individualistic cudgel of National Rifle Association sloganeering than a token and vehicle of collective civic resistance against the domestic imperialism of centralized state power.

However compelling and disturbing several aspects of Levinson's provoc-

Reprinted by permission of the Yale Law Journal Company and Fred B. Rothman & Company from *The Yale Law Journal* 99 (December 1989): 661–67.

ative argument may be, I think it is ultimately less republican than it wants to be; I think the republicanism it does harbor is of questionable value; and I think the republican subject, if he exists, is definitely a "he." In what follows, I will suggest that both the republican subject and polity invoked in Levinson's interpretation are, at best, appealing historical figures, of little relevance to our socially fragmented and politically integrated mass culture, to our bureaucratized, centralized, and nuclear-armed state, or to the relationship between them.

REPUBLICAN POLITY OR LIBERAL STATE?

The republican argument for arming the citizenry is most powerfully elaborated not by the English thinkers Levinson cites, but in that passionate republican work, Machiavelli's *Discourses on the First Decade of Titus-Livius*.[2] In Machiavelli's account, terrible ills arise from disarming the people to escape an imagined rather than real, danger instead of doing things that would give them security.[3] His beseeching tone and romantic prose almost make one forget that he is talking about deadly weapons:

> The heart and the vital parts of a body should be kept armored, and not the extremities. For without the latter it lives, but when the former is injured, it dies; and these states keep their hearts unarmored and their hands and feet armored. What this error has done to Florence has been seen and is seen every day; land when an army passes her boundaries and comes within them close to her heart, she has no further resource.[4]

What is so compelling in this account is the way Machiavelli links a state's security with the strength and independence of its citizenry. His bodily metaphor suggests a literal weakening of state power when armed citizens do not comprise the heart of the state; when state force is rooted in something other than an empowered citizenry; when state power is without "foundations" in the people; and when the policy is without civic *virtù*. In fact, Machiavelli is not talking simply about arms, but about the aggregate health of the republican polity. He recognizes that a vigorous, independent citizenry is not at odds with state power but, to the contrary, represents an indispensable resource of political flexibility, defense, and renewal. Drawing the connection between freedom and power, both individual and collective, in a manner rivaled only by Marx, Machiavelli is a marvelous antidote to our neo-Hobbesian beliefs that those practices are antinomic.

The problem with Levinson's employment of this feature of republican thought to interpret the Second Amendment is that it is not clear how much it has to do with either our Constitution or our present condition. Consider the confusion Levinson identifies in the text of the Amendment—a confusion sympotomatic of the recessive position of republicanism in the constitutional formulation of the United States as a liberal polity.[5] The preambled Second Amendment is ambiguous about whether it grants citizens the right to bear arms for protection of the state,[6] *against* the state,[7] or *against one another.*[8] Levinson calls "republican" an argument that our right to bear arms is protection against the state's potentially excessive use of its prerogative, but this argument does not really express a republican sensibility. Rather, it signifies a liberal overtaking of such sensibilities. Machiavelli's republican citizenry is not armed against the state but *as* the state—an armed citizenry in the state's heart, not its opposition or counterweight. Levinson's view of the Second Amendment as citizen protection against the state assumes a cleavage if not a hostile antagonism between state and society: "Consider the possibility . . . that the ultimate "checking value" in a republican polity is the ability of an armed populace, presumptively motivated by a shared commitment to the common good, to resist governmental tyranny."[9] In contrast to Machiavellian republicanism, Levinson's formulation is really a militarized version of Locke's "appeal to heaven"[10] and a far cry from armoring the heart of a polity. This is not republicanism but a kind of bastardized liberalism, in which a diffident and depoliticized populace squares off against the state, in which there is no political heart at all but only hands and head and feet all armed against one another.

REPUBLICAN CITIZENS OR LIBERAL INDIVIDUALS?

We may pose two sets of questions about the place held by the republican subject in Levinson's argument. First, upon what kind of political subject is republicanism premised, and what kind do we have today? What does it mean to make appeals to a republican political order when we do not have one, when our citizenry is not republican in character, values, or practices? The republican link between arms, freedom, and civic virtue (and *virtù*) depends upon the existence of responsible, active, public-minded citizens bound together in at least a modicum of civic solidarity. Machiavelli's passionate plea is not on behalf of the liberal individual—acquisitive, privatistic, concerned with hunting quail, protecting his property, or defending rights to his woman—but the republican citizen oriented toward civic, public life. And arming our citizenry, or defending our individual right to bear arms, will hardly transform us into such citizens. While Levinson's armed populace is "presumably motivated by a shared commitment to the common good,"[11] I cannot imagine a less appropriate appellation for the contemporary American citizenry, which bears a shared commitment to almost nothing, least of a common good. Ensuring the individual right to bear arms surely will not infuse the citizenry with such commitment.

The second set of questions Levinson's argument raises about the republican subject pertains to freedom. What kind of freedom does this subject claim: What kind of freedom is republican freedom? At the very least we might investigate, although Levinson does not, the classical republican links between force and freedom, arms and freedom, violence and freedom. Might there be something a bit "gendered" about a formulation of freedom that depicts man, collectively or individually, securing his autonomy, his woman, and his territory with a gun—a formulation signified in our epoch by Eugene Hasenfus flying over the forests of Central America, presidential review of the men in uniform charged with defending our freedom, or Ollie North's good intentions? Might there be something in this construction that seeks to banish the fragile, perishable feature of political freedom, something that reveals this construction's socially male as well as colonial character—subduing with force what it cannot discursively persuade, tame, or cohabit the universe with, and possessing with force what it cannot seduce? Might the republican formulation of freedom, for all its appeal next to liberalism, contains some ills in its gender-biased, imperial, and propertied moments, and might the express link between guns and freedom betoken such moments?

STORMING THE PENTAGON

Let us consider the other side of the political relationship upon which Levinson's republican interpretation of the Second Amendment depends, the problem of the state. Levinson writes:

> I do not want to argue that the state is necessarily tyrannical; I am not an anarchist. But it seems foolhardy to assume that the armed state will necessarily be benevolent. The American political tradition is, for good or ill, based in large measure on a healthy mistrust of the state.[12]

I agree that tyranny is not our problem today. But tyranny is not the only, nor most significant, mode of the contemporary state's aggression against its people or abuse of the people's trust. Indeed, bureaucratic rationalization and discipline, deregulated toxic production and dumping, arbitrary changes in welfare policy, and the Iran-Contra or HUD scandals are more significant instances of antidemocratic state arrogations of power. It is quite difficult to see how the Second Amendment empowers the citizenry to prevent these things. Even when we narrow our focus to state abuses of what Weber termed its legitimate monopoly of violence,[13] it is far from clear that an armed citizenry is a viable mode of resistance to these abuses. Think about Kent State, or more routine police brutality in breaking up militant demonstrations or arresting and interrogating America's nonprivileged and nonwhite. Or, think about the MOVE crisis in Philadelphia several years ago, in which the state literally bombed civilian households. What exactly does a republican version of our right to bear arms offer us here? The MOVE household had a cache of weapons. The mayor of Philadelphia had a bomb. Wherein lies the freedom or the republican virtue in this relationship? Of what serious value are handguns or even machine guns against the arsenal of the modern state? For that matter, of what serious assistance are handguns and machine guns for the *defense* of the state in a nuclear age? If the state militia component of the Amendment remains anything more than history, we would be wise to consign it to history through a domestic nuclear nonproliferation treaty.

If we are then left with participation in law enforcement as the sole republican rationale for arming the people, it surely requires little reflection to discern why the Guardian Angels, those most remarkable self-appointed protectors of the peace, do not carry deadly weapons, nor why the British have for so long held out against equipping their bobbies with firearms.

WHOSE RIGHT, WHOSE VIOLATION?

Finally, what does it mean to speak about the Second Amendment in the language of either republicanism or liberalism when the most routine victims of this "right" are outside both discourses: urban black men between the ages of sixteen and thirty-four, for whom homicide is the leading cause of death, and women, one of whom is raped every six minutes, one out of three at gunpoint or knifepoint. When our privately held deadly weapons are aimed neither at the state nor the lawless, but at the most marginal or violable strata of our population, is there anything more than quaintness to a republican justification of our right to bear arms?

In short, Levinson's vision of an armed citizenry, collectively resisting the excesses of state power on behalf of itself as a community, is at best nostalgic, and at worst dangerously naïve and no little bit sexist in its predication upon "a world we have lost." Levinson may be partly right in the historical argument, but the history is now largely irrelevant, not merely to our present condition, but to the prospects for reviving citizenship, public life, meaningful freedom, or political community in the United States. We cannot become republican citizens or create a republican policy by arming ourselves or defending our right to do so, and it is irresponsible to make arguments about the relationship between arms and liberty as if we did not live in a nuclear era, an era of thoroughly disintegrated public life and disintegrating social order, and an era of rampant violence within and against the urban poor and against women of all socio-economic classes. I want to be very clear here: Like Levinson, I would prefer a republican order to a liberal-capitalist one. But we do not have a republican political order; we are not a republican citizenry; we do not have republican institutions, values, virtues, or arrangements of power. And we cannot generate a republican order merely by interpreting our Constitution through a republican hermeneutic scheme. Moreover, even within republicanism, we do not have to swallow it whole. The republican intellectual tradition includes a militarism, elitism, and machismo that is past due for thoughtful critique and reworking.

Levinson began his article by mapping different stories about the Constitution and the Second Amendment. I also want to conclude with a story, yet another way of mapping our differences as citizens in relationship to this Amendment. Last summer I came out of a week-long trek in the Sierra Nevada to discover that the car my friends and I had parked at the trailhead would not start. Still deep in the wilderness, thirty miles from a paved road or gas station, I was thrilled to see signs of human life in a nearby Winnebago. These life signs turned out to be a California sportsman making his way through a case of beer and preparing to survey the area for his hunting club in anticipation of the opening of deer season. Not feeling particularly discriminating, I enlisted his aid (and fully charged battery). While his buddy and my three looked on, together we began working on getting the car started, a project that consumed our attention and combined sets of tools for the next two hours.

In the course of our work, there was time to reflect upon much in our happenstance partnership. My rescuer was wearing a cap with the words "NRA freedom" inscribed on it. This was, I thought at the time, perfectly counterpoised to the injunction "Resist Illegitimate Authority" springing from my tee shirt (a token of my involvement with a progressive political foundation called RESIST). The slogans our bodies bore appeared to mark with elegant economy our attachment to opposite ends of the political and cultural universe—he preparing to shoot the wildlife I came to revere, he living out of his satellite-dished Winnebago and me out of my dusty backpack, he sustained by his guns and beer; me, as absurdly, by my Nietzsche and trail mix.

Levinson's "The Embarrassing Second Amendment" made me rethink this assessment and consider whether for all our differences, we may have shared a commitment to resisting illegitimate authority and perhaps even occupied a shared historical tradition in this respect—one that prefers an empowered people to a state monopoly on power. However, upon still further reflection, I remember something that gives me pause about moving to a conclusion that I shared much of anything with this man or that I needed to defend his guns as part of a politics of resisting illegitimate authority. It occurred to me then, and now, that if I had run into him in those woods without my friends or a common project for us to work on, I would have been seized with one great and appropriate fear: rape. I would have harbored such fear not because he was an NRA member but because he was a man: in a culture of pervasive and normalized male heterosexual violence, the wilderness is nothing less than a Hobbesian state of nature for women, a place where the social construction of male sexual entitlement is unconstrained by law or other counterforces. Indeed, this particular man's expression of such entitlement and indifference to my reception of his innuendos was an incessant subtext of our work together. But it was his gun that could have made the difference between an assault that my hard-won skills in self-defense could have fended off and one against which they were useless.

When I consider that scene, I wonder again about the gendered constitutional subject, about shifting Levinson's cognitive mapping from a focus on the differences between an ACLU member and a New Right devotee to the differences between the social positioning and experiences of men and women in our culture. Who is the gun-carrying citizen-warrior whose power is tempered by a limit on the right to bear arms? Is he most importantly a republican citizen, or more significantly, a socially male one? Is his right my violation, and might his be precisely the illegitimate authority I am out to resist?

NOTES

1. Levinson, "The Embarrassing Second Amendment," *Yale Law Review* 99(1989):637.
2. N. Machiavelli, *Discourses on the First Decade of Titus Livius*, in *The Chief Works and Others* trans., A. Gilbert (1965).
3. Ibid., p. 410.
4. Ibid., p. 411.
5. See Levinson, *supra* note 1, pp. 643–44.
6. See, e.g., ibid., pp. 644–45 (Levinson's discussion of state militias).
7. See, e.g., ibid., pp. 648–51, 656–57 (Levinson's discussion of resistance to governmental tyranny).
8. See, e.g., ibid., pp. 655–56 (Levinson's discussion of NRA and vigilantism; emphasis that citizens should participate in law enforcement).
9. Ibid., p. 648.
10. J. Locke. *Two Treatises of Government,* ed. P. Laslett, 2d ed. (1967) (3d ed., 1968).
11. Levinson, *supra* note 1, p. 648.
12. Ibid., p. 656.
13. M. Weber. "Politics as a Vocation," in *From Max Weber: Essays in Sociology,* trans. C. Mills & H. Gerth, (Oxford University Press, 1958), p. 78.

Selected Bibliography

SYMPOSIA

"Second Amendment Symposium: Rights in Conflict in the 1980s." *Northern Kentucky Law Review* 10, no. 1 (1982).

CONGRESSIONAL DOCUMENTS

United States Congress, Senate Committee on the Judiciary. Subcommittee on the Constitution. *The Right to Keep and Bear Arms.* 97th Congress, 2d session, 1982. Committee Print.

ARTICLES

Caplan, David. "Restoring the Balance: The Second Amendment Revisited." *Fordham Urban Law Journal* 5 (1976):31–53.
————. "The Right of the Individual to Bear Arms: A Recent Judicial Trend." *Detroit College of Law Review* (1982): 789–823.
Halbrook, Stephen P. "The Jurisprudence of the Second and Fourteenth Amendments." *George Mason University Law Review* 4 (1981):1–69.
————. "To Keep and Bear Their Private Arms: The Adoption of the Second Amendment 1789–1791." *Northern Kentucky Law Review* 10 (1982):13–39.
Henigan, Dennis A. "The Right to Be Armed: A Constitiutional Illusion." *San Francisco Barrister* (December 1989):10–14.
Kates, Don B., Jr. "Handgun Prohibition and the Original Meaning of the Second Amendment." *Michigan Law Review* 82 (1983):204–73.

Levin, John. "The Right to Bear Arms: The Development of the American Experience." *Chicago-Kent Law Review* (Fall/Winter 1971):110–29.

Weatherup, Roy G. "Standing Armies and Armed Citizens: An Historical Analysis of the Second Amendment." *Hastings Constitutional Law Quarterly* 2 (1975):961–1001.